$26

B/S

Another Life Altogether

SPIEGEL & GRAU

New York

2 0 1 0

Another Life Altogether

a novel

ELAINE BEALE

Published in the United States by Spiegel & Grau,
an imprint of The Random House Publishing Group,
a division of Random House, Inc., New York.

SPIEGEL & GRAU and Design is a
registered trademark of Random House, Inc.

LIBRARY OF CONGRESS CATALOGING-IN-PUBLICATION DATA
Beale, Elaine.
Another life altogether: a novel / Elaine Beale.
p. cm.
ISBN 978-0-385-53004-0
eBook ISBN 978-0-385-53006-4
1. Girls—Fiction. 2. Parents—Mental health—Fiction.
3. England, Northern—Fiction. I. Title.
PS3552.E1366A85 2010
813´.54—dc22   2009003779

Printed in the United States of America on acid-free paper

www.spiegelandgrau.com

2 4 6 8 9 7 5 3 1

FIRST EDITION

Book design by Barbara M. Bachman

Another Life Altogether

CHAPTER ONE

———

THE DAY AFTER MY MOTHER WAS ADMITTED TO THE MENTAL HOSPITAL, I told everyone at school that she had entered a competition on the back of a Corn Flakes box and won a cruise around the world.

"How long will she be gone?" asked Julie Fraser, who sat among the girls crowding eagerly around me during morning registration.

"Months," I said. "Months and months." I looked at her slightly sad, but mostly dreamy, as if I were already imagining my mother floating across a wide blue ocean to a life of adventure that none of us there could have.

Julie made her big brown eyes even bigger and ran the tip of her tongue over her glossed lips. "God, she's lucky," she said, leaning closer to me.

"Yes," I said, wondering how I might always make her look at me like that.

"So which parts of the world is she going to?" Jimmy Crandall craned his skinny neck across his desk.

My eyes left Julie's as I let myself consider this for a moment, frowning as I tried to evoke the expression of someone struggling to recall a busy cruise-ship itinerary—all those ports of call, day trips, deck-side activities, and dinners at the captain's table. "I'm not sure," I answered, not wanting to be caught out by my uncertain grasp of geography. I knew, of course, that Britain was an island, and I had a relatively decent notion of the jumble of countries that made up Europe, but beyond that it was all a little blurred. I might have been better informed were it not for the fact that our geography teacher, Mr. Cuthbertson, had spent the entire year familiarizing us in great detail with the climatic influences, waterways, geologic history, and soil structure of our local landscape.

We lived on the banks of the River Humber, chilled by the damp air off the North Sea, on a plain scraped by glaciers that had left in their wake a land composed almost entirely of malleable and unstable boulder clay. "East Yorkshire," Mr. Cuthbertson would announce during almost every lesson, his gaunt, gray features suddenly bright with pride, "has one of the fastest-eroding coastlines in the entire world." It was as if this were an accomplishment for which we, the local inhabitants, somehow deserved credit, rather than an unhappy geologic accident that meant, even as he spoke, that the land he so loved was crumbling away by inches. Since this seemed to be the only really notable feature (geographic or otherwise) of the region I called home, by the age of thirteen, even though I had never traveled more than forty miles in any direction, I had come to regard it as one of the dullest places on the planet. So when Mr. Cuthbertson told us of villages falling into the North Sea, church spires poking above the water at low tide, and houses bought for a few pounds and change because the waves had begun eating into their back gardens, I often found myself wondering how long it would take for the sea to devour the twenty miles or so that now separated Hull, the city in which I lived, from that voracious tide.

"What do you mean, you're not sure?" Jimmy Crandall was challenging me now, his Adam's apple bobbing against his pimply throat like a bird trapped under his skin. "If my mam won a bloody cruise, I'd know where she was off to."

"She's going everywhere. It's a *world* cruise," I said, rolling my eyes at all the girls around me the way I'd seen them do so many times with one another when one of the boys said something stupid or insulting or in an obvious ploy for attention. Then I looked over at Julie Fraser, hoping to see my derision mirrored in her conspiratorial smile. Instead, I saw her glance slipping in Jimmy Crandall's direction. Inevitably, the attention of the other girls followed.

"Oh, going everywhere, is she? What, like Belfast and Biafra? The North and South Pole?" He grinned, then poked his shiny pink tongue between his lips, as if it were reaching out to taste the certainty of his victory.

The boys and the girls were all looking at me now, the stuffy classroom air filled with the school morning scents of soap, clean socks, and toothpaste-minty breath. All their eyes, even those still crusty with sleep, were intense, poised between suspicion and happy expectation.

"You can't take a cruise to the South Pole," I said, swinging my hair back over my shoulder with a toss of my head, hoping to generate an air of confident indifference. Instead, I wafted myself with the blue chemical scent of Head & Shoulders shampoo and remembered sitting in a lukewarm bath the previous night, the same bath that only hours earlier had been filled with cold, blood-tinted water before I pulled the plug and scrubbed it clean with Ajax.

"To get to the South Pole," I continued, brushing away the memory with my words, "you have to travel over miles and miles of ice." For a moment, I imagined my mother, encased in a furry parka and bearskin boots, coursing across a gleaming white landscape on a dogsled. Like so many of those explorers before her, she would disappear into a stinging blizzard and never come back.

Jimmy Crandall shrugged. "Nobody I met ever won one of those stupid Corn Flakes competitions. They're all a fucking fraud, if you ask me." He flopped back into his chair and pulled it closer to his desk with a piercing scrape that made me wince.

"Well, my mother did," I said, talking now to all the boys and girls, desperate to keep them around me, their bodies a protective nest that could somehow hold me high, above the ground, above the surging, bloody water that was threatening to wash it all away. "She's going to write to me, you'll see." My voice was too loud, too bright. It cut through the air like hands ripping fabric. Mrs. Thompson, our form-room teacher, looked over at me, arched her black, penciled-in eyebrows, and pressed her lips into a rosy little knot. I acknowledged her look with a nod. When she had turned back to the stack of exercise books she was thumbing through, I propped myself up on my elbows, leaned forward, and reached over to Jimmy Crandall. I prodded hard at his shoulder. "You're only jealous," I said as he lurched forward under my hand. I spoke even louder now, as if I could pull Julie Fraser and her friends back to me with my voice. "You just wish your family could be as lucky as mine."

PERHAPS IT SHOULDN'T have been a complete surprise to arrive home the day before to find my mother being taken away. After all, she had told us it might happen.

"One of these days, I'm going to end up in Delapole!" she'd yell, slamming doors, clattering plates. "You watch, they'll cart me away in a bloody straitjacket, they will! And then you'll be happy!"

Delapole was the mental hospital just outside Hull. It was named after a local family, the de la Poles, who, Mr. Cuthbertson told us when he'd strayed into one of his many monologues about our "rich local history," had made their fortune as merchants during the Middle Ages. He hadn't explained, however, why the local loony bin bore their name. My father had joked that all those posh families were so inbred that they had more than their share of nutcases, so it made sense that the place had been named after them. Of course, that was before my mother had fulfilled her own prophetic words and had been transported there courtesy of the National Health.

"I'll end up in Delapole!" she'd scream, her voice like a yodel that shuddered against the windows and set the sherry glasses rattling in the china cabinet. "I'll end up in Delapole, you mark my words!" she yelled when the car broke down or the milk boiled over or I spilled a glass of orange cordial across the kitchen table. As if each of these events were a calamity on the scale of the *Titanic* and it was my father or I who had just steered us slap-bang into the iceberg.

Even when I was very young, I'd realized that my mother had no sense of perspective. If anything went wrong, no matter how large or small, it constituted some ultimately threatening disaster. She might end up in the local mental institution as a consequence of my burning the house down because I hadn't turned off the electric heater in my bedroom, but she might just as easily be committed if my father forgot to put the top back on the ketchup or I neglected to put my dirty knickers in the clothes basket. I knew her reactions made no sense, but her world was also my world, so when I was small I'd feel her panic as my own. I'd try to allay her hysteria with calming words or by rectifying the problem—a six-year-old cooing, "It's all right, Mum, it's all right," while sweeping a pile of broken glass from the kitchen floor. As I grew older, however, I learned that there was no comforting or calming my mother at these moments. It was just something she had to go through, like a sneeze that has to be sneezed or an itch that has to be scratched.

Despite all this, it had been a shock to find an ambulance parked outside our house, its big wheels pushed over the curb, its light flashing like a huge bright, blinking blue eye. And I had been a little taken aback to find the neighbors gathered in our tiny front garden, nudging one another and whispering, as if they were expecting the arrival of some popular television celebrity who'd decided to drop by our house for a cup of tea and a chat. Indeed, the scene was almost festive. The women smoked ravenously, sucking at their cigarettes with big, audible gasps, while the children made wailing-siren noises as they ran up and down our path. When they noticed my arrival and parted like the Red Sea for Moses to let me reach my front door, the bitter taste of dread filled my mouth and left my stomach churning, but I felt a strange thrill of power. Here I was, a star in the middle of my own domestic disaster.

By the time I'd moved through the milling crowd outside our house and reached the front door, however, my exhilaration was gone. Instead, I felt a sickening dread in my stomach, a dread that only grew when our next-door neighbor, Mrs. Brockett, stepped from the dark interior of our hallway onto our threshold, sighing as she folded her arms across her chest. She wore a shapeless cotton dress, opaque brown stockings, and a pair of men's slippers. Her gray hair was folded around a set of pink curlers. Never known for her cheery disposition, Mrs. Brockett had a particularly grave look on her face.

In all the years we had lived in our terrace house on Marton Street, despite many valiant attempts Mrs. Brockett had never managed to get inside. In an unusual display of marital consensus, both my father and my mother hated her vehemently, though for rather different reasons—my mother because she regarded Mrs. Brockett as a relentless gossip who would "broadcast the contents of my undies drawers to the entire street if she got the bloody opportunity," my father because she hung a picture of the Queen in her front window and my father hated the Queen as passionately as he loved cricket. Mrs. Brockett was equally disdained by the children of the street. She was known among us as Cat Piss Lady because of the seventeen cats she kept inside her house and the stinging, ammonia smell that clung to her everywhere she went. I'd even heard some adults use the nickname to refer to her in whispered conversations in the queue at the butcher's or greengrocer's. But, as far as I knew, no one had ever dared to call her that to her face. Far more than the ambulance or the assembly of neighbors in my front garden, the fact that it was Mrs. Brockett who greeted me at my doorway signaled that there was something terribly wrong.

"Ooh, I wouldn't go in there if I were you, lovey," she said, placing one of her gnarly-knuckled hands on my shoulder. "Not something a girl of your age needs to see." Her narrowed eyes met mine. A wave of sighs and moans rose behind me. "Quite distressing." She pursed her lips and shook her head slowly, then turned expectantly toward the surrounding neighbors. "Anyone got a ciggy?" she inquired. There was an immediate flutter of hands and, almost simultaneously, three women reached over and held up cigarettes. "I'll take the Rothmans," she announced, snatching the longest cigarette from the hand that held it, popping it between her lips, and leaning forward as another hand reached out with a flame. She inhaled deeply before she blew the smoke into my face.

"What's going on? What's happening?" I tried to push past her.

"Just a little . . . accident. Nothing you need worry yourself about. Now, why don't you come over to my house, lovey, and I'll make you a nice cup of tea."

From deep inside the house I could hear the rumble of male voices, the clatter of metal against metal, and empty radio static. "Let me in," I said, tears welling up in my eyes. They spilled down my face and made everything around me a blur of color and noise. I fumbled blindly against the broad body that blocked my way, my hands pressing into the armor beneath the baggy dress: metal clasps, corset stays, the rigid cups of Mrs. Brockett's bra. I was lost in the smell of cigarette smoke, laundry detergent, and cat piss. I began to strike out with my fists.

"All right, all right," she said, standing aside. "But don't say I didn't warn you."

AS I LEFT MORNING registration and made toward my first lesson, I was relieved to see Jimmy Crandall skulk off in the opposite direction, his battered leather satchel hanging low on his hip and thudding against his side as he walked. But the girls who had crowded around me at the news of my mother's good fortune left me, too, drifting down the corridor in twos and threes. Wearing strappy platform shoes, they sauntered arm in arm, as if they needed one another to hold themselves up. Julie Fraser, always at the center, was oblivious to me now, her perfect blond hair reflecting the harsh corridor lights. I watched her with a yearning so enormous that it felt like a hole in my chest. As I glanced down at the sensible brown shoes my mother had bought me from the Littlewoods catalog, I imagined crashing into Julie and all her whispering, laughing friends to leave them splayed and breathless on the cold, dirty floor.

The rest of that day I was left to spend my time, as usual, with the other social outcasts: Patsy Lancey, who had twelve brothers and sisters and whose overwashed gray socks hung elasticless around her ankles and who everybody said had fleas; Janine Trotter, who had a mentally retarded sister and whose father had moved in with the seventeen-year-old girl who worked behind the counter at the newsagent's; and Gillian Gilman, who had acne and was fat and whom everyone, even her older brothers, called "the whale." Every day, we sat together in lessons and at school dinners, sneering at the popular kids and feigning interest in what we each had to say. We all knew we were in one another's company only because no one else wanted us, that if any of those other cliques had invited us to join them we would have abandoned one another in a second. When Gillian Gilman asked me if it was true that my mother had won a competition and was off on a world cruise, I told her to shut her big, fat mouth and mind her own business. She wasn't anyone I needed to impress.

When the final school bell rang, I knew I didn't want to go home. I didn't want to walk down our street trying to ignore the twitching net curtains in the front windows of all the houses or Mrs. Brockett smoking and tossing her cigarette ends into our garden as she kept vigil by her front door. Nor did I want to enter our cold and empty house. So I made my way instead to the public library, a place I visited often during the after-school hours.

The library was one of those old Victorian buildings in which even the whispered hisses of the librarian echoed against the high ceilings. It was always too hot, filled with the musty smell of aging paper and the force of suppressed coughs. The bookshelves were visited largely by pensioners—women with frosted hair and shopping bags, men who blinked behind big-framed National Health glasses and wore clothes that seemed too big. The newspaper and magazine section was inhabited by unemployed men with folded, gray faces who, despite the grimaces of the librarian, drummed their nicotine-yellow fingers against the tables, as if the library were merely a waiting room and they were impatient to get on with the real purpose of their visit in some better place beyond.

I loved the library. I loved it for its spacious quiet, the way it was possible to discern each step and shuffle and sigh against that soothing backdrop of calm. No one would yell or scream or cry there, and if they ever dared I knew that the tight-lipped wrath of the librarian would come crashing down on them, as heavy and as crushing as the weight of all those books. I loved it because it was a refuge from school, a place where I had only to navigate my way around the ingenious precision of the Dewey decimal system rather than complex and cruel social hierarchies. But most of all I loved the library because that vigorously imposed silence implied an awe of something far bigger than me, than all of us. It showed the deepest regard not for our need to talk or belch or scream—not for the silly chatter of little children, the gossip of older women, or anyone's gasping need for a cigarette—but for those stacks and stacks of books and the words and worlds that lay inside them.

That afternoon, I claimed a desk in the reference section, having planned to do the homework Mr. Cuthbertson had given us—a series of questions about the tidal patterns of the River Humber. Instead, I pulled out the *Reader's Digest World Atlas.* I thumbed through its thick pages and found myself tracing the route for my mother's cruise ship. After chugging cheerfully away from Hull Docks, I decided, she had sailed into the North Sea, around the fat-bellied coast of East Anglia, past the Thames, and into the English Channel. Soon, she'd be making her way around the coasts of France, Portugal, and northern Spain. She'd stop in Calais, where she'd do a bit of shopping and, like all the English people who went there, load up on cheap French wine, perfume, and crunchy baguettes. Then she'd find herself exploring the coast of Southern Europe and taking in the entire Mediterranean. I recognized the names of places like Barcelona, Marseilles, Nice, Monte Carlo, the islands of Corsica and Crete, the cities of Athens, Venice,

and Rome. Undoubtedly, she'd meet millionaires and high-stakes gam-
blers, racing-car drivers, fashion models, and perhaps even get to see
the Pope make a speech from a balcony in Vatican City. Then, exhausted by the excitement, she'd venture back into the Atlantic, where
her journey would continue. She'd travel all the way around Africa,
India, Burma, Thailand, the Philippines, China, Japan. Then on to the
Americas: Canada, the United States, and all those South American
cities with mysterious, multisyllabic names—Montevideo, Buenos
Aires, Tierra del Fuego. And perhaps then she might go on to the South
Pole after all, leaving Cape Horn to sail past giant icebergs toward the
massive continent of Antarctica.

When I arrived home, I found my father in the living room, sunk in
his armchair, hidden behind his copy of the Hull *Daily Mail.* I knew he
had been to see my mother earlier, and for a moment I wanted to ask
him how she was and if they were taking care of her. But that might
mean he'd ask me if I wanted to go and visit her at the hospital, and,
more than anything, I did not.

"Make us a cup of tea, can you, love?" My father spoke from behind
his newspaper. "News is on in a sec, don't want to miss it."

The BBC News was the highlight of my father's day. Normally, he
arrived home from work just a few minutes before it came on. He'd
walk through the house, discarding his overcoat and suit jacket on the
coat stand in the hall, battling the tight knot of his tie as he entered the
living room. Then he'd turn on the television, drop into his armchair,
and unlace his shiny black shoes, filling the room with his ripe, sweaty-
feet smell. Sometimes he might sigh, turn to me, and say, "All right,
Jesse, love?" But most days he just sat there silently as the BBC globe
spun around and around, and that urgent, official-sounding music
came on. Then, almost as soon as the newsreader began talking, my father would begin to yell, rolling his eyes and gesticulating, swearing and
bouncing on the noisy, worn-out springs of his chair. "Stupid bosses'
lackey!" he'd shout at Richard Baker as he talked about another miners'
strike or the Watergate scandal. Sometimes he'd throw a shoe toward

the screen when he was particularly annoyed at the BBC's account of events, or when one of the Conservative politicians he hated most came on. But usually he reserved the full force of his vitriol for those end-of-news feel-good items about the royal family—Prince Charles playing polo, the Queen Mother visiting a children's hospital, Princess Margaret opening a new shopping center. "Bloody useless parasite!" he'd shout, wagging his finger at the screen while the Queen Mum, in pastel pink and pearls, smiled benevolently and waved to an adoring crowd. "Should go out and get a real job instead of living shamelessly off the rest of us. Come the revolution, we'll make her clean toilets. That'll wipe that bloody condescending look off her face."

That evening, the headline was an IRA bomb in London, and my father was unusually subdued by the pictures of the burning skeleton of a building, the stricken faces of the bleeding survivors, the dazed ambulance men. "What'll that do to solve anybody's problems?" he said quietly as he shifted in his chair.

While my father sipped his tea and watched the rest of the news, I turned to the back page of the newspaper to find out what was on television that night. "Dad," I said when the news was over and I knew he could be interrupted. "There's a documentary on BBC Two about Spain at eight o'clock. Is it all right if we watch it?"

"Don't see why not," he said.

And so that night I embarked upon the research that would enable me to write letters from my mother to me. I sat in front of the television with a notebook scribbling down what I thought were pertinent pieces of information, like the population of Barcelona, the date Gaudi first began construction of his strange gingerbread castle of a cathedral, the number of matadors injured each year in the bull ring, a few relevant words of Spanish—señora, peso, pension, General Franco.

I liked the idea of my mother visiting Spain. It was where Julie Fraser had been for her holiday last year. She'd returned to school with her hair sun-bleached and her skin turned a deep, reddish tan. In lessons, I sat as close to her as I could, eavesdropping as she extolled the "sexy Spanish waiters" and the all-night discos. "The women go topless on the beaches there, you know," she said, giggling and peeling another piece of flaking, sunburned skin from her arm.

As I listened, I'd found myself imagining what it might be like to lie on some sunny Spanish beach next to Julie. We'd be best friends so comfortable with each other that we'd take off our tops so we wouldn't have to worry about tan lines. Later, to cool off, we'd run into the warm blue water, where we'd swim and splash until we tired ourselves out.

"What the bloody hell are you staring at?" Julie had said when she caught me watching her tell her friends, yet again, how she'd been served fried octopus one night for dinner and it was the most disgusting thing she'd ever eaten in her life.

"Nothing," I'd replied, pitching my gaze toward the geography textbook on my desk. For the rest of the lesson, while I attempted to reproduce a diagram of the East Yorkshire water table, I pondered the unfairness of a world in which Julie Fraser got to fly to the Costa del Sol for two weeks while the only holiday my family had taken was to a caravan park in Bridlington. There, our days had been punctuated by pulling out and putting away the narrow bed on which I slept that ingeniously converted into the dining table, and searching for ways to occupy our time in that confined, Formica-filled space as the rain poured down in sheets outside. While my father and I had tried to make the best of things by playing Snakes and Ladders, Ludo, and Monopoly, my mother had spent her time cleaning the caravan from top to bottom. She scrubbed around the tiny stainless-steel sink with a toothbrush, scoured the pots and pans with a Brillo pad, and mopped and remopped the kitchen floor with water she'd boiled on the foldaway stove. My father and I found ourselves soaked in the scents of Ajax, Pine-Sol, and bleach, and were finally driven out to the amusement arcade when my mother decided that she needed to take the furniture apart. "I bet it's been years since anybody's thought to take a scrubbing brush down there," she said, tossing the cushions over her shoulder. "At least the people who come here after us won't have to feel like they're spending their holidays in a cesspool of somebody else's filth."

I thought my mother might rather like Spain. It rarely rained, and since she was traveling on a cruise ship there'd be plenty of people to do all the cleaning. She wouldn't have to spend her time worrying about dirt and germs. Instead, she could happily sit on deck, taking in the Mediterranean sun and admiring the beautiful coastline. She'd disembark on the southern coast, where she'd take a day trip to see the Alhambra, and when she reached Barcelona she could spend her time in the Gaudi park, contemplating the mosaic sculptures, or sitting at a café by the harbor watching ships come in from all over the world.

"The Spanish people are remarkably friendly," I wrote in my mother's letter to me. "Like most Southern Europeans, they are deeply religious. But they don't let this get in the way of enjoying themselves. For example, the bullfights—like the one I went to yesterday—are very festive. Despite all the blood, everyone seems to have a very good time."

I stayed up very late finishing that letter, writing and rewriting until it was as thrilling as I thought I could make it, until my mother's visit to Spain made Julie Fraser's holiday seem as exciting as a rainy week in Bridlington, until I was sure that no one, not even Jimmy Crandall, would dare to question my family's good luck.

THE NEXT MORNING, during registration, I pulled out my letter. " 'Dear Jesse,' " I began after clearing my throat and noisily unfolding my several sheets of crisp white paper. " 'As I write to you, I am watching yet another glorious sunset on the crystal-clear Mediterranean Sea. It is hard to describe how breathtaking the view from my luxurious cabin is or how wonderful this trip is proving to be. But, since you cannot be with me here, I hope I can convey just some of my delight by telling you about it in this letter. Yesterday, I had the most incredible time—' "

"Let me see that!" Jimmy Crandall made a grab for the letter, but I managed to pull it out of his reach and continued reading.

" 'After having a delicious breakfast on board ship, I disembarked with a party of other passengers to go and see a bullfight in a nearby town. We arrived during siesta—a time in the afternoon when all the Spaniards like to get out of the heat and take a nap. I cannot say I blame them. The weather is quite warm, even now in late spring. I was told by one of the friendly villagers that temperatures can reach more than ninety degrees Fahrenheit during the height of the summer. Of course, we English people aren't used to anything nearly as hot as that and I am glad we are not visiting in July or August, which are the hottest days of the year. . . .' "

I lifted my eyes from my pages to see everyone in the class looking at me. Even the group of boys at the back, who had been flicking chewed-up pieces of paper onto the ceiling, had paused to listen. Almost all the girls had drawn closer, and Julie Fraser had put down her *Jackie* magazine.

" 'Bullfighting is an enormously exciting sport, far more interesting than football or rugby or cricket,' " I continued. " 'The bullfighters are extremely brave and handsome men. They have to train a very long time to become good at it. Some of them get very badly injured, and some of them even die in the ring. As I sat waiting for the fight to begin, I was hoping that no one would get hurt while I was there.' " I went on to read a long account of my mother's time at the bullring— how she watched one of the most famous bullfighters in Spain get almost gored to death by a savage, bloodthirsty bull, how she cried as he was taken off on a stretcher and screamed for joy when she later found out that he was fine and came back into the ring for a second performance. I told my classmates how she and some of her fellow passengers had dined at a local restaurant with this same bullfighter that evening, how he'd told them stories late into the night of his many near misses over the years, and how she had returned exhausted to the ship after " 'one of the most thrilling days of my entire existence.' " When I finished, ending with, " 'Fond regards, your loving mother,' " I looked up at my audience as if emerging from a dream.

"Bloody hell, Jesse," declared Julie Fraser, saying my name for the first time that I could remember. "Your mam sounds like she's having a right good time! I bet she's glad she entered that competition."

AFTER THAT, I STAYED late at the library almost every day to throw my-self into the research for my mother's letters. And each evening, while my father sat silent, I turned to the documentary programs on BBC Two about travel through the Sahara or the animals in the jungles of Madagascar. At first I approached this viewing as a chore, like my homework (which I now almost entirely ignored) or the washing of our greasy, crusted-up dishes (which I attempted every two or three days). But after a while I found myself sharing in the awed fascination of the television narrators, who invariably told about these exotic places in hushed, enthralled tones. Equally bedazzled by forests filled with butterflies, the hunting habits of lions, the hazardous swoops of flying squirrels, and the camouflage abilities of chameleons, I scribbled down names of places and species, descriptions of the immense, un-tamed landscapes that made Mr. Cuthbertson's enthusiasm for the dreary East Yorkshire terrain seem even more misplaced. And later, after the television had been turned off and my father continued his desolate vigils in the living room, I lay on my bed writing long, detailed letters from my mother that I took to school and read out loud in reg-istration each day.

This cruise-taking mother was quite a letter writer, sending me sev-eral pages almost every day. And though parts of her letters closely re-sembled entire paragraphs of the *Encyclopaedia Britannica,* providing statistics on population, gross national product, and average daily tem-peratures, they also included stories of her adventures. I thrilled at her descriptions of her trip to the Parthenon ("quite the most astonishingly beautiful place I have ever seen"), her climb up the Leaning Tower of

Pisa ("It leans at a truly incredible angle; I really was afraid it would fall over!"), her desert trek to the Pyramids ("like a trip back through time, such an awe-inspiring civilization"). And I loved her stories of moonlit rides in Venetian gondolas, drinking thick, syrupy coffee in Morocco, eating freshly made Turkish delight. I also loved this new mother of my own construction, the adventurous and dauntless spirit who wandered strange countries without fear, picked up new languages within days, and wrote gleefully about a world that no one else around me knew. She was a little eccentric, perhaps, but not nearly as odd as the woman I'd seen carried past me on a stretcher, eyes still and unblinking, limbs tucked tight under a dark wool blanket, hair sprawled behind her in a wet and matted knot.

Even more than this new mother I'd invented for myself, I loved those wide-eyed looks Julie Fraser and all the other girls gave me. Perhaps, I thought, if I could somehow keep them rapt they'd actually welcome me into their ranks.

I could tell that Julie Fraser was warming toward me. Not only had she started calling me by my name on a regular basis, she'd even invited me to sit with her and her friends in the canteen during school dinner one day. And the next day, when I walked into the girls' toilets and found her and a couple of other girls listening to the top-twenty countdown on a tinny transistor radio as they leaned against the sinks, she'd beckoned me over to listen.

I began to think that if all went well we really would become good friends. After a while, she might even invite me to spend time with her after school or on weekends. We'd really get to know each other and she'd realize that, despite my bland looks and unfashionable clothes, I was an interesting person after all.

IT TOOK A LITTLE less than two weeks for word of the real nature of my mother's journey to get around school. I was actually quite astounded that it took that long. Gossip generally traveled fast along our narrow streets, and, particularly since we lived next door to Mrs. Brockett, any unusual happenings at our house were bound to become public knowledge sooner rather than later. Somehow, the sheer horror of my mother's problem seemed to have slowed the process. But inevitably the news reached the school.

"Your mother's not on a fucking cruise, she's in the fucking loony bin," Jimmy Crandall announced during registration on a rainy Friday morning. He wore an ugly, wide-toothed grin, and every single person in the room turned to look at him. "She tried to fucking top herself, didn't she?" he continued, still grinning. "She would've done it if it weren't for one of your neighbors finding her. You must be a fucking loony yourself, making up some stupid story about her winning a competition on a Corn Flakes packet. You're as nutty as your fucking fruit-cake mother."

"That's enough, Jimmy," Mrs. Thompson said. "Sit down and be quiet." I could tell from her expression that she felt sorry for me. But I didn't need anybody's pity, and I already knew that there was nothing she could do to save me. I turned toward Julie Fraser. She and her friends were leaning across their desks, their heads pushed close together in a huddle. They were laughing, snorting as they held their hands over their mouths. I kept hoping that Julie would look at me, that she would push those girls away, smile at me, and show me that, despite my lies, despite my desperation, she'd finally seen that we were meant to be friends. But Julie didn't even glimpse in my direction. She just sat at the center of all those giggling girls, laughing until her eyes became watery and her mascara began to run in gray, jagged rivulets down her cheeks.

NOW, INSTEAD OF reading letters during registration surrounded by mesmerized listeners, I found myself surrounded by chanting boys and sneering, sour-faced girls, my days filled with their ridiculing choruses. "Batty as her mother." "Round the bloody bend." "Mad as a hatter."

"Off her rocker." "Absolutely frigging bonkers." "Mental, she's fucking mental." "Loop the bloody loop, the entire fucking family." I soon discovered that there were more euphemisms for madness than there were for sex. I also discovered that being the center of attention was not necessarily all it was cracked up to be.

Even Gillian Gilman and the other social rejects started keeping their distance. I ate my school dinner alone and did my best to avoid the playground, finding refuge in the caretaker's cupboard, where I sat on the floor amid buckets and mops and oversized bottles of bleach. At the end of the day, I made an art of lingering in the classroom so that I could avoid seeing anyone else as they walked home.

But I didn't stop writing the letters. Instead, I started writing my own letters back. Once I'd finished writing the letter from my mother for that day, I'd read it out loud to myself and then begin composing my reply. My own long missives never talked about home or school but, rather, about what I would do if I were a world traveler, the people I would talk to, the places I would visit. I told my mother how I, too, would like to journey to the coast of West Africa or visit the Taj Mahal or walk along the Great Wall of China. I told her that when I grew up I'd learn Spanish and travel in Latin America, that I'd climb the Andes to trek to Machu Picchu, and visit the Mayan ruins in Mexico. I might become an archaeologist or some kind of scientist, or perhaps I'd just become a professional traveler, plunging into dense, unexplored jungles or trekking across the Sahara just to see what it was like.

OOH, IT'S SUCH A bloody shame, it really is," Mrs. Brockett said, leaning over the brick wall that separated our two backyards, a bent cigarette dancing between her lips. I had watched her shuffle outside in her trodden-down slippers as soon as she'd seen my father walk out the door. She'd been waiting for this moment for days, lurking in her backyard at all hours, peering eagerly toward our house while she pegged up and took down so much washing that I was sure she must have laundered every item she owned.

"I mean, it's hard for me to understand," she continued. "Her with everything to look forward to. A reliable husband . . ." She pulled out her cigarette, exhaled from her nostrils, and flashed my father a squished-up, dentureless smile. "And such a lovely girl." She beamed over at me, her cheeks sinking so far inward that her cheekbones jutted out like blades.

I was leaning against the doorjamb, watching my father struggle to push our bag of kitchen rubbish into the already overfilled dustbin. I returned Mrs. Brockett's smile with a still, expressionless look.

"Lovely girl," she repeated, taking a long drag on her cigarette and pushing the smoke out the corner of her mouth as she turned to my father again. "But I suppose women—well, they just don't know when they're well off, do they?" She sighed. Then she nodded, acknowledging my father's continuing battle with the dustbin. "Looks like she left you in the lurch, eh?"

"I can do that, Dad," I said, walking across the wrinkled concrete of our backyard, taking the rubbish bag from his hands, and stuffing it on top of the other bags.

My father looked dazed, as if I'd pulled him from a dream. "Thanks, love," he muttered.

"So, how is she then, your Evelyn?" Mrs. Brockett called as my father retreated toward the house. "Go to visit her a lot out there, do you?" She craned her saggy neck sideways as my father made his way to the back door.

I willed him to step inside. But never one to offend the neighbors, even those he hated as much as he hated Mrs. Brockett, he turned slowly to face her. "I get out there as often as I can," he said.

"Yes, I'm sure you do. And I'm sure it helps. Poor woman. But of course at some point she'll have to pull herself together. I mean, she's got others to think of aside from herself. Like me—well, I don't know what my kitties would do if I gave up on them. . . ." She gazed lovingly at one of her cats, which lay across the kitchen windowsill as relaxed and shimmery as a discarded fur collar.

"Well, got things to do," my father announced, using Mrs. Brockett's distraction to hurry inside.

I remained by the dustbin, hoping she would forget my presence. Instead, she turned to look at me. "I don't know why that father of yours has to be so unfriendly. I mean, if it wasn't for me your mother would be six feet under by now. You should tell him to think about that, you should." She gestured toward me with the hand holding the cigarette, making a zigzag pattern of smoke that dissipated into the air. "If I hadn't thought to check on her when she didn't answer the door . . . well, I hate to think . . ." She pursed her lips, shuddered. "Call it a woman's sixth sense, but I just knew something wasn't right." She sucked at her cigarette. "You should remember, young lady," she said as she exhaled, "you've got me to thank that your mother is still alive."

I looked at Mrs. Brockett and felt as if something inside me would burst. Perhaps it was my head, or maybe it was my heart or my stomach, which seemed, all of a sudden, to be holding a giant fistful of fury. That fist wanted to break out and hit Mrs. Brockett; it wanted to pound Julie Fraser and Jimmy Crandall and all the kids at school. It wanted to throw all those encyclopedias out the library windows. It wanted to tear up all my letters. It wanted to beat some sense into myself.

"Why don't you just mind your own business, Cat Piss Lady," I said, relishing Mrs. Brockett's stunned expression before I turned and walked into the house.

CHAPTER TWO

—

NOT LONG AFTER MY MOTHER WAS DISCHARGED FROM DELAPOLE, my father announced that we were moving to the countryside. My mother's doctor had suggested that this might be a good idea.

"He said we might all benefit from a change of scene," my father said as the three of us sat at the kitchen table. "I mean, like they say, a change is as good as a rest. It'll be good for you, too, Jesse, living in the country. It's about time you got yourself outdoors more, some color in your cheeks. It's a damn shame all that time you're spending by yourself in that bedroom of yours."

"Yes, it's a damn shame," my mother said.

I wanted to say that, unlike her, I did at least venture beyond the backyard on a regular basis. And if anyone needed more color in her complexion it was she. She looked, as I'd heard Mrs. Brockett comment to one of our other neighbors, "like death warmed up, no pun intended, mind you." But instead I said nothing, preferring to stir another spoonful of sugar into my tea and listen to my parents above the musical rattle of the spoon against the cup.

"I don't want to move," my mother said, her words round and misshapen as she chewed slowly on a peanut-butter sandwich.

It was after two o'clock, but she still wasn't dressed. She wore the nylon dressing gown my father had bought her as a birthday present during her hospital stay. I had helped him pick it out, imagining her sweeping down sparkling cruise-ship corridors in its extravagant pink ruffles and puffy wide sleeves. Now, in our cramped, dirty-dish-cluttered kitchen, it looked garish and far too bright, like a fancy-dress costume, and it only added to my mother's off-kilter aura. "I'm happy where I am," she added, wiping crumbs from her mouth with the back of her hand and running her tongue over her chapped lips.

"You could have fooled me. If this is your version of happy, then . . ." My father faltered and took a gasping sip of his tea. "Look, Evelyn," he said after he'd swirled the liquid around his mouth then swallowed it down. "I think we all need a change of scene. I do. And Jesse's school-work's been suffering."

"No, it hasn't," I countered. It was true that my marks had slipped when I was doing all that letter writing. But the day my mother had arrived home—her face a pale moon, her arms loose and thin as sticks beneath a saggy pullover—the idea of a glamorous world-traveling mother sunning herself on the deck of a cruise ship had suddenly seemed as absurd to me as it had to my schoolmates. I'd stopped writing my letters and tried to focus on my lessons again.

"See," my mother said. "Jesse doesn't want to move, either."

This was not true. I was longing to move. Longing to go anywhere. I was tired of the teasing at school, tired of Mrs. Thompson gazing over her desk at me as if I were a sickly, abandoned waif, tired of the curtains that twitched every time I walked down our street, and tired of Mrs. Brockett peering over our backyard wall to press me for information. I was so tired of everything that I didn't even balk at the idea of moving to some country village. Perhaps, if I was lucky, my father would purchase one of those houses perched at the edge of an eroding cliff and within months we'd find ourselves pitched into the sea.

"We need a new start," my father said, letting his teacup clatter down onto its saucer. "You need a new start. And, quite frankly, I'd like to be somewhere that the whole bloody street isn't sticking their noses in our bloody business."

"Oh, right, that's it," my mother said, nodding sagely, as if everything had become clear. "That's going to suit you down to the ground." She chewed as she spoke, and I could see globs of peanut butter stuck to the roof of her mouth. "You'll put me out there in the middle of nowhere hoping everyone will forget about me. I'll be like that woman . . . what's her name, Jesse? That one in the film we saw the other day, the one they stuck in the attic until she set it on fire?"

"Mrs. Rochester," I answered.

"Yes, that's right. Mrs. Rochester," she said, wagging a finger at my father. "The mad woman in the attic, that'll be me."

We had watched *Jane Eyre* on the television the previous Sunday afternoon, and I felt ashamed to remember now that I had, in fact, imagined my mother as the first Mrs. Rochester, burning down the house and herself to make way for a sensible, Jane Eyre–like stepmother for me.

"Don't say such things in front of Jesse." My father shook his head, making the narrow shaft of sunlight that shone through the curtained window move like a spotlight above his balding head.

"Oh, come on," my mother said. "You'd be happier without me."

My father let out a heavy sigh. "Oh, for God's sake, Evelyn, don't be so stupid."

She swallowed a mouthful of sandwich. "Oh, no, don't go calling me stupid. I know you wish I'd done a better job of this." She thrust her arms out from under the puffy-sleeved dressing gown, and for the first time I saw the bold red scars across her wrists.

DESPITE MY MOTHER'S PROTESTATIONS, it became clear that we were moving, with my father exhibiting a level of determination that I hadn't quite realized he was capable of. It took him a few weeks, but finally he announced that he'd found "the perfect house" outside Midham, a village about fifteen miles northeast of Hull. He told us cheerily that it was still within driving distance of his job, adding later, when my mother was out of hearing, that his journey to work would give him "a bit of much needed peace."

The week after that, Auntie Mabel came round to help us pack. My mother's older sister, she always arrived in a cloud of cigarette smoke and thick, flowery perfume—smells that lingered in the house long after she left. Mabel was an Avon lady, and she carried one of the catalogs with her wherever she went, whipping it out of her massive PVC handbag whenever the opportunity to make a pitch for her products arose. She hosted Tupperware parties as well, and she seemed convinced that all my mother needed was a little makeup and a few fully sealable sandwich containers to set her all to rights.

"You should come over to my house next Saturday," Mabel said, flicking the ash of her cigarette with a glossy red fingernail filed to a hazardous point. She and my mother had spent twenty minutes half-heartedly tossing items into boxes when Mabel decided that it was time to retreat to the kitchen for a cup of tea. I'd been told to keep on wrapping my mother's best glasses in old copies of the Hull *Daily Mail,* but after a few minutes I got bored and followed them. Mabel had taken off her shoes and had her feet up on one of the chairs; she was wiggling her stocking-covered toes and blowing long puffs of cigarette smoke into the air. My mother sat hunched over the kitchen table, her teacup nestled in both hands.

"We're going to have cheese sticks and some of those little hot-dog sausages," Mabel continued. "And I'm going to do a makeup demo on the woman who lives next door. Ooh, you should see the state of her, Evelyn. A right bloody mess, she is. Set myself a challenge there, I have. Mind you, you've got to feel sorry for the lass. I mean, seven bleeming kids and another one on the way. If I was her, I'd make my husband tie a knot in it, I really would. Either that or chop the damn thing off." She flashed me a look. "Ooh, I suppose I shouldn't go saying such things in front of such tender young ears, should I?"

I rolled my eyes toward the ceiling. I hated it when adults pretended they felt some sort of obligation to censor themselves in front of me. At least I was past the age when they thought that spelling things out would leave me bewildered.

"Oh, I don't care," Mabel said, waving a thick ribbon of cigarette smoke from in front of her face. "You're going to have to learn sooner or later that all men are bastards, isn't she, Evelyn? I mean, I should know. I've been out with more of them than I care to mention. And not one of them was what I considered marriage material. Mind you," she said, slapping her pink, plump hand down on the table. "I might have been better off if I'd ruled out the ones that were married already." She laughed, throwing her head back so I could see the rows of gray fillings in her back teeth.

"Oh, you are terrible, you Mabel," my mother said, darting her tongue across her crinkled lips. "And you're right—you shouldn't go saying such things in front of Jesse. You know how easily influenced young girls are."

I rolled my eyes again. "Mum . . ." I protested, wanting to suggest that if she was so concerned about the influences in my life she might try exerting a few more positive ones herself.

"Oh, don't you worry, Ev. Our Jesse's a sensible lass, aren't you, love? And when she gets married, I'm sure—"

"I'm not getting married," I interrupted. "And I'm not having children." Those were two things I was certain of. As far as I could tell, people who were married were never happy. And those who had children were downright miserable. My own parents were definitely a case in point. While my mother was probably the unhappiest person I knew, Auntie Mabel—unmarried, childless, and currently without what she referred to as a "fella"—was indefatigably cheerful. Though sometimes I had the feeling that even her cheeriness was forced, slapped on with the same overstatement as her shimmery blue eye shadow.

"Of course you'll get married," Mabel said, swatting the air dismissively as I opened my mouth to protest. "I expect even I'll take the plunge one of these days. Just got to find the right man—rich, stupid, and just about to kick the bucket!" She barked out another laugh, then took a puff of her cigarette before leaning across the table to crush the lipstick-ringed butt. As she bent forward, I could see down the front of her dress, the deep slit of her cleavage and the massive pale mounds of her breasts spilling over the top of her pink lacy bra. Her whole chest was like two well-stuffed cushions, and I found myself thinking how nice it would be to rest my head there. "Everybody gets married in the end," she concluded.

"Uncle Ted's not married," I countered.

"Yes, well," Mabel said, pulling out another cigarette and tapping the end on the table. "There's not a woman on the planet stupid enough to marry our Ted."

Ted was Mabel and my mother's older brother. He didn't come to see us much, but when he did he always made an impression. Reeking of hair oil and Brut, he smoked even more than Mabel, swore incessantly, and always showed up bearing lavish or rather odd gifts. My mother said he would have visited us more often if he didn't spend so much of his time in prison.

"Yes," my mother said. "Never been anything but bloody trouble, our Ted. You're right about that, Mabel, you definitely are. I mean, you'd think he'd have learned his lesson by now. Almost forty-three and still messing around like a big kid."

"Well, he never was the brightest spark, was he?" Mabel put her cigarette to her mouth and raised her eyes to the ceiling.

Every time he got out, Ted was soon involved in what even I could see were not the most intelligent of crimes. Once, he was caught breaking into what turned out to be the local chief constable's house, tripping an alarm that connected right to the police station. Another time, he was arrested for passing forged pound notes that, according to my father, looked more like Monopoly money than the real thing. Most recently, he'd been sent away for "receiving stolen property" after he was caught trying to sell a vanload of illicitly acquired vacuum cleaners door to door in a rather upscale suburb of York. As a petty criminal, poor Ted was working at a considerable disadvantage, since he had deception written all over his boyish features. People didn't believe him even when he was telling the truth, which he swore he sometimes did.

"I hate to think of him in there, I really do," my mother said, pursing her lips and shaking her head drearily. "I mean, it must be terrible to be locked up all the time like that."

"You ask me, he must like it. Otherwise he wouldn't keep going back, now, would he?" Mabel said.

"I know, but it must be terrible. It makes me really upset at times to think about him, it does."

"Look," Mabel said sharply, "don't you go getting yourself all in a tizzy about our Ted. He can look after himself. It's you I'm worried about right now. Come on, how about it? Come over to my house on Saturday night. I know you'd have a good time. I've got some lovely stuff, Ev. You'd be amazed what they can do with plastic these days."

"No, no, you're all right, Mabel," my mother said, listlessly shaking her head. "I just don't think I'm much company. I'll be better off staying home and getting ready for the move."

Mabel reached across the table to pat my mother's hand. "What you need is to get yourself out of yourself. Have a bit of fun. I mean, it can't have been much of a picnic after . . . well, when you were away."

My mother shrugged and pulled a tight-lipped smile. "No, but I'm back now, aren't I?" Her voice fell dim and flat.

"Yes, yes you are," Mabel said. "And that's why you should come over on Saturday. We'll have some laughs. No blokes, just us girls together for a change."

"Can I come?" I chirped. I pictured myself sitting among a group of big-boned, ample-bosomed women just like Mabel, their wide arms jiggling as they lifted their cigarettes to their puckered lips. They'd swig mouthfuls of copper-colored sweet sherry and laugh from their bellies as they told dirty jokes. The idea seemed so comforting, like being wrapped in blankets on a cold winter night.

Mabel ignored me and continued. "You should come, Ev. You won't have much of a chance of that once you've flitted, now will you? You're going to be a bit out of touch out there. I mean, it's a good forty-five minutes on the bus. And fares aren't exactly cheap these days."

"Can I go to the party?" I asked again, afraid of what lay ahead of us and wondering if I'd ever see Auntie Mabel again. As far as I knew, aside from her annual trips with her bingo club to see the Blackpool Illuminations, she never ventured outside Hull.

"No, you bloody well can't," my mother snapped. "Now, why don't you get them glasses packed while me and Mabel finish off our teas."

AFTER I LEARNED ABOUT our move, I went to the library to find out some information on Midham, since all my father had been able to tell us about the place we would soon call home was that it had two pubs and a newsagent's shop, critical services as far as he was concerned. There was nothing about Midham in the *Encyclopaedia Britannica,* and it didn't even merit a speck in the *Reader's Digest Atlas.* When I'd asked the librarian if she could help me, she'd steered me toward a slim book on East Yorkshire history which noted that there had been a small Roman settlement there and that Midham had been listed as a thriving market town in the *Domesday Book.* And that was it. For almost nine hundred years, apparently, nothing worth mentioning had taken place there. Even when I finally turned to the *Royal Automobile Association Road Atlas,* I found that the village was nothing more than a tiny black dot alongside a thin strand of road. Its only redeeming feature, as far as I could tell, was that it was two miles from the coast. Not close enough to fall into the sea—at least for a few centuries—but close enough that I thought my father would easily be able to drive us for a day out at the beach.

We didn't go to the seaside much. But when we did, despite the interminable trek my mother always insisted upon in order to find the "right" spot for us to sit in, despite her complaints about other people's loud radios, snogging teenagers, the way the sand got into everything, and the tide that came in too fast, I liked it: the smell of seaweed and brine, salt crusting my skin, sand easing its way between my fingers and toes, and the sound of the waves, arcing and falling like long reluctant breaths.

The first time my parents took me to the seaside, I was three years old. My mother often told how, as soon as we arrived on the beach, I'd broken free of her arms and run, fully clothed, right into the waves. "You were a little madam, you were," she'd say, tutting her disapproval each time she told the story. "Didn't take a blind bit of notice when I shouted at you. Oh, no, you were determined to run into that water, no matter what I had to say."

I didn't remember this incident, but I loved the idea of it, loved to think of myself as a chubby-legged toddler, racing away from my yelling mother to plunge into the cold waters of the North Sea.

CHAPTER THREE

———

"WELCOME TO THE BACK END OF BLOODY BEYOND," MY MOTHER announced, stepping down from the removal van and swinging her arm listlessly across the vista of bright fields and dark hedgerows that stretched all the way to the horizon. "Welcome to the rest of my pathetic bloody life." For the first time in weeks, she was dressed—in a wrinkled gabardine mac and pearly blue stilettos, and carrying a matching blue handbag. She'd covered her hair with a silk headscarf decorated with pictures of ships and anchors. It made me think about the world-cruising mother I'd invented and I wanted to pull it off.

"It's not that bad, Mum," I said without conviction as I squinted toward the ugly brick house that was to become our new home, its crumbling façade stained green with moss, its window frames peeling paint like dead skin. I turned back toward the fields. "I mean, the air's fresh." I took a deep breath to emphasize my point and noticed the whiff of manure tingling my nostrils.

My mother wrinkled up her nose and folded her arms across her chest.

"And there's lots of space." I indicated the broad landscape, as level and uncreased as a giant map laid before us, its only vertical features the occasional trees that stretched defiantly above the flat ground. Most were green, lush with bright summer leaves, but some were bare, their dark branches stretching upward like charred and twisted bones.

"Yes, I'll not argue with you about that," she said, pursing her lips and looking longingly at the thread of gray road on which we had just arrived.

"Well, it could be worse. . . ."

"You should go into advertising, you Jesse. That's the best slogan I've heard in years. 'It could be worse.' That would sell a lot of bananas, now wouldn't it?"

I looked into her frowning face, searching desperately for something to say that would soothe her. I took a breath, opened my mouth in anticipation of finding the right phrase, but I could think of nothing.

"So, what do you think?" My father was beaming as he emerged from the other side of the van, where he'd been providing instructions to the removal men. As he approached us, the two men had begun unloading our things, noisily rolling my father's battered armchair down the ramp toward the front door. I watched flecks of its stuffing fall onto the path and float, like huge, asymmetrical snowflakes, across the weed-ridden garden to catch on the rangy stalks of purple-blooming thistles.

"What do you think I think?" my mother said, opening her handbag, fumbling about for a few seconds, then pulling out her sunglasses and promptly putting them on. Since there was no sun in sight and the clouds overhead were so dark and threatening that I worried we might not get our furniture inside before it began to pour, I suspected that she might be trying to make a point.

"Oh, come on, Evelyn. Don't be a wet blanket. I mean, what a beautiful view, eh?" His voice was jolly, as expansive as the landscape. "And we're only a few minutes from the village."

"Sorry," my mother said. "I'm afraid I didn't see a village. I must have blinked when we drove through it."

We had driven through the village of Midham a few minutes before arriving at the house, and though it wasn't quite as tiny as my mother made it out to be, it was hardly a bustling center of activity. There was a little main street that, on one side, held an old stone church, a post office, a handful of shops, and two shabby pubs; the other side looked out across open fields. The street was narrow enough that, as we'd driven through in the removal van, the couple of cars we encountered coming in the opposite direction had had to pull over to let us pass.

My father turned to me. "What about you, Jesse, do like it?" His features were animated with hopefulness, his smile a buoyant question pressed across his face.

I stood between them, my needy father and my irate mother, shifting nervously from one foot to the other, looking at each of them and then up at the ominous sky. Finally, I shrugged. "It's all right," I said, turning to walk toward the house, hoping for shelter before the imminent storm.

NOT LONG AFTER the removal men started carrying our things out of the van, the skies opened up and the rain poured, promptly revealing several holes in the steep, slate-tiled roof of our new home. While my father and I ran around frantically trying to locate enough buckets, bowls, and any other containers available to catch all the water that drip-dripped, drizzled, or simply flowed into the house, the two men worked at a leisurely pace, apparently unfazed by the rain that glided off their greased-down hair and soaked almost every item of furniture we owned. That evening, my father and I sat on our damp settee eating cold baked beans out of a tin that we planned to use afterward to capture what we hoped was one last leak discovered in the upstairs bathroom. Meanwhile, my mother, having spent the past half hour drying her side of the mattress with the hair dryer, had gone to bed.

"Now, I know there's a few things to be fixed here, Jesse," my father said, exhibiting a remarkable gift for understatement. "But nothing I can't handle, mind you." I watched an orange streak of tomato sauce roll down his chin as he leaned forward to pick up one of a stack of new handyman books he had laid in front of him on the floor. "Look," he said, flipping open the shiny cover and leafing through the untouched pages. "They explain everything in here. I'll be done in no time."

I wished I shared his confidence. The house was a shambles. Aside from the leaking roof, there were the broken sashes on the windows, drooping ceilings, wallpaper that hung off the walls in strips, rusted, dripping taps in the kitchen, and lights that flickered whenever someone walked across the room. The whole place smelled of mold and old people, and when I'd first walked inside I wondered if the previous owners had died there. I imagined them buried beneath the uneven floorboards, dead eyes staring upward between the wide gaps.

My father flipped happily through *House Repairs Made Simple,* telling me how he was going to rip out this, repoint that, take out walls, add walls, and generally transform the place into a palace of Formica and fake wood paneling. Since he didn't exactly have a track record with this sort of thing, I found myself more than a little skeptical. Apparently, though, he didn't plan to do things by himself.

"You never know," he said, smiling sheepishly. "Maybe your mother will rise to the challenge. I mean, she's quite a handywoman when she gets herself going. Remember what a transformation she did of our old place?"

How could I forget? My mother had discovered do-it-yourself right around the time I entered primary school, after she'd watched a television program that showed how to frame your favorite print. Once she'd managed to put van Gogh's *Sunflowers* in an oversized wooden frame and hang it above the mantel in the living room, there seemed to be no stopping her. She began staying up all night to regrout the bathroom, assemble a shed from a kit in the backyard, or put down new green-and-black linoleum in the kitchen. My father had spent weeks sleeping in a nylon sleeping bag on the living-room settee while she overhauled the bedrooms. I stayed up to help her, partly because I couldn't fall asleep while she played the same two records—Beethoven's Fifth Symphony and Bill Haley and the Comets' "Rock Around the Clock"—all through the night, and partly because I loved slapping on the wallpaper paste. In my first two years of school, it wasn't uncommon for my mother to spend weeks at a time working through the night to put up sliding glass doors in the living room or install a new fitted kitchen. It also wasn't uncommon for me to fall asleep in the middle of lessons, and I was almost put in the remedial class because my teacher, Mrs. Sparks, seemed to think this indicated that I might be, as she put it, "a little on the slow side." Fortunately, by the time I entered the third year my mother had completed her renovations. I was able to get a good night's sleep, and my performance at school improved.

My mother, on the other hand, went through what she and my father came to refer to as one of her "bad patches." With no more home improvements to work on, she seemed to lose all sense of purpose. It was a strange and dramatic transformation. One week she was hauling child-size stones from the local gardening shop so that she could make the patch of lawn in front of our house into a Japanese rock garden; the next she was spending hours at a time sitting at the kitchen table, staring into space. The only thing she seemed to care about was listening to the Jimmy Young and Terry Wogan shows on Radio 2. The house reverberated with the djs' bouncy voices and the Engelbert Humperdinck, Val Doonican, and Andy Williams songs they played throughout the day. It was around this time that she first began mentioning the possibility of being taken off to Delapole.

I remembered vividly the first afternoon I came home from school to find the house cold and still. It was January, the sky was filled with inky clouds, and dusk had already fallen. I had trudged home in my duffle coat and Wellington boots through snow that lay trampled and dirty on the pavements and was starting to freeze over into a layer of gray ice. A group of older boys had pelted me with snowballs that were hard as stones, and the back of my head was still aching from one that had hit me there. I had been crying, as much from anger and humiliation as from the pain, and the tears stung my cold cheeks with sudden heat.

"Mum," I called as I pushed my way through the front door and into a hall that was almost as cold as the air outside and far darker than the premature evening sky. "Mum." My voice echoed through the house. It felt hollow and unoccupied, and it was hard to imagine that this was the same place in which I had gobbled down hot porridge that morning while my father slurped his tea and my mother methodically scraped burned toast over the sink. I walked to the foot of the stairs and noticed the chatter of the radio coming from one of the upstairs bedrooms, the cheery announcer, and then the smooth gurgling of a Perry Como song. "Moon River, wider than a mile, I'm crossing you in style some day. . . ." I trudged cautiously up the stairs, stumbling on the uneven carpet, feeling my way along the banister with my fingers. When I reached my parents' bedroom, the door was closed. I pushed it open and stepped inside. The curtains were pulled shut. I could barely see anything. For a few moments I stood still, the satiny voice of Perry Como filling the emptiness. Then, as my eyes got used to the dark, I was able to make out the outline of my mother's body in the bed, the blankets pulled up to her chin and her head resting on a single, flat pillow.

"Mum," I said, venturing toward her. "Mum, are you all right? Are you feeling poorly?" She said nothing, nor did she move. Her face was a perfect mask of stillness. "Mum?" I said again, my voice shaky. I wondered if she was sleeping, but I couldn't imagine her being able to do so with the radio right there on the bedside table so close to her head. My anxiety blossomed into panic, and I had an overwhelming fear that she had somehow died since I had left her that morning. "Mum," I said, leaning over to shake her shoulder beneath the blankets. "Mum. Wake up." Her body felt loose, without will or substance under my grip. "Mum." Tears were running down my cheeks now, burning against skin that was still raw from when I had cried earlier on the way home. Still, she didn't respond. And then I remembered the film I had watched the other night, the one my mother had sobbed and sniffled at when the heroine collapsed and the doctor put his head against her chest, listened for her heartbeat, then pulled away shaking his head. I wiped my eyes on the scratchy woolen sleeve of my duffle coat and clambered onto the bed. Then I leaned over her, pressing my ear against the blankets that covered her chest. I couldn't hear anything, so I pressed my head harder against her.

"For God's sake, get off me, can't you?" Suddenly she sat up, shoving me away and pushing me to the floor. I landed, dazed, my legs splayed out in front of me. I sat there for a moment before scrambling to lift my head and peer over the bed.

"I thought you were dead," I said. "I was listening for your heartbeat."

"Dead, eh? Yes, well, I might as well be." She flopped back onto the bed again and pulled the blankets all the way over her head.

After that, it became a regular occurrence to arrive home and find the house dark, the syrupy thick melodies of those Radio 2 songs emanating from upstairs, my mother, lying weighted under heavy blankets, still as a corpse in her frigid room. I got the impression she spent most of her days like that, and it wasn't long before she stopped bothering to get up in the mornings to see my father off to work and me off to school. She sometimes got out of bed, trudging down the stairs in her yellow flannelette nightgown, dark circles under her eyes, her hair sculpted in strange and angular shapes. She never said much during these visits while my father made nervous jokes about his terrible cooking. I'd sit in a corner of the kitchen, noticing how my mother seemed each day more removed, her gestures more loose and weary. My father could barely get her to respond to his questions, never mind laugh at his jokes. She regarded us both with distant, apathetic looks, as if our voices were nothing more than the background music that came constantly from the radio in her bedroom.

It was Mabel who was finally able to coax my mother out of this utter listlessness. She arrived one evening while my father was hunched over the cooker, stirring obsessively at a pan of Heinz baked beans with pork sausages. He'd burned our previous two meals beyond any redemption, and as a result we'd dined on toast and marmalade; tonight he seemed desperate to make dinner without mishap. Mabel swept into the kitchen in a choking vapor of perfume and cigarette smoke, dropped her massive handbag onto the kitchen table, and took in the chaos.

"This will never do, will it?" she said, looking at me. "Your mam in bed, your dad cooking the dinner, and this house a right bloody mess? I mean, what kind of life is this for a lass your age, eh? She's a right moody one, our Evelyn. One minute right as rain, the next minute a face on her as long as a wet weekend." She sighed, pushing a stream of thick blue smoke out of her nostrils. "Anyway, I'm having none of this." She strode across the room to drop her cigarette into the sink. It hit the enamel surface with a hiss. "What she needs is a night on the town. Something to cheer her up. Like it or not, she's coming out with me. I'm taking her to bingo."

My father looked at her dubiously. "You and whose army?" he asked, battling a packet of Wonderloaf to place two slices under the grill. "She doesn't even get herself dressed these days, never mind out of the house. You'll be lucky to get two words out of her."

"Come hell or high water, and whether she likes it or not, that woman is coming with me to bingo."

Indeed, about an hour later and much to my and my father's amazement, Mabel appeared downstairs with my mother, who was dressed and apparently ready to go out. I had grown so used to seeing her in her nightclothes that it was strange to see her in a dress and high heels, and even stranger to see her pale cheeks striped with rosy blush, her lips glossy pink, and her eyelids tinted bright green. She reminded me of one of the cardboard cutout dolls I sometimes played with—flat and flimsy, their features painted too big and impossibly bright.

"What do you think?" Mabel asked, nodding proudly toward my mother. "Looks human for a change, doesn't she?"

My father seemed slightly bewildered, as if he'd seen a ghost. "She looks very nice. Yes, you look very nice, Evelyn."

"Right, then, Ev, get your coat on. We don't want to miss the first game, now do we?" Mabel grabbed my mother's arm and tugged her toward the hallway.

I was asleep by the time they returned, but when I got up the next morning I was astonished to find my mother in the kitchen, cooking a huge breakfast of bacon, eggs, black pudding, and fried bread. The windows were opaque with steam, and she scurried around setting knives and forks on the table, humming along as Tom Jones belted out, "Why, why, why, Delilah?" on the radio.

"Oh, hello, love," she said, flashing me a bright smile. "Are you hungry?"

I nodded.

"Well, sit yourself down, then. We're having a celebration breakfast." I took a seat at the table. "So, don't you want to know what we're celebrating?" she asked, putting a loaded plate in front of me.

"Why?" I asked, picking up my fork and pushing a piece of black pudding into my mouth.

"Because . . ." She pressed her palms together against her chest. "Because I won!" She swung her arms wide. "I won at the bingo. Twenty-three pounds three shillings and sixpence. Now, what do you think about that?" She wore a look of expectant delight.

"Is that a lot of money?" I asked, dipping a corner of fried bread into my egg yolk and watching mesmerized as the liquid yellow oozed across the plate.

"Of course it is," she answered irritably. "It's more than your father brings home in his pay packet, let's put it that way. And if I can win that in one night, who knows what I can do if I go more often. Our Mabel says they have a weekly jackpot on Friday nights. Ten thousand quid. Now, just think what we could do with that much money."

And so began my mother's bingo craze. Each morning before leaving for school, I'd sit at the kitchen table as she gave me a blow-by-blow account of the previous night's events. As she spoke, I felt as if I were there experiencing that unspeakable excitement as the bingo caller announced, "Two little ducks, twenty-two," and my mother leaped up screaming, "House! House!" and the covetous eyes of all the other women in the Astoria Bingo Hall were turned on her. She told me of her defeats, too. "I was that close, I mean that close," she said, holding out her thumb and forefinger, the smallest of space between them. "All I needed was that old bugger to call out legs eleven and that national jackpot would've been mine. Next time," she said, pushing clenched fists into her apron pockets, a fiery glint in her eye. "Next time I just know I'm going to win. You can count on that, Jesse."

She seemed so convinced that it was just a matter of time before she won the national jackpot that I began to fantasize about what we could do with that ten-thousand-pound prize. Walking to school in the rain, I'd daydream about the luxurious holidays we'd take or the brand-new car my father would chauffeur us around in. On weekends, I'd spend whole afternoons leafing through the old Littlewoods catalog that Auntie Mabel had given me, picking out clothes and furniture, keeping a running total of how much I was spending so I knew exactly what that amount of money could buy.

Unfortunately, however, it wasn't a triumphant jackpot win that brought an end to my mother's bingo obsession. After talking with Mrs. Brockett one morning, my father discovered that my mother had taken to playing three or four cards at every game, an expensive habit through which she'd managed to completely deplete my parents' Post Office savings account, and had taken to using a large chunk of the housekeeping money—which accounted for the rather skimpy dinners that had recently made an unwelcome reappearance in our household.

Much to my disappointment, the bingo (and our chance at attaining instant wealth) ended. I found myself again trudging without any distraction through gray blustery streets, and instead of compiling lists of what we might buy from the Littlewoods catalog I browsed for hours at a time through the women's underwear section, inexplicably fascinated by those coy models in their pointy bras, paneled corsets, and silky black knickers. My mother was less easily diverted. At first, she tried to convince my father that she could tone down her obsession and go only once a week to try for the national jackpot on Friday nights. But soon she began trying to sneak out to the bingo hall on other nights, only to be pursued by my father. For a while, it was almost routine for them to have an enormous, screaming fight in the middle of the street, much to the amusement of the neighbors. "Beats bloody *Coronation Street*," I heard Mrs. Brockett comment over the other side of her wall to our next-door-but-one neighbor. "Ought to start their own soap opera, that family."

Finally, my mother was defeated. But instead of taking up another hobby, as my father had been suggesting, she simply stopped doing anything at all, sinking almost immediately into another of her bad patches, far longer and worse than the last.

PERHAPS THERE WAS method in my father's madness, after all. Maybe my mother, unable to bear the decrepitude of our new home in Midham, would spring into action and throw herself into its restoration. But, as I looked up at a crack in the ceiling that ran through the plaster like a deep river, opening into a wide delta that ended above the fireplace, I couldn't help thinking he was taking a rather dubious gamble.

"Why didn't you buy a new house?" I asked.

As soon as my father announced our move, I'd begun hoping for a brand-new brick semidetached house with a neat square of lawn in the front and borders filled with pansies in the back. I'd seen pictures of such houses on television, and traveled past rows upon rows of them when we'd driven through the outskirts of Hull. I was convinced that a house like that would solve all our problems. I could come home from school and enter the basking warmth of central heating and double glazing to be greeted by my mother, who, just like the women on the Fairy Snow adverts, would be calm and smiling and made happy by a clean wash and a sparkling home.

"This is new," my father said, smiling so wide that his dimples showed. They made him look like a little boy, and I wished I could be swept up in his enthusiasm. "It's new to us," he added. "And what we don't like we can change. It will give all of us a whole new start."

"Yes," I said dully, thinking that at least with a different school to go to I might have a chance to make some friends. I'd have no history. No one would know that my mother had been in the nuthouse or that I'd made up stupid stories to try to hide that fact. And I wouldn't have to crave the approval of Julie Fraser or any of her stupid friends ever again.

THE BAD PATCH after the bingo had lasted several months but finally came to an end when my mother began watching *The Galloping Gourmet* and discovered a sudden passion for cordon-bleu cooking. She spent entire mornings scouring the shops for the appropriate ingredients (veal was something there had never been much demand for at our local butcher's, and the grocer hadn't even heard of some of the things the recipes called for) and entire afternoons in a flurry of flour and steam preparing the evening's meal. At night, in bed, she sat propped against her pillow reading recipe books. The *Galloping Gourmet* program itself was a period during which absolute silence was demanded in our household, as my mother pulled her chair to within four feet of the television, scribbling notes and sighing at the Galloping Gourmet's momentous culinary achievements.

For a few weeks, my father and I were treated almost every evening to meals like Coq au Vin, Rôti de Porc Boulangère, and Boeuf à la Mode. I quite enjoyed it, especially since my mother also insisted on "creating the appropriate atmosphere," with a red gingham tablecloth, candles, and French accordion music playing on the record player in the other room. She even made me teach her a few phrases that I had recently learned in my first year of French at school, like *merci beaucoup, c'est très bien,* and *ça c'est bon,* which she insisted on repeating throughout the meals, regardless of whether they actually made any sense at the time, and with a French accent even worse than that of any of my fellow students. Mabel, when she came over one night, was delighted at the whole scene, oohing and aahing at the paper serviettes, the white chef's hat my mother wore as she cooked, the packet of French cigarettes my mother had bought her as a treat, and the bottle of white wine she placed on the table before we began.

"I love a bit of good plonk with my food, I really do," Mabel said, gulping back half her glass of wine before lifting it into the air and declaring, "*Ooh là là,* here's to a little bit of France right here in Hull."

My father, on the other hand, was rather irritated by the whole thing and seemed to have little desire to consume meals whose names he could not pronounce, never mind understand.

"Jesus Christ, Evelyn. Whatever happened to good, plain English food?" he complained one night at the sight of a whole small bird and a pile of haricots verts in cream sauce on his plate. "I mean, what on earth is this, anyway, underage chicken? What's wrong with a nice steak and kidney pudding, a few Brussels sprouts and some chips?"

My mother's response was swift and to the point. She picked up the plate she had just placed in front of my father, screamed, "Nobody ever appreciates me! Nobody!" and hurled it at the wall. The plate shattered, the bird thumped to the floor, and the haricots verts in their cream sauce stuck to the wall for a moment before oozing slowly downward, eventually forming a puddle on the linoleum. "You'll send me to Delapole, you two!" she yelled, giving me a furious look that seemed to indicate that she regarded me as the instigator of my father's complaint.

"I like your French food, Mum," I said, lifting my knife and fork, as if I were desperate to sink my teeth into the small bird, which I, like my father, speculated was a prematurely butchered chicken. But it was too late. She leaned over me, grabbed my plate, and spun round to throw that, too, at the wall.

After that, another bad patch. That was followed, several months later, by a brief but very intense interest in dressmaking (I got a whole new, ill-fitting, and rather bizarre wardrobe), then macramé (until every available space in the house was covered in multicolored throws, blankets, tablecloths, and antimacassars), candle making, quilting, up-holstery, rug making, amateur dramatics, and, finally, a stint organizing jumble sales for the Young Wives Club until, for some reason that she never revealed to my father and me, she was asked to step down. And, in between all these things, there were, of course, the bad patches.

"I THINK I'LL TRY and fix that roof tomorrow," my father said, scraping the last baked beans from the tin and spooning them into his mouth. "First things first, after all."

I only hoped my father was up to it. He'd never been particularly good with heights and wouldn't even take me on the big wheel at Hull Fair because he said it made him dizzy. I had a difficult time imagining him scrambling over the steep slate roof, but I didn't want to be too negative, so I gave him what I hoped was an encouraging smile.

"And you'll have to do your part, our Jesse."

"Me?" I was thrilled, visualizing myself scrabbling over the tiles beside him, looking out over the fields like I was on top of the world.

"Yes—I need you to keep an eye on your mother for me while I'm busy. We wouldn't want her to . . . well, we've seen enough problems already without another little episode, if you know what I mean."

"What am I supposed to do?" I asked. "I can't stop her from doing anything." I felt the panic rising.

My father reached over and patted me on the head. "Just look out for her, that's all. I mean, it'll not be for long, love. You'll see, she'll soon be right as rain."

"She will?" More than anything, I wanted to believe him.

CHAPTER FOUR

——

FOR A WEEK OR SO, I SAT AROUND THE HOUSE TRYING TO FOLLOW MY
father's instructions and watch over my mother. I wanted to help him,
but just the idea of it made me feel overwhelmed. What was I supposed
to do? Keep her away from the kitchen knives? Guard the door so she
couldn't run out and throw herself under the wheels of one of the stray
vehicles that passed by our house? There seemed to be so many ways
that she could try to kill herself if she wanted. I looked at an electrical
cord and wondered if she could use it to hang herself from the banister,
took a bottle of Domestos from under the kitchen sink and imagined
her swigging it back, the thick, bleachy liquid making the same *glug-glug-
glug* sound when it went down her throat as it did when I poured it into
the sink. I looked at my father's hammer and wondered if it was possible to beat yourself to death, picked up one of my mother's scarves and
wondered if you could strangle yourself. Almost everything around me
became a potential instrument of death.

Thankfully, she remained relatively unperturbed, and I wondered if
the little yellow pills my father now rationed out to her each day were
responsible for this unfamiliar calm. My mother complained that it was
treating her like a child to give her medicine to her in small, daily doses.
But my father just responded to these protests with "Doctor's orders,

Evelyn, doctor's orders." I got the impression that he'd been given strict instructions not to let my mother near any large amount of medication. It was probably for this same reason, I'd deduced, that just before my mother's return an ancient bottle of aspirin and a dusty bottle of cough syrup had been removed from the medicine cabinet and my father had stopped leaving his razor blades in the bathroom.

One Thursday, a little over a week after the move, I spent the morning watching television, creeping upstairs periodically to sneak into my parents' bedroom, standing over my sleeping mother and holding my own breath until I could detect the slow and steady rise of hers. The fourth time I found myself there, I heard the loud and repeated toot of a horn. It was coming from just outside the house. Afraid that it would wake my mother and she'd find me there, I tiptoed quickly down the stairs. As the horn sounded again, I opened the front door and saw that a large blue van had pulled into our driveway and a woman was leaning out the window on the driver's side. "I'm not stopping here all day, you know!" she yelled. "If you want to join up, you'd better get yourself over here sharp."

I was about to ask her what it was that I was supposed to be joining when I saw the words COUNTY LIBRARY painted on the side of the van. I was relieved to realize that though Midham might not have much going for it, it did have a mobile library.

I bolted out the door. When I reached the back door of the van, the woman opened it up, popped out a set of metal stairs, and I walked inside.

"New here, aren't you?" she said as she looked me up and down. She was a solid woman, shapeless as a tree trunk, in a sturdy green wool dress. Her face was broad, with big jowly lines around her mouth and a deep frown etched between her eyebrows. Her hair was blue-black, the kind of color that only comes out of a bottle; it gave her skin a grayish tinge, as if she hadn't seen daylight in a while, and somehow made me feel as if, upon stepping into the mobile library, I'd entered into a fiercely guarded lair. "I heard there was some new people moving in," she said. "You'd be surprised how much I find out here in this little van. Go all over this side of the district, I do." I frowned, wondering if somehow she had already picked up some choice snippets about my family. My father would be thrilled. "So, like a good read, do you?" she asked.

"Yes."

"Reading, that's a good quality in children. Beats all that rock and roll—all that nonsense about free love and drugs. All these layabouts you get on the dole. Far as I'm concerned"—she wagged a stern finger in my direction—"you can blame most of the evils of this world on a lack of reading. If more kids these days read instead of watching the box and getting all kinds of rubbish in their heads, the world would be a much better place. Oh, no, you wouldn't find young girls unmarried and having babies if they'd been reading instead of messing about with some boy, now would you?"

I nodded in agreement. She did, after all, have a point.

"Now, you want to sign up then, do you? Want to take out some books?"

"Yes, please," I said, eyeing the shelves that lined the van.

"Oh, good, a child with some manners finally. I can't tell you how many kids these days don't know the meaning of 'please' and 'thank you.' Get you a long way in the world, do those words. Here." She pushed a form toward me. "Fill out this and you can pick five books. Keep them out no more than a fortnight. I usually come round once a week."

I filled out the form and handed it back to her. She looked it over and pointed me toward the bookshelves. "Don't take all day about it, mind. I've got to be at the Reatton church hall by twelve. They've got the pensioners coming for a browse and a cup of tea with the vicar. They're a demanding lot, them pensioners. And they'll be a bit put out today, since the Bleakwick Young Wives Club already took out half my Agatha Christies." She shook her head slowly to amplify the gravity of this occurrence. "I keep telling them over at the main library to get in more Agatha Christies. But listen to me, do they? Of course they don't. After all, they've all got their fancy degrees from some fancy university. And me—well, I'm just a lowly nobody with nothing but a few O levels and a love of literature."

I tried to pull an expression that showed deep sympathy for her plight.

"I keep trying to tell them that mysteries and romance is what goes down best with the folk round here. But what is it they send me?" She paused and seemed to expect an answer. I was about to try to give her one when she continued. "Rubbish, that's what. Well, of course they wouldn't call it rubbish, would they? But what these hoity-toity types at main think is a good book is not what interests the Reatton Derby and Joan Club, is it? And you should see some of the stuff they send me." She wrinkled her nose and lowered her voice. "Well, suffice to say it's not suitable subject matter for the young wives or the pensioners. I prefer to keep it off the shelves." She began to whisper. "Back there." She indicated a stack of books immediately behind her. "That's what I call my slush pile. And slush it is, I can tell you."

I leaned over the desk, trying to make out some of the titles on the spines of the stack of books. The librarian waved me away. "Like I said, not suitable material. Now you'd better get yourself something picked out. I've not got all day."

There were a lot of books—the tightly packed shelves lined the van from floor to ceiling—but when I began looking at the titles I couldn't see much that appealed to me. The children's section, labeled as such in big, handwritten letters, was full of the Ladybird books that I'd stopped reading when I was seven, a lot of children's novels on religious themes—*He Loves Us When We're Good, Jesus and the Snowman, The Twelve Happy Disciples*—a few other books with uninspiring titles, and picture books for toddlers. The adult section, similarly labeled, contained dozens of romance novels—*He Swept Her Away, A Distant Affair, Search for Passion*—the kind of titles I often found stacked haphazardly on Auntie Mabel's bedside table, and that I secretly skimmed through to find the parts where the heroes and heroines tussled on four-poster beds amid satin sheets, tousled hair, and torn bodices. Many of the remaining books seemed to be Westerns and mysteries. I wasn't interested in cowboy stories and though I'd read a few Agatha Christie novels and found them engaging, they weren't among my favorites. Besides, I thought it best not to reduce the mystery inventory even further and provoke a riot among the pensioners.

"Get a move on, love," the librarian commanded.

I bent down to scan the lower shelves and saw a few titles of more interest.

"Come on, come on, I can't wait forever." The librarian tapped her wristwatch.

I pulled out a copy of *Jane Eyre* and made my way to the little check-out counter.

"I'll take this," I said, handing the book to the librarian, who stood with her date stamp ready in her hand.

She opened the front page, ready to stamp the card in there, when she noticed the title. "Ooh, I don't think so," she said, shaking her head. "I don't think so at all."

I looked at her, perplexed.

"You got this in the adult section, didn't you?" she said with gravity. "You have to be over sixteen to take books out of the adult section."

"It's for my mother," I responded. "She's got a very bad illness. She's too poorly to come out of the house."

The woman shook her head solemnly. "Look, I don't care what's up with your mother, love. Rules are rules. Besides, the Brontës were considered pornographic in the nineteenth century, you know."

Pornographic? It didn't seem that way in the film my mother and I watched. If the book was pornographic, I definitely wanted to read it.

"I'm sorry," I said, smiling. "I'll put it back and pick out something else." I held out my hand. The librarian kept a tight hold on the book. "I remember exactly where I got it." I pointed to the shelf from which

I'd taken the book. "And I know all about the Dewey decimal system," I added brightly.

This seemed to convince her, and she handed it over.

I stepped back to the shelf, bent down with book in hand, turned my head to see that the librarian was no longer looking at me, and stuffed it under my sweater. I stepped over to the children's section, pulled down a couple of random titles, and took them over to her desk, where she stamped the date on their cards, put the cards into her little file box, and said goodbye.

BY THE TIME my father returned that evening, I was more than a hundred pages into *Jane Eyre,* and if there was anything pornographic in it, it had certainly escaped my attention. I wasn't disappointed, though, because it was a really good story. The awful tragedy of Jane losing the only friend she had in the world left me brushing tears from my eyes, and next to her terrible experiences in that awful school my own difficulties seemed quite small.

"I'm off to the launderette," my father announced as he shrugged off his jacket. "We need to get some of this stuff dry." He gestured toward the sweaters, trousers, and shirts that had been left strewn over every item of furniture. We hadn't been able to hang the washing outside because it had rained relentlessly ever since we moved in.

I dropped my book. "Can I come?" I began jogging around the living room, grabbing damp clothes in handfuls.

My father frowned over at my mother. "Well, I don't know . . . I mean, your mam could probably use your company and . . ."

"I'm sick of looking at that bloody face of hers; it's as long as the Mersey Tunnel," my mother said, waving a limp arm toward me. "A girl her age should get herself outside."

"But it's raining." I pointed at the window, where water drizzled down the glass in thick streams.

"Anybody would think you'd melt." Suddenly animated, she stabbed the air with the pen she'd been using to fill out the *Woman's Realm* cross-word puzzle. "Honestly, all you need to do is put a bloody raincoat on and go out there and play. When I was your age . . ."

I rolled my eyes. Anything either of my parents prefaced with those words was bound to irritate me. They had both spent their early child-hoods in the war, a time they recollected as a period of idyllic depriva-tion. The way they told it, every child would benefit from a good dose of air raids, severe food rationing, and the immediate prospect of a German invasion.

"When you were my age," I interrupted, "you didn't get moved into the middle of nowhere with nothing to do."

"The trouble with you is you're spoiled." My mother rolled up her *Woman's Realm* and threw it in my direction. It fluttered, pages splayed, at my feet. "Take her with you, for God's sake, Mike."

IT WAS A FIVE-MINUTE drive into the village, along a road bordered by thick hedgerows and grass verges speckled with the color of dandelions, daisies, and a variety of pink and purple flowers. The sky was massive, a billowing tent of gray. As my father drove, his silence punctuated every now and then with a weighty sigh, I peered through the rain-spattered windscreen at the shifting shapes of the dark clouds, the way the chang-ing light transformed their boundaries, so that they pushed and merged into one another like waves. I imagined myself falling upward into all that gloom and radiance, flying like the swallows that had their nest in the eaves of our house, soaring, arms pushed behind me in a V-shaped arrow, to somewhere else.

"I think we should do a bit of shopping while we're here, don't you, love?" my father said as he parked. He pointed toward a little Co-op supermarket across the street. "We could do with a bit of food in the house."

I couldn't have agreed more. For the past several days we'd been subsisting on baked beans, sardines, cheese, or tinned spaghetti on toast. Although I'd never been particularly fond of vegetables, even I was beginning to think at least having something green on my plate might not be such a bad idea.

I helped my father carry the clothes into the tiny launderette, the Midham Wash-It-All, push them into the machines, and place our coins in the slots. Then we dashed through the rain over to the Co-op and launched ourselves into the luster of tightly packed grocery shelves under flickering fluorescent lights.

I was quite excited to discover that Midham had a Co-op. The Co-op gave out stamps for everything you bought. These you pasted into books and could redeem for a wonderful array of items—everything from tea cozies (two books) to toasters (fifty books) and portable televisions (three hundred books). Just over a year ago, my mother had started collecting Co-op stamps. In her initial frenzy, she'd filled twenty books in a matter of weeks. She'd decided to aim for the toaster, though I'd tried to persuade her to hold out for the television.

"You could give it to me for a birthday present," I'd suggested. "Then I can watch the telly in my bedroom and I won't be a bother to you and Dad."

The way she'd refused even to acknowledge this proposal, however, implied that she had other things in mind. Indeed, she'd maintained a resolute commitment to the toaster and might well have made it were it not for my father finding out that she had taken to shopping at the Co-op almost every day, buying far more than we needed and stashing the excess under their bed. The discovery had come when he stubbed his toe on a tin of Heinz mulligatawny soup and bent down to discover that the entire floor there was occupied by an assortment of tins, packages, and boxes.

Following this, my father had decided that it was best if my mother took a break from doing the shopping. Soon he and I got into a routine of going together on Friday evenings when the Co-op in Hull had late-night closing and he could go after work. And, having inherited the twenty-seven and a half books my mother had managed to fill, I was able to begin avidly saving for a portable television. Unfortunately, at the rate my father preferred to shop, I calculated that it would take me another five years. So I was constantly trying to buy more items, or at least more expensive ones, and each of our shopping trips became a battle between the two of us, with me surreptitiously trying to place things in the basket and my father taking them out.

During our trip to the Midham Co-op that evening, I spent much of my time trying to get my father to agree to buy a package of Mr. Kipling cream cakes. "We can't afford them," he answered wearily.

Both my mother and I loved the adverts for Mr. Kipling. They were set in pretty English cottages or on wide green lawns, the kind where people played croquet following afternoon tea. And they were narrated by a man with a voice that was warm and crumbly, and made you think of a fat Victoria Sponge Cake with jam oozing from its middle. "After all," he'd say at the conclusion of every advertisement, "Mr. Kipling does make exceedingly good cakes."

"Ooh, I could do with one of those and a nice cup of tea," my mother would say, gazing longingly at the television screen. And, indeed, when she was in charge of the shopping we'd have Mr. Kipling cakes at least once a week. "I know I shouldn't, but I can't help it," she'd say, unwrapping them from the cellophane and arranging them carefully on a plate. I'd gobble mine down in a matter of seconds, but my mother would relish hers, taking small slow bites, closing her eyes and rolling her mouth around their taste. I sometimes thought she looked at her happiest when she was smacking her lips and finishing off a Mr. Kipling custard tart.

"Please, Dad," I begged, following him around the aisles as he stared glassy-eyed at rows of tinned button mushrooms and processed peas. "Just this once, can we have them? Please."

"Stop whining, Jesse, and make yourself useful," he said. "Go and get us some toilet paper, can you? We're running out." I returned carrying a packet of Andrex Supersoft toilet tissue. "Not that," my father said. "Costs a bloody arm and a leg. Get the Co-op brand."

When my father and I approached the checkout counter, and I had failed to add one single item beyond those on my father's list, I was feeling decidedly frustrated. Then I noticed a pyramid display of Mr. Kipling chocolate fingers, sited strategically at the end of the aisle, where all the shoppers queued to have their items rung up. They were even on special offer, at five pence off. "Dad," I said quietly.

"What?"

"I bet those chocolate fingers are really tasty, don't you?" I spoke cautiously, pointing at the towering triangular display. He sighed as he turned toward me, and I felt my heart sink, sure that he would deny me this one pleasure, and the extra Co-op stamps. But, to my surprise, when his eyes rested on the stack of cakes he seemed to consider them.

"You know, they'd be nice with a cup of tea, they would. I bet your mam would like them as well. Tell you what, get us a packet, Jesse, love."

"Really?" I asked, a little incredulous.

"Yeah, why not?"

I could scarcely contain my excitement. An entire packet of Mr. Kipling cakes. I could imagine the delicious smell of the chocolate as I tore them from their wrappers, the spongy softness against my fingers as I put them on a plate, my mother's delight when I set them out in front of her. "Thanks, Dad," I said, and pulled at the packet nearest to me in the display.

Unfortunately, at that moment I was far too preoccupied with visualizing my parents and me sitting around the table devouring the cakes to consider the obvious consequences of my actions. I soon found out, however, when, having removed one of the packets close to the base of the Co-op's nicely arranged pyramidal display, the whole thing came tumbling down, boxes of Mr. Kipling chocolate fingers hurling themselves onto my father and me and scattering over the floor in a wide and unruly mess.

"What on earth is going on?" Once the debris had settled, the woman at the checkout stood up. With massive shoulders, a broad face, and a short, fat neck, she reminded me of the female Russian shot-putters I'd seen while watching the Olympics on television.

"It was her," a woman queuing in front of us said, pointing at me. "She knocked it down."

"Did she, now?" the checkout woman said, peering over at me.

"It was an accident," I said weakly, sheltering behind my father, who, much to my consternation, had so far failed to speak up for me. "I just wanted a packet of—"

"Is that child your responsibility?" the checkout woman asked as if she were referring to a troublesome pet.

"Yes, she's my daughter," my father answered sheepishly. "I'm sure she didn't mean to—"

"Well," she interrupted, "we've had plenty of trouble with teenagers. Juvenile delinquents, the lot of them. Anyway, I'm sure you'll under-stand our policy, sir. Any trouble and we have to ban them from the shop."

I looked beseechingly at my father. "Yes, well, I understand," he said. "Seems like a reasonable policy." And then he turned to me. "Go on, Jesse, why don't you wait outside? I'll not be long."

"But it was an accident," I protested, my face burning. "I didn't do anything wrong."

"Outside," he said, this time more firmly. "Do as the lady says."

I hated him in that moment, for his unwillingness to stand up for me or for himself, for his desperation to not cause a scene. I turned, kicking a path through the scattered boxes and stomping across the tiled floor, until I reached the door and flung it open.

I stood in the middle of the street, waiting for him, not even both-ering to seek shelter from the pouring rain. It seeped through my hair to my scalp, drizzled down my face, and worked over the collar of my raincoat to run down my neck. But I didn't care as I stood staring into the brightness of the Co-op window, willing my father to look over at me and witness my utter misery.

"Are you all right?"

I wiped my eyes against my sleeve before turning around to face the girl standing a few feet away from me. She was dressed in knee-high black platform boots, a black leather bomber jacket, and a pencil skirt, the kind that had a slit in the back so you could walk in it without falling over. Standing under a wide red umbrella, she wore her blond hair flicked into two wings that sat at the sides of her face like pulled-back curtains, shiny with hairspray. Her eyes, outlined in deep black eyeliner, were an unusual and stunning shade of green. Her eyelashes were dark and exceptionally long. Her lips were broad and full, and moist with pale pink gloss. She was beautiful.

"Waiting for someone?" Her voice was soft. As she spoke, she pressed her lips into a sympathetic smile.

"For my dad. He's inside." I pointed toward the Co-op. My father was standing next to the checkout lady, smiling as she rang up the groceries.

"You're getting wet. Why don't you come under here with me?" She gestured toward the shelter of her umbrella. "You'll be a lot better off. You look like a drowned rat right now." She let out a laugh, and I felt myself blush as I became aware of what a sight I must look. My face was probably red from crying, and my wet hair was plastered across my forehead and draped over my shoulders in sodden strands. I tried to push it back. "Oh, don't worry," she said. "You'll dry out when you get home. But, really, you should come under here before you get worse. Come on, don't be shy."

I moved toward the girl and slipped under her umbrella.

"There, that's better. Nice and cozy." She sidled up close to me, and I found myself engulfed in the smell of damp leather and a musky perfume.

"Can you hold this for a sec?" she asked, handing me her umbrella.

I took it and watched as she rummaged around in one of her pockets, then brought out a packet of Benson & Hedges, shook out a cigarette, placed it in her mouth, and struck a match. The bristling smell of sulfur filled my nostrils, and as she held the flame to her cigarette she drew in a breath until it glowed orange, and dropped the match to the ground. She looked at me, smiling as she blew out the smoke in a sigh. For once, I found myself not minding cigarette smoke. Instead, I breathed it in avidly until I let out a harsh, spluttering cough. "You don't smoke, do you?" she said, laughing.

"No," I said, still coughing as I handed her umbrella back.

"Good thing," she said, taking another drag. She held the cigarette between her index and middle fingers, and when she pulled it from her lips I noticed that the filter bore a pink imprint from her lip gloss. I looked at the spidery lines and wondered if the print of someone's lips was as unique as a fingerprint. "How old are you, anyway?" she asked.

"Thirteen," I said.

"I'm nearly sixteen. But people always tell me I look older." She inhaled again and turned away, so that I could watch the stark silhouette of her profile as she pouted little puffy smoke rings into the air. "You think I look older than fifteen?" she asked, eyeing me sideways.

"Yes," I answered without hesitation. "You look . . . You look just like a film star." I knew I sounded stupid, but she made me think of all those old films I had watched on cold and rainy Sunday afternoons. My mother always sighed as she looked longingly at the men: Clark Gable, Cary Grant, Kirk Douglas, Victor Mature. But they always seemed stiff-jawed and graceless to me. I much preferred the women: Bette Davis, Joan Crawford, Ingrid Bergman—their long, tilted necks, loose languid movements, thrown-out chests, their fierce and watery eyes. And the way they smoked, the plumes curling away from them, making their hot breaths visible, filling a room with their fire.

"You're funny," she said, slapping my arm gently. "Very funny." She laughed, a big, delighted laugh that danced through the rainy evening and bounced across the empty street. Just hearing it made a smile tug at the edges of my mouth. "So, what do they call you?" she asked.

"Jesse," I said. "Jesse Bennett."

"Right," she said, pausing to take another drag of her cigarette. "I'm Amanda." She exhaled her name in a cloud of blue smoke.

"Amanda," I repeated. "That's a nice name."

"It'll do."

"Do you live here in Midham?"

"Afraid so. Up there, on the Primrose Housing Estate." She nodded toward the end of the street. "Marigold Court."

"I just moved here," I said.

"Did you, now?"

"Yes, with my mum and dad. My dad wanted us to move out to the countryside. To . . . get away from things."

"Well, he certainly did a good job of that. Not exactly the center of the universe round here, is it?"

I shook my head. "Not really."

"But you know what, it could be worse," she added, grinning and nudging me gently.

"Yes, that's what I said to my mum. She's not very happy here. But I told her—" I found myself wanting to confide in Amanda, to tell her something about my mother and about my family, about all the reasons I had found myself here.

"Oh, look, there he is." She interrupted me to point across the street to where a blue Ford Cortina was pulling up. "That's my boyfriend, Stan," she said, dropping her cigarette to the wet pavement, where the shimmering orange end fizzed and died. "Normally he drives a motorbike, a dead-nice one. But, with the weather the way it is, he borrowed a mate's car. He's taking me to the pictures. Going to see some horror film. *Jaws.*" She made her eyes wide and gave a little shiver. "It's supposed to be dead scary. Sorry I've got to go. And I've got to take my brolly."

I didn't mind at all about the rain, but I wanted her to remain there, standing next to me, to tell the boyfriend, Stan, to go to see the film by himself. I glowered over at the car, wishing it would pull away without Amanda.

"Tell you what," she said. "Let's tell your dad to hurry up so you don't get too wet." Before I could say anything, she grabbed my arm and pulled me over to the shopwindow. Inside, under the fluorescent lights, I could see my father standing at the checkout stand. "Is that him?" Amanda asked.

"Yes," I said flatly.

"God, he's dead slow, isn't he?" she said.

She was right. He was packing his purchases into a carrier bag, taking each item and deliberately placing it in the bag before reaching for the next. The faces of the women behind him in the queue were taut with impatience. The cashier held out his change and a sheet of Co-op stamps, but he hadn't noticed. She looked at the other women and rolled her eyes.

"Hey," Amanda called. "Hurry up." She rapped hard on the window. Everyone in the shop turned to squint in our direction. "I said, hurry up." She knocked on the window again. My father frowned and peered toward us. Amanda laughed and knocked again. "Come on, slowcoach, get moving, can't you? It's raining cats and dogs out here, and this poor lass is going to catch her death."

Everyone inside stared at us. My father grimaced, looking from me to Amanda and back to me. It was obvious that he couldn't understand what she was saying, but what he clearly understood was that he'd been shown up in public for a second time that evening. He turned to the women in the queue. Their mouths were pressed into outraged little O's. My father appeared to mutter some kind of apology, while they all scowled and shook their heads sorrowfully. There was no doubt about it. I was going to be in terrible trouble when I got home. Still, instead of trying to restrain Amanda I felt liberated by her laughter. Behind the glass barrier of the shopwindow, everything seemed too bright, filled with adults who were eager to judge, and whose world seemed as confined as that little village shop. Outside, in the cool evening, the rain spattering off the pavement and soaking everything, where sensations were real and nothing was protected, this was the place I wanted to be.

"Oh, my God," Amanda said. "Look at them. Anybody would think they'd never seen someone knock on a window before. Boneheads." Then she rapped on the window again. "Come on, get a move on," she said, wagging a finger toward my father. "If you leave her out here much longer, her feet are going to go moldy." She giggled.

"I'll grow mushrooms on my toes," I added, laughing a little myself.

"You'll have fungus feet," Amanda said, turning from the window to grin at me.

I wrinkled up my nose and then pointed toward the checkout lady, who was now standing, hands on hips, her angular face creased into a simmering frown. "Yeah, but at least I won't have a fungus face like her," I said.

At this Amanda let out a sudden gale of laughter, amusement rippling across her features, leaving her limbs loose and causing the umbrella to veer at broad angles above us. She laughed hard, a convulsion of sound that crinkled the edges of her eyes and left her mouth open, gasping, as she placed a hand on my shoulder. I watched her, for a moment stunned by the delight on her face and the fact that I had put it there. I had never made anyone laugh like that before. It warmed me, flowed through me. I began to laugh myself, leaning into Amanda so that, as I laughed, I found myself gulping her damp leather, smoke, and perfume smells.

"Oh, my God," Amanda said when she had regained her composure. "You are bloody hilarious." She slapped my shoulder with the hand she had placed there. "Hilarious," she repeated. I stood there grinning as she tried to recover her breath.

Just then a car horn sounded from across the street. I looked over to see her boyfriend roll down the window of the waiting Cortina, lean out, and yell, "For fuck's sake, Mandy, get a bloody move on!" I couldn't see him well because of the rain, but I imagined him spotty-faced and ugly.

"Christ, if I've told him once I've told him a thousand times. I don't like being called Mandy." Then, turning toward him, she shouted, "All right, Stan, I'll be over in a minute!"

"We're gonna miss the flick if you don't get your fucking fat arse over here soon," he shot back.

I expected Amanda to yell back angrily. Instead, she gave a resigned little shrug. "Men," she said, taking in the boy in the car and my father, behind the window, still gathering his shopping, in a single, sweeping look. I nodded, as if I agreed with this assessment. But, really, I didn't understand why she would ever have to put up with someone who talked to her like that. That stupid boyfriend of hers should be grateful that a girl as beautiful as Amanda would even give him the time of day.

"Look, I've got to go," Amanda said. "But it looks like your slow-coach dad is just about ready to leave." She pointed at my father, who stood next to his packed carrier bag carefully mulling over the change that the checkout woman had put into his palm. A couple of the other customers were still glaring in our direction. Stan hit the horn again. "Bloody hell, I've a good mind to make him wait longer. That'd show him," she said. "Only thing is, I don't want to miss the film." She pulled a wide grin and shrugged. "Bye, then."

"Yes, bye!" I called as I watched her run across to the Cortina, her boots slapping against the street. They made spattering explosions of water as they hit the shiny black tarmac.

She closed her umbrella and climbed into the car. Within seconds, the car squealed away. As they passed, Amanda rolled down the window and waved. "I hope I didn't get you in too much trouble!" she yelled, her voice fading in a long arc of sound as they sped down the street.

"I don't care," I called back. And, really, I didn't.

CHAPTER FIVE

———

A MONTH AFTER THE MOVE, WE WERE IN THE MIDST OF A SUMMER
that brought almost as much rain as it did sunshine. Although my father had managed to complete several makeshift repairs, there was still
a bucket on the stairway and a leak from the bathroom ceiling into the
bathtub. He seemed to have lost all enthusiasm for his planned renovations, probably because my mother, contrary to his hopes, had failed to
find an interest that would propel her back to life. Almost every night
he muttered about how he'd soon get round to fixing something, but
instead he spent most of his time hidden behind the Hull *Daily Mail* or
yelling at the BBC News. He even yelled about the epidemic of Dutch
elm disease, the blight that was killing off millions of elm trees all over
Britain and, I realized, explained the dead or dying trees I had noticed
patterning the landscape around Midham.

    If my mother happened to be in the room, she nodded vigorously at
my father's outbursts. But most of the time she was off somewhere else,
pacing the bare boards of the upstairs bedrooms or wandering the back
garden in the rain. I tried to keep track of her movements, but it wasn't
always easy. Often, I'd simply sit on the settee in the living room, anxious and afraid, knowing that I really had no idea how to stop her try-

ing to kill herself or being taken off to Delapole again. Finally, tired of worrying, I decided to focus on something I could control.

"Mum, we've got to start unpacking," I announced one weekday afternoon. After searching the house, I'd finally found her in the bathroom, peering into the mirror above the sink as she plucked her eyebrows and ate a cheese-and-pickle sandwich.

"I don't see why," she said, her breath clouding the mirror as she leaned toward it, tweezers in one hand, sandwich in the other. As I watched her, I wondered if it was possible to inflict any significant self-injury with a pair of eyebrow tweezers. "What do we need to unpack for?"

We were hardly more moved in than on the day we'd arrived. There were boxes everywhere, in leaning piles against the walls or stacked haphazardly in the middle of almost every room. Nothing had been labeled, and it was impossible to find anything. I felt too overwhelmed to try to unpack while also trying to take care of my mother, but if I got her to help me I could do both things at once, and perhaps forcing her into some activity would improve her mood.

"We've been here long enough," I said, trying not to wince as she yanked out another hair. "It's time we settled in."

"Well, I never wanted to move here in the first place. It was all your father's idea." She turned around and took a huge bite of her sandwich. Brown chunks of Branston Pickle dropped onto the floor.

"Come on, Mum. If we do it together, it'll be much quicker. What do you think?"

"Oh, all right."

I was delighted. I hadn't expected her to be so amenable. Unfortunately, my excitement didn't last very long, since I soon realized that my mother's idea of unpacking involved carrying each item—a book, a cup, or one of the menagerie of glass animals she had made a short-lived but nevertheless exhaustive hobby of collecting—singly to its designated place. I had never seen anyone move so slowly. By the end of the day, when I had managed to empty more than half a dozen boxes, my mother had unpacked one. "Make us a cup of tea, could you, love?" she said, dropping into one of the armchairs shortly before my father was due to return home from work. "I'm jiggered."

The following day, she refused to help at all, saying that all the work she did the previous day had strained her back. She lay on the settee watching television, and when I started to unpack another box, pulling plates and cups from scrunched-up newspaper, she protested that I was giving her a headache by making so much noise.

"I don't think my nerves can take all that clattering about," she said, pressing her hands against her temples. "I'll end up in bloody Delapole if you carry on doing that."

I had no choice other than to stop.

Now, in addition to worrying about my mother, I began to worry that we would spend the rest of our lives living out of boxes, scrambling every night to find the colander to drain the water from my overboiled potatoes (I was the only one doing the cooking) or eating with plastic knives and forks because we still couldn't locate the cutlery. I imagined never finding my Scrabble or books or felt-tip pens ever again, never having enough underwear because most of it was still packed, and having to watch over my mother until I finally became old enough to legally leave home.

That evening, I tried to talk with my father about it when he sat down in front of the television after work. But when I broached the matter he wasn't concerned. "Children are starving in Africa," he said, pointing to the pictures on the news of emaciated babies, their stomachs bloated like overinflated balloons. "At least you've got three square meals and a roof over your head."

"That's right," said my mother, appearing in the doorway so suddenly that she made both me and my father jump. "We had to live on rations when we were kids. The first time I saw chocolate, I was ten years old. You should think yourself fortunate, shouldn't she, Mike?"

"Yes, she should," my father muttered.

"You kids don't know how lucky you are these days." She was standing in the middle of the room now, wagging her finger at me and looking far more animated than she had in ages. I wasn't sure whether to take this as a good sign. "Bloody spoiled, you are," she said, moving toward me, stabbing her index finger into my chest.

I stepped backward and tried to shrug her off. "Stop it," I said. "I wasn't even talking to you in the first place; I was talking to Dad."

"Don't you talk to me like that, you little bugger!" she yelled, outraged.

"Why the hell not?" I was surprised at my response, the words spilling out like untamed thoughts. "I'm the one who's trying to keep some bloody order around here. I'm the one who's trying to get us moved in. While you"—I pointed at her—"all you do is sit around and complain."

"I've told you!" my mother shrieked, her hands balled into fists at her sides. "Don't use that bloody tone with me! I am still your mother, you know! Tell her, Mike, tell her I'm still her mother."

He was still watching the news, where Princess Anne, looking crisp and concerned in a nicely pressed safari suit, moved between crowds of big-eyed starving mothers and babies. He seemed so absorbed in these images that it was as if he were simultaneously inhabiting a place far away, a place where people talked in hushed BBC tones and even dying was reported on stiffly, without emotion.

"Mike!" My mother yelled so loud that it made the windows shudder. "Can you sodding well tell her!"

"Bloody bitch," my father said. For a moment, it wasn't clear whom this comment was directed at. My mother's lips tightened and she eyed him nervously. But then he added, "Bloody stuck-up bitch," and we realized he meant Princess Anne. Then he turned toward us. "Yes, she's still your mother," he muttered. My mother, her mouth pushed into a tight little bud, gave me a satisfied nod.

I found myself wondering if there had been some doubt about this matter, as if recent events should have been reason to question this biological fact that I had so often wished myself able to undo. "Of course she's still my bloody mother," I said.

"Now, you watch your language, young lady," my father warned.

"Yes, you bloody well watch your language," my mother echoed, apparently triumphant that she had got my father so easily on her side.

I could feel the heat of tears behind my eyes, the wetness in my throat, the mad thrumming of my heart in my chest. "I don't care," I said. And then, to emphasize my point, "I don't sodding well care. I'm sick of it. Sick of everything. And you," I said, pointing at my mother again. "If you want me to treat you like my mother, maybe you should start acting like one. If not, maybe you should go back to the loony bin, where you belong."

For several seconds, neither of my parents said anything, and all of us were hurled into a taut silence. I looked at their faces, which were utterly still, as if they had been slammed against thick panes of glass. No one moved. No one said anything. I felt an icy dread spread from my stomach throughout my body. Then the newsreader said chirpily, "And now on to news at home," and the spell was broken. My father blinked, my mother's lips started to twist and tighten. I tried to imagine myself shrinking.

"Did you hear that?" she screamed. "Did you bloody well hear that?"

My father sighed and pushed himself out of his armchair. He walked toward me.

"You'd better teach her a bloody lesson!" my mother yelled.

"Don't you ever talk to your mother like that," he said, his tone so dull and flat that I could barely hear him above the sounds of the television. And then he hit me. A single, hard slap across my cheek that sent me reeling backward into the wall. I saw light and crimson. I tasted the stickiness of my own saliva. I felt the sting of skin hitting skin, the slam of my backbone against the wall. "Now get upstairs, before I give you a damn good hiding," he said, already making his way back to his chair.

—

"I'M GOING OUT." It was early the next morning and I'd been standing in the hallway, waiting for my father to come out of the bathroom. He'd emerged in a cloud of thick white steam. "I'm not looking after her all the time." I gave a disdainful nod toward the door of my parents' bedroom, where my mother was still sleeping. "It's just not fair," I concluded, folding my arms and pressing them hard against my chest.

"I know, love. I know." He put a hand up to his damp, flushed cheek—the same gesture I had made after he had hit me the previous evening. The movement made my fury at him burn all over again.

"I don't care if she ends up in the hospital. I don't care if she goes away for the rest of her life. Why couldn't they just have kept her there?" If she'd stayed in Delapole, the doctors and nurses would have to watch her. I could get on with my life without having to worry all the time. I could have kept on imagining for myself a breezy world-cruising mother.

"Now, love, don't go talking that way." He looked nervously toward the bedroom door. "I know you don't mean it."

Perhaps I didn't, but I was no longer sure. Right then, I would have done anything to live alone with my father, with his quiet predictability. The few times he'd hit me, it had been only at my mother's prompting. "That child needs to be taught a lesson," she'd say, and then my father would dutifully deliver the blow.

"Look," he said, "why don't you let me get dressed and I'll come downstairs in a minute. We can have a little chat before I leave."

"All right," I said, determined not to be talked out of my decision. I couldn't bear even one more day confined there with my mother. Besides, ever since I'd met up with Amanda, I'd been itching to get out and see if I could bump into her again.

"That's better," he said. "Be a good girl and go and make a pot of tea, can you?"

He opened the bathroom door again, and I found myself immersed in steam, the lathery smells of soap and shaving lotion. I stood for a moment, my eyes closed, breathing them in, caught in a sudden stream of memory, remembering how, when I was small, I loved to watch my father shave. It was like witnessing a special, one-person ceremony, and I'd try every morning to wake up early enough so that I could follow him into the bathroom, sit down on the closed lid of the toilet, and take the whole thing in. I couldn't wake early enough every day, but when I did I'd feel an elated, nervous excitement as I tugged on my father's paisley-patterned pajamas. "Can I watch, Daddy?" I'd say.

" 'Course you can, pet," he'd reply, closing the door behind me, sealing us together in those scents.

There was something about the measured precision it took, his moving the razor through the soapy white foam, skin held taut and still as he cut the shadow of bristly whiskers from his face. On weekends, when he had more time in the morning, he'd let me stand beside him on a stool that he took from my mother's dressing table. He'd lift me there, and I'd stare at my own reflection as he soaped up my face with his soft-bristled shaving brush. He'd give me an old razor, with the blade removed, and together we'd watch ourselves in the mirror and shave. "There you go," he'd say, after I'd rinsed my face in warm water and patted my cheeks with his Old Spice aftershave. "Nice and smooth and ready to kiss your mummy." And then we'd rub our cheeks together, soft skin against soft skin.

THE NEWSREADER ANNOUNCED that a bomb in Belfast had killed two British soldiers, another thousand steelworkers were to be laid off, and the miners were threatening to go on strike again.

"What's the world coming to, eh?" my father asked, shaking his head, pressing the rim of his teacup to his lips.

I nodded and sighed, as if I felt equally world-weary. I wanted to care more about industrial strife and the war in Northern Ireland, but all I really cared about was what was happening in our house. "I'm going out today, Dad," I said.

"I know, love. I know you can't watch your mother all the time. It's not right, not for a girl your age. But, Jesse . . ."

"What?"

"Just try not to aggravate her."

"I never try to aggravate her. She just gets aggravated."

"You know how easily she gets upset. Just try not to bother her, okay?"

"Okay," I said flatly. "I'll try."

"Thanks, love."

"Dad," I said, looking at him timidly.

"What?" He glanced at his watch. I could tell he was ready to leave, already eager to be out the door and have done with our conversation.

"Are you going to repair the house?"

He grimaced. "I already told you I'm going to fix it. Who do you think I am, bloody Superman?"

"No, it's just that—"

"I know, I know. The place is a bloody pigsty." He checked his watch again, put his teacup on the counter, and began adjusting the knot of his tie. "Look, if you promise to be good, not to bother your mother and not cause any trouble, I'll start work on the house again. How's that sound?"

"All right," I said, smiling.

"Good. Well, I'm glad we can at least agree on something. So no talking back, none of your cleverness. You understand me?"

"Yes, Dad. I understand."

FOR ONCE, IT WAS sunny, the sky a pale blue, patterned by smudges of white cloud, their shadows shifting across the ground, changing the colors of the fields as they moved. Everything tasted clear and damp, and the air was filled with a ripe, earthy smell. It made me want to breathe deep, as if I could take the freshness of the morning inside me and push out all the stale air I'd inhaled inside the house.

It was a fifteen-minute walk into the village. When I got there, I walked purposefully past the short string of shops—the Co-op, the launderette, and the newsagent's on the corner—and past a series of little streets—Buttercup Close, Daffodil Gardens, and, finally, Marigold Court—that made up the Primrose Housing Estate. Each of them was lined with neat semidetached houses, almost exactly like the house I had fantasized for my own family, with orange bricks and tidy squares of lawn in the front. Some of them even had pansies in the borders; others had evenly spaced rosebushes drooping with the weight of redolent blooms. Marigold Court was a cul-de-sac at the edge of the estate, and the houses at the end of the street backed onto a grassy field.

It was just after ten o'clock, and the street was completely quiet. As I walked slowly along the pavement, I examined each house to see if it might hold a clue that would tell me if Amanda lived there. But each of them was essentially identical, the only differences being the color of the front doors, the pattern of the net curtains, and the length of the grass on the front lawns.

I began to feel foolish for having come here. What had I been expecting, that Amanda would see me and spring gleefully through her front door to greet me? She probably wouldn't recognize me, anyway. She was too old and too pretty to be interested in making friends with someone like me. Besides, she lived here, in this neat little haven, while I occupied a ridiculous shambles that would never be repaired.

"You looking for something?"

I almost bumped into the girl before I noticed her. She stood, arms crossed over her chest, bony hip stuck out at an angle, eyebrows raised in truculent expectation of an answer.

"I, er, I just moved here. I'm just looking around."

"Hmmph," she snorted, eyebrows still raised. Her long dark hair was pulled back into a ponytail. She had big cheeks, a small mouth, a perky little nose, and long-lashed brown eyes—a combination of features that left her in the uncertain territory between plain and pretty.

"I was exploring."

"What, like Christopher Columbus?" Her tone was sharp.

"No." I shook my head. "I was just trying to get the lay of the land."

"Lay of the land?"

"I meant—"

"I know what you meant. I'm not stupid, you know."

"I know. I didn't mean to—"

"You moved into Johnson's house, didn't you?"

"Johnson's house?"

"Yeah, Johnson's house—the one that's falling down, on the main road out of the village. Geoffrey Johnson used to live there."

"He did?" My curiosity about the previous occupant of our house overcame my nervousness. "Did he die there?" I asked, imagining him an old man expiring in one of our bedrooms, leaving behind the disheveled chaos.

"No. He used to own the fish-and-chip shop in Reatton. But then he bought a villa in Marbella. Been living there the last five years."

"Oh." Somehow the idea that the previous owner of our house had escaped to the heat and sunshine of Spain seemed particularly unfair.

"That place has been empty since he left. Nobody wanted to buy it. Until you moved in, that is."

"Oh," I said again. It was no wonder the house was in such disrepair. And if no one else wanted it, everyone in the village must have thought my father was a fool for buying it. We'd been here just a month and already we were probably a local laughingstock. So much for making a new start.

"Want a piece of chewy?" she asked after digging about in one of the appliquéd pockets of her wide-flared trousers and pulling out a packet of Wrigley's spearmint gum.

"Thanks," I said. I watched her take a piece, rip open the foil and paper packaging, toss it onto the ground, and pop the sliver of gum into her mouth. I did the same.

"So, what's your name?" she asked, chewing open-mouthed so that I could see the gum rolling over her teeth as she spoke.

"Jesse. Jesse Bennett."

"My name's Tracey Grasby. But my friends call me Trace." She said this in a tone that conveyed that I was definitely not to consider myself in this category. She snapped her gum a couple of times, then walked a few steps over to the fence in front of the nearest house and perched herself there. "Where did you move from, anyway?" she asked, resting her feet, in shiny black sandals with thick platform soles, on the lowest rail of the fence. Her feet were bare under the sandals, and her toenails were painted pink. I looked down at my own feet, housed in a pair of ragged white plimsolls, my ankle socks sagging listlessly, as if wilted by the sudden summer heat.

"We moved from Hull," I said.

"Really? We lived in Goole before we moved here. I didn't like it there much. But it's worse here. It's really boring." She gave me a derisive look that suggested that, despite the fact that I was new to the village, I should still be considered part of its unrelenting tedium. "We moved here three years ago, when my dad got a job in Bleakwick. Want to watch out for my dad. Says we've got to keep up the area, don't want strangers lurking about. He's liable to call the coppers on you. Either that or he'll knock you for six."

"I wasn't lurking about, I was—"

"Getting the lay of the land. I heard you the first time."

I felt myself blush again. As soon as I could reasonably extract myself from this conversation, I decided, I would go straight back home. I didn't care if I had to spend every day of the summer with my mother; it would certainly be preferable to being under the scrutiny of this girl.

"Anyway, how old are you?" she asked.

"Thirteen."

"Big for thirteen, aren't you?"

"I'm tall for my age," I said. Everyone commented on it. My mother, especially, was always complaining about how I just kept on growing. "Got the same big bones as our Mabel," she'd say as she searched fruitlessly in the sale racks for something that would fit me. Then, gesturing toward my slightly mounded chest, she'd add, "At least we can thank God you're not taking after her in the bust department. You don't want to be stuck carrying those things around with you for the rest of your life," as if Mabel's breasts were two overladen shopping bags that she'd surely choose to put down if only she had enough sense.

Tracey was remarkably thin, but, unlike me, her body curved from waist to hip, and her breasts strained against the tight fabric of her T-shirt.

"When's your birthday?" she asked.

"March."

"I'm going to be fourteen in September, so I'm older than you, but we'll still be in the same year. It's not fair, but it works out that way. We'll be third years. That means we'll get to go first for school dinner twice a week. When I was a second year, we only went in first once."

She seemed to think this was an important distinction, and it made me wonder what I should expect of the school dinners at my new school. At my old school, Knox Vale, where Spam fritters, liver and onions, and spotted dick were considered the menu's delicacies, I'd never been in a hurry to get to the dining hall.

"I can't wait to leave school," Tracey continued. "I want to be a secretary. I'm going to take shorthand and typing. You can earn good money being a secretary, you know."

I nodded in hearty agreement, though I'd always thought that typing and answering phones all day would be downright boring. I could think of a hundred jobs I'd rather do.

"Of course, that'll only be until I get married. Then I'm going to have three kids. A girl and two boys. What do you want to do when you leave school?"

"I want to go to university."

"Oh. A brainbox, then, are you?" She fixed me with a narrow-eyed stare.

"No," I said, immediately regretting this confession.

"Why do you want to go to university, then?"

"I want to go to London." For a long time now, I'd known that I wanted to live in London. It was where all the famous people lived, where anything important happened. All the headline events on the news took place in London—Princess Anne's wedding, peace demonstrations, Wimbledon, IRA bombs. And London was always on the television, on programs about history and current affairs, and in films where red double-decker buses rode by landmarks like Tower Bridge, the Houses of Parliament, Piccadilly Circus, Trafalgar Square. I'd never been to London, but I was sure I'd be happy if I lived there, pulled into that vortex of busyness and bustle, no longer someone who sat in our living room to watch the world's critical happenings.

"I went to London once," said Tracey.

"You did?"

"Yeah," she said, spitting out her gum. It landed in a tight gray ball, barely missing my right shoe. I wondered if she had been trying to hit it. "My mum is president of the Bleakwick Young Wives Club. She organized the trip. We all went shopping down Oxford Street."

"What was it like?"

"I didn't like it. We got lost on the tube, ended up getting off at the wrong stop and walking for miles. My feet were killing me. But we did see Big Ben."

"You did?"

"Yeah, and heard it as well. *Doing. Doing. Doing.*" She imitated a loud clock chime. "Just like on the News at Ten. Didn't see the Queen, though."

"I did," I chirped. "I saw the Queen."

"No, you never."

"I did. When she came to open Hull Royal Infirmary."

"What, you really saw her?" Tracey's tone softened and her eyes grew wide. Finally, I'd found something that seemed to impress her.

"Yes, I saw her. About as close as you are to me now."

It was almost true. I'd been six at the time, and the whole city was abuzz with the excitement of the Queen's visit. There were Union Jack streamers hung from all the lampposts, and the neighbors had put pictures of the Queen in their windows. (Mrs. Brockett had put up five.) My mother had been too preoccupied with installing a new water heater to pay much attention to anything beyond our front door, and I'd begged my father to take me to see the parade. But my entreaties were useless and seemed only to increase his fury at the event. The way he slammed about the house, kicking chairs and clattering crockery, anyone would have thought the whole thing had been planned not as a public celebration but as a carefully orchestrated personal insult.

Finally, Auntie Mabel appeared, a little paper Union Jack flag in her hand. "What, you can't take your own daughter to see Her Royal Highness on the one day she comes to Hull?" she'd said, looking at my father with utter contempt.

"It's against my principles," my father answered, puffing out his chest. "I'm an ardent socialist."

"More like an armchair socialist," Mabel replied. Then she turned to me. "Come on, darling, let's you and me go and enjoy our national heritage, shall we?"

When we arrived, the crowd that lined the parade route was at least ten deep, and even when Mabel lifted me onto her shoulders I still couldn't see over the rows of excited, bobbing heads. "I tell you what," she said. "Why don't you squeeze your little self to the front. I'll wait for you here. Go on. Then you'll get the best view."

I eased my way to the steel barriers to push my face into the cold metal, the weight of the crowd swaying against my back. It seemed to take forever for the Queen to arrive, and I felt my heart racing with the anticipation around me. Then suddenly the crowd surged with excitement as her massive Rolls-Royce came into view. I pushed my hand through the metal barrier, waving the little paper Union Jack flag that Mabel had given me. The car pulled alongside us and then, just as quickly, it was gone. All I saw of the Queen was a white gloved hand waving genteelly and a flash of frosted hair.

"What did she look like?" Tracey asked.

"Very . . ." I searched for the right word. "Regal. She looked very regal."

"What's that?"

"Royal," I answered.

"Well, yeah, she would, wouldn't she, her being the Queen?" Tracey shook her head slowly, as if I were the stupidest person she'd had the misfortune of laying eyes on. I could feel any hope of making her like me slip away. I could already envision her taunting me in the corridors of my new school, egged on by a gang of sneering kids. "Anyway," she continued, "I don't know why you'd want to live in London. It wasn't up to much, far as I'm concerned. This year the Young Wives did a trip to Whitby, and that was a lot better. I won two pounds on the amusements."

"You did?" It wasn't as much as some of my mother's bingo wins, but two pounds was still a lot of money.

"Yeah, on one of them one-arm bandits. But then I lost it all on one of those Penny Falls machines. They're a bloody rip-off, if you ask me." She let out a weary sigh. "Listen, I'm going to get some goodies. They've got a sale on sweets at the Co-op." She eased herself off the fence. "You coming?"

"Me?"

"Yeah, who else do you think I'm talking to?"

I was astonished at the invitation. I felt a sudden, hopeful thrill. Then the thrill abruptly abated. "I can't."

"Why not?"

My cheeks began to burn. "I'm banned. They banned me from the

Co-op." Surely now she'd think me far worse than an interloper who lurked around her neat little housing estate. I was a teenage vandal. A newcomer who was already the scourge of the village.

"They banned you?" she asked. I was surprised when the flat tone of her voice brightened and she looked at me with undisguised delight.

"Yes. This big ugly woman with black hair told me I wasn't allowed in anymore."

"Oh, you mean Mrs. Franklin. I call her Frankenstein 'cause she's such a bloody monster." Tracey laughed. "So, what happened?"

I gazed into her excitement and felt overpowered by its draw, giddy with the possibilities it promised. "She tried to overcharge me," I said, folding my arms across my chest as if still outraged by the idea. "So I got into an argument with her, but she wouldn't listen. Then I got so mad I kicked over this display they had of Mr. Kipling's cakes. And then I just stormed out of the shop."

Tracey's mouth gaped. "That was you?"

I nodded.

"Bloody hell. My mum heard about that. Her friend Doris was in there when it happened. Said there was boxes of chocolate cakes all over the floor. Said Frankenstein was bloody livid. So you're not one of those boring brainboxes, then?"

I shrugged, trying to look casual, but I couldn't help smiling. If only I could extend this moment, make Tracey want to be my friend, I knew I could leave the past behind. The taunting in the cloakroom, the hiding in the caretaker's cupboard, the school dinners spent alone—they'd be experiences I could look back on the way a traveler would regard a difficult journey in a foreign land.

"Well, then," Tracey announced, "I say bugger Frankenstein. Let's go get our goodies over at the newsagent's instead." She began clunking unsteadily in her platform sandals toward the entrance of Marigold Court.

"But I haven't got any money."

Tracey turned back toward me. "That's all right, I'll buy you some-thing. I've got loads." She stuck a hand into one of her pockets to jan-gle what sounded like a handful of coins.

"Thanks, Tracey."

"Oh," she said with a shrug, "you can call me Trace."

CHAPTER SIX

———

WHEN I RETURNED HOME LATER THAT AFTERNOON, THE DOOR OF the downstairs toilet was open and I could see my mother, a pair of blue nylon knickers draped around her ankles, reading the same battered copy of *Woman's Realm* she'd thrown at me the other day. Without looking up, she called to me as I walked past. "I'm not talking to you."

I said nothing.

She called again, this time louder. "I'm not talking to you."

"Yes, you are," I answered, continuing down the hall.

"No, I'm not."

"Well, then, what are you doing right now?"

"You know what I'm talking about, young lady."

"How can I know what you're talking about if you're not talking to me?" I stood at the kitchen door, calling back to her.

"Sometimes you're too bloody clever for your own good." She began pulling toilet paper off the roll. The holder had been there when we moved in; it was rusty and squealed like unoiled brakes with each turn. "If I'd talked to my mother like you talk to me, I would have got a good clip around the ear. Do you hear me?"

"How can I hear you if you're not talking to me?" I asked, and pushed open the kitchen door.

"Look, miss!" she yelled after me as the door shut behind me. "You'd better not start getting clever with me!"

I recalled my promise to my father that morning and cringed. This was an agreement that was going to be even harder to honor than I'd anticipated. I sighed and began searching the cupboards for some food with which to make the evening meal. It was a quarter past five, and my father would be home from work soon.

I heard the toilet flush, and the shuddering rattle of the pipes all through the house. Seconds later, my mother joined me in the kitchen. "You know, we need a towel in that toilet," she said, shaking water from her hands and spattering me with cold droplets.

"Maybe if you'd helped me unpack the towels, we'd know where to find them." I was talking back again. I wanted to stop myself, but it was just so difficult. There was something inside me that resisted silence, like a bird caught in a room battering relentlessly against the illusory freedom of glass.

My mother snorted, pulled the two sides of her dressing gown tight across her chest, and sat down in one of the chairs next to the kitchen table. "There you go again, accusing me of things I haven't done. I'll tell your father when he gets home, and we'll see what he has to say about that."

"No, Mum, don't do that. I'm sorry. I didn't mean it. After I've made the tea, I'll put a towel in there."

"I wasn't asking you to do it," she said, huffing. "I'm perfectly capable of doing it myself, you know. I was just pointing out that it's something we need, that's all. And where have you been, anyway?"

"Out. In the village. I made a friend. Her name's Tracey."

I was still giddy from my recent encounter. After buying an enormous haul of Mars Bars, Milky Ways, and Cadbury's chocolate Buttons, Tracey had shown me around the village to get "the lay of the land"—a term she'd continued to tease me about for the rest of the day. After wandering the village's limited network of narrow streets and walking out as far as one of the surrounding farms, we'd made our way to the

churchyard. There, beneath the weathered stone tower of the squat little church, we'd stretched out on a big stone slab that covered one of
the graves, while we munched on the remaining sweets and got to know
each other. Tracey had done most of the talking. She told me about
what would soon be my new school, Liston Comprehensive, which
stood in the village of Liston six miles from Midham, the teachers she
liked (her French teacher and her science teacher, who was leaving)
and those she didn't like (everybody else). She told me about her
friends—all three of whom were called Deborah, and whom Tracey
never seemed to talk about as individuals but simply referred to collec-
tively as "the Debbies." The Debbies, whom I'd visualized as identical
triplets with matching outfits and black hair worn in ribboned plaits, all
lived in Liston. Tracey told me she didn't see much of them during the
summer holidays. "So it's great you moved here," she added. "I won't be
as bored now."

She'd gone on to talk at length about some of the boys she knew at
school—a jumble of Petes, Mikes, Tonys, and Andys, who were alter-
nately "gorgeous," "dishy," or "drop-dead bloody gorgeous." When she
asked me if I'd had a boyfriend in Hull, I thought for a moment of
making one up, but somehow I couldn't work up the enthusiasm for
this particular lie.

Later, before we'd left the churchyard, Tracey wanted to take me inside the church. But when she tried the big wooden door it was locked.
"Must be after the vandalism," she said, explaining to me that the previous month someone had spray-painted "Black Sabbath Rules!" across
the stained-glass window above the church altar. The vicar had discovered the graffiti, concluded that this was the work of devil worshippers,
and, so the village gossip went, discussed the possibility of conducting
an exorcism with the verger. Fortunately, before he could go to these
lengths, someone had informed him that Black Sabbath was, in fact, a
heavy-metal group, and though spray-painting his priceless stained-
glass window was indeed a crime, it wasn't quite the desecration he'd
imagined. Still, after that he'd embarked upon a virtual inquisition, de-

manding to speak with every Black Sabbath fan within a ten-mile radius of the church. So far, no one had squealed, although attendance at the monthly Heavy Metal discos in a neighboring village hall had noticeably declined.

"Of course, if he'd asked me I could have told him who did it," Tracey said, adding, "Not that I would have, mind you."

"Who?"

"Oh, I can't say," she said, shaking her head solemnly. "It's a secret, and I wouldn't want to get him into trouble. All I can say is he's drop-dead bloody gorgeous." I sat impassively as Tracey let out a high little giggle, wondering if I would ever meet a boy who made me squirm and blush like that.

"Where does she live, then, this Tracey?" my mother asked, pulling her chair closer to the kitchen table.

"On the Primrose Estate," I answered, tearing open a plastic bag of potatoes I'd found at the bottom of one of the cupboards. I watched as they tumbled into the sink. With those and the half-dozen eggs left in the fridge, I would make egg-and-chips for tea, one of my father's favorite meals. "It's nice there," I continued, turning on the tap. "The houses are really new, and they have little gardens and flowers."

"Hah!" my mother barked. "Well, in that case they're not living in a bloody dump like this. I can tell you now, Jesse, this house is really getting me down."

Of course, I shared her sentiments, but I couldn't say that when I needed to buoy her spirits, to make sure she didn't sink even further. "Dad's going to fix it up. He told me this morning that he's going to make a start right away." I picked up one of the potatoes. It was muddy and full of eyes, and I remembered that I still hadn't managed to unearth the potato peeler from among all the boxes.

"That's a laugh, that is. Couldn't fight his way out of a wet paper bag, your father. It was always me that did the decorating in our old place. Put hundreds on the value of that house, what with all that work. You remember what a lovely job you and me did of the upstairs? Looked great, didn't it? Those lilies in my bedroom. And you loved that Rupert the Bear wallpaper, you remember?" She began singing the theme song from the television cartoon, gently swaying her head in time with the childish melody. "Rupert, Rupert the Bear, everyone knows his name. Rupert, Rupert the Bear, everyone come and join in all of his games."

"Mum." I was cringing. "That was years ago."

"Yes, but you loved that program, you really did. And the Rupert the Bear annuals, your little Rupert the Bear scarf." She sighed. "It's a shame you had to grow up, really. You were lovely when you were little. It's a pity you got so—well, let's face it, you can be a bit of a clever madam these days. It's really not very attractive, you know. I don't think the young men will find that very appealing."

"I don't care," I said, swirling the potatoes around in the sink, watching the water turn brown and murky.

"I don't believe you for a second. When I was your age, all I thought about was boys, boys, boys. Of course, your grandma had a thing or two to say about that. But then your grandma's always had a thing or two to say about everything." Suddenly, her voice brightened. "I didn't tell you, did I? I got a letter from her today." She began rummaging in the pocket of her dressing gown, pulling out a blue airmail envelope and placing it in front of her on the table.

Grandma Pearson had emigrated to Australia when I was four. According to my mother, it had been her life's dream to live there. When my mother was twelve, Grandma had pinned a map of Australia above the fireplace in her living room, and for as long as my mother could remember, Grandma had talked about the place as if it were a utopia at the opposite side of the world. Unfortunately for Grandma, Granddad Pearson hadn't shared her sentiments. A dockworker almost his entire adult life, he spent his days loading and unloading cargo from around the world but had no desire to go anywhere himself. "As far as he was concerned, paradise was at the bottom of a glass of beer down at the local pub," my mother often said bitterly. "If it wasn't for him being so stubborn, I could have grown up in Australia. Instead, I had to grow up here." She said this in a tone that suggested that a childhood spent in England was the worst fate one could wish upon a person.

After many years of complaining about the cold and damp and yearning for a land of marsupials, billabongs, and vast expanses of un-inhabitable desert, Grandma finally got her wish. Four years after I was born, Granddad was killed when a container of Australian wool fell from the crane that was lifting it onto the dockside, crushing him be-neath it. Grandma took this as something of a sign, and after collecting a sizable widow's-compensation package and spending what she con-sidered an adequate period in mourning (about three months), she sold most of her possessions, packed her bags, and left. She even man-aged to take along Granddad, who was now housed in the urn provided by the crematorium. "First thing she did when she got there," my mother told me, "was scatter that stubborn old bugger's ashes in Syd-ney Harbor. See," she said with obvious satisfaction. "She got him to Australia in the end." My mother had bemoaned Grandma's departure many times, dramatically describing how she had watched the ship that took away her beloved mother become smaller and smaller until it turned into a dot that dipped over the horizon "never, ever to be seen again."

It struck me now as strange that I hadn't thought to put Sydney or Melbourne or Perth on my mother's imaginary itinerary. After all, whenever she fell into one of her bad patches she would invariably begin talking about how Australia was as close to heaven as anywhere on earth, how happy she'd be if she lived there, and how she couldn't understand how her own mother had emigrated there without her, leaving her all alone in this awful, miserable, damp country. My father would try to reason with her, telling her that there was no such place as heaven on earth, and, even if there was, it certainly wasn't to be found in a continent that was "not much more than a wasteland with a few beaches patrolled by man-eating sharks," and, in the not-too-distant past, had been used as a dumping ground for the dregs of British soci-ety. None of this, however, had very much impact on my mother.

Throughout every one of her bad patches, she remained convinced that a ticket to Australia would be a ticket to ultimate contentment.

"It's winter there now, you know," my mother said, staring at the letter that she'd set down on the table. "Mind you, from what she says in here they have better weather in their winter than we do in our summer. That's one thing she says she doesn't miss—the bloody English weather."

My mother scanned the letter as I slid the chip pan onto the top of the cooker. I turned on the gas, struck a match, and held it close to the burner. A huge bloom of purple-blue flames burst forth. I jumped back, wrinkling my nose at the smell of burned hair.

"You know, if your father's serious about fixing this place," my mother said, wagging a finger at the cooker, "the first thing he needs to see to is that gas. One of these days we're all going to be blown to kingdom come. Your grandma's got an all-electric kitchen, you know. She said it's the best thing that's happened to her in years."

I put the pan over the burner and began slicing the potatoes into chip-size pieces.

"She says here that she went on a tour of the Sydney Opera House. And do you know what the tour guide told them? He said that when they built it they wanted it to have the best acoustics of any theater in the world. You know, so the voices of all those opera singers and such could be heard in the back rows. Trouble was, they made the sound carry so well that you could hear everything—even the sound of the loos flushing. Right in the middle of a performance. Now, will you think about that!" She started laughing as if she'd just heard the most enormously funny joke. "Oh," she concluded, slapping her hand down on the table. "Your grandma could always make me laugh. She sent us a picture of herself—you want to see?" She took a photograph out of the envelope. I peered over to see a picture of a white-haired buxom woman in a knee-length cotton dress and flat, sensible white sandals. Her legs were bare, and they looked veined and blotchy—old women's legs. "That's her house." My mother pointed to the flat-roofed oblong building that Grandma stood so proudly next to. "And those trees there are eucalyptus trees. She had a koala bear in her back garden. She saw it sitting right there. As close as you are to me."

"I know, Mum, you told me before." The fat in the chip pan was starting to sizzle and spit. I turned, lifted the wire basket out of the pan, and put several handfuls of chips into it.

"Yes, but don't you think that's brilliant? I mean, you'd never get anything like that to happen here."

"I suppose not. But maybe things like that are just normal in Australia." I placed the basket of chips into the pan and the oil rose, sputtering and hissing and covering the chips in frothing yellow foam.

"I know," my mother said, sighing and staring through the window toward our garden as if she were picturing a koala bear scrambling through the trees back there. "Sometimes I think the best thing I could do would be to go over there and live with your grandma. You wouldn't miss me, would you? And your dad—well, let's face it. Your dad would be glad to get rid of me." She began laughing again, even more hysterically than before, throwing her head back as if the thought of this was just hilarious. Then, abruptly, she stopped, letting one hand fall to her uncombed mass of hair. She began pushing her fingers into its thick tangles. "At least your grandma would appreciate me. At least she'd be glad to see me. At least she cares." Then, as if collapsing on itself, her face folded, she let out a choked little cry, and tears began rolling down her pale cheeks. "Nobody cares about me here," she said, pulling a wrinkled handkerchief from the pocket of her dressing gown.

"Do you think Dad will be home soon?" I asked, glancing at the wall clock, which was leaning against the kitchen window because no one had gotten around to hanging it yet.

"See," she said, gasping as the tears flowed copiously. "Not even my own daughter cares about me." She blew her nose in a loud, wet snort.

"Mum, I'm trying to make the tea right now." I tried to disguise my irritation, but my words came out hard and slow through tightly clenched teeth.

"I don't know what I've done to deserve this, I really don't. Am I that terrible of a mother? Am I? Tell me, am I?" She blotted the edges of her eyes.

I felt the keen ache of wanting to calm her, of wanting her hopelessness to recede into the distance like a plane jetting toward Australia, leaving only a trail of dissipating vapor behind. "No, Mum, you're not terrible," I said. I walked over to her and placed a hand on her shoulder. "You're not terrible at all."

She rested her head against me and wrapped her arms around my waist. "You don't think so?" she asked, sniffing.

"No, I don't think so. You're just going through one of your bad patches right now. You'll soon be all right." I patted her back softly, as a mother might do to coax wind out of a baby who has just been fed. Firm but soothing, as if I were trying to press the sadness out of her, ease it from the place it occupied inside her chest. I patted her like that for several minutes, feeling the shudder of her sobs against my hands. Finally, when she had calmed a little, I brushed my hand over her knotty hair. "You know, you'll start to feel better soon, Mum. I know you feel upset, but it's probably the move."

"Yes, love. You're right. It's probably the move."

"It's hard to move to a new place." As I spoke, I had an idea— a means to perhaps goad my mother out of her desperation and, at the same time, get something that I wanted. "Hey, Mum, you know what?" I said, pumping enthusiasm into my voice.

"What?" She pulled her head back to look up into my face. Her cheeks were wet and smeared with tears, her features loose and slightly askew.

"Well, I bet you'd feel better if we got settled in a bit more."

She pulled abruptly away. "But I don't want to stay here. I don't like it. It's too quiet—it's like a bloody cemetery out there." She waved her soggy hankie toward the window. "I miss my home. I miss Mabel. And I miss my mother." She paused for a moment, sighing. "Do you think she'll ever come back?"

"I don't know, Mum," I answered, though I sincerely doubted it. As far as I was concerned, anyone who had koala bears in her back garden and sunshine year-round would have to be mentally deranged to consider returning to East Yorkshire. But then, knowing my family, that level of impairment wasn't completely out of the question. "She might get homesick," I offered feebly.

"She's got a boyfriend," my mother announced flatly.

"A boyfriend?" The word seemed wholly inappropriate for a woman in her early sixties. I imagined my white-haired grandma gadding about the beach with a bronzed Australian teenager—Grandma dressed in an old-lady swimming costume with a frilly skirt to cover her puckered thighs, the boyfriend in the tiniest pair of swimming trunks imaginable.

"Yes, a boyfriend. Some chap she met at her whist club. He's retired, used to run a furniture factory. Bill's his name. They go out together—the pictures, the horse races. You ask me, it's not right, a woman of her age."

I thought a whist-playing pensioner seemed a fitting companion. "She's just having fun, Mum."

"Fun? What about me? I'm stuck here in the middle of nowhere with nothing to do but stare at four bloody walls." She buried her face in her hands and began to sob again.

"There, there, Mum," I said, eyeing the chip pan. I noticed that the burner underneath was still set on high, and I felt a little uneasy about the way the fat continued to leap and froth and spit. But I stood over my mother, continuing to loosely pat her on the back. "It'll be all right. It really will."

"Do you think so?" she asked, letting her hands slide down her face. "Do you really think so?"

"Yes," I said firmly. "And you know what I think we should do?"

"What?" She looked at me with wide eyes, the whites patterned in fine red lines.

"Well, like I said, I think you'd feel better if we got settled in more, if we got the unpacking done and got rid of all these boxes." I indicated the ten or so boxes piled in the corner of the kitchen. "Once that's done, maybe we can get Dad to drive us into Hull to go and see Mabel. We can go and visit her for tea. Now, what do you think about that?" I listened to the ringing cheeriness of my own voice. It sounded odd, distant, as if it wasn't really me speaking. "Now, that'd be nice, wouldn't it?"

"Yes, I suppose it would. We could get her one of those nice Neapolitan cakes she likes. Or you know what?" my mother said, sniffing and nudging me excitedly with her elbow. "We could splash out and get a packet of Mr. Kipling's." She looked down at the letter on the table in front of her. "And you're right about your grandma. She's entitled to her bit of fun. I suppose I can't begrudge her that." She sounded as if she was trying to convince herself.

"I'm sure she thinks about you all the time," I said.

"Yes, yes. I'm sure you're right," she said, looking up to give me a weak smile.

"Better now?" I asked, again eyeing the chip pan nervously. The oil had begun to smoke.

She wiped her eyes and blew her nose again, leaving her handkerchief a crumpled and sodden bundle in her palm. "Yes, love, I think I am." She reached up and took hold of my hand. "I don't know what I'd do without you, darling, I really don't. You're an anchor, you know that? A real anchor." She squeezed my fingers. "You're always there when I need you, aren't you? Always so sensible, always know what to do. Not like me. I'm so scattered sometimes, I—"

"Mum," I interrupted, trying to pull my hand from her grip.

"Yes, love?"

"I think I need to turn the gas under those chips down." The smoke from the pan had become thicker; it had begun to fill the room. It burned in my nostrils, and I could taste it as I spoke.

"Yes, love," my mother said again, releasing her hold on me. I launched myself across the kitchen and turned off the burner. Then, my eyes stinging, I scrambled to open a window, not an easy task, since the frame, like most of those in the house, was soft with rot and had swollen into place. Finally, I managed to force it open. After gulping in the fresh air, I turned back toward my mother, who was still sitting at the kitchen table, squeezing her hankie in her fist, completely oblivious to this culinary crisis.

"So, when's tea going to be ready?" she asked.

I strode over to the cooker and peered into the still smoking pan, where the potatoes floated in the sizzling oil, charred and blackened strips. "It's going to be a while."

"Good. Well, maybe I'll go and get dressed, then. You know, put my face on and straighten myself up a bit. I bet your dad would appreciate that, don't you?"

As I went about preparing the potatoes again, I listened to my mother clattering around upstairs, stomping across the bare wooden floors, slamming then opening then slamming doors. Then, when I'd got the chips in the pan once again (this time with the heat turned down), I sat at the kitchen table and picked up the letter my mother had left there.

My eyes scanned the introductory greetings, and then the couple of paragraphs that described the tour of the opera house. Grandma mentioned Ted briefly: "I got a letter from your brother the other day. He says he's not doing so bad, considering. I wish you'd drop him a line, Evelyn. It'd be nice for him to hear from you. He is your brother. And I hate thinking how he's stuck behind bars all day. He's not a bad lad, really. I wish I'd managed to do more to keep him on the straight and narrow. But at least my girls are doing all right! I hope your new house is nice and that you're out of the hospital and feeling much better now. I know shingles can be nasty, so I was very happy to hear you've made a full recovery."

I dropped the letter onto the table. Shingles? So that was how my mother's stay in the hospital had been accounted for. Why, I wondered, was everything in my family shaded in lies? Why did everyone, myself included, never stick to the truth? I knew the answer, of course, because it was obvious. In our case, the truth was always ugly and so very hard to swallow.

———

CHAPTER SEVEN

ONE WEEK LATER, EVERYTHING WAS FINALLY UNPACKED AND MY father had made noticeable headway on the repairs. Even my mother seemed better. She'd assisted me enthusiastically with the unpacking, and after we were finished appeared to finally find herself a mission when she decided she was going to tackle the jungle of thistles that occupied our back garden. "I'm going to put in a lawn, and some nice flowering shrubs," she said, gesturing with the massive tin of weedkiller my father had purchased for her on his way home from work.

The enormous "Poison" warning on the tin had made me a little nervous, and I'd questioned my father about the wisdom of allowing her access to several gallons of such a lethal substance. He jovially dismissed my concerns, telling me that she had obviously recovered and was now "right as rain." Unconvinced by his confidence, I eyed the giant tin apprehensively as she swung it back and forth.

"I'm going to put a fishpond and a fountain in the back," she continued describing her plans. "Maybe I'll get some of those little garden gnomes to put around it. That'll look nice, don't you think?"

"Can we have pansies?" I asked, imagining their bright yellow and purple blooms placed at perfectly spaced intervals all around the garden.

"I suppose so. But, whatever I put in, I'll have it looking lovely by next summer. We'll be able to throw one of those posh garden parties."

I couldn't imagine who she thought was going to come to this party. The only guests I could envisage were Auntie Mabel, and, if he happened to be out of prison at the time, Uncle Ted. As she continued to talk, however, I realized that my mother seemed to have illusions of making friends with the local landed gentry, going on at length about how "you get a better class of people" in the countryside and how we could "improve our social standing" if only we played our cards right. My mother's strategy in this regard seemed to be to impress them with her landscape-gardening talents and the Mr. Kipling cream cakes she'd serve with our afternoon tea.

"Sounds great, Mum," I said.

"Yes, it does, doesn't it?" she said, beaming as she unscrewed the cap of the weedkiller and strode purposefully toward the back door.

For the next week or so, my mother worked on the garden. Within days, she had reduced the thistles to a wilted, collapsed mass. After this, she talked my father into buying her a scythe. (He was a little more reluctant to purchase this particular item than the weedkiller and was persuaded to do so only after she threatened to march over to the nearest farm to ask if she could borrow one.) Scythe in hand, she began whacking away at the monstrous bramble bushes that bordered all sides of the garden. "Take care with that thing, Evelyn," my father called to her, cringing as she swung it around her in wide, menacing arcs. I watched her from the kitchen window, her eyes bright, teeth clenched, and I was reminded of those medieval pictures I had seen in my history textbook of Death, the Grim Reaper, sweeping through Europe during the plague.

The day I'd met Tracey, she'd told me that she and her family were leaving for a fortnight's holiday in Cornwall that weekend. I'd given her my telephone number, and I was thrilled when she rang the day after her return and invited me to meet up with her in the village the following morning. After we'd wandered around for a while and she'd told me about all the drop-dead-gorgeous boys she met while she was away, Tracey suggested that we go to her house and get something to eat.

"We can make some sandwiches and I can show you my David Cassidy posters," she said, grinning.

"Great," I said, trying to sound enthusiastic. During our first encounter, aside from talking about all the boys at school she liked, she had told me how, really, if she had a choice, she'd prefer to go out with David Cassidy. She also went on at great length about his looks, his songs, and how much she enjoyed watching episodes of *The Partridge Family*. I omitted to mention that I hated this particular television program and, though I knew there were boys who were far uglier than David Cassidy, I really hadn't given him a second thought. But going over to Tracey's house meant going back to Marigold Court, and I felt a flutter of excitement at the possibility of seeing Amanda again.

I hadn't mentioned Amanda to Tracey, but I had been hoping to slip her name into the conversation, to inquire whether Tracey knew her and where she happened to live. For some reason, though, it seemed impossible to just mention Amanda casually. I was afraid I'd blush when I talked about her and Tracey would think I was odd. When we came to the street, however, it was just as quiet as it had been the first time I visited, and without seeing a single one of her neighbors we made our way into Tracey's house.

Tracey's mother was at home when we arrived. Slender and peachy-skinned, she wore an Alice in Wonderland headband to hold her straight blond hair out of her face, and a flowery ruffled smock.

"Hello, Tracey, love. Didn't expect to see you back here so soon," she said, her voice so soft and melodic that it made me realize how abrasive the tones of all my female relatives were. And while all the women in my family were big-limbed and hefty, Mrs. Grasby was thin, with small fine-boned hands and guarded, delicate gestures to match. I remembered that she was the president of the Bleakwick Young Wives Club. If all the other members were like that, I thought, no wonder my mother had been tossed out. "This must be your new friend," she said, pressing her palms to each side of her face and regarding me as if I were a surprise gift that had just been delivered to her door.

"Her name's Jesse," Tracey said, rolling her eyes at me, apparently irked by her mother's enthusiasm. "She moved into Johnson's house. You know, that place on the road out of the village, the one that's falling to bits."

"Oh, Tracey, don't be so rude," her mother said, shaking her head and making a *tut-tut* sound with her tongue. "That's not how we talk to guests, now is it?" She turned to me. "Don't mind Tracey—she tends to forget her manners sometimes."

Tracey rolled her eyes again. "We just came home for something to eat. I thought you were going out."

"Oh, I was, but then I got carried away making that chicken casserole I saw in the new issue of *Good Housekeeping*. I thought your dad might want something different for a change. I think he'll like it," she said, pushing her hands into the ruffles of her smock. "At least I hope he likes it." For a moment, her voice seemed to catch in her throat and her face pressed into an uneasy tightness, her mouth bracketed by two carved lines. Then, almost as fast it came, the expression was gone and she was all soft edges and smiles. "Why don't you girls go and sit down and I'll make you some sandwiches. Ham and tomato all right for you, Jesse?"

"Yes, please, Mrs. Grasby," I said, following Tracey into the living room while her mother bustled down the hall toward the kitchen.

The furniture in Tracey's living room was very much as I'd expected—a thick-piled fitted carpet, an unscratched coffee table and sideboard, a pristine settee and matching armchairs, porcelain ornaments on the windowsills. The only unexpected element was the glass cabinet in the corner filled with gilded plates, silver trophies, bronze cups, ribbons, and medallions, and a collection of photographs and certificates on the wall.

"I didn't know your mum and dad did ballroom dancing," I said, walking over to take a closer look at the photographs.

Tracey shrugged. "Yeah, that's how they met."

In the pictures, they were beautiful. Mrs. Grasby, her hair coiffed in elaborate, twisty piles, her body sheathed in sparkly, sequined gowns, looked glamorous. And Mr. Grasby was dark-featured and ruggedly handsome in a black suit, white shirt, and black bow tie, his hair slicked back and shiny as patent leather. Some of the photographs were posed, but most caught them in the exuberance of dancing—their bodies arced in elegant lines, heads tilted, faces shiny with perspiration and the brilliance of the ballroom's lights. My eyes flitted from photograph to photograph, fascinated by the way, in those dancing shots, they cut such a dazzling spectacle, their two bodies converging in a single fluid motion, so that there was no doubt that they were meant to be to-gether. I thought of my own parents, both terrible dancers in their own particular way: my father so robotically stiff that dancing hardly seemed the right word for the wooden movements of his limbs; my mother frenetic and out of sync with any rhythm in the music, making it obvious that in dancing, as in everything else, she occupied a world of her own.

For a moment, I felt such envy that it was a liquid filling me. Here was the neat little house I imagined for myself: a mother who baked casseroles, presided over the Young Wives, and looked glamorous on the dance floor; and a father who was good-looking and won trophies in the quickstep. It was all so perfect, so perfectly normal, that I wished that it were mine. Of course, I knew I couldn't have it; I couldn't step into Tracey's life. But if I remained her friend, attached myself to all this perfection, perhaps I'd be able to shed my own aura of social fail-ure and bask in Tracey's glow.

"God," Tracey huffed. "I'm bloody starving. Mum! Mum! Have you got them sandwiches made yet?" She pushed herself up from the settee and made for the door. "Come on, let's see what's taking her so bloody long."

I followed her down the hall and into the kitchen, where her mother stood over the counter buttering slices of bread. Tracey walked over to her to look out the kitchen window. "Oh, God. What the bloody hell is she doing here?"

"Tracey," her mother said, "there is no need for that language! And, anyway, don't be like that. She's your sister, for goodness' sake."

"Who?" I asked, walking closer to the window.

"Our bloody Amanda, that's who."

"Tracey!" Her mother exclaimed.

I leaned over the kitchen counter and, gripping its edge, peered through the window. The back garden was a square of lawn surrounded by a border filled with rosebushes, sweet peas, and geraniums. In the middle of the grass, on a vinyl sun bed, reading a book, lay the girl I had met outside the Co-op. Wearing the smallest bikini I had ever seen anywhere except, perhaps, on the girls who draped the beaches on *Hawaii Five-O*, her whole body was glossy with suntan lotion.

"You didn't tell me you had a sister," I said, turning to Tracey.

"Yeah, well, she's horrible and I don't like her. So I don't talk about her much. All right?"

Mrs. Grasby looked at me and sighed. "They used to get along perfectly well. I suppose it's a teenager thing. Do you have any sisters or brothers, Jesse?"

"No, it's just me," I answered.

"God, what I wouldn't do to be an only child," Tracey huffed. Then she stomped toward the back door, swung it open, and stalked into the garden. I followed close behind.

"What are you doing home?" she demanded, standing over Amanda, hands on hips. "First I find Mum at home and now you're here as well. You told me you were going out."

"What business is it of yours what I get up to?" Amanda said without lowering her book. It was a romance novel. "Now go along and play like a good little girl."

"Oh, piss off, Amanda."

"You piss off. Can't I get even five minutes' quiet?"

"God, anybody would think you were the queen of bloody everything the way you carry on. You said you were going out."

"I changed my mind, didn't I?" Amanda dropped her book to her lap. She was wearing sunglasses but pulled them off to give Tracey a challenging stare. Then she noticed me. "I know you," she said, picking up the book again and waving it toward me so the pages flapped loose and open. "You're the one I saw outside the Co-op a couple of weeks ago. The one that was all wet."

"She's my friend," Tracey declared, as if she thought this was in jeopardy.

"Oh, don't get your knickers in a knot," Amanda responded. "She's quite a laugh, this one. Got a good sense of humor. Maybe she'll get you out of your permanent bloody bad mood. What's your name again?"

"Jesse," I answered.

"Right. Nice to see you again, Jesse."

I wished that I could find something to say that would make my name, myself, as memorable as she was to me. "Did you have a nice time at the pictures with your boyfriend?" I finally asked, hating the feebleness of my question as soon as I uttered it.

"It was all right. Of course, all he wanted to do was snog in the back row," she said, lowering her voice and looking toward the kitchen, where Mrs. Grasby was standing by the window assembling the sandwiches. "Me, I wanted to watch the film. Spent as much time fighting Stan off as that bloke in the film spends fighting that damn shark." She laughed and tossed her book so that it fell, splayed open on the grass. Then she picked up the bottle of suntan lotion that sat next to her on the lawn, shook some of the brown liquid into her palm, and began to rub it on her neck. "Sometimes I think I should give up men altogether," she said as she pulled down each of the straps of her bikini top to smear lotion on her shoulders. "Become a nun, go and live in a convent."

"Really?" I asked.

"No, of course she's not going to be a nun," Tracey said. "They wouldn't take her. She's too much of a slag."

"Yeah, well, takes one to know one," Amanda said, scowling at Tracey. Then she looked at me again. "So what do you think I should do, Jesse? I do get sick of lads. They're only after one thing, anyway. Don't you think?"

"I, er, I don't know," I said, shuffling awkwardly on the grass.

Amanda laughed. "Yeah, well, keep it that way. Stay sweet and innocent for as long as you can." She gave me a wink.

I felt color flood into my cheeks. I stood there wordless while Amanda squeezed lotion across the top of her breasts.

"Come on, Jesse," Tracey said, grabbing my sleeve. "Who wants to listen to this rubbish? Let's go and get a sandwich." She tugged me toward the kitchen.

"Hey, Jesse, before Miss Nasty Knickers here drags you away . . ." Amanda waved her hand loosely in my direction.

Without thinking, I shrugged Tracey's hand off me. "Yes?"

"I think I want to turn over—you know, get some sun on my back. Do you think you could rub some lotion on me?"

"Okay," I answered, ignoring Tracey's loud grunt, her stomping retreat toward the kitchen.

"I don't know why you bother—you only burn," Tracey called over her shoulder. "Got Irish skin, to match your Irish brain, haven't you, Amanda? You'll never get a tan, you'll only end up red as a beetroot. Who knows, maybe Stan will finally realize how ugly you are, see some bloody sense, and dump you." Then she marched through the door, slamming it behind her.

"Don't take any notice of her. She's only jealous."

"Jealous?"

"Yeah, she doesn't like it when I get on with her friends. She's very possessive, is Tracey. And bossy, in case you hadn't noticed. Of course, having an older sister makes it difficult for her. It's not like I'm going to let her tell me what to do. Get more than enough of that from certain other people round here." She paused and looked toward the house. Then she smiled up at me. "Now, can you make sure and do every inch of me? One thing Tracey's right about is that I burn something terrible if I'm not careful." Amanda eased herself over to lie on her stomach.

I picked up the bottle and poured out the lotion so that it pooled in my palm. Then I put my hand on Amanda's shoulder and began rubbing it over her. The lotion was warm, warmer than her skin, and it seeped so easily into her flesh that I kept having to pour out more. I found myself fascinated with the way it oozed over her, following the curve of her spine, dripping down the valleys below her shoulder blades. It ran in little brown rivulets, washing over the tiny golden hairs that patterned her legs.

"You've got very soft hands, you know." Amanda let out a long breath and shifted her hips sideways. "Hey, I'll have to get you to come round and do this more often." She laughed a soft throaty laugh.

I didn't say anything. I didn't think I could. My heart was beating too hard, thumping like an immense timpani drum against my chest. My throat felt dry, and though I was trying desperately to control them as they slid across Amanda's slick and freckled skin, my fingers were trembling.

THAT EVENING, MY MOTHER announced that she needed a break from doing the garden. I had to admit that she'd made remarkable progress. After she'd hacked away the thistles and brambles, she telephoned a local nursery. The following day, a man had arrived with a petrol-powered rototiller in the back of his van, hauling it out to the driveway and providing my mother with detailed verbal instructions and a spare can of petrol before he drove away.

"Just don't let her do anything stupid, will you, Jesse?" my father said as he eyed my mother pulling on the rototiller's starter cord before he left for work.

"No, Dad," I answered, imagining myself trying to prise my mother's hands away from the machine's handles if things went awry or throwing my body in its path if that strategy failed.

Fortunately, everything went smoothly and my mother worked until dusk, pushing the chortling machine back and forth, churning up the heavy dark clay. By Friday, she had mapped out a plan and begun digging the fishpond, which she had decided, along with a fountain surrounded by fishing gnomes, would form the centerpiece of her new garden.

"I'm jiggered," she said, walking into the kitchen and throwing herself into one of the chairs. "I'm taking this weekend off. I thought we'd get your dad to take us to see Mabel on Saturday. What do you think about that?"

I was delighted at the idea, but I'd already made arrangements to meet Tracey. "I can't, I'm seeing my friend. Tracey."

"That's all right," my mother said breezily. "You can bring her with you."

Hoping to prevent Tracey wanting to visit our house or meet my family, I'd told her that my mother had a very serious case of shingles and it was absolutely imperative that she remain in isolation until she had fully recovered. I had also told Tracey that that could take a very long time.

"What time are you meeting her?" my mother asked.

"Who?"

"Your friend, this Tracey."

"Oh, I don't remember."

"Well, that's not much good, is it? I mean, how are you going to meet her if you don't know what time you're supposed to be there?"

I shrugged. "I'll probably remember by tomorrow. I'm not meeting her until tomorrow."

"Does she have a phone?" my mother asked, pushing herself out of her chair and making her way toward the hallway, where our telephone sat buried under a sheet my father had put over it to protect it from the paint he'd been applying to the walls.

"I don't remember." I followed her into the hallway, panicking.

"What do you mean, you don't remember? What's wrong with you, anyway?" She pulled out the telephone directory. "What's her name?" she asked, leafing through the directory's flimsy pages.

"Tracey."

"Look, madam, don't you get funny with me. You know full well I mean what's her surname. Here am I trying to do you a favor and invite your friend to come out with us for the day and there you are acting like a big useless dollop. Now, you'd better get some sense into yourself soon, miss, or I'll be giving you the back of my hand to think about. Am I making myself clear?"

"Yes."

"Good. So what's her name?"

"It's all right, Mum," I said. "I'll phone her."

"Oh, so now you remember her number, then? God, you're as bad as your father. You'd forget your own head if it wasn't screwed on." She picked up the phone and thrust it toward me.

I had been hoping that she would leave me alone to make my call, allowing me to make up an excuse to Tracey for not being able to meet her and afterward to report that, sadly, Tracey was unable to join us. This, however, was not to be, and with my mother standing over me I found myself inviting Tracey to accompany us on a visit to my Auntie Mabel's. Despite my best attempts to make this outing sound like the dullest way to spend an afternoon, Tracey eagerly accepted the invitation.

"IF WE'RE GOING TO Mabel's, then we're going to visit my dad," my father said as my mother announced the news of our impending journey later that evening. He was slapping pale blue paint onto one of the hallway walls and my mother had to stand well back to avoid being spattered. His own face was already covered in tiny speckles of blue, making him look as if he had some kind of strange skin ailment.

"Oh, no, we're not! I'm not spending one minute with that miserable old bugger."

My mother usually refused to accompany my father when he visited my grandfather. For as long as I could remember, she had never liked him. And, from what I had witnessed of their limited interactions, it was obvious the feeling was mutual.

"Well, in that case I'm not driving you to see your Mabel." He said this somewhat gleefully, apparently enjoying the power he had as the only one who could drive. My mother had tried to learn. Indeed, she had taken the driving test six times but had failed to pass. It wasn't clear if she would try again, since the last time she took the examination, over two years ago now, she drove through a red light, narrowly missing an elderly pedestrian but managing to broadside a Mini before finally coming to a stop when the car she was driving hit a lamppost. The last we'd heard, the poor examiner was still out on disability leave.

"If you don't want to see my dad, you'll have to take the bus," my father concluded.

"But it takes forever."

My father shrugged. "It's up to you."

"Oh, all right, then. But we're only stopping for an hour and not a second longer, right, Jesse?"

I turned toward the stairs and the relative safety of my bedroom. I didn't want to get involved in their argument. I was already dealing with enough anxiety thinking about dragging Tracey along on this excursion.

CHAPTER EIGHT

—

WE PICKED UP TRACEY OUTSIDE HER HOUSE EARLY THE FOLLOW-
ing afternoon. She was wearing a pair of short-shorts, her big black
platform sandals, and a tight red tube top. As she walked down the path
toward our car, my mother muttered, "See, Jesse, at least I'm not the
type of mother that would let you out of the house dressed like *that*."

I wasn't sure that Mrs. Grasby was particularly thrilled about
Tracey's choice of outfit, either; she hadn't exactly seemed like the kind
of mother who would sanction such revealing clothes. But from our
visit the other day I'd got the impression that Tracey's mother was
fighting a losing battle in controlling certain aspects of Tracey's behavior, and that Tracey took particular delight in defying her. Still, as I
looked down at the nondescript cotton trousers and shapeless T-shirt
I was wearing, I wished that I had the courage to dress in outfits that
would make my mother scream.

"Extremely nice to meet you, Tracey," my mother said, peering
through her window as Tracey drew near. She talked in her put-on posh
voice, the one she always used to impress strangers and whenever she
picked up the telephone. I found it excruciating. Fortunately, she could
never keep it up for long and three sentences into any conversation she
usually reverted to her normal accent.

"Yeah, thanks for inviting me." Tracey pulled a smile and opened the car door. She clambered in beside me, arranging then rearranging her bare legs on the sticky vinyl of the backseat. As our car pulled away, I searched for signs of Amanda, but she was nowhere to be seen.

We turned onto the main road, and Tracey leaned toward my mother. "So I bet it's a relief not be infectious anymore, Mrs. Bennett." She spoke into my mother's stiff mound of hair, which occupied most of the space directly in front of her.

"What did you say, dear?" my mother asked, cocking her head slightly.

I shot Tracey a fierce, wide-eyed look, pushing my lips tight together in an effort to silently communicate that it was critical that she drop this line of conversation right away. Tracey, however, was oblivious. "I said, it's good that you're not infectious anymore."

My mother shifted around in her seat. "Infectious?" It was hard to gauge her expression. She had donned her sunglasses for this outing, the lenses reflecting back distorted round images of whatever she was looking at.

"Yeah," Tracey said, ignoring my elbow dig to her side. "Jesse said you had the shingles. She said you've been quite poorly."

"Did she now?" my mother said, turning toward me so that I could see a tubby, squat version of myself in her glasses, leaning as far into the corner of the backseat as possible. My father gave my mother a nervous glance. When he turned his attention back to the road, he let out a long, weighty sigh.

"Yeah, she said you've been poorly for what, a couple of months, right, Jesse?" Tracey looked from my mother to me. I said nothing. My mother continued to cast her silent, shaded scowl in my direction. "When I told my mum you had the shingles," Tracey continued, "she said a friend of hers had it and was off work for months. Caused her all sorts of problems, she said." Tracey's ability to remain completely unaware of the frosty atmosphere that had filled the inside of the car was astounding. I quite envied her this talent.

"Well, Tracey," my mother responded in an icily cheery voice, "you can tell your mother and anyone else that Jesse has broadcast the news of my illness to that I'm feeling all better now. And as for you, miss," she said, stabbing an index finger in my direction. "I'll be talking to you later." And with that she spun around to stare solidly in front of her, as still as a statue until we pulled up, half an hour later, outside Granddad's house.

GRANDDAD BENNETT WAS A retired trawlerman who'd spent thirty years going out on deep-sea fishing boats for three weeks at a time to trawl for cod. He had a raw, gravelly voice and a face that looked as if it had seen the kind of weather that was common off Iceland, with skin as gnarled as old leather, lines worn by salt and gales and one-hundred-foot waves. "He must have raked in a fortune over the years," my mother had said. "Earned good money on them fishing boats back then, they did. But the stupid sod drank and gambled it all away. Sent your poor grandma Bennett to an early grave." I'd never met Grandma Bennett; she died two weeks after my parents were married. Their wedding photographs contained the last pictures of her—a dumpy, frizzy-haired woman with a tight-lipped smile that stretched like an inked-in line across her face. From these photographs, I surmised that she was as pleased about my father's marriage to my mother as Granddad Bennett was.

When we arrived, we found Granddad sitting in his cramped living room, ensconced in the winged armchair that stood a little more than arm's length from the television. He wore a white shirt, open to show sprouts of gray chest hair poking through the holes of his string vest, and red braces that bowed outward over his expansive belly and held his baggy trousers high above his waist. We had traipsed single file down the narrow hallway of his two-up, two-down terraced house, not bothering to knock before we let ourselves in, because Granddad wouldn't have heard us anyway, since he was rather deaf. He had been in the navy during the war, and his left ear was damaged when his ship hit a mine and sank. In recent years, his disability had worsened considerably, but he refused to wear a hearing aid. Whenever someone suggested that he might benefit from one, he'd respond, "That water was cold enough to freeze the bollocks off a brass monkey, and I managed to survive eight hours in it. I've lived through worse things than you can imagine. So I'm not about to start wearing some prissy bloody hearing aid." I failed to see the logic of this argument. I did suspect, however, that he enjoyed being able to tune in and out of any surrounding conversation and sometimes rather liked making people repeat three or four times what they were saying to him.

"Hello, Dad," my father said, bellowing loud enough to be heard above the blaring television. "Just thought we'd stop round for a visit, see how you're getting on."

"I'm all right," Granddad bellowed back. "You've got no reason to worry about me. I'm watching the sports." He waved us vaguely toward the settee and the other armchair across the room. "It's a right good match, this." He picked up the roll-up cigarette that lay in the ashtray balanced on the arm of his chair, took a long, audible drag, and turned back to the television, where a shifting pile of black and red—jerseyed men were scrambling and kicking at one another in what appeared to have started out as a rugby scrum.

"So who's winning, then?" my father yelled, taking a seat in the second armchair. My mother, Tracey, and I sat down on the settee, our bodies pressed unwillingly together on the uncomfortable and uneven cushions.

"Eh?" Granddad said, looking quizzically over at my father.

"I said, who's winning?" As he shouted across the living room, my mother closed her eyes, pursed her lips, and shook her head.

"They are," Granddad answered. "But don't you worry," he said, giving us all a reassuring nod. "We're going to catch up soon."

I was far from clear who the "we" in this particular match might be. England, perhaps? Yorkshire? Hull Kingston Rovers? When I noticed the vague expression on my father's face, I realized that he was probably just as clueless. He'd never been much of a rugby fan. I spent several frustrating minutes trying to work out exactly who the opposing teams were, but with no scores announced and the commentator speaking in unintelligible rugby-related jargon, I was having no success. Tracey seemed indifferent to the game itself, but she kept leaning into me and making remarks about how good-looking some of the players were, what firm legs they had, and how she wouldn't mind finding herself in the middle of one of their scrums. I studied the players she admired, trying to create within myself a similar enthusiasm for their mud-streaked muscled bodies, but as much as I tried it just wouldn't come.

Aside from Tracey's animated whispered commentary, no one spoke until, during a break in the action, my mother yelled toward Granddad, "This is Jesse's friend, Tracey!"

"What?" Granddad said, frowning.

"This is Jesse's friend, Tracey!" she yelled again, this time even louder.

Granddad let his gaze slide slowly up Tracey's legs and torso. "Aye, I didn't think I'd seen her before," he said, his eyes finally resting on her face. "But I thought she might be one of your lot. I mean, it's hard to keep track of them, isn't it? Half the family flitting off to Australia, the rest of them in and out of the nick." He flicked the ash from the end of his cigarette, pulled a smile, and turned back to the television.

I felt my mother's body stiffen next to me, her knuckles pressed white into the settee cushions. She glowered at my father, who seemed suddenly intensely interested in the sufferings of an injured rugby player. Tracey crossed, uncrossed, and recrossed her legs. Even she, it appeared, had noticed the discomfort of this interaction.

"Right, then," my mother said. "I'll make a pot of tea, then, shall I?"

"Ooh, that'd be lovely," Granddad said. "Nice of you to offer, Evelyn. And there's some tinned salmon in the pantry. A plate of sandwiches would be nice, don't you think?"

My mother swept wordlessly out of the room, slamming the door behind her and then clattering and banging around in the kitchen with what was considerably more fervor than was required to make a pot of tea and a plate of tinned salmon sandwiches.

Tracey looked curiously around the cramped and cluttered little room. "Who's that?" she asked, gesturing toward the numerous framed photographs arranged on the mantelpiece, along the sideboard, and on top of the television. Almost all of them showed the same person, as a baby, a child, and a teenager. In many of them he was pictured kicking, holding, or heading a football.

"My uncle Brian," I responded. "He's dead."

Brian was my father's only brother, older than my father by a little more than three years. I had never met him, but I'd heard about him often enough. He died before I was born, on his eighteenth birthday. After downing several pints at the local pub, to celebrate his attainment of legal drinking age, he'd stepped into the road and been killed by a passing delivery van, driven by an off-duty grocer's assistant who was somewhat under the influence himself. I had taken for granted being surrounded by images of this dead uncle in Granddad's house, but now that Tracey had pointed out his omnipresence I saw it with a stranger's eyes and realized that it was a little odd. I scanned for any pictures of other family members and found only two: a smiling portrait of my grandmother and a small picture of my father and mother holding me as a baby. We occupied the far end of the sideboard, in a particularly shadowy corner of the room.

Tracey stood up and went over to the mantel. "Was he a football star or something?" she asked.

"What did you say?" Granddad said, turning toward her when he noticed her picking up one of the several trophies and medals that interspersed the photographs.

"She asked if Uncle Brian was a football star!" I yelled.

"Oh, yes, he was going to be," Granddad answered, nodding vigorously at Tracey. "No doubt about that. He was a genius at football, was that lad. A bloody genius. Could have been as good as Bobby Charlton. Could have played for England in the World Cup."

"You don't know that, Dad," my father said, keeping his gaze fixed on the television screen.

"Of course I do. I saw our Brian play. He was a natural. More moves on that playing field than Fred Astaire has on the dance floor. Two days after he died, he was supposed to try out for professional."

"For Hull City," my father added scornfully but not quite loud enough for Granddad to hear. The local football team wasn't exactly known for its stunning achievements. In recent years Hull had been lucky to avoid demotion to the Third Division. Even their most loyal of fans had started to become embarrassed about sporting the amber-and-black of the Hull City colors.

"Everyone said he had talent," Granddad continued. "If he'd lived, he'd have been making millions, just like that Kevin Keegan and the like. But, even though he died young, at least he achieved something."

My father groaned, rolled his eyes, then spoke, this time loud enough for Granddad to hear. "He died rolling out the pub, drunk as a bloody skunk. I'd hardly call that an achievement, would you? And, besides, it wasn't as if he was destined for a career as a rocket scientist, is it? I mean, all he could do was play football, for Christ's sake." He pronounced the word "football" with such utter derision, it was as if he'd declared that my late uncle Brian had nothing more than a talent for cleaning sewers. My father had always regarded the game with particular disdain and would begin to fume if he so much as heard the theme music for *Match of the Day.*

"Don't you talk about your brother like that," Granddad said, leaning forward in his chair and gesturing toward my father with a newly rolled unlit cigarette. "Your mother would turn over in her grave to hear you say such a thing, she really would. Broke her heart, losing Brian like that." He turned to the television. The room was once again filled with the cheers of the rugby crowd and the babble of the commentator.

"He was right good-looking, wasn't he?" Tracey said, picking up one of the photographs, a close-up of Uncle Brian kneeling with a football in his hands and smiling broadly into the camera. His hair was combed back, with a wave overhanging his forehead. His eyes were narrow, like my father's, and his cheeks dimpled in the same way. But it was true— the combination of his features made him handsome, while my father's made him merely ordinary, and Brian looked cheerier, somehow more at ease, his toothy grin filling the picture with its confident brilliance. Tracey stared into the photograph dreamily, as if it were a picture of David Cassidy and not my long-dead uncle Brian she was holding.

"Oh, yes, he was definitely the looker of the family was our Brian," Granddad said. "And he had all the get-up-and-go."

My father shifted in his chair and muttered something under his breath. I wanted Tracey to sit down, to stop mulling over the photographs and trophies, to leave my dead uncle alone on the mantel. But she continued to pick up and examine the trophies. "They're a bit dusty, you know," she said, running her finger over a large silver cup and then indicating the patch of gray dirt on her fingertip. "It'd be nice to clean them up, don't you think? Honor his memory."

My father closed his eyes and sighed.

Granddad, on the other hand, seemed delighted at the idea. "Aye, you're right about that, young lady. They do need polishing up. Your mam used to do it once a week," he said, turning to my father. "But me, I'm no good with things like that. Maybe I'll ask Evelyn to do it for me. What do you think?"

"You can ask her," my father answered dubiously. A resounding bang followed by several smaller crashing noises emanated from the kitchen.

"Maybe I'll wait," Granddad said, pushing back the top of his brass lighter, striking the flint with a flick of his thumb and lighting his ciga-rette. "I just hope that's not the best china she's messing about with."

"I'll do it," Tracey said. "I'll give them a dusting. And I know how to polish things. I watch my mum polish her and my dad's ballroom-dancing trophies all the time."

"That would be champion, would that," Granddad said.

"No, Tracey, it's all right. Just leave it," I said. I saw the annoyance on my father's face, the way that all this talk of his dead brother seemed to upset him, make him sink further into himself.

"No, I want to," Tracey insisted. "I think it's important."

"You're a good lass," Granddad said. "It's a pity it takes a stranger to take care of the lad's memory, it really is. There's a tin of polish and a duster somewhere in one of them cupboards in the kitchen. Ask Evelyn. She'll help you find it."

Half an hour later, the room was filled with the caustic smell of Brasso, Uncle Brian's trophies were sparkling, and the rugby match had ended. When the final scores were announced, I finally realized that we had been watching England playing New Zealand. And, as seemed the norm for almost every international sport, England had lost.

"No wonder this country's such a mess," Granddad declared. "Wasn't so long ago those people were living in our colonies. Now they're beating us at the sport we bloody well invented. I don't know what this country's coming to. If you ask me, it all started to go down the drain when we ended national service. Well, that and letting all those Pakistanis and West Indians in." He puffed on his cigarette for a few seconds, then, as an afterthought, added, "At least *they* don't play rugby."

"But they're damned good cricket players," my father said.

"Yes, well," said Granddad, stabbing the air with his cigarette. "That proves my point then, doesn't it?"

"What point?" I asked.

"That we should keep England for the English," he responded. "None of this colored immigration. None of this racial mixing. They're sneaking in everywhere these days."

My father heaved a sigh. This was a theme that Granddad revisited almost every time we saw him.

"Watering down the English culture, they are," Granddad continued. "And that's what made England great, you know. The culture. There's only one Shakespeare. Only one Winston Churchill. Only one . . ." He cast about for a few seconds, frowning and taking a puff of his cigarette. "Only one Tom Jones." He gave a satisfied nod.

"Tom Jones is Welsh," I said.

Granddad shrugged. "Aye, well, British, though, isn't he?"

"And he's got a lovely voice," my mother said. "But that's what they say about the Welsh, isn't it? They might have a bit of a funny accent, but they don't half know how to sing."

Granddad let out a loud dismissive snort.

"We read Shakespeare at school," Tracey said. "It was dead boring."

"Yes, well, I've never read him myself," Granddad admitted. "All those to bes and not to bes, all that wherefore art thou Romeo rubbish. It's a bit much, really." He paused to take a loud, long sip of his tea, wiping his lips with the back of his hand before going on. "But it's the English have made the biggest contribution to world literature, there's no denying that. I mean, England's produced all the world's best poets. I mean, there's . . . Wordsworth . . . Keats, and that bloke—you know, the one they have as the poet laureate, the one that writes poems for the Queen's birthday. It's not as if them West Indians have produced any great writers."

"How do you know?" I asked, guessing that Granddad was even less qualified to make pronouncements about foreign literature than of his native tongue.

"Yes, how would you know?" my mother echoed, leaning toward Granddad in an effort to ensure that he heard this particular question quite clearly. "I mean, you already said yourself you're not much of a reader." She gave a triumphant nod.

"You know, you're right about that, Evelyn," Granddad said, turning toward her slowly, a smile itching at the edges of his pale lips. "But then I don't have the time. Not like some people. I mean, if I managed to get myself put in the nuthouse for a couple of months, then I'd have plenty of time to catch up on my reading." He looked at Tracey, smiling wider now. "Yes, that'd give me enough time to get through the entire works of Shakespeare, don't you think?"

"Well, I suppose so . . ." Tracey began, looking a little confused as she eyed my mother, then me.

I began pulling at a loose thread in one of the settee cushions. As I felt the heat of Tracey's questioning eyes on me, I tugged hard and a wide patch of the cushion's fabric began to work loose. I feared that our friendship would unravel as easily as that thread. Within seconds, Tracey would learn the awful truth about my mother and she'd run screaming from the house. I wanted to do something to stop it, but I felt paralyzed. Instead, I watched the stitching on the settee come undone and waited for the inevitable.

"I don't think people in nuthouses are allowed to read," Tracey said matter-of-factly as she turned back to Granddad. "I mean, don't they lock them up in straitjackets and padded cells? I saw one on the telly once, and it looked a bit like a prison, it—"

"Right, then," my mother declared, springing up so abruptly that Tracey and I knocked against each other at the other end of the settee. "I think we'd better be leaving. Come on, Mike, we've got to get over to Mabel's now. Jesse, you and your friend get yourselves ready. I'm off outside. I think I need a breath of fresh air. Bye, now, Dad," she said, the words falling behind her as she strode down the hall.

Tracey gave me a bewildered look. I shrugged and stood up.

"Shame you've got to go," Granddad said, rising from his chair. I thought he was getting up to wish us goodbye, but instead he walked over to the television and switched the channel to the wrestling and went back to his armchair. "This should be a good match," he said, waving his big weathered hand toward the screen.

IF THE ATMOSPHERE in the car had been chilly before we arrived at Granddad's, it was positively frozen when we left. My father, true to form, seemed determined to pretend that everything was fine, while my mother fumed silently. If she'd been a cartoon character, there would have been steam coming out of her ears.

"Right, then, let's get off to Mabel's then, shall we?" my father said cheerily, turning the key in the ignition and putting the car into gear. "I bet she's going to be pleased to see us." He beamed toward me and Tracey in the mirror. "Do you want to pick up a cake or something on the way, Evelyn?" he asked, smiling at my mother now.

"No," she answered stonily.

"But I thought you wanted to get Mabel a cake," my father said. "You know your Mabel likes a nice bit of cake." I sat directly behind him, pressing my knees into his seat and willing him to shut up.

My mother turned to him. "Are you deaf?" She had put her sunglasses on for the car journey, but she took them off now, widening her eyes at him expectantly. "Don't tell me you've inherited that from your father as well? I said"—she began speaking very slowly and very loudly—"I don't want to get a cake, and that means I don't want to get a cake. Understand?"

"For God's sake, Evelyn, I was just trying to be helpful."

"Well, don't bloody bother." She looked out the window, paused for a moment, and then swung around to look at me in the backseat. "And you, Jesse, make sure you behave yourself when we're at our Mabel's, can you? I'm sick of this family showing me up."

"I didn't do anything! Don't go blaming me just because Granddad upset you."

"Too clever for your own good, that's what you are," she said, turning toward the front and putting her sunglasses back on.

"But I didn't do anything," I repeated. Neither of my parents responded.

It took us twenty minutes to get to Auntie Mabel's house—twenty minutes of stiff, angry silence that was beginning to take its toll even on Tracey. As we clambered out of the car, she whispered to me, "Did I say something wrong at your granddad's house?"

"No," I said, desperately hoping that this excursion wouldn't put an end to our friendship, though at that moment I wouldn't have blamed her for demanding to be driven back to Midham and declaring that she never wanted anything to do with my family again. I only wished I had that option.

"Well, it's just that I don't think your mam likes me very much."

"It's all right, she doesn't like anyone," I said, hoping that she might find at least a little comfort in this, and then adding, in a tone that sounded more desperate than I had intended, "But I like you. And I really, really want you to be my friend."

"EVELYN, MIKE, JESSE! By heck, this is a lovely surprise." Despite her exclamation, Auntie Mabel didn't exactly sound thrilled to see us standing on her doorstep. In fact, she looked somewhat perturbed— perturbed and a little disheveled. It was very out of character. Mabel was the kind of woman whose very first actions of the day (after lighting a cigarette) were to remove her hairnet and curlers, tease and shape her hair, and apply her makeup. In all the years I'd known her, I'd never seen her without eyebrow pencil and mascara, her hair vigorously styled, her body pressed into a Playtex Cross Your Heart Bra and Eighteen-Hour Girdle, her tamed curves straining against the seams of a tight dress. Now here she was at half past three in the afternoon, her hair flattened against her head, wearing a red nylon dressing gown and last night's faded makeup. In fact, her eyebrow pencil and mascara had come off almost completely and I was struck by how amazingly small her eyes appeared without their usual adornment.

"Did you just get out of bed?" my mother asked accusingly, apparently forgetting that she was in the habit of rising well after the noon hour herself.

"Well, how was I supposed to know you were coming round? What, don't they have phones where you moved to? I mean, couldn't you have given me a ring?" Mabel put her hands in the pockets of her dressing gown and leaned her shoulder into the doorjamb. In the bright sun-shine, her shrunken eyes narrowed to flickering slits as she peered be-yond her tiny square of yard to the massive concrete edifices of the tower blocks beyond.

Mabel had moved to her new council estate only a year before. The city had grand plans for slum clearance, and forced from the terrace house, almost identical to Granddad's, that she'd occupied for as long as I could remember, she'd packed up her things and settled into this box-shaped little home. She didn't care for it much, but she counted herself lucky, since a past relationship with one of the men in charge of the re-location plans had meant she'd been able to avoid moving into one of those immense buildings that now blocked her view of the sky.

"We wanted to surprise you," my mother replied. "And, besides, you haven't exactly been ringing night and day yourself. I don't remember the last time I heard from you."

Mabel gave a guilty shrug. "I know, I know. I've been a bit busy re-cently, what with one thing and another. You know how things can be, Ev."

"Well, are you going to invite us in, then?" my mother demanded. "Or are you going to leave your own sister standing on your doorstep?"

Mabel shot a look over her shoulder down the hallway, then turned back to us, sighing. "You're right. I'm terrible, aren't I? Come on, come in." She gestured us into the house. "Ooh, it is lovely to see you, our Jesse," she said, pulling me toward her as I stepped into the hall. She kissed me on the cheek and pressed me into her shoulder. "And is this a friend of yours, then?" she asked, releasing me and gesturing toward Tracey.

"This is Tracey," I said.

"You're a bonny lass," Mabel said. "But you could do with a bit of meat on them bones, love." She reached out and gently pinched one of Tracey's skinny arms. "See, hardly anything on you. Come on, I'll give you something to fatten you up a bit. But first I need a minute to put my face on and make myself decent."

While Mabel went upstairs, my mother went into the kitchen to make a pot of tea. My father slunk off into the living room, where he turned on the television and commenced watching the wrestling. Tracey and I followed him, sat down on the settee, and began leafing through the copies of *Woman's Weekly* that Mabel kept in a stack on her coffee table. We turned to the "problem pages" in the back.

Most of the problem-page letters were filled with words like "menopause," "ovaries," "infertility," questions about bodily functions that seemed dull, and a little disgusting, older women's problems that we knew didn't apply to us. The ones we searched for were about sex. Some actually used the occasional "penis," "vagina," and "sexual inter-course," and when Tracey or I came upon one of these forbidden words we nudged each other and read the letters in furtive, giggling whispers.

"Hey, listen to this one," Tracey said, jabbing me with an elbow. " 'Dear Jill, I have a very difficult and embarrassing problem to share with you. But I have decided to write because, quite frankly, I really don't know what else to do. There's a woman who moved into the house two doors away from mine about a year ago. In the last few months we've become very close friends. She understands me in a way my husband doesn't. Recently, I've begun thinking about her all the time—and not just as a friend, if you understand what I mean.' " Tracey barked out a laugh before pressing her hand to her mouth and snigger-ing into her palm.

I laughed, too, but it was cautious, soft-edged, and went no further than my throat. "Let me see," I said, leaning over Tracey's shoulder, wanting to read the words for myself.

"No." She pushed me away and continued reading. " 'Last week, when I told her how I felt, she responded by kissing me.' " She burst into a fit of uncontrollable giggles.

I watched, irritated by her laughter, uneasy but not quite sure why. "Go on," I said, nudging her. "Finish the letter."

Tracey sputtered out another laugh before taking a deep breath and continuing with difficulty. " 'I just don't know what to do. My husband

and I don't have a bad marriage, and we have two delightful young children. But I just can't stop thinking about my friend. Do you think I'm
a lesbian?' " At this, Tracey began to laugh so loudly that even my father
looked at us for a moment, frowning, shrugging, and then turning away.

I wasn't laughing nearly as hard as Tracey, and after a few moments
I stopped to mull over the letter. I'd heard the word "lesbian" before,
yelled at girls in the school corridors, girls who were unpopular, girls
like me that none of the boys liked. And sometimes, when two girls
walked arm in arm across the playground or played with each other's
hair in the classroom, boys would goad them with "lesby-friends, lesby-
friends," as if touching each other somehow tainted them, as if that was
the worst thing they could be. I knew lesbians were girls who didn't like
boys, that they liked girls instead, but up until that moment I'd never
really thought that they actually existed.

"What does the answer say?" I asked, trying to tug the magazine
from Tracey. I wanted to read the response. Would the woman be told
to put a stop to her thoughts, to stop seeing her friend? Would she be
told that her impulses were unnatural, that she needed to confess them
to a doctor or a priest?

"No," Tracey said, tugging back. "I'll read it."

"You can't, you're laughing too much." She was doubled up, tears
streaming down her face. I could feel my irritation turning to anger. It
really wasn't that funny.

"No, I can, just give me a minute." She took a deep breath and wiped
away her tears in an effort to compose herself. " 'Dear Confused,' " she
began. Then, looking solemn, she dropped the magazine to her lap.
"Yeah, she is confused, all right. Confused and bloody queer. Can you
imagine that, kissing a woman?" She slapped the page and contorted
her face into an expression of disgust. "Yuck. She needs to be put away.
It's repulsive."

I nodded, a quick, soft bob of my head.

"Revolting," Tracey added. "Sick, sick, sick."

I felt my chest tighten and my stomach knot up, as if my torso were a rag being twisted and squeezed. "Let's read what the answer says," I said, making a grab for the magazine.

"What are you two up to?" My mother entered the living room carrying a tray loaded with teacups, saucers, and a plate of fairy cakes.

Tracey and I scrambled to close the pile of magazines we had strewn across the settee and tossed them onto the coffee table. "Nothing. You want a hand with that tray, Mum?" I leaped up and took the tray from her while Tracey straightened up the pile of magazines.

"Thank you, darling," my mother said as I began placing cups in their saucers. Then, looking at my father, she commented acidly, "Nice to see someone around here can manage to lift a finger to help."

My father didn't pay her any attention. He was sitting on the edge of his seat, watching as one of the wrestlers sat astride the chest of his opponent and the referee pointed down at them and counted steadily to ten. "One-a, two-a, three-a, four-a . . ."

"Well, you can stop watching this bloody rubbish for a start," my mother declared, marching over to the television and turning it off. The wrestlers flickered, then disappeared to a white dot in the middle of the screen.

"Aw, bloody hell, Evelyn," my father protested. "I was watching that." He thrust himself backward into his chair, expelling air from his mouth like a punctured tire.

"Well, you're not now, are you?" my mother replied, standing defiantly in front of the television, hands on her hips. "Show some respect, can't you? We're visitors."

"God," he huffed. "Anybody would think we'd dropped in on the lord mayor or something. It's only your Mabel."

"Oh, that's it, is it? My family not good enough for you?" She folded her arms across her chest now. "It's all right when your father treats me like rubbish, isn't it?"

"Oh, for God's sake, Evelyn."

"Don't you 'for God's sake' me," she said, waving her index finger toward him. "I know you think you're better than me. But you're not, you know. Despite what that sodding father of yours has to say, you're not." Her voice began to break, and I was afraid that she was going to burst into tears in front of Tracey. "And I don't care if he's on his bloody deathbed next time we're supposed to go round. I'm never going to visit that nasty old bugger again."

"Mum," I said, desperate not to let things deteriorate any further. "Why don't I pour you a nice cup of tea? You don't want to get upset in front of Auntie Mabel, do you? It'd be a shame to spoil your time here. I mean, you haven't seen her in ages."

Much to my relief, she gasped a couple of deep breaths and took a seat on the settee next to Tracey and me. "Thanks, darling," she said as I handed her a cup of tea. Then, turning to Tracey, she said, "I only hope you're as nice to your mother, Tracey, as Jesse is to me. She's a saint sometimes, she really is."

A few minutes later, Mabel made her entrance. Reeking of hair spray and perfume, she wore a fluorescent orange sundress, her makeup now carefully applied, her hair a big shiny brown helmet on her head. On her feet she wore a pair of red wedge-heeled slippers decorated with fluffy pompons. "Here I am, back to the land of the living," she beamed. "Ooh, pour us a cuppa, would you, Jesse, love?"

"Here you are, Auntie Mabel," I said, handing her a cup of tea just the way she liked it—the cup almost half filled with milk, three heaping spoonfuls of sugar stirred into it.

"You've made me a very happy woman, darling, you really have," she said, after taking her first sip and sinking back into the armchair. "Now all I need is a fag and I'll be able to die in peace." She jostled a cigarette out of the packet of Benson & Hedges she had been carrying and popped it into her mouth.

"Yes, well, you might not die so peaceful if you end up with lung cancer," my mother muttered grimly.

"Anybody ever tell you you're a right bloody killjoy, Evelyn?" Mabel asked, lighting the cigarette, throwing her head back, and blowing a column of blue smoke toward the ceiling.

"My uncle Desmond died of a heart attack," chirped Tracey, leaning forward to take a fairy cake. "My dad said it was because he smoked. I was only little when it happened. He was thirty-four," she said, biting into the sponge so that her words came out thick and crumbs sputtered from her mouth.

"Oh, that's terrible. And so young," my mother said, shaking her head sympathetically, then turning to Mabel. "See, I told you, if you don't watch it you'll be popping your clogs before you see the other side of forty. And let's face it, Mabel, that's not that long off for you, now, is it?"

"If I'd known you were going to come round and cheer me up like this, I wouldn't have bothered opening the door."

"Pardon me, I was only trying to help you improve your health," my mother said haughtily.

"Well, don't bloody bother." Mabel took a long drag of her cigarette and exhaled, loudly. "I mean, everybody's got to have some pleasures in life. Even you, Evelyn."

My mother huffed and wrapped her arms tightly around her chest, taking a sudden interest in the slightly askew print of a buxom parlor maid above the mantel, the puppy calendar behind the television, the velvet painting of Blackpool Tower above Mabel's head.

"Did you make these fairy cakes?" Tracey asked, stuffing another one into her mouth, chewing as she spoke. "They're very nice, Mrs. . . ." Her voice trailed off as she realized that no one had briefed her on how to correctly address Auntie Mabel.

Mabel opened her mouth to respond, but my mother interjected. "Mabel doesn't bake," she said derisively, as if she spent hours each week in the kitchen virtuously turning out delicious homemade delicacies. "Doesn't cook, either. And she's not a Mrs. She's a Miss. A spinster, really, right, Mabel?"

Mabel responded by shaking her head slowly and taking another drag on her cigarette. I sank lower into the settee while Tracey, still apparently unperturbed by any of the tensions around her, munched on another fairy cake. I was relieved that she seemed so unaffected. If our friendship could survive this particular family outing, there really was a chance that she'd stay friends with me for a lot longer.

"For a skinny lass, you can't half put those things away," Mabel commented. "Or maybe you store it all in them shoes of yours, eh?" She laughed, gesturing toward the towering platform heels on Tracey's sandals. "What do you think, Ev, maybe I should get myself a pair? Now, that'd be a lark, staggering around in them!"

"You'd look like mutton dressed as lamb," my mother said flatly.

Mabel said nothing. We sat in silence for a few moments, the only sound Tracey's chewing. Finally, my father, who had been making a concentrated study of his feet for the past few minutes, shifted in his armchair. "Mind if I put the wrestling on, Mabel?" he asked.

"No, no, you go ahead, Mike," she answered. "To tell you the truth, I don't mind watching the wrestling myself. Don't mind doing it every now and again, either," she added, waggling her eyebrows. Tracey and I laughed along with her, but my mother, who was now busy glaring daggers over at my father, ignored her comments. "Oh, come on, Ev," Mabel said. "Cheer up, for God's sake. You look as miserable as sin. What have you been doing to her out there in the country, Mike?"

"What?" My father had already turned on the television and slumped back into his chair. He was staring intently at the screen, where a man wearing a black mask and built like a small tank was body slamming his opponent, a rather more slender gentleman dressed in Union Jack shorts. The crowd around the ring was booing and hissing frantically.

"Oh, never mind," Mabel said, waving him away. Then to my mother, "Men, they're all the same. Put them in front of a telly and they go into a trance. They're like kids really, aren't they? But at least it keeps them quiet for a while. Leaves us girls to have a conversation by ourselves, eh?" She beamed hopefully at my mother. "So, how are you keeping out there, then, Ev?" she asked, crushing her cigarette in one of the half-dozen ashtrays that ornamented the room. "Like it, do you?"

My mother shrugged. "Could be worse, I suppose."

"Dad's decorating the house and Mum's doing the garden, aren't you, Mum?" I said. "You should come out and visit us, Auntie Mabel. We could have you over for tea."

"Ooh, I don't know, darling. I'm not used to traveling that far. It was bad enough when they moved me out of my old house and onto this bloody estate. Felt like they'd sent me to the end of the world, it did. I'd be even more out of my element visiting you in the country. I'd probably go into shock seeing all them trees and fields."

"It's really not that far," I said.

"We'll see, love," she answered. "We'll see." She paused for a moment, then her face lit up. "Oh, Ev, I almost forgot. I've got a right bit of news for you, I have. Actually, I suppose it's more than a bit of news. This'll knock your socks off, will this."

"What?" my mother asked, frowning.

"Well, I only found out yesterday myself. And I was going to ring you, but I was on my way out when I got the news and then, well, as you probably guessed, I had a bit of a night on the town last night. So, what with one thing and another, it's probably just as well you dropped round, because given the state of my head today I might've forgotten to ring you."

"What?" my mother said impatiently. "What's the news?"

"It's Mam. She phoned me from Australia. She's getting married! To that fella Bill she's been hanging about with. Used to own a factory or something like that. According to Mam, he's loaded with money. Hey, Evelyn, do you think he'll pay our tickets over to Australia for the wedding?"

"Married? She's getting married?"

"That's what she said. They haven't set a date yet. But they're going to do it next year, in the summer, probably—which is their winter for some reason, though I have to say I've never been able to work that one out."

"Why did she ring you?" my mother asked. "I mean, if she's getting married, then the least she could do is tell both her daughters."

"I don't know, Ev. Maybe she didn't have your new number."

"I sent it to her. Wrote it plain as day for her in one of my letters."

"It's expensive to make those overseas calls, you know, Ev. And she did tell me to pass the good news on to you as soon as I could. It's my fault I didn't ring you yesterday. But, like I said, I was on my way out and I—"

"That's not the point," my mother interrupted. "*She* should have told me. *She* should have told me that she's hitching herself to a bloke over there. That she's planning on stopping in Australia, that she's never coming back. To England. To her home. To her family!" And, with that, my mother leaped up from the settee and made a hurried exit from the room.

We heard her as she scurried up the stairs, apparently making her way to the bathroom. Then we heard a loud scream and her thundering steps as she turned tail and ran downstairs again, this time moving so fast that it sounded as if she stumbled several times before finally making it to the ground floor.

"Ooh, heck," Mabel said, rapidly firing up another cigarette before my mother burst into the room.

"Mabel!" My mother was white as a sheet, her eyes as wide as saucers.

"What, Ev?" Mabel asked, attempting to look coy. "Something wrong?"

"I found a naked man in your bathroom."

Tracey and I turned to each other, hiding gleeful expressions behind our hands. A smile tugged at Mabel's lips, but she managed to suppress it. "You did?" she asked with exaggerated innocence.

"Yes, I did."

"Well, there's some women might not consider that such a bad thing, you know."

"How can you say that?" My mother was outraged, grinding her heels into Mabel's green-and-orange carpet. "It's . . . it's . . . well, it's disgusting. He was standing right there. Not a stitch on him. Not a bloody stitch."

"Yes, well," Mabel said, hitching up the straps on her sundress and looking away from my mother. "That'll be Frank."

"Frank?"

Mabel nodded. "He was the bloke I went out with last night, the one I—"

"I always knew you had loose morals, our Mabel. But this . . ."

"Oh, for goodness' sake, Ev, calm down." Mabel rolled her eyes. "It's not like you've not seen anything like that before. I mean, I'm sure Mike—"

"Don't you bring my married life into this. At least I respect myself. At least I don't cheapen myself like other members of this family. What with you frolicking with every bloke left, right, and center, and now my mother gallivanting around with some Australian gigolo."

"Look, Ev, I know you're upset that Mam's getting married, that she's staying in Australia—"

"That's nothing to do with it. Nothing to do with it at all. Suffice it to say, if you choose to have men wandering about your house in the altogether—well, that's your affair. But I don't have to stay here and put up with it. Come on, Mike, we're leaving."

"Leaving?" my father asked, looking up from the television with an expression so startled it was as if he'd abruptly been brought out of a trance.

"Yes, leaving. Come on, girls. Let's go."

"But we only just got here," my father protested, giving my mother, then Mabel, then me a distressed look.

"And now it's time to go," my mother responded, already making her way out the living-room door.

"But the match isn't over. Can't we just stay for the end of the match?" He rose reluctantly from his seat, all the time gazing at the television screen, where the two wrestlers were now taking turns flinging each other from one side of the ring to the other, bouncing back and forth against the ropes. As they did so, each roared at the top of his lungs and shook his head like some kind of demented animal. "Hope we see you again soon, Mabel," my father said when he had finally reached the door after backing his way out of the living room, eyes fixed on the hyperactive performance on the television. "You must come and pay us a visit."

"Maybe. But I think I'll wait until she's calmed down a bit," Mabel answered, indicating my mother, who was pacing back and forth across the front garden like an overwound toy soldier. "And, judging by the state she's got herself in, that might be a while."

CHAPTER NINE

———

I DIDN'T SEE MUCH OF TRACEY DURING THE NEXT FEW DAYS, TURN-
ing her down several times when she telephoned and asked me to meet
her in the village. I even said no when she suggested we spend the afternoon at her house, despite the opportunity this presented of basking
in the comfortable normality of her household, and the thrill that came
over me when I considered the possibility of seeing Amanda again.
Even in the face of these temptations, I didn't feel comfortable leaving
my mother alone. Immediately following our visit to Mabel's, her
mood had plummeted. She had taken to her bed and stayed there, re-
fusing to rouse herself when I went into her room to try to coax her out
of bed. "I might never see my own mother again," she sobbed, buried
under blankets. "I've got nothing to look forward to. Nothing."

I felt I had no choice other than to stay at home and make sure she
didn't do anything foolish. While I watched over her, I sought refuge in
the books I'd sneaked out of the mobile library. Since my initial foray,
I'd perfected my skills at sneaking books from the adult section, making sure I put on a particularly baggy item of clothing before running
down the driveway to the van. I didn't feel too guilty about deceiving
the librarian because she didn't seem to notice the absence of any of the

items I took, and I always sneaked them back onto the shelves within the regulation lending period of two weeks.

When the mobile library arrived that week, however, I was a little disturbed to find that I'd almost exhausted the potentially interesting titles in the adult section. After finding only one volume there that even vaguely interested me, I waited to check out the little stack of children's titles I always took out to avoid arousing the librarian's suspicion. As I stood there, I found myself eyeing the slush pile of titles she didn't approve of that had been sent by the staff at the main library. I hadn't heard of any of the authors, but two of the titles on the top of the pile looked particularly interesting: *Sons and Lovers* and *Brave New World*. So when the librarian dropped her date stamp and bent awkwardly behind the checkout counter to pick it up, I took the opportunity to grab the two books and stuff them down the front of my anorak. After I got them home, I was thrilled to find that I enjoyed these books, and to realize that if I could continue to poach from the librarian's slush pile the horizons of my reading would broaden significantly.

Despite the distraction offered by my new reading, however, I was becoming increasingly concerned about my mother. The only time she got out of bed was to go to the toilet, and five days after we'd visited Mabel the only thing she had eaten was a packet of cream crackers and a bowl of Heinz cream of mushroom soup. Otherwise, she'd refused to eat, and I was beginning to wonder whether she might have decided to starve herself to death, wasting away so that I'd barely be able to distinguish the outline of her body from the ripples and ridges in the blankets, and she'd end up being carried out of the house again on a stretcher, this time a bundle of loose skin over jutting-out bones.

It was distressing, too, that my father seemed unconcerned. "Oh, she'll pull herself out of it," he said, slapping on another coat of paint in the hallway. "She's just sulking after she got the news about her mother. But she'll get over that soon enough." Then he turned up the radio so he could listen to the cricket match.

Maybe he was right, maybe this was just a minor hiccup in my mother's recovery; maybe she'd get back to landscaping the back garden once she'd got over her initial shock. But, really, I never knew with my mother. What I did know, though, was that if she didn't have any food she wasn't going to get better. And though I might not be able to control her mood, I might be able to persuade her to eat.

"Mum," I said, entering her room soon after my father had left for work. "Are you awake, Mum?" The curtains were closed and I found myself immersed in a grainy semidarkness, able to make out my mother's undulating form beneath the bedclothes only after I'd been standing there for several seconds. She lay on her side, facing me, silent, unmoving. "Come on, Mum," I said. "It's time you got up." I could make out her features now; they looked pale and smooth as paper in the dim light. Her eyes were closed, the lashes unflickering, her mouth without tension. I knew she wasn't asleep; her breathing was too shallow. "Come on, Mum," I said again, running my hand over her hair. I'd expected it to be soft, but it was crisp and springy with matted-in lacquer, a hard sheen-repelling touch. I stood up and walked over to the window. "Wakey, wakey," I said, pulling back the curtains, dazzling myself with the bright morning light.

"Bloody hell, Jesse," my mother said, pulling the bedclothes over her head. "Shut those curtains. You'll send me blind."

"It's time you got up," I declared. "You can't spend the rest of your life in bed."

"Who says I can't?" she snapped, her voice stifled by the bedclothes. "It's my life, I'll do as I bloody well please."

"You'll end up with bedsores," I said. This was true—I'd read about it in an article in one of my mother's *Woman's Realm* magazines about a woman who was in a coma for eight years before she woke up. "And your legs will stop working." This was also true, or at least I thought it was. I seemed to recall reading how they had to keep moving the woman's legs or the muscles would turn to jiggly slabs of fat.

"I don't care," my mother said, hiking the blankets farther over her head.

"Of course you care. If you can't walk, I'll have to push you around in a wheelchair. And you won't be able to work on the garden anymore."

"Hmmph . . ." She pulled the covers down, so that I could see one eye peering at me. "I don't have the energy to take care of a garden. I don't have the energy for anything."

This was my opening. "Well, if you got some food inside you, Mum, don't you think you'd feel much better?"

Her eye stared at me, unmoving, glassy, like a marble.

"And I was just thinking that if I went and got you some of your favorites—you know, made you some cheese-and-pickle sandwiches and bought you a packet of Mr. Kipling cream cakes . . ."

"Mr. Kipling's?" She shifted her head, so that I could see both of her eyes now. They seemed to hold a slight glimmer.

"Yes, Mr. Kipling's. You know how they always cheer you up." I beamed, hoping to shift some of the jaunty hopefulness in my words into her.

"Oh, I don't know," she said, letting out a long, hefty sigh. "To be honest with you, love, I'm not sure there's anything that could cheer me up right now. It'll take more than a packet of Mr. Kipling's."

"I could get you the vanilla slices or, if you like, the chocolate éclairs." I could feel my cheeriness slipping.

"Well . . . I suppose I could . . ." My mother raised herself onto the pillow and I felt my hope rise with her.

"So what do you want, then, vanilla slices or chocolate éclairs?" I pumped the enthusiasm back into my voice.

"I'll have the vanilla slices," she said, pushing the blankets from her chest to reveal her yellow flannel nightdress and her bare arms, still tan from spending all that time out in the garden. "No, I tell you what, why don't you get the slices and the chocolate éclairs. After all, I haven't had a decent meal in days."

Ten minutes later, having raided the sparse contents of my piggy bank, I was out the door and on my way to retrieve my mother's beloved cakes. Of course, I couldn't go to the Midham Co-op. I'd have to go to the next nearest Co-op, two miles away in Reatton-on-Sea.

I pulled my bicycle out of the garden shed and set out. It was a beautiful day, warm and breezy, the sky pale blue, the clouds huge snow-white cumulus that patterned the fields with fat, ever-shifting shadows. As I cycled along the winding, narrow road that led to the coast, I felt exhilarated by the wind and the sun on my face, the steady pumping of my legs against the pedals. I was almost able to leave my worries behind as I breathed deep and hard, took in the smells—earth and grass and the drifting perfume of summer flowers and, when I was almost there, the briny ripe smell of the sea. And then I saw it, a line of dark blue horizon against the paler sky. I pedaled faster as I came to a slight hill, huffing upward and then, after reaching its crest, freewheeling downward until I reached my destination.

Despite its name, the buildings that made up the village of Reatton-on-Sea weren't right on the coast, and I was a little disappointed to realize that, so far back from the cliffs, it wouldn't be Reatton-in-Sea anytime soon. It was, though, a little more lively than Midham. The village's little high street curved away from the main road in a meandering S, and, in addition to the Co-op, there was a pub, a launderette, a post office, a bank, a butcher's, a greengrocer's, and a couple of poky little shops that sold seaside souvenirs. Next to the Co-op was a dingy-looking amusement arcade, with a row of flashing bulbs above its shabby marquee.

I bought my two packets of Mr. Kipling cakes without incident, pocketed my treasured Co-op stamps (despite being banned from the Midham Co-op, I was still collecting them, taking care to make sure that my father handed them over to me after each of his shopping trips), and headed back along the high street on my bike. I had planned to go back home immediately to deliver my mother's cakes, but as I reached the junction with the main road I found myself irresistibly drawn toward the cliffs and the place where the land met the sea.

By the Reatton cliffs, the asphalt of the road became a sandy path

down to the beach, and right beside it stood the Holiday Haven Caravan Park, identified as such by a big painted sign. Below, there was a
wide swath of sandy beach, dotted with holidaymakers who lay sun-
bathing on bright blankets and striped deck chairs; at the shoreline, the
little figures of children bounced in the frothy white of the unfurling
waves. I pulled to a halt next to the Holiday Haven entrance, climbed
off my bike, and leaned it against the sign. The caravan park must have
suffered some serious erosion, because the cliff there looked as if a huge
voracious monster had taken bites out of it, with big clumps of dark
clay spilling like crumbs down those jaw-shaped indentations to the
beach. All the caravans were a good hundred yards away from the cliff
edge, except for one, a particularly old and weathered-looking speci-
men, its sides patterned with rust. It was sited on its own narrow
peninsula, within less than thirty feet or so of the tumbling cliff edge. I
imagined myself within its thin metal walls on a stormy night, a cold
east wind bawling outside, the waves roaring hungrily below. What
would it be like, I wondered, to be inside that caravan if it was pulled
down into the swirling cold water of the North Sea?

Just as I was pondering this, the door of the caravan was pushed
open and a stringy boy wearing flip-flops, shorts, and an oversized
bright blue T-shirt emerged. He slammed the door behind him, making the windows shiver noticeably in their flimsy aluminum frames,
then began to make his way to the park's entrance. He moved with a
loose-jointed gait. The breeze, which was so much more vigorous here
at the coast, tugged at his clothes, pulling them around his body so that,
under the thin fabric of his T-shirt, I could make out the bony shape of
his rib cage and the scrawny outline of his shoulders. His hair, dark and
wild, was sent flying back from his head like a spiky mane. He didn't
notice me watching him, because as he walked his face was bent over
the book he was holding in both hands to prevent its pages from flapping in the wind.

"Excuse me," I said as the boy reached the gate of the caravan park.

"Argh!" He gave a start, jumping back and fumbling, then dropping his book. "Bloody hell, do you always go creeping up on people? You could scare a person to death like that."

"Sorry," I said, regretting that I hadn't thought to cough or clear my throat to warn him of my presence. "I didn't creep up, I was just here."

"I've lost my place now," he said, giving me an irritated look before bending down to retrieve the book. I noticed the title, *Animal Farm,* and a cartoony picture of some pigs on the cover. The boy retrieved the book, then stuffed the slender volume into the waistband of his shorts. He looked to be at least my age and must be embarrassed, I thought, to be reading what looked like a fairy story.

"Sorry," I said again. "Really, I didn't mean to make you jump."

"Well, I suppose there's no harm done." He had a neat little nose, broad cheeks, and watery blue eyes.

"I'm sorry to bother you, but I saw you come out of that caravan. And I was just wondering . . . well, what's it like to stay there? You know, right on the edge of the cliff like that. Is it scary?"

"Not really." He bunched up his eyebrows, which were slender and tidy, and looked at me as if I was a little odd.

I ignored his look and continued. This was a topic I was determined to explore. "Aren't you frightened, though, that it'll fall into the sea?"

He barked out a high laugh. "Maybe, but that might not be a bad thing. It might make my dad buy us a new place to live."

"You're not on holiday? You live here?" I asked, even more intrigued.

"Yeah, my dad owns the caravan park."

"God, that must be great, being right on the sea like this. I mean, being able to watch the waves all the time and see the ships and imagine all the places they're going to."

"You think so?" he asked. He seemed a little taken aback at my enthusiasm, but also a little pleased, his bright mouth easing into a smile.

"Yes," I answered. "I'd love to live here." It might not be a neat little street with neat new houses, but it had a view that stretched all the way to the horizon. How could anyone not want to live in such a place?

"Are you having me on?" he asked, resting his hand on his hip and eyeing me suspiciously.

"No," I answered. "Really, it must be great."

"Well, yeah, actually, there is something nice about looking out at the sea. And hearing it. I *love* the sound of the waves."

"It must be very soothing." I listened to the lulling softness of the waves behind us on the beach. They rose and fell so steadily, like the slow exhale and inhale of a peaceful sleeper.

"Yeah, exactly! It's really, really soothing," the boy said, apparently delighted that I understood. Then he added with a shrug, "But living in a caravan can get a bit cramped. There's only the three of us—me, my mum, and my dad. But, still, it's a bloody tight squeeze."

I recalled my own family's week in a caravan in Bridlington—how I'd had barely an inch of privacy, how the rain had thrummed on the roof as loud as bullets, the unbearable claustrophobia after the first few days. On second thought, perhaps living in a caravan on a cliff edge might not be as wonderful as I'd thought. Still, it did have some advantages. "It must be exciting seeing the erosion," I declared. "East York-shire has one of the fastest-eroding coastlines in the world, you know." I shoved my hands into my pockets and gave a slow, authoritative nod. After all, this was a subject I was well versed in—Mr. Cuthbertson had seen to that.

"I know," the boy said, raising his eyes skyward, as if he'd heard this piece of information a thousand times. Then he grinned. "But you're right—it can be sort of exciting sometimes. There was a big storm last year and about fifteen feet of the cliff went down in one night. I actu-ally heard it fall."

"You didn't," I said, amazed.

"I did," he said. "It went *thunk.*" He gave an exaggerated nod, as if to imitate the fall of the cliff. "And the next day, when I went out, there was this giant piece of the cliff just gone. Disappeared." He swept his hands in front of him, like a magician performing a trick.

"Really?" I said, looking wistfully toward the cliff edge.

"Yeah. And not long after that we had to move all the caravans away from the cliff. This man from the council came and said it was dangerous if we left things the way they were. We didn't get round to moving ours, though. My dad said he'll do it when he feels like it. He can't stand the council telling him what to do. He thinks they're a bunch of busybodies. But to be honest," he said, glancing back at his family's caravan then turning to me and lowering his voice, "I think they know what they're talking about. Maybe you're right," he said, laughing. "I should be scared, living right near the cliff edge like that. I mean, every year there's a little bit less of the caravan park. And though my dad won't admit it, eventually we won't have anything left."

"Really?" I surveyed the caravan park. It seemed strange that this entire grassy stretch would be pulled into the water. Perhaps, I thought with a thrill, it would be Reatton-in-Sea sooner than I'd thought. "Have you ever had a caravan go over the edge?" I asked.

"No," the boy said. "But I'd like to give ours a shove."

I laughed. "It does look a bit the worse for wear."

"Bloody ancient," he answered, sighing. "I'd love to live in a normal house." He waved a loose hand to punctuate his statement.

"So would I."

"What, you don't live in a house, either?" He seemed excited, as if he'd been longing to find someone else who lived in a situation as strange and different as his own.

"I do, but it's not a normal house. It's falling apart. My dad says he's going to fix it up, but I don't think he'll be able to. He's not very good at those sorts of things."

"I just wish my dad would move us into any kind of house. Four walls, a roof, a real foundation—I'd settle for that. But he's stubborn, is my dad. Once he gets something into his head, well, he just won't give up. But fighting the North Sea—well, that's a bit stupid in anybody's book."

"I suppose so," I said, thinking of my own father. In some ways, he was just as stubborn. While this boy's father had set himself up to battle the inexorable erosion of the coastline, my own father fought the forever-shifting tide of my mother's moods. And the house he'd bought, supposed to be a bastion that would keep us safe, was falling apart, crumbling, as surely as those clay cliffs lashed by the relentless waves of the North Sea.

"What's your name?" the boy asked.

"Jesse, Jesse Bennett. What's yours?"

"Malcolm Clements. I'm thirteen. How old are you?"

"I'm thirteen as well."

"So where do you live, then, thirteen-year-old Jesse Bennett?" He folded his arms across his chest.

"I just moved to Midham."

He laughed. "Well, no wonder you think it's exciting here in Reatton. Midham's even deader than it is here."

He slapped at the air, and I realized that I'd never met a boy who made such wide and unrestrained gestures, whose hands moved so animatedly with his words. There was something almost girlish about Malcolm—his soft and energetic features, his bright and uncontained voice, the way he amplified everything he said with a gesture or a look. I rather liked it, and found myself enthralled by the drama he put into his conversation. And he seemed so eager to talk, willing to tell me about himself. Boys generally weren't like that; they hid themselves behind bluster and bravado, seemed to think they were somehow better than girls. But Malcolm was different.

"I'm sorry you ended up there," he continued, pursing his lips. "If they gave awards for the most boring place on earth, it would probably go to Midham."

"I'm going to move to London when I'm older," I said.

"Really? Oh, my God, so am I," Malcolm said, making his eyes big and round. "London's where everything happens, don't you think?"

"Oh, yes. Have you ever been there?"

He huffed. "I wish! I'm stuck here most of the time. Farthest I've ever been is Scunthorpe. And, believe me, that wasn't worth the trip. I've read all about London, though. The history, the buildings, all about the different areas, about the River Thames. I got a whole stack of books about it from the main library."

"You go to the main library?" I asked. The main library was seven miles from Midham, in Bleakwick. Given the mobile librarian's avid disapproval of everything they sent from there, I imagined it stacked, floor to ceiling, with deliciously illicit reading material.

"My dad takes me there when he has to go into Bleakwick," Malcolm said. "While he goes to the bank and the shops, I go there and get my books."

"Do they let you take books from the adult section?" I asked, scarcely able to contain my excitement.

"Yeah, why wouldn't they?" he said, Then he laughed. "Oh, no, you've been using the mobile library, haven't you? You're wasting your time there, having to put up with that old battle-ax. Anybody would think she was born in the bloody Stone Age, the attitudes she has. Did she tell you not to read stuff because it was pornographic?" he asked, grinning.

"Yes. She wouldn't let me take out *Jane Eyre*."

Malcolm rolled his eyes. "She's off her rocker. You ask me, she spends far too much time in that van by herself. You can't borrow anything worthwhile from the mobile library. Even if you *can* find any decent books there, she'll make sure you don't get them out the door."

"Actually," I ventured, "I found out how to borrow good books from the mobile library. It's just that the librarian doesn't know." I explained to him my new strategy of sneaking books from the librarian's slush pile out under my anorak. Malcolm seemed impressed.

"God, I never thought of that," he said. "But, even if I had, I probably wouldn't do it. She scares the life out of me. You're a lot braver than I am." He gave me a gentle shove, then chewed on his lip a moment, as if considering something. "You know, if you wanted you could come with me to Bleakwick. You could come to the main library and you wouldn't have to worry about sneaking things out. They let you take six books out at a time."

"Really?" Just the idea of getting out of Midham to somewhere as busy as Bleakwick would make a welcome change, but going to the main library, having the chance to borrow whatever I wanted, that was definitely something to look forward to.

"So you want to come?" Malcolm beamed.

"All right," I said. "I'll just have to . . . well, I'll have to check with my mum." I had no intention of missing this opportunity, but I wanted to make sure that at least my mother had started eating before I went off to Bleakwick.

"Oh, don't worry. I won't be going until after school starts, and you can let me know when I see you there. You will be going to Liston Comprehensive, won't you?"

I nodded.

"Good!" He grinned. "So you want to come with me for a walk on the beach? I can show you the spot where that chunk of cliff fell down."

I wanted to walk on the beach with this odd, interesting boy along the tide line, examining the sea's debris—seaweed, bleached wood, seashells, and all the other fascinating items the waves churned up and disgorged onto the shore. It would be nice, too, to take off my shoes and socks and wade out into the water, leaving behind the colorful little gatherings of holidaymakers and that narrow ribbon of sand. I remembered the story my mother had told of my three-year-old self charging, oblivious to any restraint, into the water. For a moment, I let myself imagine doing it again, racing down the beach, galloping into the waves, gasping at the sudden cold, my heart sent racing, my body light and buoyant in the liquid vastness of the sea. And then swimming, sleek and slippery like a sea mammal, farther and farther from the shore.

But, just as I was about to take up Malcolm's invitation, I remembered my mother's cream cakes and that she was waiting, helpless, for them under the bedclothes. "I'm sorry, but I have to go," I said. "I've got some shopping that I've got to take home for my mum."

"All right," he said, shrugging. "Well, I suppose I'll see you at school, then, Jesse Bennett."

"Yes," I answered. "I'll see you at school." And with that I hopped on my bike and, feeling a lot happier than I had when I set out, began pedaling toward home.

———

CHAPTER TEN

THE SATURDAY BEFORE I WAS DUE TO START AT LISTON COMPREHEN-
sive, my father drove me into Hull to buy my new uniform. That morning, I'd asked my mother if she wanted to come with us, but she'd told
me no. Unfortunately, although I'd succeeded in luring her out of bed
with the Mr. Kipling cakes and her appetite had soon returned to normal, she hadn't taken up her gardening as I'd hoped. Instead, she spent
her days lying on the settee in her nightclothes, indiscriminately watching whatever was being shown on television. In the afternoons, it
wasn't unusual for me to come upon her staring blankly while the hyperactive presenters of *Play School* or *Romper Room* pranced about the
screen, their big-gestured antics and exaggerated enunciations making
my mother appear even more lethargic, like a limp cloth draped across
the furniture. Still, I felt it was probably all right to leave her alone
while we went to buy my new uniform. I was going to have to leave her
on Monday, anyway, since I had no intention of missing the first day at
my new school. After all, those first few days were crucial if I was to
have any hope of making friends and establishing myself somewhere
above the bottom of the student pecking order.

While I'd always considered shopping for clothes with my mother
something akin to torture, going with my father was relatively uncom-

plicated. We went to one shop, the one recommended in the letter sent to us by the school secretary at Liston Comprehensive listing all my uniform needs, I picked out what I needed, and my father bought it. The one exception was the blazer.

"Bloody hell," my father declared when he looked at the price tag hanging from the blazer I tried on. "Do these people think we're made of money?" He gave the shop assistant an outraged look. She was an older woman with unnaturally bright auburn hair. She wore orange lipstick and thick orange powder that had sunk into all the lines and crannies in her face. She reminded me of the shriveled tangerines that sat uneaten in our fruit bowl after Christmas.

"Well, it is one hundred percent wool, sir. And I'm sure you're aware that the school requires it." She talked in a posh, plum-in-her-mouth kind of accent that I knew irritated my father no end. After the revolution, no doubt, he would want anyone who spoke like that to join the royal family in their toilet-cleaning duties.

"Yes, I am well aware of that," he said, then turned to me. "The rate you grow, Jesse, that thing won't fit you in three months."

"It's not my fault," I protested.

"If it would help, sir, we do have a larger size that the young lady could grow into. That might make it a little more, erm, affordable." The assistant smiled, her eyes shining with sympathetic disdain.

"But this one fits," I said. Too late. The woman was already pulling down a larger size from one of the hangers. My father took it from her eagerly. I scowled at her, but she didn't seem to notice.

"That's better," he said when I'd reluctantly tried it on, huffing and puffing as I slid my arms into its massive sleeves. It felt like wearing the jacket of an overweight gorilla. The shoulders hung down to the tops of my arms, it was far too wide, and the sleeves ended far below my wrists. When I looked in the mirror, my worst fears were confirmed. It looked ridiculous.

"I can't wear this," I said, staring at my hideous reflection. But no one was listening.

"It is an excellent brand, sir," the shop assistant reassured my father.

"Bloody extortion, it is," he muttered, plunging his hands into his trouser pockets.

"It will wear extremely well, sir. And with room for the child's growth, then—"

"I'm not 'the child,'" I said. "I'm thirteen. I'm old enough to make my own decisions and I don't think I—"

"When you start paying for your own clothes, you can make your own decisions," my father interrupted me. Then, with a defeated sigh, he pulled out his wallet and turned toward the shop assistant. "We'll take it," he said.

IT WAS COOL THAT first morning I headed out to the bench at the bus stop on Midham's main street, where the school bus would pick us up at quarter past eight. As I approached, there was already a small group gathered—Tracey, three boys of various ages who looked equally bleary-eyed, and a short, robust girl with ruddy cheeks whom everyone called Dizzy because of the way her eyes wandered in opposing directions behind the thick lenses of her glasses. I'd seen her a couple of times when I was out with Tracey. She lived in one of the shabby council houses that lined the road at the edge of the village. Dizzy had smiled and greeted Tracey each time, but Tracey had merely mumbled, "Hiya, four-eyes," before marching past her. I'd felt a little guilty as I followed Tracey's cue and walked on down the street, but clearly Dizzy wasn't someone I wanted to be too friendly with if I didn't want to end up on the social-reject pile again.

This first day of school was particularly important in the remaking of myself. I'd been nervous for days, had slept little the previous night, and that morning had been unable to down anything other than a cup of milky tea before heading out the door. As I made my way to the little crowd, I felt painfully self-conscious in my new school uniform—

my shiny, lace-up shoes, my white knee-high socks, my black pleated skirt, and, of course, my hideous, oversized blazer. It didn't help that as soon as Tracey saw me she started to laugh.

"Jesus Christ, Jesse, what's that you're wearing?" she said as I reached the bench. She was sitting on its back, her feet (clad in a new pair of the most fashionable buckle-up platform shoes) resting on the seat. Two of the boys sat beside her. They had already started to giggle. Even Dizzy had a smile tugging at the edges of her thin-lipped mouth. "Looks like a cast-off from a giant. Bet you must have searched high and low for that thing. What, get it from the church jumble sale, did you?"

"No," I blurted, trying to hoist up the blazer's sleeves to reveal more than just my fingertips. But it was a vain effort, and when I tried to re-arrange the sleeves it only made the blazer's padded shoulders fall down my back. "My dad bought it," I said.

"What, for himself?" Tracey laughed harder, and all the boys joined in.

"No," I said again, this time more weakly, as I let my arms drop and my hands disappeared once more into the vast cavities of the blazer's sleeves. I scanned the laughing faces around me and felt a sickening dread.

"Well, in that thing we'll have to think of a good nickname for you," Tracey said. "Now, what would fit?" She pursed her lips as she consid-ered this. The boys creased their faces into pensive frowns. Dizzy re-garded me with something close to pity in her blinking blue eyes, magnified behind her thick-lensed glasses. I glared back at her—the last thing I needed was sympathy from someone like her.

"What about Monster Mash?" one of the boys suggested.

"Don't be stupid," Tracey said. "There's already a Monster Mash in the fourth year. Can't you think of anything original?"

"We could just call her Monster," another of the boys suggested, but Tracey dismissed him without comment.

"I've got it," the third boy said, jumping off the bench, dangling his arms monkey style as he staggered forward and groaned. "What about Yeti?"

Tracey considered this for a moment, then beamed. "Yeah, that's perfect. Jesse the Yeti. That's bloody brilliant!"

My future at Liston Comprehensive became radiantly clear. I could already see scores of my fellow students sniggering at me in the cloakrooms, tripping me in the corridors, flicking food at me in the canteen. I'd live my life to choruses of "Jesse the Yeti," my big, ugly, clumsy self acclaimed by everyone around me, so that no amount of trying to blend into the background could help. It had been foolish to think it would be otherwise.

"We could even make up a song about you," Tracey continued. "We'd have to find a good tune, though." She looked sparkling, alive, thriving on my spiraling despair.

I wanted to grab her arm, to pull her from the bench and drag her to me. "But you're supposed to be my friend," I wanted to say to her. Instead, I stood silent. After all, she was only pointing out what was apparent to anyone who looked. I was hopelessly flawed. I could never really be good enough to be her friend.

"Jesse the Yeti," the boy who'd made up the name said. "Jesse the Yeti, Jesse the Yeti," he began to chant, finding his rhythm, stamping his feet. The other boys joined him. "Jesse the Yeti, Jesse the Yeti, Jesse the Yeti," they chanted together, their dull, early-morning faces transformed with gleeful animation. "Jesse the Yeti, Jesse the Yeti," Tracey repeated, adding her voice to the chorus.

I wished I could stand there, distant, unaffected. Or I wished I could come up with some clever retort, some way of making myself bigger than this stupid name-calling. But I couldn't. Instead, I felt myself sucked under, into a whirlpool of humiliation. Their chorus melted into all that taunting in my memories. I saw myself standing in a playground utterly alone, or with the other glum-faced rejects like Dizzy, wishing for acceptance and inclusion more than anything in the world. "Leave me alone!" I yelled. "Leave me alone!" Even as I tried to sound fierce, my voice was breaking and the tears were coming. I didn't want to cry in front of them, so I considered turning around and running home, loping away like a terrified animal. Like a yeti, too monstrous to be seen.

"Jesse the Yeti, Jesse the Yeti, Jesse the Yeti," they continued. Only Dizzy hadn't joined in. She stood back, frowning, watching, her eyes flickering back and forth between Tracey and me. But her sympathy was no comfort; it only made me feel worse.

I imagined myself arriving at my house, scrambling upstairs to my room, diving under the bedclothes and spending the day there. When my father came home from work that night, he'd find that both my mother and me were going through bad patches.

"Jesse the Yeti, Jesse the Yeti, Jesse the Yeti," the chant went on. Tracey had started to clap her hands to its rhythm. She was smiling in my direction, but looking through me. I was nothing more than ugliness and air.

"Shut up!"

When I heard the voice, I spun around. At the same time, the chorus ground to an immediate halt.

"How old are you lot, anyway? You should be bloody well ashamed of yourselves." It was Amanda; she stood with her hands on her hips, her gaze moving across each of the now silent faces. One of the boys sputtered out a giggle. "One more bloody peep out of you, Nigel Curtis, and I'll knock your bloody teeth out," she said, prodding the air with her index finger. The boy opened his mouth as if to speak. "Or maybe I'll get someone to do it for me." The boy snapped his mouth shut. "I know for a fact there's a couple of fifth-year boys would like nothing better than to beat the living daylights out of you."

"Oh, leave off, Amanda," Tracey said. "We were only having a laugh. It was just a laugh, wasn't it, Jess?"

I blinked back my tears. Maybe I should have been able to go along with it. Maybe I shouldn't have taken it so seriously. Perhaps I was too sensitive. It was, after all, only a joke. "I suppose so," I answered.

"See?" Tracey said, looking at Amanda defiantly.

"Yeah, well, some people don't always appreciate your sense of humor, Tracey. You've got a nasty streak, and you know it. Just don't start taking it out on Jesse. I like her, and I don't want anybody picking on her. And if I hear any one of you lot has bothered her, I'll make sure you're sorry about it. All right?" She paused and folded her arms across her chest. No one said anything.

I looked around at their faces, no longer bright and taunting, now tight, eyelids flickering, mouths stretched silent. They didn't look ashamed, exactly, but it was as if they had been slapped into silence. Stung and brought up short. I felt the fear slip off me, the way I might shrug off my awful oversized blazer, leaving a dark pool of rumpled fabric at my feet. No one, except teachers, who, after all, did it only out of a sense of obligation, had ever stood up for me before. When I looked at Amanda, she gave me such a broad, reassuring smile that I couldn't help smiling back. But, really, I wanted to throw my arms around her, murmur "Thank you, thank you" over and over into her smooth and milky neck.

"Kids," she said, making her eyes wide, implying that she and I together were somehow above their silly antics. I shrugged, hoping to indicate my own mature exasperation, but the gesture made the shoulders of my blazer fall backward so that the garment lolled over my body even more ridiculously than it had before. Someone behind me coughed out a laugh. Amanda spun around. "I told you lot," she said. A couple of the boys nervously shuffled their feet. She turned back to me. "Let's see if I can make that a little better," she said, and began rearranging my blazer, straightening it up on my shoulders, then turning up the ends of the sleeves into cuffs so that they no longer hid my hands. As she worked, I breathed in her scents—her shampoo as her hair brushed across my face, the perfume she wore that wafted over me as her hands moved busily, and the smell of her, her body, as she leaned across me, raw and slightly sweet. I breathed deep, pulling all of that inward, and it was as if something inside me eased up, let go—something at the center of me that I hadn't even known had been coiled tight. I felt the urge to sink, fall into her, knowing she would hold me up.

"There, that's better." Amanda smiled approvingly as she gave the shoulders of the blazer a final adjustment, then stood back to admire her own handiwork.

"I bloody hate you, Amanda," Tracey said. "You should mind your own business, keep out of things that don't concern you." Then she turned toward me. "And you should learn how to take a joke, Jesse," she said, scowling. "People don't like being friends with people who can't take jokes."

—

CHAPTER ELEVEN

AFTER STOPPING AT SEVERAL OTHER VILLAGES TO TAKE ON MORE children, our bus pulled into the car park in front of Liston Comprehensive and I was greeted by a sprawling complex of redbrick, flat-roofed buildings with big windows that looked out onto acres of playing fields in the back and well-kept gardens in the front.

"Here we bloody well are," Tracey groaned as the bus rumbled to a halt and its aisles became a heaving, jostling mess of dark uniforms, swinging satchels, and shouts.

Tracey had sat next to me during our ride—something I'd had mixed feelings about since, when the bus arrived and Amanda was making adjustments to my blazer, I'd found myself hoping that I might sit beside her. But when the doors of the bus sighed open, Amanda had simply patted me on the shoulder, saying, "See you later, Jesse," as she headed to the back of the bus to take her place among a group of older girls. I'd watched Amanda yell enthusiastic greetings to her friends and press herself between them on the backseat, so that they were all a bright and laughing mass of waving limbs, excited eyes, and talk. For a moment, I'd imagined myself squeezing in among them, next to Amanda, tucked between the warmth of their laughter and their bodies, letting their giggles roll over me like warm waves. But there really wasn't any room and, besides, I knew that wasn't where I belonged. So instead I'd eased into one of the seats in front, a cold stone of fear in my chest. Amanda had abandoned me, Tracey was angry at me, and I was alone, friendless again. But then Tracey had stopped by my seat and muttered, "Shove over, then," and I'd eased myself over to the window and she'd taken the seat beside me. During the ride, she didn't mention the incident at the bus stop, nor did she call me by that dreadful nickname. By the time we reached the car park outside Liston Comprehensive, I realized, with profound relief, that we were still friends. When I stepped off the bus into the throng of uniformed bodies and Tracey threaded her arm through mine, I felt, for the first time, that I did not have to push my way through a seething school-day crowd alone.

"Look, look, it's the Debbies," Tracey said, waving toward three girls standing next to the school entrance.

"Hiya, Trace," the tallest of the girls said as we joined their group. "God, can you believe we're back at school already?" She smiled and knocked her hip into Tracey's.

"Yeah, I know," Tracey said, shoving the girl back. "And seven bloody more weeks until the half-term holiday. God, seems like forever."

"Never mind, at least we can hang around together again. And, to tell the truth, I was bored to bloody tears after the first two weeks at home." The girl peered around Tracey to look at me. "So, who's this, then?" she asked. I met her look with a hopeful smile.

"This is Jesse," Tracey said. "Jesse Bennett. She just moved to Midham." At least she hadn't introduced me as Jesse the Yeti. Though, from the dubious up-and-down looks the three girls gave me, she may as well have. I could see that their approval wasn't going to come easily.

"Oh, yeah?" the tallest Debbie said, narrowing her eyes to scrutinize me further. "So, where you from, then?" She gave her hair a backward flip.

"Hull," I answered warily, sure that she would find me wanting. Rejected from their little clique, I'd lose not only their approval but

Tracey's as well. And then I'd definitely become known as Jesse the Yeti.

"Hull, eh?" The girl put both hands on her hips.

"Oh, leave off, Debbie," Tracey said, issuing a slap to her friend's arm. "She's all right, is this one. Me and her have been hanging about together over the holidays. She's my new friend." Miraculously, with this seal of approval from Tracey the look on all three of their faces shifted. They smiled and introduced themselves to me.

Contrary to my earlier imaginings of the Debbies as identical triplets, the three could not have been more physically different: the tallest, Debbie Frost, was blond and big-boned; the second, Debbie Green, was olive-skinned, short, and pudgy; and the third, Debbie Mason, was a petite thread of a girl with dark hair and enormous brown eyes. Nevertheless, they did seem, in a way, to be a set, with all three of them—in obvious defiance of the strict uniform regulations outlined in the letter my parents had received—wearing tartan scarves around their necks, tartan socks, and huge white platform shoes that added at least three and a half inches to their height, making Debbie Frost tower over everyone like a giant and the tiny, skinny-legged Debbie Mason look about as unstable as if she were walking on stilts. They all wore their hair in the "shaggy dog" style of the band whose members were obviously their idols, the Bay City Rollers, and each of the three had the image of a different tartan-clad pop star on a huge round badge worn on her school blazer.

"So, who do you like best, Les or Woody or Derek?" the diminutive Debbie Mason demanded almost as soon as she had told me her name. I frowned and looked over at Tracey, hoping for guidance. I had no idea what she was talking about. "Les or Woody or Derek?" she asked again. This time she nodded toward the badge on her chest, and I realized that she was talking about the members of the Bay City Rollers.

Since I really had not given this very much thought until that moment, I was genuinely bewildered. Certainly, it had been impossible to escape the Bay City Rollers—their pictures in magazines, the television footage of frenzied fans chasing them down the street, their songs on the radio or trilled by groups of girls at my last school—but I'd never actually looked at the faces of those band members to rank who might be better-looking, and I certainly hadn't remembered their names.

"I'm not sure, I . . ." I stalled, made increasingly nervous now that the three Debbies were staring eagerly at me, wondering which of them would end up hating me when I picked the wrong name. It occurred to me that my future social success could rest on this one decision. I had no idea what to say. Fortunately, Tracey spoke up.

"God, are you three still going on about that bunch of Scottish morons? How can you think any bloke who prances about in trousers six inches above his ankles is sexy? Besides, their music is a pile of bloody crap."

I looked from Tracey to the three girls, all of whom were glowering and gripping both ends of their tartan scarves so tightly that I could see blue veins pushing against the skin on the backs of their hands. For a moment, I was afraid they might explode at Tracey, pounding her with those veiny fists. Instead, Debbie Mason again turned to me. "So, who do you like best?" she demanded.

"Oh, David Cassidy," I said, this time without hesitation. "I think he's sexier than them all."

The three girls scowled at me, but Tracey was grinning. "See, I told you she was all right," she said. And, much to my surprise, all three girls shrugged an acquiescent agreement.

The Debbies, Tracey, and I were all in Form 2D, and our form-room teacher was Mr. Davies, a Welshman with a big, booming voice and an enormous belly that, if he hadn't been a man, would have convinced me that he was pregnant. After he took registration, he handed out our new timetables, made a few remarks about the critical importance of quiet and orderly conduct when moving about the school, and told us to make our way to morning assembly. At that, there was the deafening shriek and clatter of thirty chairs pushed back and a rampaging rush to exit the room. Battered by swinging satchels and bags, I followed Tracey and the Debbies as they flew, with everyone else, toward the door.

By the time I reached the corridor, I found myself detached from Tracey and the Debbies, trailing at the very back of the crowd heading toward the assembly hall. Then, as I reached the corridor that led to the hall, I saw someone I knew. "Hiya," I said.

"Hiya, Jesse Bennett." It was Malcolm. He was standing in a little alcove away from the river of moving students, leaning against the wall, his face pressed into a book. It was much fatter than the one he'd been reading the first time I saw him, and it had a more mature title, too: *Crime and Punishment.* Something I might find in the adult section of the mobile library, I thought—if the librarian didn't deem it pornographic.

"Aren't you going to assembly?" I asked Malcolm, gesturing toward the crowd of students flooding past us.

He shrugged. "What's the rush? All it's going to be is a few boring hymns, the Lord's Prayer, and the headmaster giving us a lecture about working hard and obeying school rules." He made a theatrical cough and adopted a pompous expression. "Though you might be descended from apes," he said, in a voice clearly meant to imitate that of an elderly teacher, "this does not mean that you should act like apes. So, I'd appreciate it if you'd cease swinging from the coat hooks in the cloakroom."

I laughed. "Sounds like the headmaster here is a lot like the one at my old school."

"They make them all out of the same mold," Malcolm said. "Doddery and boring. If that old fart tells one more story about how he served his king and country in the war and we should think of Liston Comprehensive as our country and bad reports as the enemy we have to conquer, I think I'll shoot myself." He put two fingers to his temple and mimed pulling a trigger.

I laughed again.

"So, what class are you in?" he asked.

"2D."

"Oh, with Taffy Davis. He's all right, is Taffy. I'm in 2J with Jefferson. He's a little fascist. But maybe you and me will have some lessons together. I hope so. And listen, you're still invited to come to the library with me if you want."

"Oh, yes, I—" I was just about to tell Malcolm how I could definitely come next time his father planned a visit to Bleakwick when I noticed Tracey stalking down the corridor toward us, a deep scowl on her face.

"Bloody hell, Jesse, first you disappear and then I find you talking to the biggest bloody poofter in all Yorkshire."

"I just—"

"Stop hanging about in the corridor, nancy boy," she said, ignoring me and turning to Malcolm.

"Don't tell me what to do, Tracey Grasby," Malcolm said, a bright flush flooding his face. "Who died and made you queen, anyway?"

"There's only one queen round here, and it's not me," Tracey said, her face twisted in disdain. "What are you doing here, anyway? Hanging about in a dark corner so you can wank off while you think about little boys?"

"God, you are so ridiculous," Malcolm said, trying to dismiss Tracey with a haughty look. But I could see how those words stung him. Poofter. Nancy boy. Queen. Suddenly, I realized that this was how a boy like Malcolm was summed up. There had been a few other boys like him at my last school, boys whose movements were sweeping and fluid, whose voices weren't big and booming, whose expressions were more animated than boys' were supposed to be. They were the boys who stood on the sidelines when the others played football or rugby, whom everyone laughed at when they ran or threw a ball. Those boys were teased far more relentlessly than I ever had been. They were not just mocked; they were hated. And no one, not even the teachers, ever stood up for them.

"Malcolm lives on the edge of a cliff," I said, hoping somehow to ease Tracey out of her animosity. "In a caravan. The council said they're going to have to move it or it'll fall off."

"Bloody hell," Tracey said, laughing. "Is that true, nancy boy? Hey, with a bit of luck maybe you'll be in it when it goes over the edge."

"Hah, hah, very funny." Malcolm's voice was flat, his face now a blazing beetroot red.

"It is as far as I'm concerned. Right, Jesse?"

She peered at me, belligerent, expectant. Malcolm stared at me, a question folded into his face. I bit my lip.

"Hey, what's that you're reading?" Tracey made a grab for the book nestled under Malcolm's arm. Malcolm tried to turn away, but he was too slow and she wrenched it from his grip. "*Crime and Punishment?*" She began flipping through the pages. "A book about poofs and homos, is it? Now, that's a crime that needs to be punished."

"Give it back," Malcolm demanded, his voice high and thin, his arms scrabbling at the air. I watched while delight bloomed across Tracey's features and Malcolm's twisted in distress. "Give it back, you bloody cow," Malcolm said again.

"Right, that's it," Tracey said. "I'll teach you to call me a cow." And with that she turned and ran down the corridor to a window and began wrestling it open. Malcolm stumbled after her, slack-limbed and uncoordinated. He did run like those boys that everyone laughed at, and in my mind I could hear the taunts: "poofter," "nancy boy," "the homo runs just like a girl."

Before Malcolm caught her, Tracey managed to open the window and hurl the book outside. I watched it glide in a single sweeping arc, its pages fluttering like flimsy futile wings as it curved upward, then plunged onto the hard asphalt of the playground outside.

Malcolm shuddered to a halt, staring, open-mouthed, through the window as the book made its hopeless trajectory. "What the hell did you do that for?"

Tracey grinned. "Because I felt like it, you little poofter."

"God, you really are a bloody cow, Tracey Grasby," Malcolm said, his voice cracked and hollow. Then he turned away from her and began walking back toward me. He marched, his shoulders hunched, his face folded in defeated fury, so that his eyes seemed nothing more than flickering lashes and his lips were compressed into a hard, flat line.

I knew that look. It was the one I had worn so many times myself. I also knew the helpless anger and humiliation that Malcolm carried, the way he must be struggling to hold back tears. I glanced at Tracey, her eyes wide and shimmering, her smile a crescent of satisfaction across her face. I had seen that look, too—on the faces of the girls and boys who had taunted me, their pleasure rising like heat as my hope plummeted as fast and inevitably as Malcolm's book had fallen and hit the ground.

"What the hell are you doing hanging around with *her?*" Malcolm demanded when he reached me.

I pictured his battered caravan. I saw myself standing beside it on a crumbling cliff edge, where the soft boulder clay of the East Yorkshire coast cascaded down to the sea. I could stay in place, on safe ground with Tracey, or I could step toward Malcolm, to the very edge of that cliff, and risk tumbling into the relentless waves. It was a choice that was easy to make.

"Tracey's my best friend," I said, folding my arms across my chest and looking into his eyes.

I saw him flinch, step back. Then he looked me up and down, as if he was conducting a quick reassessment of me. When he was done, he let out a disgusted snort. "I thought you had more sense than that," he said before he turned away and continued his march down the corridor and through the door of the main entrance.

For a moment, I felt a pang of regret as I watched him stride onto the playground to retrieve his book. I had an odd sense of having lost something, and it wasn't just Malcolm; it was something intangible, something inside myself. But then Tracey strolled back to me and placed her arm across my shoulder.

"Hah, that showed him, didn't it?" she said. "Good job, Jesse." She leaned into me, and any sense of loss was gone. "I can't bloody well stand him. Such a little homo," she said. "And such a bloody know-it-all. Always has his head in some stupid book. I never knew he lived in a bloody caravan on the edge of a cliff, though. I bet he has fleas as well as being queer. You want to watch it, Jesse—you were standing a bit too close to him. Maybe you've caught something." She jumped away from me, a look of mock horror on her face. "Hey, maybe we'll have to have you fumigated." She let out a sharp laugh.

"You think so?" I asked, making a performance of scratching my head, my arm, my stomach, and, as Tracey started giggling, my buttocks.

"You're funny, Jesse."

"But not half as funny as Malcolm Clements," I said, making my voice high. "Funny peculiar, that is." In an exaggerated imitation of Malcolm, I took a limp-wristed slap at the air.

Tracey sputtered and folded forward, wrapping her arms around her stomach and laughing helplessly. And although I couldn't quite find it in myself to laugh along with her, I watched her, smiling, buoyantly happy that I was with her, on firm ground.

OUR FIRST LESSON OF the day was history, and the teacher, Miss Nutall, spent the lesson lecturing us about the triumph of William the Conqueror at the Battle of Hastings. History was followed by maths, taught by a tall man named Mr. Whitman, who simply wrote a series of problems on the blackboard, told us to solve them, and then sat at the front of the classroom, his feet up on his desk, perusing a magazine with a racing car on its cover. While history had been painfully boring, I quite enjoyed this lesson, since my ability to solve all the problems without much difficulty seemed to greatly endear me to Tracey and the Debbies. "I told you she was a brainbox," Tracey said, addressing her three friends as they passed my exercise book among them to copy my answers.

The school dinner menu was unspectacular, the choices being very much the same as those at my old school: Spam fritters and chips, toad-in-the-hole, or liver and onions, with treacle pudding or pink blanc-mange afterward. But I wouldn't have cared if we had nothing to eat at all, because there, in the dining room, I felt utterly content. While I sat between Debbie Mason and Tracey, the other two Debbies opposite us, I watched as several other girls vied to sit closer to us, battling one another with their dinner trays, leaning across the table to try to interject themselves into the conversation, their eyes wide and yearning for approval. I sat, mostly quiet, listening as the giggling and the gossip flowed over me, basking in this newfound safety, never wanting to leave it again.

The first hour of the afternoon crawled by as Mr. Livingstone, our religious-education teacher—a skinny man with big ears and a red bow tie that made him look as if he were planning to host a television quiz—droned listlessly through the story of the Good Samaritan. Our final lesson of the day was English, and I only hoped that the teacher, who, Tracey told me, was new to the school, would prove to be a little more inspiring. As we trudged along the corridor to our classroom, we looked at her name on the timetable.

"It says here, 'M S Hastings.' 'M S.' What the bloody hell is that about?" Tracey asked.

I shrugged. "Maybe they wrote it wrong, maybe it was supposed to be Mrs.," I suggested. "Or maybe it's her initials."

"What, like Mary Samantha?" Tracey said.

"Or Marks and Spencer," I offered, delighted when Tracey sputtered out a giggle.

At my old school, our English lessons had involved grammar exercises, spelling tests, and long diatribes from our teacher, Mr. Knighton, on the shrinking vocabulary of today's teenagers, the dreadful, corrupting influence of American television on the English language, and the long-forgotten virtues of the semicolon. Like everyone else in Mr.

Knighton's lesson, I'd spent most of my time gazing out the window onto the playground. Almost from the first moment I stepped into Ms. Hastings's room, however, I realized that English lessons at Liston Comprehensive were going to be very different.

I had never seen anyone quite like her. Big-boned, broad-shouldered, and towering above six feet in a pair of knee-high black leather boots, she wore a patchwork skirt with a jagged hem and a billowy red cotton blouse. Her hair was cropped so short that it lay against her scalp like a shiny little cap, and her ears, wrists, and neck were adorned with beaded silver jewelry that clinked and jingled as she moved. She took up more space than any woman I had ever seen, and, judging by the way she moved around the classroom—in big-booted, jingling strides, making broad, audacious gestures as she spoke—she seemed to delight in the immensity of her own presence. Even Auntie Mabel, who always managed to fill up whatever room she entered with her brash energy, seemed at times ashamed of her own size and impact, pressing the force of herself into smoking cigarette after cigarette, as if she were somehow trying to make herself fade into the cloud of smoke that filled the air about her. But there was no shame in Ms. Hastings.

"Right you lot," she thundered as soon as we were all seated. "First things first. I'm Ms. Hastings, your new English teacher."

"Hello, Msssss," one of the boys at the back of the room yelled, extending the S into a long, hissing syllable that echoed against the bare classroom walls. The entire class fell about in high, shrieking laughs. Ms. Hastings raised her eyebrows and shifted an icy gaze over our faces. Within seconds, the laughter died in our throats.

"And what's your name, sonny?" she asked the boy who'd yelled.

"Erm, Paul Kitchen, Ms. Hastings." This time, he added no extra hiss to her name.

"Well, Mr. Kitchen, it's a pleasure, I'm sure." A few scattered giggles moved around the classroom, but with a single look from Ms. Hastings they petered out into throaty coughs. She turned her attention back to

Paul Kitchen. "And just so we understand each other, Mr. Kitchen, I'm going to tell you why I've chosen what you seem to regard as a humorous form of address. See, while you, Mr. Kitchen, for your entire life will never be expected to change your name, we women are. When we're single we're supposed to use our father's surname, because we're seen as our father's property, and when we marry we have to change our names and call ourselves Mrs., because then we're supposed to belong to our husband. So, by calling myself Ms. I am demonstrating that I have my own independent identity and I'm not the property of some man. Is that clear?" She gave him a cool, expectant look.

"Yes, Ms." He nodded sheepishly.

"Good, because I'd hate to have to punish you by making you write 'I must not be a male chauvinist' a thousand times after school. I've never liked giving out lines."

"No, Ms.," Peter Kitchen said.

I watched with utter fascination as Ms. Hastings chastised Peter Kitchen, whose face, as she continued to stare at him, became an ever-deepening shade of red. I had never even heard the term "Ms." before, but as soon as she explained what it meant I thought it made complete sense. Why should women change their names when they got married? She was right. Of course, women shouldn't be regarded as men's property. It was wrong and unjust, and it made me even more determined that I would never, ever marry. What's more, I resolved that I was going to start calling myself Ms. immediately. As I considered this, I peered around the classroom to see if anyone else was as thrilled as I was with Ms. Hastings's remarks. I was disappointed to see that most of the other students, including Tracey and the Debbies, had perplexed expressions on their faces, but in the very back there were a couple of smiling and nodding faces—Dizzy and Malcolm. I hadn't realized that Malcolm was in my English class, so I was a little surprised to see him there. For a moment I wanted to try to catch his eye, to show him that among all these other ignoramuses he and Dizzy and I were the only ones who understood the important point Ms. Hastings was making, but then I remembered our encounter in the corridor, the decision I'd made, the line I had crossed, and I turned away.

"All right, so let's get some work done," Ms. Hastings boomed as she lifted herself onto her desk and sat there, legs apart and swinging. "Today we're going to start by reading one of the most important allegories of our time. This," she said, holding up one of the books that sat in a stack on her desk, "is essential reading for anyone who wants to understand the twentieth century." I thought I recognized the cover and leaned forward to see it better. When I did, I realized it was the book I'd seen Malcolm reading that first day I'd met him. It was a copy of *Animal Farm*.

AN HOUR LATER, as we filed into the corridor, I turned to Tracey and the Debbies. "So, what did you think?" I asked, excited to hear their assessment of the fascinating Ms. Hastings.

"Jesus, what a bloody dippy hippie," Tracey declared without hesitation. "I mean, look at the state of her. You'd think she got all her clothes from the rag-and-bone man. And, my God, her hair. Looks like she had a fight with a pair of garden shears."

"I sort of liked it—it's different," I ventured, having imagined cutting my own hair short like that during the lesson, running my hands over its fine and silky sheen.

"Different? Yeah, it's definitely different all right!" Tracey rolled her eyes. "Ugly and different. God, I can't stand women like her!"

"Really?" I asked, genuinely perplexed at Tracey's vitriol.

"Yeah, really."

"Well," I said hesitantly, "I did think she had a good point when she talked about not being a man's property."

"Now, that was a load of old crap," Tracey countered. "She must be one of those bloody women's libbers. But, like my dad says, they only say that stuff because they're too ugly to get a man."

"You're dead right about that," Debbie Mason said, while the other two Debbies chorused their agreement.

When I didn't join in, Tracey narrowed her eyes and studied me. "God, Jesse, don't tell me that you *like* her."

"No," I said cautiously. "I don't *like* her. I just thought she was, well, I thought that she was interesting."

"She's a bloody freak, if you ask me," Tracey said. "And really, Jesse, only freaks like freaks."

CHAPTER TWELVE

———

WITH THE SCHOOL DAY OVER, TRACEY AND I WALKED TO THE SCHOOL gates to say goodbye to the Debbies, who, because they all lived in Liston, could walk home. I'd been looking forward to the end of the day, when I'd get a chance to see Amanda again, and had spent much of my time planning what I might say to her when I finally saw her again. Unfortunately, I needn't have bothered. When we got to the school gates, Amanda was there with a couple of her friends, smoking and throwing back her head to blow long puffs of smoke into the air between bouts of giggling conversation. I tried to catch her eye and even wiggled my fingers toward her in a feeble wave, but despite my efforts she didn't notice me. What finally got her attention was the harsh buzz of a motorbike coming down Liston's main street. As soon as she heard it, she turned toward the sound. "Oh, look, it's Stan," she said, waving an outstretched arm.

I watched the bike veer around an elderly couple who were in the middle of the zebra crossing. The woman's coat lifted visibly in the bike's wake, and the man's flat cap was blown from his head. "That's Amanda's boyfriend," Tracey said, tugging on my sleeve. "Frankly, I have no bloody idea what he sees in her."

I remembered the evening I'd first met Amanda and the boy in the

Ford Cortina who'd yelled at her from across the street. I'd already decided I didn't like him. Now that he seemed to be on his way to interrupt my opportunity to talk to her, I liked him even less. "Does he always drive like that?" I asked. "It looks dangerous."

"Motorbikes *are* dangerous," Tracey said with unrestrained enthusiasm. "Really dangerous. Last year Larry Kirk came off his bike and had to have both his legs amputated. He's in a wheelchair now." She said this with delight, as if Larry Kirk had won some sort of competition. "You might have seen him; he works at the newsagent's. It's a bit weird, him with no legs and that. Can't help feeling sorry for him. But don't worry, nothing like that will happen to Stan." I was about to tell her that it wasn't Stan I was worried about as I observed the elderly couple, pale and open-mouthed, apparently immobilized by shock or fear or both, standing stock-still in the middle of the street. But Tracey continued. "Stan's not like Larry Kirk. He's a really, really good driver." This, clearly, was a matter for dispute.

With Stan rapidly approaching, Amanda waved vigorously, while next to me Tracey patted her hair, pinched her cheeks, and smoothed her hands over her skirt. As the bike came closer, its rider didn't reduce his speed, and, for a moment, I felt relieved as I thought Stan planned to continue right by us. At the last moment, however, he steered the bike toward our little crowd outside the school gates, mounted the pavement, and drove at full speed toward us. It was hard to take it in at first, but it soon became apparent that he really didn't plan to stop and would inevitably hit us. Simultaneously, all of us—Tracey, Amanda, Amanda's friends, and I—let out high screams and began running away like a throng of panicked mice. We were a mess of limbs, fast breaths, and shrieks scattering in front of the bike when, at the very last second, it came to a halt right in the spot where we had been standing.

"Ha, that got you good and proper, didn't it?" Stan Heaphy was laughing so hard that the black full-face helmet he wore jiggled unsteadily. It made him look like a baby struggling to support its big, lolling head.

I leaned against the school fence and tried to get my breath. My heart was racing so loud and fast, it felt as if it occupied my entire chest. I was furious. He could have killed us, or left one of us with no legs like the unfortunate Larry Kirk.

"God, you should've seen your faces." Stan slapped his thigh with a leather-gloved hand and looked around at all of us. "I wish I had a camera, I really do." He was still laughing as he took off his gloves, unbuckled his helmet, and eased it over his head to reveal his face, smooth-skinned and angular, with a straight nose and large brown eyes. He had glossy blond hair that was long enough to rest below the collar of his studded leather jacket. That night outside the Co-op I hadn't been able to see him in the rain and I'd imagined him pimply and ugly. But now I could see that he was actually very good-looking. In fact, he might have seemed girlish, with his long eyelashes and full, red lips, but for his thick eyebrows and the way his mouth, as he laughed, stretched into a wide, arrogant sneer.

"Oh, Stan, you're such a joker," Tracey said, laughing and flipping back her ponytail. "You really had us going there for a while. I thought you were going to run right into us." I stared at her, astounded. Surely she didn't think being terrified like that was funny.

"Christ, Stan," Amanda snapped, "what did you have to go and do that for? You could have bloody killed somebody with an idiot trick like that." Around her, Amanda's friends, still breathless, nodded in agreement.

"Ah, come on, Mandy, I was just having a laugh," Stan said as he dismounted his bike and balanced it on the kickstand.

"Oh, I knew that, Stan," Tracey said, beaming in his direction.

"Shut your cake-hole, Tracey," Amanda said.

"Shut up yourself," Tracey mumbled. Then she turned to smile at Stan again. "You all right, then, Stan? Got a job yet?"

"Job? What do I want a fucking job for?" Stan said, moving past her and swaggering over to Amanda. He put his hand on her shoulder. "How was school, then? Boring as ever? Teachers still a bunch of wankers?" I noticed that the back of his leather jacket was decorated with studs and clumsy, hand-painted letters that read BLACK SABBATH RULES across his back. I remembered Tracey's story about the vandalism in the Midham church. Surely the vicar must be a complete fool not to have found the culprit. The evidence was literally written on him.

"Get lost," Amanda said. I watched her, delighted, as she shrugged his hand away.

"Oh, don't be like that, Mandy. Like I said, it was just a laugh."

"I told you I don't like being called Mandy. And I don't like being almost run over by your bloody motorbike, either."

Silently, I egged Amanda on. Stan was clearly an idiot, and she was clearly far too good for him. It was ridiculous to imagine that she'd want him as a boyfriend. The sooner she sent him on his way, the sooner I could talk to her.

"Is this a new motorbike, Stan?" Tracey asked. "It's a Suzuki, isn't it? God, I just love Suzukis." She spoke in the same dreamy tone she usually reserved for her pronunciations about David Cassidy.

Stan ignored Tracey and put a hand on Amanda's arm again. "I'm sorry, darling," he said, his tone more conciliatory now. "Really, I didn't mean to scare you. It was just a laugh, that's all."

I watched, eager to see Amanda push him away again. Instead, I was surprised to see her let him rest his hand there, and even more surprised when, a second later, she turned to him. "Just don't do it again, all right?" she said, her voice softer now. "You scared the living daylights out of me. Really, you did, Stan."

"Come here," he said, wrapping his arm around her waist. For a moment, Amanda stiffened and pulled back a little, then she let Stan ease her toward him. He took the cigarette she'd been holding, placed it in his mouth, and took a drag. Then he blew the smoke out sideways, tossed the cigarette to the ground, and, in a move that made my heart beat even harder than when he'd been pursuing us on his motorbike, leaned into Amanda to deliver a chomping kiss.

I wanted Amanda to push him away, to slam her arms against his chest and declare that she couldn't stand him. I wanted her to yell at him, the way she'd yelled at Tracey and the boys who'd teased me that morning. Instead, she closed her eyes, leaned into Stan, wrapped her arms around his neck, and kissed him back. As I watched this, I felt first a jolt of utter outrage, but, within moments, I was surprised to feel my anger melt, replaced by another heat that filled my body and made my face burn. While Stan pressed himself against Amanda, I imagined myself standing there in his place, my arms wrapped around Amanda, kissing her on the mouth.

"MUM," I CALLED AS I stepped into the house after walking home from the bus stop. "Mum." I pushed open the living-room door. "I like my new school, Mum."

"Not now, love," my mother said. "I'm watching this." On the television screen a group of three- and four-year olds were dancing in a ring around a grinning, wide-eyed woman. My mother was watching *Romper Room.*

I walked over to her and dropped my satchel to the floor. It fell with a heavy thud. It was full of new exercise books, textbooks, my new timetable, and the year's school dinner schedule. It contained a map of my life for the next ten months. I wanted to tell her about all of it. I wanted to talk to her about my day—Mr. Davies and his oversized stomach, Miss Nutall and her boring history lectures, my outstanding performance in maths, and, of course, the fascinating Ms. Hastings. But my mother didn't care about any of this. She was more interested in watching children's television.

"I made some new friends, Mum," I persisted. "I had my school dinner with them, and we sat together in every lesson." I wanted her to care, at least, that I was safe, that she didn't need to worry about me the way I always needed to worry about her. But my mother said nothing. She lay across the settee, her face squished asymmetrical, pressed half flat against a cushion as she stared steadily at the jovial bustle on the television screen.

I stood over her, the solidity of my body blocking her view. "I said, I like my new school."

Her lips parted slightly, she took in a breath, her eyelids quivered. Then she closed her eyes and exhaled. But she said nothing.

I felt the anger in me flare, like one of the brilliant fizzing fireworks set off on Bonfire Night. Dazzling, incandescent against the wintry darkness. "Say something!" I yelled. She opened her eyes, but still she remained silent. "Why can't you even act like you bloody well care?"

I watched her face carefully, eager for her reaction, for a twitch of her lips, a jerk in the muscles under her eyes, a clenching fist, a hiss of fury as she rose to strike me. I wanted her to leap up, yell in my face, slap my arms and legs and cheeks, pull my hair until my scalp was burning. Then I could scream and cry and yell back. Pummel her flesh, feel the clash of my knuckles against her bone. Bruise her, mark her. Make her feel my anger instead of feeling nothing. Instead of lying there, dazed and utterly limp, a pathetic excuse for a mother.

But she didn't jump up, nor did she hit me, nor did she yell. Instead, she turned her head, achingly slow, like the cogs in a flagging clockwork toy, until, after an age of waiting, her eyes finally met mine.

"I'm sorry," she said, her voice a whisper in her throat. "I'm doing my best, love. I know you can't tell. But, really, I am. And I'm sorry."

The blistering conflagration inside me died, sputtering to nothing. It was as if I had been gearing up for a fight and my opponent had gone running down the road, out of sight. The least she could do was stand up to me, meet my anger with her own, let me have the satisfaction of battering myself against her.

I stared down at her. And I knew that the same loathing and disdain burned in my eyes that I had seen in the eyes of the children who had taunted me after she'd been taken to the hospital, who had mocked my pathetic lies about her cruise. "I don't care if you're sorry," I said. "I don't give a bloody damn." I drew out the words, wrapping my lips and tongue around them, pushing all my energy into those long, wide sounds. I pulled back my foot, balancing one-legged for a moment as I imagined the hard, sharp toe of my shoe slamming into her cheek, knocking her head loose and unresisting against the cushions of the settee. Then, I let my foot fly, landing a fierce and almighty kick against my satchel. It skidded across the room, the unbuckled flap flying open and my new books and pens and pencils scattering over the floor like a body blown apart by an explosion. Then I turned on my heels and marched toward the door. When I looked back, my mother was staring at the television, expressionless again. I pulled open the door and let it slam behind me, hoping the shock of the noise penetrated her insides and took her breath away, the way a punch to her stomach would.

LATER THAT EVENING, I sat on my bed. Downstairs, I could hear the melodic rumble of the news announcer's voice and then my father's thunderous yells. As I sat there, my father's voice reverberating through me, I understood his feelings of anger and futility, knowing that they were also my own. There was so much to rage at: the entire unfairness of the world. For my father it was the royal family and rampant inflation, factory closures, unemployment, the killing of innocent people in places like Northern Ireland and Vietnam. For me it was this ugly house, my mother's utter inability to be the normal mother I longed for, and the fact that Amanda had spent her time after school snogging the awful Stan Heaphy.

But what was I expecting, really? My mother had never been the mother I wanted. And Amanda was far out of reach. Even if she decided tomorrow that she didn't want to go out with Stan Heaphy, she'd doubtless take up with some other boy she'd kiss outside the school gates. She'd hardly start wanting to be my friend. She might like me enough to defend me from Tracey's teasing, but she didn't even want to sit with me on the bus ride to school. I was simply a girl she'd felt sorry for when she found me out in the rain and whose name she couldn't remember, a girl she could order to rub suntan lotion over her back. It would make so much more sense if I could make myself stop thinking about her, if I could be infatuated with David Cassidy or one of the Bay City Rollers, if I could be like all the other girls. But clearly, and now more than ever, I knew that I was not.

I had finished my homework, doing my maths first because Tracey and the Debbies were relying on me to get the answers to them the next morning so they could copy them before the lesson later that day. And I had finished the assignment that Ms. Hastings set us, a story about ourselves, because, she'd told us, she wanted to know her students better. At first, when she'd told us about this homework, I'd been eager to get home and write about my interests in world exploration and all the fascinating things I'd discovered during my research on my mother's cruise. But on the bus ride home, when I'd mentioned the assignment and Tracey declared that anyone who wanted Ms. Hastings to know them better was probably trying to be teacher's pet, I'd lost my initial enthusiasm and had instead written a couple of careless pages about our move from Hull to Midham, a story that bored me even as I wrote it. Now I had nothing to do but brood.

Then I had an idea. I might not be able to tell Amanda how I felt. And she might not even care how I felt. But I could write her a letter. Of course, I would never actually give it to her. Like all that correspondence between me and my cruise-taking mother, it would remain unsent. And, having learned my lesson about sharing those letters with other people, I would keep this letter completely to myself. But I wanted to write to her—I felt compelled to. I was so filled with bursting emotion and confusion that somehow I needed to get it out. So I found an empty notebook on the table beside my bed and began to write.

"Dear Amanda," I wrote, "the first thing I want you to know is that you are the most beautiful person I have ever known. The second thing I want you to know is that Stan Heaphy might be good-looking but underneath he is ugly and you deserve someone much better than him. The third thing you should know is that even though I know this is probably wrong, I love you and I would do anything for you. In fact, from the moment I met you outside the Co-op on that rainy night, I loved you. I think you are the nicest person I ever met in my entire life." I sat back, looked at those few sentences, and felt an immediate urge to cross them out. Once the words were on the page, they seemed ridiculous, and I knew anyone reading them would think so, too. But no one would ever read them. Ever. Whatever happened, I was determined to make sure of that.

And so I continued. I recalled our first meeting, telling her how I'd been utterly miserable there in the rain until she invited me under her umbrella and everything had changed. I wrote about how wonderful it had been to discover that she was Tracey's sister, how stunning she'd looked out there on her sun bed in her garden, how much I admired her pretty little house and her parents' photographs, and how if she ever dressed up in a glittery ballroom dress like one of her mother's she'd look far more glamorous than any film star I'd ever seen. I wrote about how grateful I was that she'd stopped Tracey and those boys from teasing me, how she'd changed my life by saving me from a terrible fate.

As I continued, I felt my embarrassment at my words fall away. It started to feel good, cleansing almost, to get it all out there on the page. Though I knew it was terribly wrong to want to kiss another girl, when I wrote about wanting to take Stan Heaphy's place, to wrap my arms around Amanda, it made me feel calm, less troubled, as if putting my desires in writing took the shamefulness out of them, transformed them into sentences made up of nothing more than words.

When I finished my letter, signing it "All my love, Jesse," it was several pages long and the time was after ten o'clock. I tore the pages carefully out of the notebook, folded them, and looked around the room. For a moment, I considered hiding them under my mattress, but I decided that might not be such a good place. Despite my mother's current apathy, there was always a chance she'd find some new frenzied energy and take it upon herself to clean the bedrooms from top to bottom, single-handedly turning the mattresses on all the beds. After giving it a few minutes' consideration, I took one of the books down from my bookshelf, pressed the letter inside its pages, and put it back on the shelf. Though in a sudden fit of housework my mother might dust off my books, she was very unlikely to look inside. Then, my confession made and hidden away, I changed into my pajamas, climbed into bed, and promptly fell asleep.

—

CHAPTER THIRTEEN

I USUALLY GOT A CHANCE TO TALK TO AMANDA IN THE MORNING AT the bus stop, but she never took the bus home with us after school. She would stand outside the school gates with Stan and ride back to Midham on his motorbike. They argued frequently, but just as frequently they engaged in long snogging sessions, eyes closed, mouths squished together and moving as if they were chewing on each other. During the first couple of weeks of school, Tracey and I watched them from the school car park until our bus arrived, Tracey huffing and mumbling under her breath about how Stan was far too good for Amanda, how she hoped it wouldn't be too long before he moved on to some other, better girl. I said nothing, guiltily imagining myself there instead of Stan, Amanda in my arms.

Within a short time, however, Tracey got over her fixation on Stan Heaphy when she developed a crush on Gregory Loomis, one of the boys who regularly hung out with Stan by the school gates. Greg was a lanky fifth-year who tottered around school on platform shoes sporting a feathered haircut, wispy sideburns, and flares so wide he could have held a disco inside his trousers. He had a precociously hairy chest, which he attempted to reveal at any opportunity by walking around school with his tie loosened and his shirt undone even when the rest of the Liston Comprehensive student body had donned pullovers to keep off the deepening October chill. "Don't you think he's bloody gorgeous?" Tracey oozed each time we passed him in the corridor (an event that happened with great frequency after she obtained a copy of his timetable and began dragging me and the Debbies on circuitous detours to our lessons so that our movements would coincide with his). I thought he had decent enough looks, but I wasn't convinced that he had much in the way of personality, since the only thing he seemed capable of talking about was his favorite football team, Liverpool; he became positively fanatic when the subject of their star player, Kevin Keegan, came up. It wasn't long, however, before Tracey became an avid Liverpool fan herself, replacing the pictures of David Cassidy she'd pasted on the front of her exercise books with photographs of Kevin Keegan and his teammates.

There were times, during the first few weeks of school, when I had to admit I found the endless conversations about Greg Loomis and Kevin Keegan a little tedious, and the Debbies' endless choruses of "Bye Bye Baby," and "Shang-A-Lang" were starting to convince me that I could quite easily grow to hate all the members of the Bay City Rollers equally. But these things were, after all, the things that girls were supposed to talk about, and if I wanted to keep my friends, putting up with this seemed like a small price to pay. I felt similarly about letting Tracey and the Debbies copy most of my homework and, when the teacher wasn't looking, the work I did in class. Most of the time, we all got B's and C's—a considerable improvement for the four of them, since, they told me, they used to get mostly C's and D's. Before my mother was taken to Delapole, I'd almost always got A's, but that seemed an age away.

The only lesson in which I might have wanted to do better in was English. I kept hoping that Tracey and the Debbies would warm to Ms. Hastings, but they never did, complaining before, during, and after her lessons about what a "bloody hippie weirdo" she was. Though I didn't say so, I thought she was a breath of fresh air, and I loved to watch her stride down the corridors. With her big boots, bright clothes, and the constant jangle of her jewelry, she made the rest of us in our dull school uniforms look washed-out and dim. The other teachers, too, in their conservative tweeds and sensible shoes, all looked faded beside her. Her lessons were also far more interesting than any others, involving avid discussions in which Malcolm, Dizzy, and a handful of others talked about what motivated a particular character or the writer of the book. Sometimes I felt a brief ache to jump in and say what I thought, but I stayed silent. And when, outside in the corridor, the other girls shoved against Dizzy and ran off with her glasses, or the boys tripped up Malcolm, laughing at him as he stumbled, and called him a "clumsy little queer," I was glad that I'd stayed sheltered within my little group of friends, that I hadn't drawn any attention to myself.

After school, because I wasn't working particularly hard on my homework, I had quite a lot of free time. So, while my mother spent her evenings sleeping or curled up silently in bed, and my father sat alone ranting at the television, I sat in my bedroom filling first one and then a second notebook with letters to Amanda. Soon, I had so many that it became more difficult to hide them between the pages of my books. So instead I retrieved an empty Teatime Assortment biscuit tin from the kitchen, shook out the remaining crumbs, and placed my letters inside. Then I pulled out all the old toys, shoes, and the boxes of Monopoly and Snakes and Ladders that covered the bottom of my wardrobe, put the box of letters there, and piled all those other things on top.

My early letters talked mostly about how wonderful it had been to see Amanda that morning at the bus stop, recalled the short conversations we sometimes had, and included long paragraphs in which I tried to convince her that Stan Heaphy was utterly undeserving of her attention. But as I continued to write, my letters began to change course into imagined days I might spend with her, and soon I found myself writing letters to Amanda that barely touched upon reality, stories that were, instead, long, delicious fantasies of the life we might have if we ran away together or lived in another time or place. The first of these were inspired by an episode of *Star Trek.*

Star Trek was one of my favorite programs. Fortunately, my father liked it, too, and over the years we'd developed our own little ritual in preparation for watching it. Just before *Star Trek* started at eight o'clock, we'd make a fresh pot of tea and set out a plate of biscuits on the coffee table. Then, even in the summer when it was still light outside, we'd close the living-room curtains so we could shut out the mundane world of the present and immerse ourselves in a future where people wore bright-colored stretchy pantsuits and traveled faster than the speed of light. "Space, the final frontier," my father and I would both chorus along with Captain James T. Kirk against a background of swirly, space-age music, as we shuffled to get more comfortable in our respective seats. The only parts of *Star Trek* I had never liked were the scenes where some dazzled female alien with bouffant hair and sparkly eye shadow fell into the arms of Captain Kirk and demanded to be taught how we humans show affection. My father equally disdained these scenes, muttering, "Bloody Americans, always got to get some sex in somewhere."

On that particular Monday, however, I was all attention as Captain Kirk and his latest alien love interest snogged. Instead of itching for the scene to be over, I watched intently as I imagined myself as James T. Kirk and Amanda as the female alien who fell into my arms. In fact, the fantasy became so vivid that when my father turned to me with some disparaging comment about Americans and their vulgar sensibilities, I found myself avoiding his eyes, worried that he'd be able to tell what I was thinking just by looking at me. As soon as the episode was over, I charged upstairs to my bedroom, where I took out my notebook and began a letter to Amanda in which I suggested that we might become space travelers together. I'd be Captain Jesse T. Bennett, commander of the spaceship, while Lieutenant Amanda Grasby would be my second in command.

I wrote my *Star Trek*–inspired letters for quite a while. They were full of all kinds of dangers—flesh-eating plants, toxic gases, hostile shape-shifting aliens. Despite these terrible hazards, I'd always manage to save Lieutenant Grasby, and she, of course, would always thank me by throwing herself into my arms and landing a grateful kiss on my lips. Then, one Saturday night, I stayed up late to watch a Vincent Price horror film and started writing letters that involved haunted castles, marauding peasants, and wicked counts determined to spread terror throughout the land. In these letters, I became the vampire- and ghost-hunting hero who prevented the triumph of whichever evildoer was threatening to take over the land, while also rescuing the beautiful Amanda, who had been taken captive and, without my intervention, faced a fate as one of the living dead.

Immersed in these letters, I found that my life at home became far more tolerable, an inconvenient backdrop to the adventures I took myself on every night. And even though it was still agonizing to see Amanda climb onto the back of Stan Heaphy's motorbike every afternoon, on the bus ride home I comforted myself with the thought that later I could create stories in which Amanda and I always ended up together, where even space aliens and vampires couldn't keep us apart.

ON THE FIRST SATURDAY of the half-term holiday, Auntie Mabel rang early. "How's your mother?" she asked after inquiring about my new school and the progress of my father's renovations.

"She's all right."

"All right?" Mabel said dubiously. "What's that supposed to mean, eh, Jesse? Let's face it, when was the last time our Evelyn was all right?"

"She's sleeping a lot," I said. Above me, my parents' snoring reverberated through the ceiling. It was like listening to the grumbling melodies of two steam locomotives as they chuffed slowly along parallel railway tracks.

Mabel was, of course, correct. My mother wasn't all right. She wasn't anywhere approaching all right. For the past several weeks she hadn't stirred out of her terrible inertia, barely got dressed, and bathed so infrequently that even from a distance I could make out her sour and musky smell. And though she hadn't mentioned Delapole or made reference to any plans to do herself in, she'd started going on at length about how maybe she should buy a ticket and fly off to Australia, where, even if being with her mother didn't cheer her up, at least the change in the climate would.

Sometimes I tried to talk to her, sitting beside her on the settee, taking her hand, and telling her how nice it would be if she started working on the garden, how the exercise and the fresh air would do her good. "It's too wet and too bloody cold," she'd say, pulling her hand away. "And, anyway, it'll be winter soon and everything in the garden will be dead." Then she'd go on to tell me how it would be summer soon in Australia, and there would be lovely weather in Sydney and how her mother and "that bloody Australian gigolo" would celebrate Christmas with a barbecue on the beach.

"Well, listen," Mabel continued, the sound of her lighting a cigarette and taking a sighing drag audible over the telephone. "You tell Evelyn to get herself up and out of bed, because I'm coming over."

"You are?" I was delighted. I'd been missing Mabel terribly, longing for her to stride in and brighten up our dull and ugly house. If anyone could talk my mother out of this bad patch, it was Mabel. "What time will you be here?" I asked.

"Oh, tell your mam and dad I'll be there around one o'clock. And I'm bringing someone with me."

"Who?"

"My new fella, Frank."

"Frank?" I repeated, hoping this wasn't the same Frank who had startled my mother in Mabel's bathroom.

"Oh, don't you worry now, Jesse," Mabel said. "I'll make sure he puts some clothes on before he comes along."

When Mabel arrived that afternoon with Frank in tow, both my parents were a little surprised. I'd decided, after my mother's disastrous first encounter with Frank, that perhaps it was best that I didn't mention Mabel's intention to bring him. That way, my mother might have a little more of a positive attitude toward her sister's approaching visit and my father wouldn't be left anxiously awaiting another social catastrophe in the making. The prospect of seeing her sister had miraculously propelled my mother out of bed. She'd even managed to take a bath, get dressed, do her hair, and put on some makeup. When she went to answer their knock, she looked as full of fearsome energy as she had when she'd been swinging that scythe around the garden to clear the weeds a couple of months before. As I watched her pull open the door with rediscovered vigor, I let myself hope that perhaps Mabel could inject some liveliness into her that would last beyond the brief few hours of this visit.

"Evelyn, this is Frank," Mabel said, smiling cautiously at my mother. "Frank, this is Evelyn. I know the two of you have met before, but I thought a more formal introduction might be appropriate."

Frank looked a little older than Mabel. He had jet-black hair, graying just slightly at the temples, and a craggy, narrow face with generous lips, dark bushy eyebrows, and a small, cherublike nose. It was an interesting combination of features that was not entirely unattractive. The same, however, could not be said of his clothing. He wore a pair of bottle-green polyester flares that were far too long, sagged over his thin hips, folded over his ankles, and almost hid his shiny Winklepicker shoes. He carried a matching jacket over his shoulder, and his big-collared, big-cuffed shirt, billowing across his insubstantial chest, was bright green satin. As he stood next to Mabel, shifting his weight from foot to foot, I wondered what he looked like when my mother stumbled upon him naked. All I could imagine, however, was a man in green underwear with the green, scrawny body of a stick insect.

Frank seemed to be doing his best to look apologetic in front of my mother, but I could tell from the glint in his gray eyes that he was thinking back on their first encounter with amusement. "Nice to meet you, Evelyn," he said, and pushed a solid, wide hand toward my mother. He was holding a large paper-wrapped package.

My mother regarded Frank, then the package, frostily. "What's that?" she said, narrowing her eyes and taking a couple of steps back, as if Frank were proffering a hand grenade.

"It's a peace offering, like," Frank replied.

"A peace offering?" My mother looked down the long, straight line of her nose at Frank and then at Mabel. "There a war going on around here that I don't know about?" I could already tell that she was intent on directing her renewed energy in a furious belligerence toward Frank. She must have been storing up her anger ever since she stormed out of Mabel's house.

Mabel smiled. "It's to make up for that little . . . misunderstanding we had. I know the two of you got off on the wrong foot and I thought—"

"So, this is *your* idea, then?"

Mabel began rifling through her handbag. "No, Evelyn. It was Frank's idea. He thought you'd appreciate a little gift, that's all." She retrieved a packet of cigarettes.

My mother frowned, thoughtful for a moment, and then extended her hand toward Frank. "Well, in that case, thanks very much." She took the package and pressed it to her chest. I breathed a sigh of relief. Perhaps things would go better than I'd thought. "It's been quite a while since anyone's been so thoughtful as to get me a present," she said, giving me a sideways but nevertheless pointed look.

"Open it then," I urged her. I imagined a pretty pearl necklace, a pair of gold earrings, a flowing silk scarf—the kinds of things I might buy my mother if it occurred to me to get her anything besides the talcum powder and bath crystals I always ordered for her out of Mabel's Avon catalog for Christmas and birthdays.

"All right, all right," my mother said. "Ooh, I wonder what it could be." She didn't have to wonder long, however, for having deftly torn back the paper in only a matter of seconds, she found herself holding a large mound of mottled pink sausages.

"Best pork sausages you'll find in the whole of Yorkshire," Frank announced. He had a deep, throaty voice—the kind men get from smoking too many cigarettes, the kind that makes them sound careworn and wrung out by life. "And probably the best you'll find in the whole country, if I'm not mistaken. There's three pounds there. That should last you a while."

My mother regarded the sausages with the expression of a person who had just been handed a package of someone else's vomit. When she looked up at Frank and Mabel, her expression remained unchanged.

"Frank's right," said Mabel, an unlit cigarette now dangling from her lips as she scrambled about in her bag again, presumably to locate her lighter. "Best sausages you'll find anywhere in the world. And Frank should know. That's where he works—Tuggles Sausage Factory. Been there for seventeen years now, haven't you, Frank?"

Frank nodded, his face a picture of saddened confusion as he met my mother's disdainful expression.

"I see," my mother said flatly, lowering her eyes toward the sausages again. "So, this is how you spend your days, then, Frank? Making sausages?"

"Aye, like Mabel says, I've been there seventeen years."

"Yes, well, I've never been much of a pork person myself," my mother said, folding the paper back around the package as if she could no longer bear the sight of all that raw, pink meat. "Beef is much more my cup of tea. You could have asked Mabel and she would have told you that. I've always had a preference for beef." She shook her head slowly, as if to say that had Frank only had the sense to bring along a package of beef sausages, this whole sorry interaction would have gone perfectly.

"I like pork sausages," I said, desperate to rescue the only visit we'd had at our new home from complete disaster. "And so does my dad. We'll eat them, won't we, Dad?" I looked over at my father, who was lurking behind my mother and me in the hallway. He gave a noncommittal shrug.

My mother handed the package to me. "Yes, well, you'd better put them in the fridge then, hadn't you? If it's not stored properly, you can get all kinds of diseases from pork. That's why them Muslims and Jews won't touch it. I mean, I don't know about you, but I wouldn't want to end up with tapeworm."

"Oh, there's no chance of you getting anything like that," Frank said solemnly. "Use the best sanitary practices, we do."

"I'm not taking any chances, thank you very much," my mother said. "Jesse and Mike can eat pork, but I'd rather not, if you don't mind."

"You've eaten it plenty of times before," I chimed. Indeed, next to Mr. Kipling cream cakes, pork pies were one of my mother's favorite foods. She loved to eat them in thin slices, buried under shiny mounds of Branston Pickle and mustard, leaving brown and yellow stains around her mouth. It didn't surprise me, however, that she conveniently seemed to have forgotten this particular passion. I felt sorry for Frank. Though he might keep us in meat products for the rest of our lives, he would never be forgiven his faux pas in Mabel's bathroom. If Mabel had any compassion, she'd never have raised his hopes in the first place.

"Well," my mother said, turning away from the doorway, "I suppose you want something to eat. I'm sorry, but I just haven't had a chance to make it to the shops this week." She sighed as if she'd had one of those excessively busy weeks that hadn't included a spare moment to get some shopping done. "I think we might have some custard creams in the biscuit tin. . . ."

"Oh, that's fine. We're not hungry," Mabel said, the unlit cigarette still in her mouth as she followed my mother down the hall. Frank, his hands pushed into the pockets of his big green trousers, tagged along behind next to my father. "We got something to eat on the way. Frank drove me over, you know."

"Aye, that's right," Frank called toward my mother. "Came over in the Tuggles delivery van, we did. Let me use it outside of work hours, they do. And quite a ride it was. More curves on them there roads than on your Mabel!" He let out a loud raspy laugh.

At this, my mother turned on her heels, gave Auntie Mabel a sour look, and muttered, "Pick up the village idiot on your way, did you, Mabel?"

Mabel looked at Frank, exasperated. He swallowed his laugh and shrugged. "Just trying to lighten things up a bit," he said, looking toward me and my father. I gave him a wan, apologetic smile, thinking that someone, at least, should let him know not to waste his energy. My father looked steadily at his own feet.

When we reached the kitchen, Mabel removed the still unlit cigarette from her mouth, grabbed me, wrapped me in a tight hug, and placed a greasy lipstick kiss on my cheek. "By heck, Jesse, I'll swear you get bigger every time I see you. I bet you grow out of your clothes like nobody's business."

"You can say that again," my mother said sternly as she filled the kettle. "You ask me, it's a bit abnormal. When we were younger, we never grew like that."

"Aye, well, kids these days, they're a lot different," said Frank. "My kids—"

My mother turned around abruptly. "You've got kids?" She waited for Frank's nod of affirmation, then turned to scowl at Mabel.

"For God's sake, keep your hair on, Evelyn," Mabel said, sighing. "He's divorced. His kids live with his ex-wife, don't they, Frank?"

"Aye, nine and eleven, they are. Want to see a picture?" He gave my mother a hopeful smile, pulled his wallet out of his back pocket, and rummaged around until he found a creased photograph. He handed it to her. Eyebrows raised, lips pursed tight and small, she gave the photograph a cursory glance before passing it to my father.

"Hmmph," she said. "I expect those poor little things must really miss their daddy. It's awful, what happens to children of divorce." She looked meaningfully over at Mabel, who, once again, popped the cigarette back into her mouth and began scouring her handbag for her cigarette lighter.

"Nice photo," my father said, handing the picture back to Frank. My mother let out a snort.

For a moment, Frank held it in the flat of his hand. He was gazing at the photograph the way someone might if he were trying to read the lines in his palm, hoping to discern some hidden meaning from the deeply familiar.

"Can I see?" I asked, reaching for the photograph.

"Here," he said, handing it to me.

It showed two dark-haired children, a boy and a girl. They were sitting on a beach, building a tilting, clumsy sandcastle, squinting and smiling as they looked toward the camera. The girl had two of her front teeth missing and a solid, pudgy body. She wore a canary-yellow swimsuit, and her hair was tied in two long, stringy plaits that hung limply over her chest. The boy, a little older, had Frank's same skin-and-bones build. In the picture, as if immensely proud of his sandcastle, he was puffing out his chest to show the rigid arc of each of his ribs pressed against his pallid skin. "What are their names?" I asked.

"The girl's Karen," Frank said. "And the boy's Bobby. Bit of a good-looker, just like his dad, don't you think?"

"You wish!" Mabel laughed.

I had never known a man to carry a photograph of his children around in his wallet. All the men I knew, like my father, left it to their wives to put their holiday snaps in albums or place the photographs that were taken annually at school in frames and set them on the sideboard. Children were something they left at home when they went out into the world, part of the domestic burden they shed as soon as they stepped out the front door. I wondered if once men got divorced and were freed of their children as a daily responsibility, they began carrying pictures of them around like some distant memento of the past. Was it easier to be proud of them, to love them, I wondered, if you didn't have to see them every day?

"They look nice," I said, still studying Frank's children, the way the sea shimmered so blue behind them and the sand glinted as it reflected back the sun. They looked happy in the picture, and I wondered if they continued to be, now that their parents were apart.

"Interested in Do-It-Yourself, Frank?" my father asked chirpily. "Fancy a look at some of my handiwork? I've been doing quite a lot of repairs."

"Aye, that'd be nice, Mike," Frank answered, giving my father a grateful look as they both beat an exit into the hall.

When the kettle boiled, my mother set out a plate of the biscuits that had been languishing in a tin in the back of the pantry since we moved in. I, for one, didn't plan on eating any—they looked crumbly and stale.

Mabel searched about in her handbag again, finally looking up with a sigh. "I don't know what the heck I've done with my lighter, and I'm gasping for a ciggy. You got any matches in here?" she asked, looking around the kitchen.

"Just run out," my mother said stonily. "And, anyway, didn't I tell you to give that dirty habit up?"

Mabel ignored her, turning to me. "Jesse, be a love would you and go and ask Frank to let me borrow his lighter?"

"All right, Auntie Mabel," I said, and went out into the hallway, where my father and Frank had apparently graduated from discussing my father's talents as a handyman to more personal things. I stood in the shadows by the kitchen door, reluctant to interrupt and a little curious to find out more about Frank.

"So, you work at Tuggles, then, Frank?" my father said. "They make good sausages, do Tuggles."

"Aye," Frank said. "Like I said, been there seventeen years."

"So you must like it, then?"

"It's all right," Frank said, stuffing his hands into his trouser pockets. "It's a job. Though I have to say, with paying the ex-wife and the kids' maintenance, well, there's not much left over. With two incomes coming in, mind, I wouldn't be so bad off."

"You thinking about getting another job as well?" my father asked, surprised.

"Bloody hell, no. One's enough for me, thank you very much. But, well, Mabel makes a decent bit of cash with all that makeup and Tupperware she flogs. And she's got a right nice little house on that new estate. I mean, if we pooled our resources . . . Right now I'm stuck in a poky little bedsit over a betting shop on Holderness Road. It's handy if I want to make a flutter on the horses, but not much of a home. And, anyway, what do we men know about making somewhere feel like home, eh?" He gave a raspy little laugh. "Need a woman to take care of that kind of thing. A man my age, I wasn't meant to live by myself. I can't cook, not much for cleaning, and I bloody hate doing my own washing."

"Yes, well," my father said, scratching the back of his neck and looking thoughtful. "I'm not sure there's anyone really likes cleaning and washing, Frank. Evelyn, well, when she gets in the mood she can be like a flipping tornado going through the house. But I don't think she'd ever tell you she likes doing housework. She did get into a bit of a cooking phase for a while, mind you. She seemed to like that." He lowered his voice to almost a whisper. "Made all this bloody French food. Can't say I really cared for it."

"Don't blame you," Frank said. "Me, I prefer a nice plate of meat, gravy, and potatoes. Thankfully, that's what Mabel makes best."

"So, Frank, how come it didn't work out with your ex-wife, then? I mean, divorce—that's a serious step." Though my father might be a little less vocal than my mother in his judgments, he'd never approved of divorce.

"To be honest with you, Mike," Frank said, "my ex, she was a bit of a bitch. Always complaining that I was going to the pub with my mates too much, spending too much on the horses, not giving her enough money to make ends meet. Nag, nag, nag." He flapped his thumb and fingers open and shut to imitate a chattering jaw. "Finally, I just got sick of it. I miss the kids sometimes, but I can't say I miss motormouth one bit. That's what I used to call her, motormouth—and a few other things besides."

I thought of those two children smiling proudly at the camera, and of how photographs never showed more than one captured moment—how, after that picture had been taken, the tide would inevitably have come in and washed away their sandcastle, and how, at the end of that day, they'd have changed out of their swimming costumes and been driven home by Frank. I thought about how they'd have sat behind bedroom walls listening to their parents argue, and I wondered if they'd been relieved when their father walked out on them, or if they still kept hoping that he would come back.

"In contrast to my ex," Frank continued, "Mabel's a bloody breath of fresh air. She's more easygoing, knows how to have a laugh. And, like I said, she's got a nice setup there on the estate and I could use a bit of home cooking."

"Yes, well," my father ventured, "Mabel's always been quite an independent type, you know. I'm not sure she—"

"Oh, Mabel knows what's good for her," Frank interrupted. "When it comes down to it, every woman wants a man around the house."

"No, they don't," I said, moving out of the shadows.

"Aye, well, you tell that to your husband, love," Frank said, his voice half laugh, half growl. "When you get married—"

"I'm not getting married," I interjected. "I'm not going to be the servant of some lazy man who can't be bothered to do his own washing and cleaning." I had no doubt, also, that while Frank might have aspirations to settle down and be waited on in Mabel's little council house, she would send him on his way soon enough. As my mother said, Mabel went through men the way other women went through nylon stockings.

For a moment, Frank held my gaze, the slow burn of indignation in his eyes. "Got yourself quite a little firebrand here, don't you, Mike? Sent out to spy on us by the women in the kitchen, were you?"

"Mabel told me to ask Frank for his lighter," I explained, turning to my father.

"See, Mike," Frank said, laughing. "Women, they always need a man for something."

"YOU KNOW, IT'S LOVELY out here, it really is."

I'd returned to the kitchen. After lighting her cigarette and taking a couple of long, hungry drags, Mabel stood by the window, looking out over my mother's abandoned garden. In the churned-up soil, the thistles and other weeds had started to grow back, the bright yellow heads of dandelions peering through a thickening carpet of green.

"All them trees, all this nature," Mabel continued. "And you could have a lovely garden out there if you get back to it, Ev. I mean, you've got so much space here. Me, I look outside and all I see is concrete and that eighty-year-old bloke across the street who likes to stand in his window in nothing but his Y-fronts. Bloody old pervert. Not a pretty sight, I'll tell you that. But you, well, you've got it all here, haven't you? You could get yourself out—maybe you could take your driving test again and . . ." Mabel frowned for a moment, apparently remembering the outcome of my mother's last failed driving test. "Or maybe you could get yourself a bike," she added brightly. "You know, cycle out on them lovely roads. Go into the village, do a bit of shopping. And let's face it, Ev, you've got your work cut out for you here, haven't you?" She gestured around the kitchen, still desperately in need of renovation. "I don't see how you could possibly get bored."

"Well, I am," my mother said, dropping her teacup into the saucer with a clatter.

"Jesse's not bored, are you, love?" Mabel said, gesturing me over to her with her cigarette. I walked to her side and she put an arm around my shoulder, pressing me into her soft, springy flesh.

"No, I like it," I said.

"And did you make some friends?"

"Yes. I made a few. But my best friend is Tracey."

"Oh, that's that skinny lass that you brought over to my house, right?"

I nodded.

"See, Evelyn," Mabel said. "If Jesse here can adjust, I'm sure you can."

My mother sat back and folded her arms across her chest. "You know, I haven't heard one word from our mother since she phoned you about getting married. Not one bloody word."

"Well, I'm sure she—" Mabel began.

My mother slammed her hand down on the table, making the cups and saucers there dance noisily over its surface. "I just don't understand how a woman could treat her daughter like that, I really don't. Flitting off to another country, leaving her to fend for herself." She pondered this for a moment, then looked over at me, watery-eyed. "Don't you worry, love, I'd never leave you in the lurch like that."

Mabel sighed. My head against her, I could hear her breath as it moved through her chest. I pressed closer into her, into the warmth beneath her clothes. If my parents ever divorced, I thought, perhaps Auntie Mabel would take me in. We could live in her little council house, laughing together at the neighbor in his underpants. Unlike Frank, I wouldn't expect to be waited on. I'd even help out with Mabel's Tupperware and Avon makeup parties if it meant she'd let me stay.

"But Jesse's only a kid," Mabel responded. "You were a married woman when Mam left. And she left me as well, you know. I miss her, of course. But you've got to decide to get on with your life—"

"But that's not the point, is it?" My mother thumped the kitchen table again. "You're not like me, Mabel. You know that. Nobody understands what I go through. Nobody. Not Mike, not all those bloody doctors, not even my own sister or my own mother. You should try being me sometimes. I bet you couldn't stand it for a day." She paused for a moment. Beside me, Mabel took a couple of tense puffs on her cigarette. "Come to think of it," my mother continued, "our Ted is better off than me."

"What are you talking about, Ev? You're just being daft now." Mabel waved away the smoke in front of her as if she were trying to wave away my mother's words.

"No, I'm not. At least he gets out every once in a while. Gets a bit of freedom. But me, my prison's in here." My mother jabbed her forehead with her index finger. "On the inside. I can't help the way I feel, you know. I can't. People are always saying cheer up, or pull yourself together, or other such bloody rubbish. They smile at you and tell you how it'd be so much better if you did this or you did that. Hah! That's a bloody joke, that is!" Her voice was getting louder and her features seemed twisted, as if she were pulling something hard and painful from deep inside herself. "Get yourself a hobby, they say. Then, when I do get myself a hobby, find something I want to do, they tell me to calm down, take it easy, don't get so overwrought. And you know what's so ridiculous about all this?" She was yelling now. "Do you? Do you?"

Beside me, I felt Mabel shake her head.

My mother stood up, her chair scraping the floor with a shriek. "There's not a damn thing I can do about any of it! That's what! I mean, don't you think I'd change the way I am if I could?" Her hands gripped the edges of the table now, her eyes wild and teary. I stepped away from Mabel, feeling the urge to go to my mother, to put my arms around her shoulders, to try to ease her sadness and her anger, as if by touching her I could let it soak into myself. But it was hopeless; she had said so herself. Her moods were as inevitable as the tides that ate away cliffs and knocked over sandcastles. I remained by the kitchen counter.

"I know, Ev, I'm sure it must be hard," said Mabel, her voice a syrupy calm. "But I'm sure you'd feel better if you got back to your gardening."

"I don't give a toss about that bloody garden. I don't give a toss about anything right now." She dropped back into her chair.

"Oh, Evelyn," Mabel said. "Honestly, I don't know what to say. And comparing yourself to Ted, well that makes no sense to me. I mean, you're out here with all this space and countryside and he's stuck in some poky little cell. Mind you, he'll be out soon enough. He wrote to me last week, said they're releasing him early next year. Cheeky bugger, wanted to know if he could come and stay with me. Fat chance of that! Hey, did I tell you what he did last time I let him kip at my house, Jesse?" She took an eager puff on her cigarette, then gestured toward me with it. "I made the mistake of saying I'd help him get on his feet. Well, the telly went on the blink, so he goes out and gets me another one. I was pleased as punch, I was. Pleased, that is, until Mrs. Waverly from down the street comes in to borrow a cup of sugar, sees my new telly, and tells me that it's the one she'd had nicked from her house just the week before. Of course, it had been our Ted." She shook her head. "Took months before I could hold up my head on my street again. You're nothing like our Ted, Evelyn. Not one jot. He's got real problems. You—well, you've got a nice house and a lovely family. You couldn't really want much more than that." She beamed at my mother, but my mother simply stared into her empty teacup. Mabel stubbed out her cigarette. "So, what do you think of Frank, then? Bit of all right, don't you think?"

"How should I know?" my mother said, pouring herself another cup of tea.

"Well, I mean, you did see him in the altogether, didn't you?" Mabel said. "You'd have as good an idea as anybody."

"I'd rather not be reminded about that, if you don't mind," my mother said dully.

"Sorry." Mabel looked at me and pulled a guilty smile.

"Not all that glitters is gold, you know," my mother said with a sudden spark of energy, pulling the spoon from the sugar bowl and pointing it ominously at Mabel.

"What the heck is that supposed to mean?"

"I'd have thought you'd know full well. Let's face it, you've kissed a lot of frogs and you've not found yourself a prince yet, have you?"

"To be honest with you, Ev," Mabel said, "I gave up on finding a prince long ago. These days, I'd settle for a decent-looking frog." I felt tempted to make a joke about Frank resembling a frog in his green suit and shirt, but I didn't want to hurt Mabel's feelings. And I certainly didn't want to give my mother any more ammunition to hurl at her.

"Yes, well," my mother said, gesturing toward the hallway, from which we could hear the reverberating bass of my father's and Frank's voices. "You certainly haven't picked Prince Charming this time. I've never heard a story about a prince that works in a sausage factory, who's divorced, and has abandoned his poor little kiddies." She dumped a couple of spoonfuls of sugar into her tea and began stirring it so vigorously that I thought she might break the cup.

I expected Mabel to make some sharp and funny comeback, to repel my mother with a loud, strident joke. Instead, she took another cigarette out, lit it, and took a thoughtful drag. "You know, you might be right, Evelyn," she said, her words enfolded in smoke. "But as you've said yourself, I'm not getting any younger. And, despite my Platex Eighteen-Hour Girdle and Cross Your Heart Bra"—she planted a hand on one of her breasts—"things are heading more south than north these days. So, while I've got a little bit of spring in my step—and in a few other places—I'd better play my hand. Otherwise, I'll be all washed up and this"—she jiggled her breast with the hand that still rested there—"won't do me one bit of good."

I felt my stomach lurch. I hated the defeated tone in her voice, the way it suggested that she was going to have to settle for something far less than she'd hoped for. I sidled back up to her and wrapped my arms around her broad waist, hoping that by pressing myself against her I could will her to remain herself. "You don't need a Prince Charming, Auntie Mabel," I said. "You don't need any man. You could call yourself Ms., like my teacher Ms. Hastings. She thinks if you get married you just become some man's property."

Mabel laughed softly. "Crikey, the things they teach them at school these days! Next thing I know, you'll be telling me to burn my flipping bra, Jesse. I can just see myself walking into the Snail and Whippet on a Saturday night with my boobs down to my knees. Ooh, I'd be the talk of the town, I would."

"I wouldn't care about what other people said about you, Auntie Mabel. I'd love you if you didn't have a man *and* you didn't wear a bra." I clasped my arms tighter around Mabel's waist, as if the fierceness of my grip on her could seep all the way through the thick armor of her underwear, down into her flesh. I had the dreadful feeling of something slipping away from me, something I needed to hold on to to keep me afloat.

"Bleeming heck, Jesse, you're going to squeeze me to bloody death if you carry on like that!" Mabel said. "I can hardly breathe."

—

CHAPTER FOURTEEN

MABEL'S VISIT HAD NO POSITIVE IMPACT ON MY MOTHER'S MOOD.
During the following weeks, she rarely left her bedroom, and, as the
days became shorter and the leaves turned a glorious array of gold,
crimson, orange, and a hundred shades in between, she did not even
look out her window to notice the change in the seasons. When the
clocks went back at the end of October, plunging the days into a lingering gray dusk soon after four o'clock, it made no difference to her, since
she rarely got out of bed. And when the weather became cold, frost
leaving a glimmering layer of white over everything in the mornings,
she simply piled more blankets on her side of the bed, eventually lying
under a stack so heavy and thick that I wondered that it didn't suffo-
cate her.

My father continued his indifference to my mother's decline, although, after giving Frank a tour of all his half-finished projects, he did
take a renewed interest in repairing the house, throwing himself into it
with an enthusiasm I had never witnessed in him before. He stayed up
late into the night stripping the wallpaper in the living room, patching
cracks in the ceiling, painting the walls, and installing new light fix-
tures. His weekends were fully occupied, too—ripping out frayed and
rotted carpet, putting down new floorboards, replacing the dry rot-

riddled window frames outside. It was as if, with my mother's failure to leave her bed, he was trying to evoke her old ferocity, as if he had decided that if he couldn't force her to get back to her former, frantic self, he would imitate it.

While I still spent most of my evenings writing letters to Amanda, the highlight of my days came before school started, at the bus stop in Midham, when I could actually spend some time in her company. I looked forward to this with such fervor that just the thought of it was the thing that propelled me out of bed. And the hope of talking with her meant that I usually got to the bus stop far too early, always several minutes before everyone else. I waited in blistering winds that tore the leaves from the trees and scattered them in swirling piles while my coat whipped about my body, or on days when fog shrouded the fields and made the whole world bone-deep cold and impossibly still. When it rained, I stood under an umbrella, watching the leaping dance of raindrops on the street, letting the damp seep into my skin. But none of this mattered when Amanda appeared, and those few minutes that I got to spend with her filled me with a heat that, no matter how cold and inhospitable the weather, I carried with me for the rest of the day.

One morning in mid-November, when the sky was a stunning cloudless blue and the ground was silvered with frost, Amanda appeared at the bus stop earlier than usual, so that I had the luxury of a full fifteen minutes to talk with her before the bus arrived to sweep us off.

"Hiya, Jesse," she said as she approached. Though she smiled at me warmly, she looked a little ragged, tired, and not quite as immaculately groomed as she usually was.

"Hiya," I said, light-limbed at the sight of her. I was particularly pleased because, apart from one of the younger boys who preoccupied himself with smashing his heels into all the iced-over puddles at the side of the road, there was no one else at the bus stop yet. Usually, Tracey was already there by the time Amanda showed up, and I was always aware of her standing somewhere close, making disgruntled huffs and muttered comments while I spoke with her sister. Most of the time, I ignored her. Though I followed Tracey around faithfully at school, this was the one time in my day when I didn't care what she thought.

"It's a lovely day." Amanda let out a wistful sigh and looked out beyond the trees across the street from us to the fields surrounding the village. Those that were fallow were covered in a sheen of white, but a nearby grassy meadow sparkled as the sun, lurking just above the horizon, caught on the frosted blades of grass as if they were jewels. "Cold, but pretty," she said, shivering as she pushed her gloved hands into the pockets of her coat and shuffled closer to me.

"Yes," I said, breathing in the scent of her perfume, sweet and almost overpowering against the stark, odorless cold.

"So, what lessons have you got today?" She knocked her hip against mine.

"Maths, history, English, and PE," I recited. By now I knew my timetable by heart.

"You've got that Ms. Hastings for English, don't you? I don't have lessons with her, but I've heard Tracey moaning about her, complaining she's a hippie and all that. What do you think of her?"

"She's all right," I said, trying my best to sound noncommittal. I didn't want Amanda to think I liked a weirdo.

Amanda laughed. "Well, she might have got right up our Tracey's nose, but she seems like a bloody breath of fresh air, you ask me."

"You think so?" I was surprised to hear her say this, and more than a little pleased. Maybe it wasn't such a dreadful thing after all to like a female teacher with big boots, shorn hair, and hippie clothes.

"Yeah. God, I wish I had her instead of Mr. Forrest. You should hear him, Jesse. Just the sound of his voice is enough to put me to sleep. And he's always complaining about something. Come to think of it, he sounds a bit like our Tracey." She laughed. "The only thing I haven't heard her complain about is that idiot Greg Loomis."

I smiled. "She does go on about him a bit, doesn't she?"

Amanda rolled her eyes. "Non-bloody-stop. It's Greg this, Greg that, Greg the other. Honestly, sometimes I don't think she speaks one sentence without the word 'Greg' in it. She drives me mad. I expect she drives you a bit mad as well."

"Sometimes," I admitted. "The worst thing is having to follow him around school all day, though." I told Amanda about Tracey dragging me and the Debbies in search of Greg as he traveled from lesson to lesson.

Amanda barked out a laugh. "Bloody hell, she's got it worse than I thought. And you, Jesse Bennett, have got the patience of a saint." She pulled her hand out of her pocket and ruffled my hair. Her touch sent an immediate bolt of heat charging through my body. "So, how's your dad's house repairs coming along, then?"

I had told Amanda about my father's efforts to repair the house. I had also confessed my frustration with his sporadic interest in this activity. "He's finished the hallway, done the living room, and painted all the windows," I said. "He's working on the kitchen now."

"That's great."

"I suppose so, but I don't think our house will ever be as nice as yours."

"Yeah, well," she said, pulling her lips into a tight, flat line, "there's a lot of things more important than appearances, Jesse."

She said this with such heaviness that I was tempted to ask her if anything was bothering her. But the next moment she tugged her mouth into a smile. "So, Stan's taking me for a trip on his bike this weekend," she said, shuffling against me again. The weight of her body against mine made me want to lean all the way into her, so that there would be no space or cold air separating us at all. "Guess where we're going."

"Where?" I asked, trying to sound enthusiastic.

"We're going to Sheffield, to a Black Sabbath concert."

"Oh."

"Yeah, I know, I know. All that head-banging music's not my cup of tea, either. But it'll be great to get away. Of course," she said, lowering her voice and looking warily down the street, "I haven't told my dad. He doesn't like me having a boyfriend. Doesn't like me doing anything, really." She shrugged. "He thinks I'm staying at a friend's house this weekend. So does Tracey. Don't tell her, will you, Jesse? She'll only go and tell tales to my dad. And then there'll be hell to pay."

"Don't worry, I won't tell her," I said, feeling torn between pleasure at having Amanda confide in me and jealousy at the thought of Amanda clinging tightly to Stan along all those miles of road to Sheffield.

"To tell you the truth, Jesse, I'm really only going so I can get out of the house. I need to . . ."

"What?"

"Oh, nothing." She took a breath and seemed to push something from her thoughts. "It doesn't matter."

"Is it Stan?" I asked. "Have you been arguing?"

"No," she said. "It's not him. Mind you, he has been getting on my nerves."

"He has?" I tried not to sound too gleeful.

"Yeah. Frankly, sometimes he acts almost as full of himself as that bonehead Greg Loomis. And he's dead stupid on his bike sometimes. Scared me to death the other day, he did. He was driving me home from school, and he overtook this car on a bend and there was this lorry coming right at us. He almost had to swerve off the road to miss it. God, Jesse, I tell you, I thought I was going to wet myself I was so frightened."

"Maybe you should take the bus home," I suggested.

"Maybe you're right," she said. "Though sometimes, to tell you the truth, I have a good mind to give him the shove."

"The shove?" I had the sudden image of Amanda standing on a roadside with Stan, pushing him into the path of a speeding lorry.

"You know, pack him in. Break up."

"Really?" It was almost impossible to contain my delight now.

"Yeah," she said, gazing up toward the jagged silhouette of an elm tree that had been stripped bare not by the changing seasons but by Dutch elm disease. It had stood there, overlooking the bus stop and the high street, a sad skeleton among its verdant companions all summer. Now, though, it blended perfectly into the winter landscape, stark against the yellow light of the ascending sun.

"So why don't you? Why don't you give him the shove?"

"It's complicated and, well, I suppose it's because I love him."

"Oh," I said, my voice suddenly thin. "Well, then, of course you can't give him the shove." I turned to look at the disease-ravaged tree, noticing the way its smaller branches reached like knotty fingers pointing to the vast blue sky.

"Of course, you're probably still too young, Jesse, to understand love and all that."

"No, I'm not," I said quietly, still staring at the tree, because I didn't dare to look at Amanda.

I felt her turn to study me, and for a moment I was afraid that she might tease me or, as Tracey or the Debbies would have done if I'd said such a thing to them, interrogate me about which boy at school I was infatuated with. Instead, Amanda reached out and placed her hand gently on my arm. "Yeah," she said, "you're right. You are old enough."

As she touched me, I felt as if I could melt forever in that moment. And I wondered if, despite her declaration of love for Stan, there was a chance that Amanda might soon come to realize that he wasn't the person she deserved. Realizing this, she would also see that I was the only one who truly loved her and, filled with this knowledge, she would have to love me in return. And though we'd have to keep our love secret, because no one else would understand it, the two of us would know that there was nothing terrible about the way we felt. While I had to hide my love from her, it was a terrible, shameful secret. But if Amanda returned my feelings I'd have no reason to be ashamed.

DURING THE LAST WEEK of term, there was a Christmas pantomime, a carol service, and Mr. Davies held a party for his class on the final afternoon. But the social event that elicited the most excited anticipation from Tracey and the Debbies was the disco that would be held on the Saturday before Christmas in the Reatton-on-Sea church hall. Hosted by Reverend Mullins, the vicar of Reatton—who was apparently rather more in touch with current youth culture than his counterpart in Midham—it was an annual event that attracted teenagers from miles around.

I'd been to a couple of school-run discos when I was at Knox Vale—a Halloween party and the Christmas dance—and found them excruciating. While the teachers seemed to think they were giving us an enormous treat, I would far rather have spent all afternoon drawing cross sections of the Humber estuary for Mr. Cuthbertson, memorizing vocabulary for Mr. Knighton, or even playing hockey on the frozen playing field than being herded with two hundred and fifty other students into the dimly lit assembly hall where Gary Glitter, singing "I'm the Leader of the Gang," blared from a couple of speakers on the stage. Standing with the other social rejects in the darkest corner we could find, I'd made myself queasy on fizzy drinks and salted peanuts while I watched the other girls dance in ritualistic circles, all moving in the same rhythm, making the same gestures, following one another's steps. I'd hated those girls, but I'd hated myself more for longing so hard for inclusion in their tight, satisfied little groups. But now, though I still anticipated the Reatton disco with trepidation, the sea change in my social standing meant that I didn't have to await it with utter dread. Besides, after Tracey told me that she and her family were leaving the next day to spend the entire Christmas holidays with her grandparents, who lived in Cleethorpes, I realized that the disco would be the last time I'd be able to see Amanda for a while.

In preparation for this pivotal event, I'd managed to talk my father into buying me a pair of orange bell-bottoms and a yellow-and-beige shirt that I ordered from the Littlewoods catalog that Mabel had left with us during her last visit. On the model in the catalog, of course, the vivid colors and lustrously smooth polyester had looked stunning, and I'd imagined transforming myself into a similarly bold and stylish girl who didn't mind standing out in a crowd. When the clothes arrived, however, the effect was a little less impressive and I couldn't help feeling that their oversized buttons, billowing lines, and glaring brightness only declared my desperation to fit in. Nevertheless, the evening of the disco, I put on my new outfit and my least hideous pair of shoes and readied myself to leave.

When I walked into our newly decorated living room to announce my departure, I was surprised to see my mother sitting in her dressing gown in one of the armchairs, her legs draped over the side of the chair, slippers dangling from her toes. There was a powdery ring of icing sugar around her mouth, evidence that she had joined my father in finishing off the plate of leftover mince pies he'd brought home that evening from the Christmas party at his job. It had been quite a while since I'd seen her under the living room's bright lights, and for the first time I noticed how astonishingly thin and pale she'd become. Her skin had a grayish tinge and seemed pressed tight over her bones, so that her eyes, nose, and chin seemed bigger, more prominent, while her legs, sticking out from under her dressing gown, appeared impossibly white and etched in pale blue veins.

"We got a Christmas card from your grandma today," she said, waving a card at me. It held a picture of a group of beaming children building a snowman. I wondered if my father had used news of this correspondence from Australia to coax my mother out of bed.

"That's nice," I said.

"Yes, well, it's also signed by that bloody Australian gigolo of hers. Look at this," my mother said, opening the card and flapping it at me again. " 'All our love,' it says, 'Mam and Bill.' Like he thinks he's part of the bloody family now." She let go of the card and it fluttered to the floor. "I mean, who the heck does he think he is?"

"It's only a card, Mum. He's only trying to—"

"And where do you think you're going, madam?" she interrupted, giving my new outfit a once-over and again making me doubt the wisdom of my purchase.

"I'm going to a disco," I said calmly, not wanting to aggravate her. If she felt like it, she could easily decide to make me stay at home.

"You're going to a disco?" she repeated, her tone so appalled anyone would have thought I'd just announced that I was planning to attend a get-together of the local Hells Angels. It infuriated me that she could spend literally weeks hidden away in her bedroom with no clue about my daily whereabouts and now, barely out of bed and still in her nightclothes, she was playing the part of a conscientious parent concerned about my moral welfare. "Does your father know?" she asked, implying that if he did he'd put a stop to this outrageous plan.

My father didn't seem to hear her. He was chewing on a mince pie and watching *Look North,* the local news program that always followed the BBC News.

"Yes," I said. "He's picking me up after." Tracey and I planned to walk the two miles to Reatton, but, since the disco didn't end until half past ten and I didn't fancy walking back on a freezing December night, I'd recruited my father to give us a lift home.

"Is he now?" My mother looked to my father for confirmation. As she did so, the *Look North* announcer introduced a report on "a surprise royal visit to South Yorkshire," and my father leaned eagerly toward the television. The screen was filled with the stark silhouette of the gear at a coal mine's pithead, and then the dazed and grinning face of Prince Charles.

"That's it, that's what they should do!" my father yelled, spitting mince-pie crumbs across the carpet and pointing at Prince Charles. "They should send him to work down the bloody mine. That'd bloody teach him." His words were noticeably slurred, and I deduced that there had been more than just a few mince pies consumed at his work's party.

"Dad," I said loudly, hoping to get his attention before he inevitably got into another anti-royalist rant.

"What?"

"Tell Mum you're picking me up after the disco tonight."

"I am?" he said, looking at me, perplexed, before turning back to the television.

"Yes. You're supposed to come and get me. You said you'd take Tracey home as well. Remember?" I gave him a beseeching look.

"Oh, right, yes." Barely taking his eyes off the screen, he reached over and picked up another mince pie. "God, look at him, the bloody tosspot," he said as Prince Charles walked along a line of hard-faced miners' wives, stopping occasionally to shake a hand and exchange a few words.

"At half past ten. You're to pick us up in Reatton, outside the church hall." I pronounced the words in the kind of slow yell that people generally reserved for foreigners, the deaf, and the senile.

"I know, I know. I'll be there," he said.

"See," I said, turning toward my mother. "I told you he was picking me up."

I fully expected her to put some obstacle in my way, to perhaps assert that it just wasn't appropriate for me to go to a late-night event where there'd be loud music and boys, or to suggest that I was bound to catch my death if I ventured out on such a cold night. I was tensed up and ready to do battle. But I didn't have to bother, since she seemed suddenly to have lost any energy for belligerence or pronouncements, or, in fact, anything at all. Instead, she shrugged and pressed herself deeper into her chair, so that, in her newly angular body, her legs dangling over the arm of the chair, I imagined her folding all the way into herself until she disappeared. And though I was relieved that I could escape the house without having to fight my way out, as I looked at my mother I felt afraid. Instead of killing herself, I wondered, could a person just shrink and crumple until she became nothing, until her traits and quirks wasted along with her body, until one day you realized that she had faded away?

I walked over to my mother, leaned down toward her, and kissed her on the cheek. "Bye, Mum. See you later," I said, letting myself take in the texture of her skin against my lips and her pungent body smells. At least for now, she was still solidly herself.

I thought about going over to kiss my father, too. But, as the *Look North* reporter waxed lyrical about how "so near to Christmas, the gift of a royal visit has lifted everyone's spirits in this little mining town," and my father hurled his mince pie toward the television screen so that it landed with a *splat* right in Prince Charles's face, I decided it was best to leave him alone to his seasonal enjoyment.

CHAPTER FIFTEEN

———

REVEREND MULLINS WAS ONE OF THOSE TRENDY VICARS, THE KIND I'd seen only on television. He wore his dog collar under a wrinkled corduroy jacket and atop a pair of carefully pressed jeans, and bore a fixed, beatific smile that made him look, in the words of several of the kids at the disco, "a bit retarded." He wandered around, enthusiastically greeting the teenagers under his supervision, slapping backs, nudging ribs, patting shoulders, and infusing his conversation with liberal use of words like "cool" and "wow." He was like a new kid at school, so desperate to impress that he was oblivious to the disdainful looks and mumbled insults he managed to provoke everywhere he went.

When Tracey and I finally arrived at the Reatton church hall, our ten-pence admission in hand, he greeted us with a painfully sincere smile, told us how wonderful it was to see young people turn out for a church event, and said how very much he hoped we'd make it to the Sunday service and the special teenagers' Sunday school class afterward. "And maybe you two young ladies will consider coming on the trip to Lincoln Cathedral in January," he added. "It has some amazing stained glass, and the choir is simply wonderful."

"Right, I bet it is," Tracey said, looking in my direction and rolling her eyes. I made a similarly scornful expression. From down the corridor, we could hear the thump-thump-thump of the disco music. Neither of us wanted to stay here at the door making polite conversation with the vicar.

"Oh, yes, they're very cool," he continued earnestly. "Now, I don't know if you've ever thought of joining a choir yourselves, but I'm putting one together here in Reatton and I'm sure you two young ladies have angelic voices. . . ."

Tracey gave another impatient roll of her eyes, then interrupted. "Look, Vicar," she said as she crossed her legs and began shuffling about noisily in her immense platform shoes. "I've got to take a piss something rotten. And if I don't get to the toilet right now, I swear I'm gonna wet myself. So, if you don't mind—"

"Oh, no, by all means, you should . . ." he stuttered, his face turning a startling shade of crimson. "Erm . . . it's down the hallway, through the cloakroom door, and then to your left."

"I hope I can make it," Tracey said, jigging about even more and pressing her legs together so tight that it looked as if her knees might buckle under her.

I concentrated on trying to stop myself from giggling, pressing my lips together and my face into fierce contortions until, thankfully, Tracey grabbed my arm and pulled me down the corridor after her. As soon as we plunged through the cloakroom door, she relaxed her needing-to-pee stance and spat out a loud wide-mouthed laugh. I laughed along with her.

"God, what a wanker," she declared. "Who the hell does that bloody vicar think he is? Jesus bloody Christ himself?"

"He's a fucking poofter, that's what he is." It was Stan Heaphy. He leaned lazily against the cloakroom wall, gesturing with a lighted cigarette under a big, hand-lettered sign that read, "No Smoking, Please!" In his other hand he held a bottle of Johnny Walker Red Label whiskey. He tipped the bottle to his mouth, his Adam's apple moving visibly in his throat as he *glug-glugged* the liquid down.

"You think so, Stan?" asked Greg Loomis. He stood among a group of boys assembled around Stan. He was dressed in a billowy orange shirt undone almost to his navel, a pair of trousers with an enormous, multibuttoned waistband, and platform shoes that made his legs look disconcertingly long. Upon catching sight of this paragon of male style, Tracey took a sharp breath and issued an elbow to my side.

I ignored her and instead looked about urgently to see if Amanda was there. Unfortunately, all I could see aside from the throng of boys surrounding Stan was a single empty bench in the middle of the room and the open door to the girls' toilet beyond. Clearly, Amanda was elsewhere. Upon realizing this, my first instinct was to drape my coat on the nearest hanger and leave the cloakroom to Stan and his little gang, but when I turned toward Tracey to see her gazing at Greg with the most pathetically adoring expression on her face, I realized it was unlikely we'd depart the cloakroom soon.

"Tell them poofs a fucking mile off, you can," Stan declared, lazily wiping his mouth on the sleeve of his leather jacket before handing the bottle to Greg.

"Really? You think so, Stan?" Greg asked again. He grabbed the bottle and took an enthusiastic swig, screwing his face up and almost choking as he swallowed it down, prompting several of the boys around him to laugh. Tracey turned to scowl at them.

"Only a fucking poofter would want to be a vicar," Stan pontificated, sucking on his cigarette and then forcing the smoke out through his turned-down mouth. "I mean, who else would want to ponce around in a white dress on Sundays? What do you think he's recruiting a choir for? So he can slip it to one of the choirboys afterward, that's why. You want to fucking watch him. Turn your back on him and he'll stick it up your arse in a second." He made a sweeping gesture with his cigarette and launched it toward the buttocks of a pudgy-faced younger boy. The boy had entered the cloakroom a few moments earlier and, his back to Stan, was hanging his coat on one of the hooks on the wall. The cigarette end landed against his backside, sending out a small shower of sparks and ash. Everyone around him burst into fits of bellowing laugh-

ter. I didn't know his name, but I recognized him from school. He was
a first-year, and I'd sometimes seen him eating at the same table as
Malcolm and Dizzy in the dining hall.

"Bloody hell!" the boy yelled as he leaped away, dancing around the
cloakroom while he brushed frantically at the seat of his pants. Stan,
Greg, and the rest of their friends roared, doubling over and slapping
one another on the back as they watched. Next to me, Tracey giggled,
digging me with her elbow again as the boy tried to look over his shoulder to assess the state of his rear end. Though I was determined not to
find anything that Stan Heaphy did amusing, I couldn't help laughing.
After all, the boy looked ludicrous, leaping around like a character in a
slapstick comedy.

"Christ almighty," the boy said when he'd managed to ascertain that
his trousers weren't on fire. "What the hell did you have to do that for?
These are brand-new bloody trousers. If you've scorched them, my
mam will kill me."

His trousers, with their unfaded fabric and perfect creases, did
look new. But the rest of his clothes—frayed denim jacket, shrunken
sweater, and scuffed shoes—looked sad and worn. He didn't look as if
he came from the kind of family that could afford to replace clothes
easily. I felt a fierce pang of guilt for having joined in his humiliation at
the hands of Stan.

"Just trying to teach you a lesson, Ken, that's all," Stan said, stepping
over to where the cigarette still burned on the floor and grinding
it under one of his black Dr. Martens boots. "It's for your own good.
Got to keep an eye out for those poofter types. Can't turn your
back for a second. I mean, not with a delicious chubby little arse like
yours." There was another ripple of laughter. This time I did not
join in.

Greg, whose laugh was by far the loudest, slapped Stan on the back.
"Good one, Stan. Hah, that's a bloody good one," he brayed, hooking
his arm over Stan's shoulder and leaning into him so closely that he was
almost hanging off Stan.

"Yeah, Stan, that was a good one," Tracey echoed, gazing hopefully at Greg.

Grabbing the whiskey from Greg and shrugging him off, Stan took another long drink, removing at least an inch of the copper liquid from the bottle. As soon as he finished, he let out a theatrically loud belch and grinned proudly at the crowd assembled around him. Then he handed the bottle back to Greg, folded his arms, and regarded Ken with an arcing grin. "What's up? Getting poked in the arse like that, did it bother you, Kenny boy?" The joking tone was gone from his voice, and his words came out in a slow and lazy snarl. I saw the muscles in Ken's face tighten. He glanced at Stan's face and then toward the door. I noticed how the air in the room felt stale with cigarette smoke and the heat of all those jostling boys' bodies. Like Ken, I wanted to get out.

"More like nancy boy," Greg Loomis crowed.

"Yeah, he's definitely a nancy boy," Tracey agreed, barking out an awkward, overloud laugh. "A fat little nancy boy." Her eyes darted over to Greg, and for a moment her features seemed stung with intense neediness.

"Yeah, he's got to be a fucking poofter," Stan said. "Doesn't like me messing with him 'cause he'd prefer it up the arse from the vicar, wouldn't you, nancy boy?"

"That's not true," Ken said, his voice flimsy and suddenly higher, precipitating an immediate chorus of vociferous laughter—the boys, mouths wide, lips curled, showing teeth and tongues and gums, and Tracey, clapping her hands together as she tossed her head back. I took a step back from the heaving circle, aware of how the stillness of my own face and my secrets set me apart.

"That's not true," Stan mimicked, making his own voice high-pitched and jiggling his head from side to side.

"But it's not." Ken seemed to find some anger within himself, raising his fists so that I thought he actually might try to hit Stan. I felt myself willing him to do it, even though I knew it would be a hopeless endeavor. At least then there'd be someone willing to defy Stan, to go down fighting. But Ken kept his fists clenched close to his chest, and under Stan's sneering gaze he soon dropped them to his sides. "Just don't do that again," he said weakly, pressing his lips into a pout. "You shouldn't do things like that. It's not right." Then he turned and scuttled toward the door.

I had already decided to follow Ken out. The little room felt as if it was getting smaller—I was dizzy with the bellowing laughter, with the smoke and sweat and alcohol smell. But just as Ken, head down, shoulders hunched, was pushing past one of the grinning boys, Tracey piped up.

"You hear that, Stan?" she said, her voice stark and bitingly shrill. "He went and threatened you. You're not going to let him get away with that, are you?" Her features were fiery, animated. The desperate look I'd seen only seconds earlier was replaced by a glistening appetite in her eyes. "Go on, get him, Stan, teach him a lesson. Shouldn't let a fat little fairy like him show you up."

"She's right, Stan," Greg said, looking directly at Tracey. "We should teach the little dickhead not to talk to you like that."

As Ken reached for the door handle, one of the boys closest to him grabbed his hand and jerked it away. Then, in a single movement, he twisted Ken's arm around his back. Ken gasped, grimaced, and cried out. The blood drained from his features like liquid poured away.

"Not so bloody fast, you chubby little poof," Greg said, striding toward Ken. As he moved past Tracey, he handed the whiskey bottle to her.

"Show him, Greg," Tracey said, almost breathless. She looked utterly focused, gleeful in her rage. "Show him that he needs to watch what comes out of his big fat gob." She gestured toward Ken with the bottle.

Greg took over the hold on Ken's arm from the other boy and marched him toward Stan. Across the room, Stan took out another cigarette, lit it with a flourish, and tossed the burning match to the floor. He took a long, languorous drag, the calm in his movements belied by the greedy anticipation in his eyes.

"Stop it, stop it," Ken wailed, squirming loosely against Greg's grip. "I haven't done anything to you." His body contorted, with his arm still twisted high up behind his back, he looked awkwardly at the gawping crowd. All the boys, leaning into one another, were a single shuddering wall of laughter, angled limbs, blotchy skin, and oversized hands. When I caught the eye of one of the older boys—long-faced, with a strand of greasy hair falling over his forehead—I felt the cold heat of his stare press into me and I looked away, knowing that he could see my fear.

Having marched Ken across the room, Greg released his grip and shoved him toward Stan. "Hello there, Kenny boy," Stan said. "Back so soon?"

"Just . . . just, let me go, Stan. I'm sorry—really, I am. I . . . I . . . didn't mean to bother you." Ken's voice was so shaky he was almost stuttering.

"But, see, there's your problem right there, Ken," Stan said, shaking his head and letting out a long sigh. "See, fat little poofs like you—well, they always bother me. I know you can't help it, Kenny, but the trouble is, no matter what you do you just get on my fucking nerves."

"Yeah, you get on everybody's nerves, actually, Ken," Greg agreed.

"So, Ken," Stan said, sucking on his cigarette and then waving it in the air over Ken's head. "What do you think the right kind of punishment for you would be?"

Ken, looking upward at the cigarette, didn't answer.

I wanted to rescue him. I really did. I wanted, more than anything, the courage to speak out, to release my fury against Stan. But I also knew that speaking out would make me a target. And perhaps then they would somehow see all the things about me that had so far gone unnoticed. After all, if I stood up for Ken, who everyone thought was a fat poof, a hideous little nancy boy, what did that say about me? In my panic, I looked at Tracey. Perhaps this was enough for her, too. Perhaps she hadn't thought that things would go so far. Surely, now she saw that Stan might really hurt Ken, she would want it to stop? But when I looked into her face her features were energized, ravenous, like someone watching a late-night suspense film, utterly transported, thrilled. She put the whiskey bottle that Greg had handed to her to her lips, tipped it back, and took a swig. Her face twisted as she drank down the copper liquid, then, as she let the bottle drop to her side, her eyes blazed wider and her cheeks were bathed in a sudden flush.

Stan took another puff on his cigarette and then, this time, as he exhaled a breath of thick gray smoke, he moved the cigarette deliberately, slowly, until its burning end was just a couple of inches from Ken's cheek. "Feel the heat, Kenny?" he said, easing the cigarette closer still to Ken's face.

There was a single snort of awkward laughter among the surrounding boys, and then an empty perilous silence against the insistent beat of disco music coming from down the hall. The beat merged with the throb of my pulse in my temples. My mouth felt dry, my whole body frozen and breathless, as I watched Ken's horrified eyes blinking rapidly, his eyelashes fluttering like tiny, nervous wings.

Stan pulled the cigarette away and everyone sucked in a breath. As he took a drag, I noticed a couple of the boys shuffle awkwardly, eyeing Stan and then the door. "Hey, Stan," one of them said warily, "maybe you should take it easy. I mean, the vicar's only just down the hall."

"Yeah, Stan," said another. "You don't want him to chuck us out."

Ken, apparently sensing a shift in the mood of the room, began to back away.

"Like I give a fuck," Stan said as he reached out and grabbed Ken by the arm. "Not so fast, Kenny boy." And then, in a swift and unexpected movement, he plunged his cigarette toward Ken's face.

I stood motionless, unable to move. Ken let out a sound like a bleat, and, his face crumpling like a piece of balled-up paper, he stumbled backward and began to heave out jagged, thunderous sobs.

"Shit, Stan," one of the boys said as the room was filled with the acrid scent of burned hair. "Did you burn his face? You'll get the fucking cops on you if you burned his face."

For a moment, Stan's face was a mask of joyous fury, his eyes narrowed and still and filled with delight. Then, as if pulled from a dream, his expression changed. "He's all right," he said, eyeing Ken. "You're all right, aren't you, Ken?" He put his hand on Ken's shoulder and pulled him upward. "See, I didn't touch him," he said, pointing at Ken's damp but apparently undamaged cheek. The cigarette must only have burned a wayward strand of hair.

At that moment, the door swung open and everyone turned to see who had come in. Even Stan bore a look of alarm. I had a sudden jolt of hope, desperate for rescue by the vicar or one of the other adults supervising the evening's activities. My hope plunged as Malcolm and Dizzy walked into the room.

Oblivious at first to the scene they had intruded upon, they were talking in fast and excited tones, their features animated. They were all blazing color, Dizzy in a knee-length red velvet dress that settled over her body like a billowing crimson cloud, Malcolm in a pair of pastel blue trousers and a shocking-pink satin shirt. In that first moment I saw them, I felt a streak of envy as bright as their clothes—for the normality that they still occupied, while I stood there horrified. But I saw their faces plummet as they took in the scene around them, and I felt the dread inside me swell.

"Oh, look," Tracey sneered. "It's four-eyes and her little fairy friend. What you two doing here? Close the freak show early, did they?"

Greg chuckled. "Hah, freak show—yeah, that's a good one."

Tracey beamed. Malcolm and Dizzy exchanged looks.

"You all right, Ken?" Malcolm asked.

"He . . . he . . . he tried to burn me. With his cigarette." Ken gestured shakily toward Stan.

Malcolm looked at Stan, his expression a mixture of confusion and anger. "Jesus Christ!" He began to move toward Ken, past the line of silent onlookers. "Come on, Ken," he said, his voice soft and soothing. "Maybe we should get you out of here, eh?"

"Mind your own fucking business, you fucking fairy," Stan said.

"Ken's my friend. It *is* my business," Malcolm said. "And if you tried to burn Ken, that's the police's business."

Stan laughed, but this time he seemed uneasy, taking a hasty drag on his cigarette. "Who the hell do you think you are? Policeman Plod? More like Sergeant Fairy. Look at you—you're a fucking embarrassment." He reached over and tugged on one of the flouncy sleeves of Malcolm's shirt. "Who the hell bought this? Your mummy? Maybe next time she can send you out in a nice frilly little dress." At this, the other boys sniggered. "But for fuck's sake don't take any fashion advice from this ugly slag," Stan continued, nodding toward Dizzy. "Put a paper bag on her head and even Greg here still wouldn't shag her. Right, Greg?" He slapped Greg across the shoulder.

"Of course I wouldn't shag her," Greg huffed.

"You're both fucking weirdos," Stan said.

"Nobody asked for your opinion," Malcolm responded.

"Nobody asked for your opinion," Stan imitated, making his voice high and flapping his wrist. He began mincing about the room. "Because I'm a little poof," he continued in the high, ridiculous voice. "And I'm just here to spoil everybody else's fun." He stopped and leaned his face into Malcolm's. "Just what do you think you're doing?" he said, resuming his normal snarl.

"I'm taking Ken here into the other room," Malcolm replied. "And I think it'd be wise to let me. Otherwise, we might have to talk to the police. With your reputation, Stan Heaphy, I doubt they'd show much sympathy for you."

Stan seemed jarred. As Malcolm edged past him, Stan didn't even try to stop him. The boys gathered around were nervous again, cowed by the mention of the police.

I was amazed at Malcolm's daring. A reedy wisp next to Stan's leather-clad bulk, he was defiant, propelled by something that seemed to make him impervious to fear. When he reached Ken, he put an arm around his shoulder and began to guide him toward the door.

"Aw, isn't that sweet, they're giving each other a girlie hug," Greg sneered. Tracey giggled.

"God, what is wrong with you?" Malcolm said. His eyes swept the room. "Is this funny to you? Scaring people? Hurting them? Making them cry? Calling them names just because they're different, because they're not like you? It's pathetic!" I looked away, my fear almost completely replaced by shame.

"No," Stan said, stepping in front of Malcolm again. "You're pathetic, you scrawny little poof. You and blubber-faced fatty here. And you'll be even more pathetic once I've beat the fucking shit out of you." He took a final drag on his cigarette and tossed it over his shoulder so that one of the boys behind him had to duck to avoid getting hit in the face by the still burning butt. Then he rolled his right hand into a fist and pressed his left palm over his folded fingers so that his knuckles sounded an aching crack.

I could see now the fear in Malcolm's features—in the clench of his jaw, the taut skin around his mouth, the bloom of sweat across his forehead. I was amazed that he didn't flinch or try to get away. Instead, he kept looking steadily into Stan's face and pulled himself broader, taller, announcing his bright and satiny presence without shame.

"Get him, Greg," Tracey urged, gesturing toward Malcolm with the whiskey bottle.

Greg puffed up his chest and curled his lip. "You're in for it now, you little poof."

Tracey beamed proudly at Greg, and then, as if toasting his bravado, she lifted the bottle to her lips to take a swig. Unfortunately, she tipped back the bottle with a little too much force, taking in a larger mouthful of whiskey than she'd anticipated, so that almost as soon as she tried to swallow she choked, coughed, and sputtered out most of the liquid in Greg and Stan's direction.

"Fucking hell!" Stan shouted, jumping back as a shower of Tracey's whiskey spittle hit him. "Christ almighty, don't drink that fucking stuff if you can't take it."

A smile tugged at the edge of my lips as I watched Stan brush at the spatters on his jacket and Greg frantically wipe the whiskey that had hit him in the eyes. For a second, I looked across at Malcolm. Our eyes met only briefly, but in that moment I felt as if he saw into me—my hatred of Stan and the agony I felt at witnessing this scene. He looked away toward Dizzy. She was moving slowly backward, toward the door.

"God, I'm sorry, Stan, I really am," Tracey said, trying to help wipe his jacket.

Stan pushed her away. "Stupid fucking bitch," he muttered.

Tracey stepped back, swinging the whiskey bottle in my direction. Without even thinking, I reached for it. "Here, Trace, I'll take that for you," I said. I grabbed the bottle with loose enthusiasm, swinging it widely so that, with the bottle's mouth pointed outward, whiskey splashed in a wide, liquid arc around the room.

"Jesus! Fuck! Shit! Christ almighty!" A chorus of expletives sounded as everyone around me was doused with a generous spray of whiskey. And then a chaos of churning bodies and flailing limbs as boys wiped dripping liquid from their faces and pushed wet hair out of their eyes.

"Jesse, you idiot!" Tracey yelled, rubbing at the splotches darkening the fabric of her blouse.

"Yeah, she's a fucking idiot, all right," Stan barked. "There's hardly any fucking drink left, and that fat bitch has got away." In the anarchy prompted by the whiskey shower, Dizzy had fled the cloakroom.

"You think she's going to tell the vicar, Stan?" Greg asked.

Stan rolled his eyes. "Where do you think she's gone, you fucking bonehead? To powder her fucking nose? Of course she's gone to tell the vicar."

"Christ," Greg said. "I hope he doesn't chuck us out."

"I'm not worried about that," another boy added. "I just hope he doesn't phone my dad." At this, a disconcerted mumble traveled around the room.

"I'm sorry, Stan," I said. "I didn't mean to . . ." I let my words fade as Stan turned to look at Malcolm and Ken.

"You breathe a fucking word about someone trying to burn you, Kenny," he snarled, "and I promise you that I will make you sorry you were ever fucking born. Besides, everybody here will say it was you that was causing trouble, right, lads?"

Everyone around me nodded.

"I won't say anything, Stan, I promise," Ken said. "Malcolm won't say anything, either, will you, Malcolm?" When Malcolm remained stonily silent, Ken tugged on his arm. "Don't say anything, Malcolm. Please. I don't want any trouble. And Stan didn't really hurt me. It was just an accident."

"All right, Ken. For you, I won't say anything."

Relieved, Ken scurried toward the exit. But Malcolm paused before he made to leave, sweeping the room with a look of disgust. When his eyes finally met mine, I thought I detected a subtle shift in his expression—a hint of curiosity and, possibly, recognition—before he turned away and marched out the door.

THE ROOM IN WHICH the disco was held had that oppressive, institutional feeling that comes with khaki-green walls and narrow windows that have been painted forever closed. It was stuffy and crowded and its innate dust and disinfectant odors blended with the smell of bodies and breath. In the front, on a stage backed by a banner that read FRIDAY NIGHT IS BINGO NIGHT: JOIN US AT THE REATTON DERBY AND JOAN CLUB, the dj stood behind a console of three colored lights that flashed in rhythm to the thumping music. Most of the dancers were girls assembled in little circles on the dance floor. The boys flanked the walls, their hands stuffed into their pockets, their heads bobbing with the music's beat.

Tracey and I wandered out of the cloakroom and found the Debbies sitting on a row of chairs near the stage. Dressed in full Bay City

Rollers regalia (tartan-trimmed jackets and half-mast trousers, tartan socks and shiny platform boots), they were easy to spot. "Where the heck have you two been?" demanded Debbie Masters.

"Getting a bloody lecture from the vicar," Tracey responded, plunking herself down in one of the empty chairs. I sat down beside her.

"Why? What happened?" All three of the Debbies looked eagerly toward us.

Tracey rolled her eyes. "This idiot," she said, sticking her elbow in my side, "managed to spray whiskey round the entire room. So when the vicar comes in it smells like a bloody brewery. God, you should have heard him go on and on."

"It wasn't my fault," I protested. "And it wasn't me who brought the whiskey here in the first place. Besides, the vicar was just as bothered about the smoking—"

"Oh, shut up, Jesse," Tracey snapped.

I felt stung. "No need to be like that. If Stan and Greg hadn't started trouble in the first place, if they hadn't been picking on Ken—"

"Don't you say a word against Greg! Him and me were getting on great until you went and ruined everything."

"But I didn't mean to," I said weakly.

Of course, Stan and Greg hadn't been very happy with me, either. As soon as Malcolm and Ken left the cloakroom, Stan commanded me to put the top on the whiskey bottle and hide it, saying, "I don't fucking care where you put it—up your bloody arse, for all I mind. But if I get the blame from the fucking vicar, you'll be getting the blame from me." Almost tripping over myself, I'd scrambled to find somewhere to stow the bottle. The only real place to hide anything in the otherwise bare cloakroom was among the coats hanging all around the wall, and I'd shoved it into my own coat pocket and then pulled the other coats over it to hide it from view in time for Reverend Mullins's entry. Not that I needed to be afraid, since Reverend Mullins's idea of discipline was to subject us to a cheery little pep talk about how turning to God would provide us with far more solace than could ever be found in alcohol and how, though smoking might seem "cool" to us teenagers, it really wasn't "cool with Jesus." He delivered his lecture to a chorus of scornful snorts and barely suppressed giggles, and, upon suggesting that we might want to attend the Christmas Day service, by Stan's bellowed, derisive laughter. At this, the vicar seemed finally to understand that he needed to take a firmer hand and concluded his chat by telling us, "If I hear so much as a whisper of trouble tonight, I'll have the police down here as fast as you can say 'Jack Robinson,' and your parents on the phone within five minutes of that."

Fortunately for me, the vicar had prattled on for so long that by the time he was finished, everyone seemed to have forgotten that it was my apparent clumsiness that had saddled us with this lecture. Spirits deflated by the prospect of having the local constabulary swoop down on them, Stan, Greg, and the rest of the boys drifted sulkily out of the cloakroom into the main hall.

"I'm sorry, Trace," I said, pressing my hand against her arm. "But, really, don't you think things went a bit too far with Ken? I mean, he really could've got hurt."

"Oh, for God's sake, Jesse, don't be so bloody stupid. I mean, what kind of idiot cares about pudgy-faced little Ken? Never mind that ugly pervert Malcolm Clements. Me and Greg were getting on really good in there. Didn't you see? And then you had to go and spoil it."

"I'm sorry," I said again, terrified of the anger that showed in Tracey's face. "I didn't mean to." I tugged against her sleeve and looked at her imploringly, but she simply pressed her eyes into burning slits and turned away.

For most of the evening, Tracey and the Debbies ignored me. When they got up to dance with all the other girls, I wasn't invited. When Tracey went to buy pop and crisps, she asked the Debbies what they wanted but didn't even look my way. While the four of them huddled together to chat, not only was I not included but, from the way the Debbies kept snickering in my direction, I got the distinct impression they were talking about me.

This was it, I realized. I had fallen from grace. I couldn't believe how stupid I'd been. If I'd only stood by and done nothing, Tracey wouldn't be angry at me. She was right—why should I care about Kevin or Malcolm? They weren't the people I wanted to be my friends. I could see them now, across the dance floor, in their pathetic little group. Dizzy and Malcolm dancing together, as mismatched and comical as Laurel and Hardy—Dizzy gyrating around in her big velvet sack while Malcolm, head thrown back and eyes half closed, pranced about like a pixie. From the sidelines, his eyes still swollen from crying, Kevin watched them enthralled. Everyone else thought they looked ridiculous. Being laughed at like that, being made the butt of everybody's jokes, was awful; it was the worst thing I could imagine. Except, I thought as I watched Malcolm spinning round and round, what if you really didn't care? What if you were somehow able to let the mocking slide off you? What if it made no difference to you at all? For a moment, I felt the possibility touch me, the idea of that solidity, that confidence—knowing you were different but embracing it, occupying it, and being utterly immune to the derision or hatred of anyone else. But then, when Malcolm toppled outward, fell against another boy, and the boy shoved him away so that he staggered back and hit Dizzy, I felt that possibility fall away. No matter how carefree you might be, there was always someone on the sidelines wanting to push you around.

SHAKEN BY THE SCENE that had played out in the cloakroom and cold-shouldered by Tracey, I felt my longing for Amanda's presence intensify. I watched the entrance of the dance hall, willing her to arrive. When she finally entered the room, she looked stunning, wearing a calf-length emerald-green dress made of a thin, silky material that draped itself in shiny folds over her frame and infallibly outlined her impressive curves. Her hair, styled so that it rippled back from her face in shiny waves, was crowned by a tiara she'd fashioned out of silver

Christmas tree tinsel. Even in the dimly lit hall, her features were bright and flushed, as if she had only just come in from the cold. My stomach turned somersaults at the sight of her. The air seemed to crackle around her, as if charged. As she moved, all the eyes in the room followed her.

"God, look at the bloody state of her," Tracey said. "She looks like a bloody Christmas tree gone wrong. Should stick some bloody ornaments on her fat backside—that'd complete the picture perfectly."

"I think she looks fantastic," I said.

"Fantastic? Maybe to an idiot without any fashion sense," Tracey huffed.

I felt myself shrink, but then my heart began to race as Amanda veered away from her friends and toward us.

"Don't bother us, Amanda," Tracey said. "We've got better things to do than talk to you."

"Didn't come to talk to you, did I?" Amanda said. Her words slid together, and she had a glazed, loose look on her face. "Came to see Jesse." She turned to look at me, and as she did, her dress swished around her, a glossy emerald wave. "Having a good time?" she asked, giving me a broad but slightly slack smile.

"Yes, it's all right," I said, barely able to get the words out.

"Good, that's good." She wrinkled up her nose and moved her head up and down in a jerky nod.

"Yes," I agreed, searching desperately for something interesting or amusing to say.

"You had a dance yet, then?"

I shook my head. "I can't really dance."

"Can't dance?" She furrowed her brow. "Don't be daft!" She batted at the air with her hand, stumbling forward slightly.

"You're drunk!" Tracey declared, flashing Amanda a contemptuous look.

"No, I'm not. And it wouldn't be any business of yours if I was. Anyway, Stan already told me you had a go at his whiskey earlier, so don't be such a bloody hypocrite."

"At least I didn't spray most of the bottle around the room."

Amanda laughed. "Yeah, I heard about that, Jesse. Managed to piss Stan off, you did. Don't worry, though. I told him not to get his knickers in a twist. He's got a couple of dozen more where that bottle came from. Got them dead cheap, from a mate of his. He brought three bottles with him tonight. Stashed the rest outside near his motorbike. We've been having a bit of a booze-up outside. Had to come in, though. It's bloody freezing now out there."

I wondered if Stan had told Amanda about the rest of the happenings in the cloakroom, about his efforts to burn Ken with his cigarette or his threats to Malcolm and Dizzy. I wondered what Amanda would think if she knew. She'd been quick to jump to my defense when Tracey and the other kids at the bus stop had been tormenting me; maybe she would be angry at Stan for being a bully, too. For a moment, I considered telling her. But while I wanted nothing more than to convince her of Stan's unworthiness, the experience in the cloakroom had left me fearful of him. He was capable of really hurting someone, and capable of enjoying it. I didn't want to give him a reason to want to burn me with his cigarette.

Abruptly, the music changed. Apparently, the dj, whose last several records had been a series of chirpy melodies, had decided on a change of mood, and the booming bass of the Rolling Stones' "Satisfaction" sounded out across the room.

"Oh, come on, Jesse, you've got to dance to this." Amanda gestured toward me.

"Me? Dance?"

"Yeah. Come on," she said, reaching over to grab my arm. "Don't be shy."

"But I can't, I . . ." I wanted to explain that, after my parents, I was one of the most inept dancers in the world, that I'd only embarrass myself beyond hope if I were to try to get up and follow her. At the same time, though, I longed to glide onto the dance floor with Amanda. Hadn't I written about it in my letter to her? Surely I wasn't going to let this chance go by?

"Oh, come on, don't be daft." She pulled on my arm, moved backward unsteadily, and I let her drag me after her, into the crowd.

She pulled me into the center of the floor and, letting go of my hand, closed her eyes, tossed back her head, and started to dance. While the music pulsed and swam, I stood there watching her. She moved within a shimmering sheen of green, clapping her hands, swaying her hips, moving her feet in time to the music's rhythm, her face—eyes still closed—rapt. She was utterly mesmerizing.

"Come on, Jesse," she said, opening her eyes, looking indignant. "You can't just stand there, you've got to dance." She moved closer.

"I can't dance, I—"

"Everybody can dance!" she yelled over the pounding music. "Come on!" She grabbed my arm and started to swing it.

I wanted to do this, but at the same time I had never felt so self-conscious in my entire life. I started to sway unsteadily from one foot to the other. "That's it," Amanda said, smiling enthusiastically. She dropped my arm and I moved beside her, all uncoordinated limbs. I knew I looked completely ridiculous, and right then I would have run from the dance floor if I'd thought I could do it without her noticing. Except, after a minute or so, I felt something shift. The dance floor had become more crowded. We were surrounded by dark and moving bodies in a flashing half-light. No one was paying attention to either me or Amanda. Within that hot cavern of energy and bodies, it was almost as if we were alone. I felt myself begin to loosen as the bass flowed through me, and, as I did, I remembered the way Malcolm had danced—unrestrained, oblivious to everyone around him even though he clearly had no rhythm at all. As I thought about him, I found that I, too, could let myself fall into a similar oblivion, into the sensation of

Amanda beside me, the brush of her dress against my hand, the enraptured expression on her face.

When the record ended, she fell against me, laughing and panting. "See, I knew you'd like it," she said, wrapping an arm around my shoulder and leaning into me. Her breath was hot; it made me shudder, a thread of electric energy that bristled through me. "I knew you'd like to dance with me," she said, pushing her lips closer, so that I felt them brush against my ear.

As I made my way back through the crowd, I felt the urge to throw my arms in the air, to yell, to celebrate. I had danced with Amanda. I felt light, buoyant, as if my body were made of nothing but air.

"What the heck are you grinning about?" Tracey demanded as I took my seat beside her once again.

"Nothing," I said, "I just . . . I just really like this song." The dj was playing something raucous, with a lot of crashing guitars.

"It's rubbish. And if he keeps playing all this loud stuff I'll never get a chance to dance with Greg. Of course, with you messing things up with him, Jesse, he'll never ask me to dance."

"Tracey, I'm sorry." I put my hand on Tracey's arm. She shrugged it away.

I felt a flash of hatred—for Tracey, for her stupidity for caring about an idiot like Greg Loomis, while she found it so easy to cast me aside. But, almost as soon as the hatred came, I felt a surge of desperation. I needed Tracey.

"You're not being fair, Trace," I said, detesting the whine in my voice, wanting, in fact, to slap some sense into her, to tell her to stop being so petty and cruel.

"Life's not fair, Jesse," she said.

For the rest of the evening, I sat nursing the hope that Amanda might ask me to dance again. My hope finally expired, though, when the dj switched to playing slow songs, and I saw Stan swagger across the room, take Amanda's hand, and pull her onto the dance floor. Then, together, they shuffled about, Amanda's arms around Stan's neck, her head resting dozily against his shoulder while he wrapped his arms around her waist and let his hands rest on the curve of her buttocks.

I couldn't stand to watch them, and for a moment I let myself imagine stomping across the floor, pulling Stan away, kicking him, knocking him down. But this fantasy was just as futile as all my others, and so, rather than torture myself further, I stood up and threaded my way through the dancing couples toward the cloakroom. When I stepped inside, I was surprised to find Greg Loomis sitting on one of the low benches, smoking. He rolled his eyes when he saw me. "You! Thanks to you, I still smell like a fucking booze factory. Ruined my bloody chances with the lasses, you have. I should give you a fucking good hiding. I should—"

"I didn't think you'd be so brave without Stan Heaphy to back you up," I said. Instead of feeling afraid, I just felt irritated. The things that were bothering me were far more significant that Greg Loomis.

"Hey, if you don't watch it—" He began to rise from the bench.

"God," I said, past caring, "you think you're such a big, bloody man. And you can't even see what's in front of your face."

"What you talking about?"

"My friend, that girl that was in here earlier. Tracey Grasby. She really fancies you."

He dropped to the bench again, taken aback. "Really?"

"Yes," I said, wanting to add that he had to be blind as well as vain and immensely stupid if he hadn't seen it himself.

He took a thoughtful puff on his cigarette. "This your idea of a joke? Because if it is, I'll—"

"Look, all I know is she might stop her nonstop talking about you if you just go out there and ask her to dance."

"Oh." He took another drag on the cigarette, held it in, frowned deeply, then blew the smoke out in a fast stream. "Well, maybe I will, then," he said, dropping his cigarette to the floor and standing up to make his way to the door. Before he left the cloakroom, though, he stopped to look in the mirror at the end of the coat pegs. He patted his hair smooth with both hands, straightened his eyebrows with a moistened finger, and turned his face to admire his profile. "All right, Greg," he said, smiling at his reflection. "Go out there and knock her dead."

When he was gone, I sank to the bench, listening to the music echoing down the corridor and realizing that the outcome of this evening had been inevitable from the start. It was stupid of me to even think that I could fit in here. I was a misfit and a failure, and even when I tried my best to buy the right clothes and be like the other girls it was still obvious that I didn't belong. Tracey hated me, Amanda was dancing with the hideous Stan, and here was I, again, pathetic and alone.

When I heard the music stop, I stood up, pulled on my coat, and pushed my way into the corridor. Staring glumly at the linoleum floor, I didn't notice that someone had just stepped out of the door that led into the boys' toilet until I almost bumped into him. When I looked up, I found myself face to face with Malcolm. Still flushed from all his exertions on the dance floor, his hair was damp and plastered across his forehead, and I could see tiny beads of perspiration at his temples.

"Excuse me," I said instinctively as I started to edge around him.

"Hey." He grabbed at my arm.

"What?"

"I just wanted to say, well, thanks for helping out earlier—you know, in there." He gestured toward the cloakroom door.

Just then, I heard a loud peal of laughter echo down the corridor. I looked over to see Tracey marching toward us.

"That was really quick thinking, I—"

"I don't know what you're talking about," I interrupted.

"But you . . . I saw you."

"I said, I don't know what you're talking about," I repeated, pulling my arm out of his grip.

Just then, Tracey reached us. "Out of my way, poofter boy," she said, barging into Malcolm and pushing past him. Then, much to my delight, she leaned into me and hooked her arm through mine. "Did you see, Jesse? Did you see?" She was bouncing up and down beside me. "Greg likes me! He likes me! He's going to give me a lift home on his motorbike!" She looked about as thrilled as someone who'd won a ten-thousand-pound bingo prize. "And he told me, Jesse, he told me that you said he should ask me to dance. God, I'm sorry I wasn't very nice to you earlier on because, really, you are absolutely the best bloody friend in the world."

"Thanks, Trace," I said, beaming at her, only noticing, out of the corner of my eye, Malcolm turn around and stalk off.

CHAPTER SIXTEEN

—

WE EXITED THE CHURCH HALL TO FIND THAT A LIGHT POWDERING of snow had fallen and the world had been dusted a luminescent white. The air tasted different, a cold, sharp burn. I stood on the steps as everyone spilled past me into the street. All the voices were filled with the thrill of snow, the girls' squeals and the boys' shouts seeming to travel forever across the silvery open fields. I watched as the haphazard pattern of footprints multiplied and boys hurled snowballs and the girls screamed and ran. I watched Tracey climb onto Greg's motorbike and wrap her arms around his waist before they eased away. And I watched as Stan revved his bike so that it bucked up and down like a rodeo horse while he waited for Amanda to make her way unsteadily toward him. "Come on, slowcoach!" he yelled. "Let's get going." As she climbed on behind him, she noticed me watching her and gave a little wave. "Merry Christmas, Jesse," she called as she pulled on the bike helmet and fastened it under her chin.

"Merry Christmas," I called back, my voice a forlorn thread in the wide-open night. Stan revved the engine again, released the brake, and, after the bike skidded back and forth on the slushy road for a second, they sped off. I watched the bike rush into the darkness, its shape and the shapes of the figures on it rapidly fading until it became nothing but its red rear light gliding through the darkness, like a single discon-nected eye.

All the others were gone, either picked up by parents or walking home fast through the bitter cold. In the distance, I could hear their voices, loud and strident against the subtle insulation of the snow. My father still hadn't arrived.

After only a few minutes my whole body tingled with cold. I stamped my feet, wrapped my arms to my chest, and looked up at the stars. They shone scattered and gleaming, like salt grains on a frozen road, and I imagined myself stretching out to run my fingertips over them, rough crystals against a tarmac black. A car came, its lights sweeping over the thick, intertwined branches of hedgerows, the stripes of other tires made through the snow. It slowed as it approached the tight curve in the road in front of the church hall. I began to move toward it, cursing under my breath at my father for taking so long. But, once around the curve, the car sped up again and I was left to watch its lights swing around another bend and disappear from sight. I looked at my watch. It was almost eleven o'clock. My father had forgotten to pick me up.

Behind me, the lights in the church hall flickered off, and I heard Reverend Mullins humming "Silent Night" as he pulled the doors closed and pushed a key into the lock. For a moment, I considered ask-ing him if I could use the telephone in the church hall to call my father, but I didn't want to have to wait with him, trapped in some inter-minable conversation about joining the choir, visiting Lincoln Cathe-dral, or the benefit of prayer upon the tumultuous teenage soul. Besides, I had become very conscious of the bottle of Johnny Walker Red Label that I had stowed away in my coat pocket. I decided to walk the two miles home.

As I walked, the whiskey bottle banged so insistently against my thigh that it started to hurt, and when I'd got far enough from the church hall to no longer fear being bothered by the vicar, I pulled it out.

There were about three inches of liquid left. For a moment, I considered drinking it down, wondering what it would feel like inside me, wondering if it might take away my misery and set me free in the steely cold night. Then I thought about Stan and Greg and Tracey and how they guzzled it down and spat out meanness, and I considered tossing the bottle into one of the surrounding fields. But I decided against this and slid the bottle back into my pocket. I simply stood there, taking in the wide-open emptiness of the dark. In the stillness, I became aware of the sound of the sea—the waves lifting, churning, falling, as if the world itself were breathing slow and sleepy breaths. The whispery roar made me think about Malcolm and how by now he was probably tucked under blankets in his little caravan being soothed by that steady sound of the sea.

It was then that I heard a harsh buzz, as incongruous as the drone of a fat summer bluebottle fly in this winter landscape. It was the sound of a motorbike and it came closer, growling around the curves behind me until its headlamp swept up from the bend in the road, illuminating a narrow swath of yellow. Then I heard a voice, shrieking higher than the buzz of the bike, echoing out across the snow-sheened fields.

"Stop! Stop!" It was Amanda.

But the bike didn't stop. It seemed to speed up, charging forward like a raging insect. I could clearly see its silhouette and its two riders— the driver, Stan, leaning far down and forward, while Amanda, the passenger, held on tightly and kept screaming, "Stop, stop!" at the top of her lungs.

Just before it reached me, the bike came to a particularly tight bend in the road. It was the sort of bend that, even in the daylight in the best of conditions, a vehicle would have to slow down to take. Now, with the snow and the darkness, it was a bend that it was easy to miss until you came upon it. And that, it seemed, was exactly what happened.

I watched it all as if in slow motion. The bike jerking when Stan leaned his body backward as if he were trying to pull up a galloping horse, straining against the strength of the unruly animal he rode. Then the wheels of the bike slipping sideways, out from under them, the bike sliding fast and gracelessly, while Amanda and Stan were tossed in a high, tumbling arc, into the ditch at the side of the road.

Without a thought, I ran to them. I found Amanda lying on her back, arms splayed, crucifixion style, legs tucked up toward her body. "Are you all right? Are you all right?" I called, frantic. I leaned down, my breath clouding the air between us. I looked into her face under the big bulb of her helmet and saw that her eyes were wide and still. She said nothing and seemed not to be breathing.

Then she groaned, thumping one of her outstretched fists against the snow. "Oh, for God's sake," she said. "What a bloody idiot." Then she struggled to push herself up from the ground. I reached out to help her, but she seemed oblivious and so, still leaning over her, I was almost bashed in the head by her helmet as she abruptly sat up. "What are you doing here?" she asked.

"I was walking home. My dad forgot to pick me up."

"Oh." She sat with her legs splayed out in front of her, like a doll set upright in the snow.

"Are you all right?" I asked again.

"Me?" She looked along the length of her arms, body, and legs, slowly examining herself. "Yeah, I think so. Can you give me a hand?"

"Are you sure you can get up?" I was concerned. She had landed with considerable force.

"Yeah, come on, Jesse." She reached out and I took her gloved hands and pulled her upward. She winced but made it to her feet. "Thanks," she said, swaying unsteadily before gaining her balance. She brushed the snow from her coat and took a couple of shaky steps forward.

"Are you sure you're all right?"

She paused, sighed, and then moved forward again. "Yeah, I'm okay. Where's Stan?" I pointed to where he lay, a few feet away. I followed her as she stumbled toward him. He, too, had been flung from the bike to lie on his back and was staring wide-eyed at the sky. As I looked down on him, I felt a little quiver of excitement at the thought that he might be dead.

"Are you all right, Stan?" Amanda asked, wavering back and forth a little as she stood over him.

I was disappointed to see him manage a lolling nod.

"You sure?"

He nodded again. "Yeah, I think so."

"Get up, then, show me." She gestured with both hands, urging him up.

He rolled with great effort onto his side and from there struggled to his feet. He looked a little dazed, blinking fast and glancing around as if to get his bearings. When he finally seemed to get himself oriented, he looked down and, seeing snow clinging to his trousers, stamped his feet to shake it off. As he did so, he noticed a tear in his trousers. His skin was grazed beneath, but he wasn't badly hurt. "Aw, look, my best trousers. Fucking ruined, they are."

"Christ, Stan, is that all you care about? Your bloody trousers? We're lucky we're still walking. I can't believe you, I really can't."

"Where's my bike?" he asked, ignoring Amanda's outrage to stagger about in the snow, looking for signs of his motorbike.

"Over there," I said, pointing toward the ditch beyond. Once it had discarded its riders, the bike had continued its long, leaning skid, finally stopping when it fell into one of the ditches at the side of the fields. In the winter, those ditches were always full. His bike had doubtless plunged through the thin layer of ice there and was now immersed in green and murky water.

Wordlessly, Stan lumbered through the snow-covered grass to peer over the side of the ditch. "I don't think I'll be able to get it out tonight," he called to Amanda.

"Really? And there was me all ready to go and fish it out for you," Amanda responded as she battled clumsily to undo her helmet.

Stan turned toward her. "Well, tomorrow we could—"

"Tomorrow you can fuck off. And the next day. And the day after that." Having finally undone the buckle of the helmet, she pulled it off. "I told you I wanted to go straight home. It's too bloody cold and too bloody icy to be driving around. But did you listen to me?"

"Oh, come on, don't be daft, I—"

"Daft?" Her voice was thin and shrill in the freezing emptiness of the night. "You've got the nerve to call me daft. Don't you realize you could have got us killed? You're an idiot. A stupid bloody idiot. And I don't want to waste my time with a bloody idiot. I'm finished with you, Stan. That's it."

I was elated. She'd finally given him the shove.

"But, Mandy—"

"And if I've told you once, I've told you a thousand times. Do not call me Mandy."

"But—" Stan looked at her, open-mouthed.

"Here," Amanda interrupted, lifting the helmet above her head in both hands, holding it up in the air for a moment, and then throwing it with all her might at Stan. He clearly hadn't expected this, and when it reached him it hit him full in the chest, knocking him down again. He sat on the ground, stunned.

He looked pathetic. I felt a little guilty that I had so recently wished him dead. "What the fuck are you staring at, you stupid cow?" he demanded.

"Nothing," I said, my guilt immediately gone.

"Oh, shut up, Stan. She's not done any harm, which is more than I can say for you," Amanda barked. She backed away a couple of steps, turned unsteadily, and then lurched toward the road. "Come on, Jesse," she said. "Let's leave him to his fucking motorbike. I don't know about you, but I want to get home."

Amanda said nothing as we made our way toward Midham. Her anger seemed to puff out in the big clouds of her breath, and every now and then she let out a long, exasperated sigh. She looked so indignant that I imagined her untouched by the shock of the accident. It wasn't until she stopped to take off her gloves, pull out her packet of cigarettes, and tried to strike a light that I realized how shaken up she actually was. Even the cigarette in her lips was shaking, and her hands quivered so much that she couldn't get the flame to stay in one place. "It's the cold," she said, trying once again to put the flame to the cigarette end. It was freezing, all my muscles seemed to ache, and my fingers and toes were burning with it. But I knew that it wasn't the cold that was making Amanda shiver. "Jesse, do you think you could do it for me?" She handed me the box of matches and the cigarette. "I really need a smoke, I really do."

I put the cigarette to my lips and Amanda pressed herself close, shielding me from the bitter wind that had started to blow, burning any exposed skin, freezing our faces still. I started to shake myself, and with the stiffness in my hands it was difficult to get the match alight. After a couple of failed attempts, I managed to strike it, hold it to the cigarette end, and breathe its end orange and alive. It was my first cigarette and, in the fashion of all first-time smokers, I began coughing so fiercely that I thought my lungs would seize up. I was afraid that Amanda would laugh at me, but she didn't. Instead, she took the cigarette from my grasp, put it hungrily to her lips, and rubbed her palm soothingly over my back. "I'm sorry, Jesse," she said between big, urgent drags. "I shouldn't have made you do that. It's bad enough that I've got this dirty habit, never mind encouraging you to pick it up."

"It's all right," I said when my coughing fit was done. "I don't mind, I really don't." It was true. At that moment, I would have done anything for Amanda. If she had asked me to throw myself into the path of the next oncoming car, I probably would have. I was so thrilled to be with her, nothing else mattered. Nothing. "I'm glad I was around when you fell off the bike. I mean, I wouldn't want you to hurt yourself and have no one there. Well, I suppose Stan was there—"

"Stan? Stan is history."

I tried not to smile, but it was impossible. I'd never been so happy.

She turned, put her arm through mine, and we began to walk home again. We were moving in unison now, as I timed my steps to match hers. She walked slowly, a little clumsily. I wasn't sure if she was bruised from the accident or this was the effect of all that whiskey she'd drunk at the disco. But all that mattered was that she was there, holding on to me. Even through my coat I could feel the heat of her against my side. I wished that it was ten miles rather than two from Reatton to Midham, so that we could walk together for hours along a winding road in the dark.

When we reached the village high street, she pulled me toward the enormous Christmas tree that stood in front of the Co-op. Its lights were still on, illuminating the thick night with yellow, red, orange, and green.

"Pretty, isn't it?" she said. She drew in a deep breath through her nose. "And the smell—I love that smell. Always makes me want to be in the middle of a pine forest. I've never been in a forest." She looked at me and pulled a soft and slightly crooked smile. She still wore her silver crown of tinsel, though now it sat askew, pulled down over her tangled and unruly hair. Still, with the lights of the tree behind her and the glaze of snow over everything, I saw her as an angel, smiling down at me, pulling me into her beatific light. "Have you ever been in a forest, Jesse?"

"No," I said, though I had written about riding through a forest with Amanda in one of my letters, when we'd been fleeing vampires together.

"I think it would be nice." She looked up at the tree and then at me. "You go home that way, don't you, Jesse?" She pointed to where the high street veered away from the village.

"Yes, but I can walk you home if you like." I did not want to leave her. I really could have stayed there with her all night. The accident had made her seem so vulnerable, fragile—the way I'd imagined her in so many of my letters, needing me to take care of her, rescue her, make sure she was safe. "I'd feel better if I walked you home," I said.

She laughed. "It's all right, Jesse. I'm a big girl, I can find my way back. And me getting home this late—well . . . there's going to be bloody hell to pay. I wouldn't want you to get stuck in the middle of that."

"But it's not your fault, you—"

"Yeah, well, you try telling my dad that." She pressed her lips together and sighed. Then she smiled again. "Anyway, it's nice of you to offer. More than Stan would ever do. Bloody wanker. Mind you, that's all most lads are, you know, wankers. Most men are, when I come to think of it. But you—" She took off one of her gloves and raised her hand, impossibly cold, to my face and pressed it against my equally frozen cheek. "You're nice. Really nice." Her words were drawn out, limp. She looked into my face, smiling. Then she leaned toward me, sending me reeling in the swirling scent of her cigarette-and-whiskey breath before she landed a soft, wet kiss on my mouth.

—

CHAPTER SEVENTEEN

"JINGLE BELLS, JINGLE BELLS, JINGLE ALL THE WAY." MY FATHER DANCED into the kitchen on Christmas morning wearing his brown wool dressing gown, paisley patterned pajamas, and red slippers. His hair, usually carefully combed in a vain attempt to cover his ever-expanding bald patch, hung in loose, jagged strands over his right ear. "Oh what fun it is to ride on a one-horse open sleigh, hey!" He stuck his hip outward and his hand into the air. Clearly, he was in good spirits and determined to inject our Christmas celebrations with an appropriate degree of cheer. I was considerably less jolly as I stood at the sink peeling what felt like an infinite quantity of potatoes. We were having them roasted and mashed to go with Christmas dinner. Mabel, Frank, and Granddad Bennett would be joining us, and I was preparing two five-pound bags to make sure there would be enough. "Merry Christmas, love," my father said, stopping to plant a kiss on the crown of my head before dancing over to the cooker. "By heck, I could kill for a cup of tea. My mouth feels like the inside of a bloody birdcage. And, speaking of birds, how's that turkey coming along, eh?"

The previous evening, while my mother had lain lifeless on the settee watching *Val Doonican's Christmas Show*, my father and I had prepared the stuffing for the oversized bird, gratefully following the instructions from the recipe for roast turkey that Auntie Mabel had clipped out of a December issue of *Woman's Weekly* and sent to us with the Christmas card signed by her and Frank. At seven o'clock that morning, my alarm had gone off and I'd got up to stuff the bird and hoist it into the oven. Now the turkey was roasting away in its massive roasting pan and I was basting it every half hour.

"It smells great," my father said, dreamily sniffing the air as he filled the kettle with water. "When you grow up, you'll make some man a lovely wife, Jesse."

"I've told you before," I snapped. "I am not getting married."

He laughed. "That's probably your best plan, love." Leaning over the gas burner, he turned it on, struck a match, and leaped back when it burst into a ball of blue flame. "Bloody hell, another damn thing to fix," he muttered, shaken as he brushed a few singed strands of hair that had been hanging perilously close to the gas burner back over his ear. "Anyway," he said, putting the kettle over the flame and then searching the kitchen counter for the tea caddy. "You ask me, marriage isn't all it's cracked up to be. Certainly not the riding-into-the-sunset-happily-ever-after rubbish they make out, I'll tell you that for nothing."

He laughed again, but there was a sadness to it that made me wonder how many times he had regretted marrying my mother. I wondered also whether, given the chance now, my father would still choose to have me. But I knew the answer. My father's ideal life would consist of a quiet house, an armchair, a television and a newspaper, and regularly but anonymously delivered cups of tea. If things went well, he'd get to watch the downfall and then humiliation of the royal family on the BBC. In that little cocoon, there wouldn't be any room for a daughter who demanded his attention, who wanted more than he could possibly give. After all, he had so easily forgotten me the other night at the disco, and if Amanda and Stan hadn't had that accident I would have been left to walk home completely alone in the dark.

"Of course, when I was young," my father said, "that's what you were supposed to do—get married. Never occurred to us to do anything else. But the world's changing now. There's lots more opportuni-ties for you, love." I saw my father as a much younger man—the young man he had been in his wedding photographs, dimple-faced with a full head of hair, grinning for the camera as he stood next to my mother outside the church after the ceremony. He had looked so happy, so full of hope. I wondered how he felt about that day now.

I brushed the thought away and tossed a peeled potato into the colander. "When are you going to pick up Granddad?" I asked.

"After Mabel and Frank get here," he said. "Your granddad doesn't like to wait for his dinner."

"So when are Mabel and Frank coming, then?" I asked.

"About eleven o'clock. Mabel said she'll take care of the cooking if your mother's not up to it—which I can't see that she will be, given the state she's been in recently. I told Mabel I want to have the dinner on the table by half past one at the latest," my father continued, taking a mug down from the kitchen cupboard as he waited for the kettle to boil. "That way, your granddad will be happy and I can be sure of see-ing the Queen's speech at three o'clock."

My father loved the Queen's Christmas speech. He'd probably never admit it, but it was one of the highlights of his Christmas—his annual chance to rant at the Queen, not just when she was waving from her carriage leaving Buckingham Palace or pictured having tea with some foreign dignitary but face to face as she addressed us in our living room.

I much preferred the perennial showings of *A Christmas Carol*. This year, it was being aired on BBC One on Christmas night, and I had cir-cled it in bright red ink in the Christmas edition of the *Radio Times*. There was something about the transformation of Scrooge from miser and Christmas curmudgeon to generous humanitarian and jolly party-goer that I found irresistible, and I always got tears in my eyes when he raised the salary of his poor beleaguered clerk, Bob Cratchit, who for some reason reminded me of my father. But my favorite character was the Ghost of Christmas Yet to Come. I longed to be visited by a spirit like that, someone to tell me what lay ahead so I would know the worst to expect.

My mother finally came downstairs after ten o'clock. Though she had clearly made an effort to dress up, with a set of fake pearls around her neck, matching earrings, and a silver charm bracelet, she looked decidedly off-kilter. It was partly her dress, a silver-flecked outfit that resembled an oversized, stretched-out sweater, with an uneven hem that hung just below her thighs. Then there were the black seamed stockings and high-heeled silver sandals, which made me expect to see her put her hands on her hips and start kicking her legs in the air like a music-hall dancer. And finally the makeup, fiercely bright hues on her eyes, lips, and cheeks that made Mabel's choice of cosmetics look minimalist by comparison. She looked ridiculous, like a child in dress-up clothes trying to imitate what she understood as adult sophistication.

"Are you all right, Mum?" I asked as she strutted into the kitchen, pausing to examine her reflection in the shiny curve of the kettle.

"Of course I'm all right," she said, puckering up her lips, patting her hair, then turning toward me, beaming to reveal a smear of lipstick on her teeth. "Couldn't be better. I mean, after all, it's Christmas." Her voice was high and overwrought. "Merry Christmas, love," she said, sweeping me into her arms. "A merry, merry Christmas."

"Same to you, too, Mum," I muttered as she pressed my face into the mothball smell of her dress. I tried to sink into her, to relax into her embrace, but I felt stiff and prickly and, without really wanting to, I pushed her away.

"Oh, I see you've got the turkey in already," she said in a disappointed tone, as if she'd been planning to prepare the meal herself and I'd beaten her to it. She flopped onto one of the kitchen chairs. "Any tea in that pot, love?" she asked, indicating the teapot that my father had filled earlier.

"It'll be cold by now," I answered.

"Oh, well, make another one, will you, love? You know me, can't do a thing without my morning brew."

Mabel and Frank arrived shortly afterward. They came bearing gifts. Three pounds of beef sausages, a box of Milk Tray, and a bottle of Harveys Bristol Cream sherry for my mother, a bottle of brandy for my father, and a book for me. My mother accepted the package of sausages from Frank without even a murmur of ingratitude and shoved it into the fridge. My father opened the bottles and offered Mabel, Frank, and my mother a drink.

"I'm not sure Mum should have anything," I said softly as my father took the top off the Harveys Bristol Cream. I'd read the label on the bottle of pills he administered to her. There, along with the dosage instructions, it said very clearly: "Not to be taken with alcohol!"

"Don't be daft, Jesse." My father waved me away.

"But it says on her pills—" I said as I looked at my mother, who, having already torn the cellophane off the box of Milk Tray, had popped two chocolates into her mouth and was chewing loudly.

"It's Christmas—everybody deserves a drink at Christmas," my father said grandly.

"Oh, aye, you can say that again, Mike," Frank agreed. "Nowt like a nice bit of booze to get the celebration started."

I stood by silently watching as my father poured out a glass of sherry for Mabel and then for my mother. "Merry Christmas, everybody!" he toasted. The four of them lifted their glasses into the air, clinked them noisily together, then pressed them to their lips. Mabel, Frank, and my father took two or three fast little sips, while my mother swallowed the entire contents of her glass in one decisive gulp.

"I'll have another one of them, Mike," she declared, slamming her glass down on the kitchen table with all the gusto of a cowboy in a Wild West saloon. Playing the part of the cowed bartender, my father obediently filled her glass.

As soon as she'd taken a few sips of her sherry, Mabel commandeered the kitchen. "You've done a grand job, our Jesse," she said, peering into the oven at the sizzling turkey. "But I'll take over from here. It's a real woman's touch you want with your Christmas dinner, right, Frank?"

"Oh, aye," said Frank, nodding sagely. "And, believe me, Mabel is definitely a real woman, one hundred percent." He nudged my father and wiggled his eyebrows. My father responded with an awkward laugh.

I turned and made a prompt retreat to the living room. There, I curled up on the settee and examined the book that Mabel had brought me: *The Girl's Book of Heroines,* a volume that was a little young for me, perhaps, but as I flipped through the pages I found it was filled with fascinating stories. Against the drone of my father's commentary in the hall and on the stairs as he gave Frank another tour of the house, providing updates on his latest do-it-yourself accomplishments, I reveled in stories of the Virgin Queen, who never married despite being pursued by suitors far and wide; Saint Joan, who dressed in men's clothing so that she could fight a war but was burned as a witch afterward; and Lady Jane Grey, queen for a mere nine days until she was deposed by Mary Tudor and sent off to the Tower of London to have her head chopped off.

Looking at the illustration of the tragic and beautiful Lady Jane Grey made me think of Amanda and what had been almost constantly on my mind since the night of the Reatton disco—the kiss that she had placed on my lips before we parted in the village. It wasn't a long kiss, not like those lock-lipped, endless smooches that the girls and boys had been giving one another at the disco earlier. Nor was it like those open-mouthed kisses that the heroes of Sunday afternoon films planted on the lips of struggling and then suddenly limp-limbed women. And it wasn't like the swirling kisses that Captain Kirk gave those female aliens. But that kiss by the village Christmas tree was the longest and softest kiss I had ever had. Not the fierce dry peck of my great-aunt June or the whiskery rub of my father or the oily lipstick smear that Auntie Mabel greeted me with. This had been my first real kiss. Tender,

lingering, so that I could still conjure up that sensation of the unexpected softness of Amanda's lips, the astonishing warmth of her mouth
against mine in that freezing night.

Afterward, I had been unable to meet Amanda's eyes, afraid of what
she might see there. I longed for her to say something, a comment that
might make it real. But when all she said was "Well, see you then, Jesse,"
and turned to walk away, I wondered if I had imagined it. I stood a long
time there in the snow and the silence, watching the meandering track
of her footprints as if it were the only evidence of what had just occurred.

"Jesse! Jesse! For God's sake, how many times do I have to call you?"
It was my mother. She stood in the doorway, leaning loosely against the
doorframe. "Are you deaf?"

"I was reading."

"Well, a lot of good that will do, won't it? Your auntie Mabel needs
you to set the table."

"Can't you do it?" I asked, resenting her sudden intrusion.

"No, I can't. I'm busy. I'm making the sherry trifle." Her expression
was even slacker than it had been earlier, and I guessed that she had
probably consumed at least as much sherry as she had put into the trifle. "Come on, you've got to do your part, you know. This is a family
dinner, after all." As she turned, she hit her shoulder against the doorframe and reeled back a moment before she launched herself out of the
room. I followed unwillingly.

"Are you all right, Mum?" I asked as she barged into the kitchen and
knocked into the table.

" 'Course I'm bloody well all right," she said, steadying herself with
a palm pushed against the Formica before flopping down into one of
the chairs. "Never been bloody better. Mabel, pour us another sherry,
will you?"

"Don't you think you've had enough, Ev?" Mabel said.

"Enough?" My mother laughed. "Yes, I've definitely had enough.
Had enough of everything, I have. Had it up to here." She jabbed her

index finger clumsily against her temple. "That's why I could use another drink." She laughed again. "That'll wash the cares away—oh, yes
it will. Oh, yes it will indeed."

I gave Mabel a beseeching look.

"Why don't you at least wait until you've had some food in you, Ev?"
she said. "It won't be long until it's ready." She took a slurp from the
gravy spoon.

"I'm not a bloody child, you know," my mother said, slamming her
hand down on the table, making it wobble from side to side. "You
might have been able to boss me around when we were kids, but you
can't tell me what to do now." She pouted and added, "Anyway, I have
been eating. I've polished off them chocolates you brought." The box
of Milk Tray sat ransacked on the counter.

Mabel gave a hopeless shrug. "Oh, go on, Jesse, pour your mother
another drink. At least it'll shut her up while I get the rest of this dinner cooked."

My mother watched me with narrowed, expectant eyes. "Go on, you
heard your auntie Mabel," she said, hitting the table even harder. This
time it groaned slightly as it wobbled.

I poured about an inch of sherry into my mother's glass and pushed
it toward her. She looked at it scornfully, then heaved herself up, leaned
across the table, grabbed the bottle, and filled the glass to the top.

Half an hour later, I looked out the kitchen window to see my father pull into the driveway and Granddad emerge from the passenger
side. His gray hair was so shiny with Brylcreem that it looked wet, and
as he crossed the front garden, swathed in an oversized black wool coat,
he made me think of a massive sea mammal—a walrus or one of those
elephant seals I'd seen on a BBC Two wildlife documentary—fearsome
and inelegant, and ready to butt chests with anyone who got in his way.
When he got within a few yards of the house, he stopped and appraised
it. He didn't seem impressed.

For a while I stayed in the kitchen while Mabel bustled around like
a woman possessed. She stirred and agitated pans, put things in and

pulled things out of the oven. Moving through clouds of steam, her face was damp and rosy, and her chest—revealed by the plunging neckline of her skintight orange sweater—was flushed a patchy red. I offered to help, but she brushed me away. And since my mother, now staring foggy-eyed and wordless at her empty sherry glass, wasn't exactly my idea of good company, I left and wandered into the living room. There, while my father stared at a Bugs Bunny cartoon, Granddad and Frank were engaged in a somewhat one-sided discussion of the character-building merits of military service.

"I mean, just look at the state of youngsters these days," Granddad said as I entered the room. "All them lads with hair past their shoulders. And the lasses, my God. When I was young, the lasses put some effort into their appearance. Not anymore—oh, no. Far as I can tell, they sleep in their clothes and never so much as run a comb through their hair." He looked at me and shook his head disapprovingly.

I had on the same outfit I'd worn at the Christmas disco. And though it probably didn't match Granddad's antediluvian fashion taste, I had carefully ironed it the night before. I'd also taken care to brush and style my hair and had thought I looked quite presentable before I descended the stairs that morning. I opened my mouth to protest Granddad's pronouncements, but it was hard to interrupt him once he was in a flow.

"This country, going to the dogs, it is," he continued. "It's all them hippies and peaceniks or whatever they call themselves. No wonder England's in such a mess. Can you imagine it, if we'd been the same when I was younger? Hitler about to kick in the bloody door and us responding by growing our hair and preaching free love. We'd have all been speaking German and living on sauerkraut by now. I'll tell you one thing, erm—" He narrowed his eyes and waved at Frank. "What's your name again, laddy?"

"Frank. Frank's the name and I—"

"Like I was saying," Granddad interrupted, "lads need to look like lads. Need to act like them as well. Best thing you could do for them is give them a short back and sides and make them do their national service. Never did Mike any harm." He looked over at my father and bellowed, "Did it, Mike?"

"What?" my father asked, still staring at the television.

"He said national service never did you any harm," Frank said.

My father shrugged. "Bloody waste of time, you ask me."

"Eh? What did he say?" Granddad asked.

"He said he thought it was a waste of time," Frank repeated, louder. "I never felt like that, mind. Too young to serve in the war, I was, but not too young to serve my country. I—"

"Should be proud of serving your country," Granddad said, scowling at my father. "If you'd appreciated your time in the army, maybe it would have made more of a man of you. See, our Brian . . . Did I tell you about our Brian, erm—" He waved vaguely toward Frank.

"Frank, the name's Frank," he said, a strain of irritation in his voice.

"Right, Frank." Granddad repeated. "Well, Frank, did I tell you about my lad Brian? Grand lad, he was. Now, if he'd had a chance he'd have served his country. But killed, he was. On his eighteenth birthday." Granddad breathed a heavy sigh, shook his head, and folded his arms over the huge curve of his belly.

"What, in the army was he?" Frank ventured.

"He was a football player," I chirped. "He was run over by a delivery van." For some reason, I enjoyed supplying this particular item of information.

"Oh, aye," Granddad said. "Terrible it was. Best bloody football player you've ever seen. And if his life hadn't been snatched away from him so young there's no doubt he would've played on the national team. Lad like Brian, he'd have gotten the England squad out of the bloody doldrums. He wouldn't have let us lose three nil to the bloody krauts."

At that moment, the door burst open and Mabel propelled herself into the room. "Right, then, lads," she said, breathless. "I hope all this sitting around has worked up your appetite because your dinner's ready."

As if on springs, both Frank and my father bounced to their feet and followed Mabel into the kitchen. I launched myself after them, leaving Granddad, who continued to extol Brian's football-playing skills, muttering behind me in the hall.

Once assembled, we all sat, a cramped little bunch, elbows touching, around the piles of steaming food on the kitchen table. I had covered it with a big white tablecloth and had managed to make it look quite festive, with holly-patterned serviettes. In an effort to enhance the party atmosphere, my father had unearthed a box of Christmas crackers that Ted had given us on one of his previous visits. At some point, apparently, the crackers had been stored in the sun so that, on one side, the colors on their crepe-paper coverings were washed-out and streaky. The fatigued colors gave our gathering a rather sad air. Like the crackers, my mother looked as if she had passed her prime. No longer gleefully drunk, she sat glum and barely verbal, staring down at her empty plate and playing with the edge of the tablecloth, as a nervous guest might, wrapping it between her fingers and around her hands.

"Cheer up, Evelyn," Frank declared, knocking against her with his shoulder. My mother flinched slightly and glowered at her plate. "Crikey," he muttered to Mabel. "Doesn't seem like I can do a bloody thing right."

"It's all right," Mabel said, lowering her voice to a whisper, as if my mother wouldn't be able to hear her across the tiny table. "She's just in one of her moods, that's all. She'll get herself out of it, you'll see." I was glad for her optimism, but I wasn't so sure. I'd seen my mother like this before, and it seldom ended well.

"Some people, they don't know when they're onto a good thing, really, do they?" Granddad pronounced, unfurling his serviette, tucking a corner into his shirt collar, smoothing the rest over his chest, then picking up his knife and fork. Not known for his willingness to stand on ceremony, Granddad was apparently eager to get started on the food. "Most women—well, they have to make Christmas dinner themselves, don't they? Don't have a loving sister like you to come in and make everything for them, do they now, Mabel?"

"I helped," I said. "And Dad. We made the stuffing, and I peeled the potatoes. It took ages."

"Aye, well, there's some men what would think it's a wife's job to take care of all that," Granddad said, pointing his knife at my father. "Your mam, God rest her soul—well, she would never have expected me to help out in the kitchen. Oh, no, a woman's job, is that."

"Maybe women don't want to be stuck in the kitchen, maybe they want to do other things instead," I said.

"See, I told you, didn't I?" Granddad said, giving Frank a knowing look. "Listen to it, the voice of the younger generation. Don't know what the world's coming to. I tell you, young lady, the way you're talking there's no man will want to marry you."

"Good," I said decisively.

"Now, now," said Mabel, "it's Christmas, remember. No time for disagreements. And, besides, we need to tuck in—it's getting cold."

"You're right there, Mabel. But before we start noshing," my father said, his voice booming with false jollity, "why don't we pull our Christmas crackers? That'll be a lark, now, won't it?" He looked hopefully at my mother. She did not respond.

"What a lovely idea," Mabel said.

"Come on, Ev, pull a cracker with me, won't you?" my father said. My mother said nothing and merely worked her fingers more fiercely into the tablecloth.

"Will you pull mine with me, Dad?" I asked, picking up my Christmas cracker and holding it across the table so that my father could take the other end.

"Of course, love," he said. I took the crepe-paper ruffle of the cracker in my hand and searched with my fingers for the cardboard strip inside. "All right, now, let's give it a good tug, eh?" my father said.

We both reached across the table, pulled hard, and the cracker tore apart, sounding its short, sudden bang. My father and I burst into laughter, but my mother, who had been steadily staring down at the table, still entranced by her empty plate, hadn't anticipated the noise, and, jolting with shock, leaped from her chair, gripping the edge of the table and pressing all her weight against it.

The table creaked, shifted slightly to one side, then to the other. All of us watched with held breath as it performed this gentle wobble and the plates, cutlery, and food in front of us wobbled with it. Then, as my mother let go and reeled backward and the table seemed to right itself, we all let out our breath in relief. But, with that collective exhaled breath, the table creaked again and shuddered as two of its legs buckled outward from under it and the entire thing toppled sideways, falling hard against Frank and knocking him from his chair as it made its fast and inevitable journey to the floor.

The plates, food, and everything else that had been on the table were hurled around the room in a deafening cacophony of clattering metal and shattering china. Frank, sprawled on the floor next to his chair, shrieked as the gravy boat landed on him, spilling steaming turkey gravy into his lap.

For perhaps a second, the rest of us sat there stunned and I had the sensation of sitting within a frozen tableau, watching from some out-side viewpoint: my father white-faced and open-mouthed; Mabel, a palm pressed hard against each of her cheeks; Granddad, a bemused frown on his face as he held his knife and fork expectantly aloft; while I looked over at my mother, horrified, and she stared at the collapsed table, her face a picture of dazed bafflement. And, as I observed the scene, I wondered why I hadn't been able to prevent this calamity. I'd known my mother shouldn't drink, and I'd witnessed the precipitous decline of her mood. I'd even seen how the kitchen table hadn't seemed as steady as it should have when she slammed her hand down on it ear-lier. If I'd been brought to witness this chaotic scene by the Ghost of Christmas Yet to Come a couple of hours before, I would not have been surprised. Like Scrooge, I might have asked if this version of the future was inevitable or if I could make different choices that would change the outcome. But now it was too late. And, as the turkey, which had fallen off the table to balance precariously on Frank's vacated seat, dropped to the floor with an enormous thud, that frozen moment was ended and I was no longer distant, observing, but fully occupying my horror.

Everyone began to move. Frank scrambled to his feet and half hopped, half ran over to the sink, where he began frantically dabbing at his trousers with a wet cloth. Mabel jumped up and dashed over to help Frank, Granddad loosed his grip on his knife and fork and let them clatter to the floor, and my father, speaking through clenched teeth, said, "Jesus bloody Christ, Evelyn, you've gone and done it now."

"Are you all right, love?" Mabel said as she reached Frank.

"Oh, it's nothing," he said bitterly. "Of course, I may never have a normal sex life again." He looked, incensed, over at my mother, who had backed away to the kitchen counter and slid down to the floor. She sat there, legs folded under her, shoulders sunken, as if she had crumpled.

"I'm sure you'll be all right, love," Mabel said, grabbing another wet cloth and starting to dab at Frank's trousers herself. "Just a bit of gravy."

"Gravy? More like frigging molten oil. It's not right, Mabel. I come here for Christmas dinner and I end up losing my bloody manhood."

After his first muttered comment, my father had remained silent. But now, as I looked at him, I realized it would not be for long. He stood up slowly, visibly shaking, the muscles in his face tensed. His hands were clenched, white knuckled, with one fist still wrapped around the remnants of the Christmas cracker we had pulled. He spoke softly at first, glaring down at my mother as if his eyes could burn right through her. "You have to spoil everything, don't you?" he began. "Bloody everything. Can't bloody well stop yourself, can you?" Gradually, his voice became louder, his words faster. I felt myself pressed against my chair, as if I had been slammed there by a wild and irresistible gale. "We can't even have a bloody Christmas dinner without you causing chaos," he continued, while my mother looked at him, her face pale and expressionless. "If it's not one thing, then it's another. I mean, what more do you want? I try my best. I bloody well do. I go out to work every day. I come home and I try to fix up this bloody house. I put up with your moods—your bloody ups and your bloody downs, your crying fits, your screaming bloody rages, your bloody weeks in bed. I take you to the doctor's. I try to play the nice bloody husband. The caring bloody spouse. Hah!" He let out a short, sour laugh, shaking his head as if laughing at his own stupidity. "But nothing works, does it, Evelyn? Nothing ever does. And what I want to know is, what is wrong with you? What the bloody hell is wrong?" He was yelling now, but he stared at my mother imploringly, as if he really expected a response. His question hung in the air between them, the force of his words and his need for an answer filling the room. My mother dropped her gaze to the floor and began running an index finger along the zigzag pattern in the shiny linoleum my father had laid a couple of weeks before. My father sputtered and turned away. "I don't know why I bother, I really don't," he said, closing his eyes and shaking his head so slowly that it was as if he could barely move it for all the misery it held. "I mean, what's the bloody point?" Then he scowled over at my mother again. "Are you bloody well listening to me?" he yelled. My mother flinched, as if a sudden shock had coursed along her spine, but she did not look up. "Might as well not waste my breath." He shook his head. "I'm sorry, Mabel, Frank, Dad," he said, his voice suddenly soft and utterly defeated. "I really didn't mean to spoil your Christmas like this." Then he looked at me. "I'm sorry, Jesse, love," he said. His face looked as worn out as I had ever seen it, his skin pale and sagging, as if, after finding the energy for all this anger, the muscles beneath had lost all their strength. "Sorry, love," he repeated, "but I've got to go." He turned away and began walking to the door. Halfway across the room, he realized that he was still holding the ragged remainder of the Christmas cracker. He paused, lifted it up and looked at it for a moment, then threw it to the floor. Then he walked out of the kitchen, down the hallway, and out the front door.

AFTER MY FATHER LEFT, Auntie Mabel and I bundled my mother up the stairs and into her room like a heavy sodden sack. She fell onto her bed, pausing only to kick off her shoes before clambering under the covers, resisting both my and Mabel's efforts to make her undress. Within a minute or so, she had fallen asleep, her breaths coming out in soft, chortling snores.

I ate my Christmas dinner on my lap in front of the television with Granddad, Frank, and Mabel—a plate of salvaged turkey, stuffing, Brussels sprouts, and mashed potatoes, all of it cold and rather dry without the benefit of any gravy. Frank had apparently found a pair of my father's trousers to change into. They were far too big and hung around his thin hips in huge folds. A belt kept them from falling to his ankles when he stood up.

"Well, I don't know about you three, but I could do with a cup of tea," he said, still chewing on a final Brussels sprout, his teeth flecked green as he spoke.

"Ooh, yes," declared Mabel. "That'll do the trick. Thanks, Frank."

"Aye, tea would be nice," Granddad said. "Would be nicer with a bit of Christmas pudding, though." He looked meaningfully at Mabel.

"You want Christmas pudding, Harry, you'll have to make it yourself. There's some sherry trifle in the fridge that our Evelyn made, but last time I looked at it, it didn't look like it was going to set."

Granddad turned and scowled at the television. "Should have stayed at home and ordered bloody Meals on Wheels."

Frank carried his and Granddad's plates to the kitchen while Mabel pushed hers onto the arm of the settee, lit a cigarette, and began flicking her ash into a pile of uneaten mashed potatoes. "I honestly don't know where your dad's gone," she said, leaning forward and craning her neck to look out the window, as if she might see him lurking in the front garden. "A bit daft taking off like that, if you ask me. Don't you worry yourself, though, darling," she said, reaching over to pat my knee. "I expect he'll be back when he gets hungry enough."

A loud crash came from the kitchen. "Ooh, heck," said Mabel. "I hope Frank's not broken any more dishes. You'll be lucky if you have any left, the rate things are going today." She took a final puff on her cigarette, then dunked it into the pile of mashed potatoes on her plate. "Do me a favor, can you, Jesse, love, and go and give him a hand?"

I got up to make my way to the kitchen, quickening my stride when I heard another crash. When I got there, Frank was on all fours by the kitchen counter, picking up the pieces of a broken cup and saucer, his scrawny backside shrouded in my father's pants. "Bit of a clumsy dollop, I'm afraid. Flew right out of my hand, they did. You mind giving us a hand down here, love?" he asked, crawling across the floor with all the agility of an arthritic baby. "Can't say I'm as nimble as I used to be. Not after I put my back out at work last year." He groaned as he reached toward a shard of china. "I'll have to have Mabel rub some liniment on me after this. What with your mam spilling boiling hot gravy on my bloody privates, I feel like I've been through a war and not a Christmas dinner. Things always like this at your house?" He sounded jovial enough, but there was a prickly undertone.

"Only sometimes," I said as I knelt down beside him and began gathering the shattered pieces of the cup.

"Mabel said your mam tried to knock herself off. Cut her wrists in the bath."

"Yes," I said softly. He had stopped picking up the pieces now, and I could feel his eyes on me.

"Carted her off to Delapole, didn't they? Kept her in there awhile."

I felt the color rise in my face. I hated that Frank had this information about my mother, and I felt a flare of anger at Mabel for telling him this shameful fact. Frank had no right to know. And he had no right to bring it up.

"Yeah, well, she's always seemed like a bloody nutcase to me. No wonder your dad cleared off. Though God only knows why he put up with her until now. Those things tend to run in families, you know."

I reached for the cracked-off curve of the cup handle that lay next to Frank's knee. As I did, he put his hand on top of mine. I tried to pull away, but he pressed his hand down hard, pushing my palm against the sharp edge of the broken cup handle. I winced at the sudden burn of pain and looked into his face. He was still smiling, his narrowed eyes glinting like deep-set jewels. "Get off," I said.

He pressed down harder. "So, are you a nutcase like your mother?"

"No."

He held my hand down, and the cup handle's serrated edge cut deeper into my skin. "Good, because I wouldn't want to get myself too involved in a family full of crackpots. I mean, Mabel's all right, but a man can't be too careful. And that bloody mother of yours—"

"Let go," I said, trying to pull my hand away again. But I was pinned. The world narrowed to the sharpness of the pain and Frank's growling voice.

"Frigging humiliating, not to mention the real harm she could've done. I've never been one to put up easily with being made a fool of. But by a bitch like that, well—"

"Frank! Frank!" Mabel was shouting from the hallway. Within seconds, the kitchen door swung open. "Where's that— For God's sake, what are the two of you doing down there?"

As soon as he heard her voice, Frank let go of my hand to begin picking up pieces of broken china from the floor. "Oh, hello, love," he said. "Jesse here was helping me pick up a cup and saucer I dropped. Silly butterfingers me." He barked a throaty laugh.

"Well, me and Harry are still waiting for our tea."

"I know, love. And I was just about to bring it in." Frank reached up to grab the edge of the counter and slowly eased himself to standing. As he did so, he pressed a hand into his lower back. "I think I've done myself a right injury down there, I have."

"Should take more care with the dishes, then, shouldn't you? Men,"

Mabel said, rolling her eyes at me. "They can't even make a pot of tea without creating a bloody crisis. I say, love, what happened to you?"

I realized my hand was bleeding, the blood seeping across the bright shine of the new linoleum.

I looked up at Frank to see him staring at me, the skin at the edges of his eyes puckered and his eyelids fluttering slightly, as if he was try-ing to contain his rage. I thought of telling Mabel what he had done, but I felt the weight of that look. I didn't want to provoke him into more meanness.

"It's all right, Auntie Mabel," I said, holding my palm upward so that the blood rolled in a thin stream over my wrist and down my arm. "It's just a little cut. It will heal."

CHAPTER EIGHTEEN

—

ALL THAT AFTERNOON, MABEL INSISTED THAT MY FATHER WOULD return soon, but as afternoon shifted rapidly into dusk she seemed to have doubts. "I just don't know where he's got to," she said as she looked out the window at the last weak threads of sunlight shimmering at the western edges of the sky. "I mean, even the pubs aren't open on Christmas Day."

Of course, the pub was the only place we could imagine that he had gone. There was nowhere else I could think of that he might seek refuge. In the pub, he could sit in a darkened corner, nursing his wounds and a pint of warm, frothy beer. But if there were no pubs open I had no idea where he might be—except driving along empty roads, away from us.

When he'd yelled at my mother in the kitchen, all that anger he usually directed at the television had found its true mark. For the first time, I realized that he resented my mother as much as I did. Perhaps he had shocked himself with his anger as much as he had shocked me. But surely, now that he had admitted it, he would not return. I knew that if, like him, I was able to drive away and put miles and miles between me, this house, and my family, I'd find another life altogether and never feel the urge to come back.

After he'd eaten, Granddad dozed in his armchair. Across the room, Frank stared stonily at the television, and, on the settee next to me, Mabel's eyes moved ever more anxiously to the window, which, with the sky now completely dark, only reflected back our cheerless gathering.

When A Christmas Carol came on, rather than wishing for Scrooge's redemption I found myself despising Bob Cratchit for his ridiculous subservience and for burdening himself with such overwhelming responsibilities. When the Ghost of Christmas Yet to Come arrived to visit Scrooge, pointing to the future's possibilities with its outstretched, spectral hand, I wished instead that it had visited the penniless clerk to warn him of his life ahead when he was still a young man and had a chance to make different choices.

Almost as soon as A Christmas Carol ended, Granddad roused himself. "That useless dollop come back yet?" he asked.

"He's not a useless dollop," I said, feeling, more than ever, that there was nothing to keep my father here.

Granddad ignored me and checked his watch. "I don't know about you, Frank, lad," he said, "but I wouldn't mind getting a move on. Can't wait all night for our bloody Michael. I've got to get home. And, anyway, maybe he's finally found himself a bloody backbone and left that lunatic. . . ." He nodded toward the ceiling.

"I'd be grateful if you didn't talk about my sister in that manner, Harry," Mabel said, grabbing her cigarettes and shaking one from the packet. "That's no way to talk about family, and especially in front of Jesse here."

"Harry's got a point, though, Mabel," Frank said. "I mean, the woman's a danger to herself and others, she—"

"Frank!" Mabel flashed him a beseeching look. She pressed a cigarette into her mouth, lit it, and took a gasping drag.

"All right, all right," Frank said. "But we had better get home. It's late. Time we hit the road." He slapped his hands down on the arms of his chair and stood up. "Come on, Mabel. We'll drop Harry off on our way."

I turned to Mabel. "You're leaving? You're leaving me here by myself?" I was surprised at the way my voice rose, high and thin and quavering.

"Well, no, love, I . . ." She looked uncertainly over at Frank.

I hadn't anticipated this moment, the moment when, my father not having returned, decisions had to be made. And, after my mother's meltdown in the kitchen earlier, I certainly hadn't anticipated that I would be left alone with her. Naturally, I didn't want Frank to stay, and I wasn't that keen for Granddad to remain, either, but surely Mabel wouldn't leave me.

"Can't hang around here all night, can we?" Frank said, shoving his hands into the pockets of my father's oversized trousers. "She'll be all right." He nodded in my direction. "What, thirteen, isn't she? That's old enough to take care of herself. Come on, Mabel, get your coat."

Mabel rolled her lips together, her eyes moving to Frank and then to me.

"Oh, come on, Mabel. It's not like we're leaving her by herself, is it?" Frank said, his tone indignant. "I mean, after all, her mother's upstairs."

I looked at him, incredulous. "You already said yourself she's a danger to herself and others."

Mabel still sat on the settee, taking fast, urgent puffs on her cigarette. "Jesse's got a point, Frank. I mean, Evelyn was a bit beside herself today. And we all know that"—she paused—"well, she can go over the edge when she gets like that."

"Oh, don't be daft, Mabel." Frank said. "Besides, I came over here for my Christmas dinner, not to bloody babysit."

"It's not me that needs a babysitter," I protested. "Someone's got to help me take care of her." I could feel the tears welling up behind my eyes. I felt desperate, helpless, but I didn't want to let Frank see me cry. "Don't go, Auntie Mabel," I said. "You could stay in my bed. I wouldn't mind sleeping down here on the settee."

"Come on, Mabel, I said get your coat," Frank growled. "I'm not waiting here all bloody night."

"Oh, Frank, I just don't know that I should leave the lass. I could stay, I—"

"This is bloody ridiculous," Frank interrupted. "I've had boiling bloody gravy poured over my privates and my sodding Christmas ruined. If you think I'm going to stop here until Boxing Day, Mabel, well, you've got another thing coming. She'll be all right. It's not like she doesn't know how to use a phone. Come on, Harry," he said, turning to Granddad. "Let's me and you get our coats on. I'll wait for you, Mabel. Out in the car." He turned and left the room, Granddad following close behind.

As soon as he left, I reached over to Mabel, brushing my fingers over the pudgy softness of her forearm. "You're not going to go, are you, Auntie Mabel?" I wanted to tighten my grip around her wrist, to pin her down, refuse to let her go the same way Frank had held my hand on the kitchen floor.

Mabel sighed, her expansive chest heaving outward then sinking as if deflated. "I'm ever so sorry, darling," she said. "But I know what Frank's like and he'll be in a nasty mood for days if I don't go. He's got a bit of a temper on him, I'm sad to say."

I wanted to tell her that I'd seen his temper, and his cruelty, and that I knew exactly how nasty Frank could be. I wanted to ask her how she could possibly leave me now to follow after a man like that. But I didn't. I felt too dazed, too panicked, to speak.

"I tell you what," Mabel offered, "I'll pop upstairs before I go and take a look at your mam and make sure she's sleeping soundly. And first thing in the morning I'll give you a ring. If you need me to come over then, no matter what Frank says, I'll come. Even if it means I have to get a taxi all the way." She took my hand and pressed it into hers, wrapping my fingers in her clammy warmth. "You know I wouldn't leave you if you really needed me, darling."

After Frank, Mabel, and Granddad left, I tried to make myself feel better by writing to Amanda. I lay on my bed, *The Girl's Book of Heroines* by my side, and I wrote a letter to her telling her that if I lived in the past I'd dress like Saint Joan in a suit of armor. I'd travel astride a trusty mare, swinging my sword wildly above my head as I chased villains and invaders away. Peasants would bow down in my presence and ladies would swoon at the mention of my name, but it would be Lady Amanda who won my heart. I would rescue her from an evil Catholic pretender to the English throne, and, in her fervent gratitude, she'd throw herself into my arms, plant her lips on mine, and declare her undying love.

For the first time, however, composing a letter to Amanda was little distraction. And, as much as I tried not to, I kept thinking about my father, wondering if he was gone forever or he was really coming back. Through all the terrible events of the day, I had forced myself not to cry, but now big tears rolled down my cheeks and fell onto my letter so that the blue ink bled across the paper. Finally, I just lay down, next to my sodden letter, curled my knees to my chest, and let myself sob.

At some point I must have fallen asleep, because I woke, a few hours later, splayed on my bed with my cheek pressed into my wrinkled letter. I looked over at my alarm clock; it was just after two o'clock. I felt clammy and cold, and I was still wearing my clothes. I sat up and was about to get into my pajamas when I heard the door of my parents' bedroom ease open and my mother's soft patter along the hall. The bathroom light clicked on and then I heard the clink of bottles, glass clattering against the hard enamel of the sink. I sat there listening as the noise went on for a while, wondering, in my sleepy haze, if she had decided to rearrange the bathroom cabinet in the middle of the night. But then, recalling the catastrophe of our Christmas dinner, I had another thought, and, suddenly alert, I jumped off my bed, ran down the hall, and into the bathroom.

My mother was still wearing the ridiculous dress she'd donned for Christmas dinner, but she had taken off her stockings and, her bare feet planted on the floorboards, she was sitting on the closed lid of the toilet, a bottle of aspirin in one hand, a bottle of something the doctors at Delapole had prescribed for her in the other. They were both empty.

She had tipped their contents into the valley that her dress formed between her legs and was frowning down at them, a bright pile of tiny yellow and white disks, as if trying to determine how many pills she held. I guessed there were at least a hundred.

"Where did you get those tablets, Mum?" I asked, moving to perch on the side of the bathtub close to her. I shivered as I felt the hard cold of the enamel against my palms.

She ignored me and continued to stare down at her cache of pills.

"Mum," I said, more insistently, "where did you get them?" I had no idea where my father had been hiding my mother's medicines. All I knew was that he'd stashed them away and had been dispensing them to her. My mother must have scoured the house to find them. I imagined how she must have waited for my father and me to depart before she leaped out of bed to search for them. The thought made me furious.

"What are you doing?" I demanded. "What are you doing, sitting here like this in the middle of the night?"

"Your father's gone," she said, defeated.

My anger evaporated. I felt my father's absence like a cavern inside me. "He'll be back, Mum," I said. "Really, he'll be back. I think he just needed to get a break." I didn't believe it myself, but I felt the urgency of making her believe it.

"You think so?" She looked up. Under the harsh, unshaded bulb of the bathroom, her face looked colorless, almost gray. There were big dark circles under her eyes and, for the first time, I noticed the fine pattern of lines fanning out from beneath her eyes, like tiny channels carved by water across rock. She looked older, as if age had washed over her in the night. It made me aware of my mother's utter vulnerability. She could never, no matter how hard I wanted it or willed it, rise above the capricious tides of her moods. I was the one who had to hold her up.

I looked down at the pills, which were bright and shiny; small children would want to put them into their mouths. And, for a moment, I could see their attraction. All those innocent little tablets could take my mother into oblivion. She wouldn't have to flail and fight. And I could let her go, a lost swimmer falling through my arms, going under. I wouldn't have to try to save her anymore.

"I didn't mean to spoil your Christmas, you know, love," she said, her bleary eyes beseeching me.

"I know, Mum. I know." I took a deep breath, filling my lungs with air the way someone might before diving underwater, holding it in me, before I let it out in a steady sigh. Then I reached over and took the two empty pill bottles from her hands, brushing her fingers; they were icy cold. I placed the bottles on the floor.

I stood up and began looking around the bathroom. Behind the sink, I spotted one of the buckets that we had used to catch the leaks. I pulled it out and took it over to my mother. "Stand up," I commanded, tugging her up from the toilet so that the pills spilled into the bucket as I held it next to her. They fell like the sound of a downpour. A few missed the bucket and bounced over the floor, dancing brightly until they rolled into the cracks between the floorboards or settled silently against the bath and the sink. I bent down and began picking them up, tossing them into the bucket until I could find no more. Then I took my mother by the sleeve. "Come on, Mum," I said. "Let's get you back to bed."

After I had accompanied my mother to her bedroom, I went back to the bathroom, took the bucket of pills into my bedroom, tipped them into a pillowcase, and stuffed the pillowcase into the bottom of my dirty-laundry basket, the same place I'd hidden the whiskey I'd brought back from the disco a few days earlier. Then I undressed, put on my pajamas, and went back into my mother's room. I climbed into bed with her, pushing myself against her and wrapping my arm across her shoulder. Her whole body was cold, and her feet—curled up beneath her so she lay next to me pressed into the shape of a shrunken

S—were like little slabs of ice. But after a while we both began to warm, and eventually my mother fell into soft, steady breaths and then rhythmic snores, before I, too, drifted into sleep.

I woke to such familiar smells—my parents' musky blankets, the scent of their room (a blend of my mother's makeup and hair lacquer, my father's aftershave, and the polish on their chest of drawers)—that I had the sensation of having fallen back into my early childhood, when I was three or four years old and I'd climb into my parents' bed in the morning, squirm between them, and listen to their snuffles and groans as they folded themselves around me until I fell into a warm and delicious sleep. But then I opened my eyes and the recollections of the previous day's events came to me, and I wished that I could have stayed in that moment of memory. My mother, I was relieved to see, was still sleeping, but when I got up and peeked through the curtains there was no sign of my father's car.

For the rest of the day I watched television, feeling increasingly stupefied as I sat in front of the gas fire, snacking on the remnants of our Christmas dinner and staring at the Boxing Day programming, indifferent to everything I watched. When the telephone rang, I picked it up hoping that it was my father calling to tell us that he was coming back, but it was only Mabel, asking me how my mother was. I didn't tell her about the pills; I didn't want to ruin Mabel's Boxing Day as well as her Christmas, and though I would have liked, more than anything, for her to come over and take care of me, I knew that if she did she would bring Frank with her. The cut on my hand still hurt, reminding me of his brittle anger. I knew I'd be thrilled when he went the way of all Mabel's other boyfriends and she moved on to someone else.

Early in the afternoon, I coaxed my mother out of bed and got her to take a bath. She obeyed me like an automaton, moving about wordlessly. Once she was dressed, I had her come downstairs, where I made her a plate of leftovers and told her to eat it. She picked up a knife and fork and began pushing mouthfuls of food into her mouth, chewing so lethargically and swallowing with such effort that it was as if I were forcing her to eat poison—though, given her interest in taking all those tablets, perhaps she would have eaten poison more eagerly.

I wondered what I was going to do if my father didn't return. Should I call my mother's doctor and tell him what had happened? And if I did, would they take my mother off to Delapole again? And if they did that, what would happen to me? Would my father come back and take care of me, or had he simply had enough of everything and gone off to find a place that would give him solitude and peace? If it weren't for Frank, I'd want to go and live with Auntie Mabel, but with him around I'd need to go somewhere else. Maybe I'd be sent to live with Granddad, which, in some ways, wouldn't be so bad. After all, as long as I delivered his tea and regular plates of sandwiches he probably wouldn't bother me very much. Or perhaps I could ask to be sent to Australia, where I could live with Grandma and her fiancé in all that sun and heat. Or maybe I'd get sent to live with a foster family who lived in a neat little house on a neat little street? I found myself wondering if Tracey and Amanda's parents might take me in.

For a while, I managed to buoy myself up as I thought about these possibilities, but then, as darkness began to ease over the dull gray sky outside, I felt my optimism deflate. It was ridiculous for me to think that anyone would really want me. The other night, I'd been ignored by Tracey at the disco, and my father had forgotten me and left me to walk home alone in the snow. Yesterday, if he had wanted, he could have taken me with him, but he didn't care about me enough for that. He'd left me with my mother so that he could become someone like Frank— a man who carried a photograph of his children in his wallet, looking at their picture with fondness when he was no longer burdened by them every day. I would become a smiling face, frozen in a remembered moment, so that he could think of me as happy when, really, I was miserable and raw.

All of this seemed too much to bear until I thought again of how I had walked home with Amanda and how, beneath the warm lights of the village Christmas tree, she had placed that kiss on my lips. And I realized then that Amanda had not left me. In fact, she had given me something to hold on to, a piece of certainty in this baffling and desolate world. I knew that this meant that Amanda must like me, must really care for me—and, in a way, that wasn't so different from the way I cared for her. Girls didn't kiss girls unless, like those housewives on the problem page, they had different kinds of feelings for them.

I saw all the ways that Amanda had signaled this to me—how, that first time we'd met, she'd invited me to stand close to her under her umbrella, and how, the second time we saw each other, she'd asked me to smooth suntan lotion over her skin. How she'd defended me when everyone had teased me, how she'd confided in me at the bus stop about all her difficulties with Stan. How she'd pulled me up to dance with her at the disco, and how she'd leaned so close to me I'd felt her breath against my ear. It seemed no coincidence that, immediately after breaking up with Stan, she had kissed me. Clearly, she had been trying to tell me something. Clearly, she knew how I felt about her and she felt something similar in return. At the thought of all this, my hope rose, no longer held down in the terrible reality of this day.

IT WAS LATE WHEN I heard a car growl up the driveway. I ran over to the window, and as I saw my father pull up in front of the house I wanted to wave, bang on the window, shout in excitement. But I didn't. After all, he might just be coming back for his things. I turned and took a seat beside my mother, who had been making a study of her lap. "Dad's here," I said. She looked up, her eyes showing a slight glimmer, and then she turned expectantly toward the door.

He entered, his clothes rumpled and clearly slept in, his pullover stretched out and saggy at the elbows. His hair was windblown, exposing his bald patch. While the skin under his eyes was dark and saggy, his face had a waxy tinge.

"I've been thinking," he said after lowering himself into his armchair. "I've been thinking a lot. And I've decided that things can't go on like this."

I looked at him steadily, my stomach a knot, knowing that he was about to announce his permanent departure, that he was going to leave my mother and me alone. It was all I could do to stop myself jumping up and throwing myself on the floor in front of him, pleading, "Take me with you, take me with you. Don't leave me here with her." Instead, I gripped the edges of the settee cushion with both hands.

"I think things call for drastic measures," he continued.

I felt hot, woozy. I thought I might be sick.

"So," my father said, looking at my mother and sweeping a wayward strand of hair from his face. "I've had a word with your Ted, Evelyn. He's getting out of the nick in the middle of February, and when he does he's coming to live here."

"And where are you going, Dad?" I asked, trying to keep my voice calm while panic rose in me in swirling, frantic waves.

"Me?" he asked.

"Yes. Where will you go when you leave us?"

"I'm not going anywhere."

"You're not?"

"No," he said with a shrug. "Just needed to get away for a bit to get a chance to think. And while I was thinking, well"—his lips extended into a smile—"I realized that if Ted came to stay he could keep your mam company, cheer her up, help her out, while we could help him get on his feet. Seems like it's an arrangement that could benefit all of us and—"

Unable to control myself any longer, I pushed myself from the settee and launched myself across the room toward him, landing against his chest with a thud and wrapping my arms around his neck.

"Bloody hell, Jesse, what on earth's got into you?" I heard his words echoing through his chest as I pressed my cheek there, and then, when he put an arm around me and sat there wordless, I could hear the unwavering rhythm of his heart.

—

THE NEXT MORNING, I was woken at six o'clock by the sound of furniture scraping over floorboards. When I got up to investigate, I discovered my mother in the spare bedroom at the front of the house, dragging an old armchair into the middle of the room, where she had already piled boxes, cartons, and other miscellaneous items. "What are you doing, Mum?" I asked, bleary-eyed under the glare of the unshaded bulb that hung from the flaking ceiling.

"Decorating," she said. "If we leave it to your father, it's going to take forever. And I'll not have our Ted thinking that we live in a pigsty. It's bad enough him having to be in prison. Last thing he needs is to get out and find himself in a dump like this." She swung an arm to indicate the chaos around her. "Now, that would be depressing."

"Are you all right, Mum?"

"All right? Of course I'm all right," she said, setting the chair beside an ancient lamp with a moth-eaten shade. "I've never felt better in my life."

I looked at her, mouth agape. Just over twenty-four hours ago, she'd been on the verge of swallowing several dozen pills, and now here she was telling me she'd never felt better, as if that moment in the bathroom had never taken place. I imagined myself holding on to the rear bumper of a wildly careening car, a fool for thinking I might slow a speeding vehicle or prevent it from colliding with whatever was in the way.

"I'll have to take a lot of this plaster down," she said, pointing at the crumbling ceiling. "And that window frame needs replacing as well. Of course, I'll have to put a carpet in. But I already know what color scheme I'm using. I'm going to do burgundy walls with a light red on the woodwork. And I'll make some nice purple curtains and a matching bedspread. I'll see if I can get a nice red carpet as well. What do you think?"

"Sounds nice." Actually, I was more than a little dubious about the aesthetic merits of a room done entirely in shades of red and purple, but I'd long given up on either of my parents exhibiting even the tiniest skill in interior decorating. And, if it was going to help her remain in her present mood, that was fine with me.

"I know our Ted will love it," my mother continued, gazing dreamily up at the blotchy ceiling. "Men like strong colors. And I bet those prisons aren't exactly painted nice and bright. This'll cheer him up. And if he's going to be here in a few weeks, then I'd better get started right away."

After that, my mother engaged herself in a whirlwind of activity. She managed to change out of her nightclothes, but now she wore the same paint-spattered slacks and oversized shirt every day. (I suspected that she also slept in this outfit, but since she never went to bed until after I'd gone to sleep and was up before I ventured out of my bedroom in the mornings I couldn't be sure.) She stopped watching television altogether; instead, she hummed the tunes of songs sung by Engelbert Humperdinck, Tom Jones, and Perry Como while she knocked down the ceiling, banged away at the window frame, and hauled bags of plaster up the stairs.

While I was pleased that my father's decision to invite Ted to stay with us had energized my mother, I wasn't convinced that this was my father's best plan. Ted, after all, was not known for his stabilizing influence on anyone. And, after hearing Mabel's anecdote about his stealing her neighbor's television, I wondered if having him here was really worth the risk. For the first time, I found some consolation in the fact that our house was in the middle of nowhere, with no neighbors nearby at all. Perhaps without those kinds of temptations Ted would behave himself. I decided to cling firmly to this flimsy hope.

CHAPTER NINETEEN

——

DURING THE REST OF THE CHRISTMAS HOLIDAYS, WHILE MY MOTHER
was consumed with fixing up the spare bedroom, I was equally consumed by a need to write my letters to Amanda. Fueled now by my certainty that she returned my feelings, I felt compelled to compose
ever-longer and more elaborate stories about our imagined adventures.
Everything that I had been holding back spilled out onto the page.
After all, if Amanda felt the same way that I did, I didn't need to feel
ashamed or guilty about anything I wrote. Even if we would have to
hide our feelings from the rest of the world, together, secretly, we could
revel in them. I would no longer worry that I was the only girl who was
in love with another girl. By the time school started, I had almost filled
my biscuit tin with letters and I'd tied them in a tight fat bundle, folded
neatly and sorted in chronological order. Sometimes I'd pull them out
and reread them, and sometimes I'd simply sit on my bed and hold
them, as if their collective weight was proof of something solid, something I could rely on when everything else seemed in flux.

It was still dark when I awoke that first morning of the new term.
When I peered out my window, the world below was silent, silvered
and furred with frost. When I'd fallen asleep the night before, my
mother had still been working in the spare bedroom, but now I could

hear her snores along with my father's. I was relieved to know that she was at least getting some sleep. As I made my way downstairs after washing and dressing, I heard the harsh ring of my father's alarm clock and his angry muttering as he fumbled to turn it off. In the kitchen, I made tea and a big pan of porridge for both of us, but before my father had even made it downstairs I was out the door.

I was ridiculously early for the bus that morning, arriving in the village almost half an hour before it was due to arrive. Of course, I expected to be the first one there. No one else in their right mind would want to stand outside in such fearsome cold. So I was surprised when I turned the corner onto the high street and saw someone standing by the bus stop. I was utterly thrilled when, as I drew closer, I realized it was Amanda.

"Hiya, Jesse," she called, giving me an enthusiastic wave.

"Hiya," I said, my heart pounding as I neared.

"God, I'm glad you're here," she said as I reached the bus stop. "It's bloody freezing this morning." She gave a shudder and wrapped her arms about her. "But I wanted to see you before our Tracey comes."

"You did?" My heart raced and my stomach flipped. It was as much as I could do to stop myself from throwing my arms around her neck.

"I just had to tell you something." She stamped her feet, in part to keep herself warm, it seemed, and partly out of excitement. Her face, ablaze with the cold, was intensely animated. "But first you have to swear to keep it a secret."

I knew that I'd been right. That kiss really had meant that she cared about me. What else would she want to talk to me about in secret? And why else would she brave this bone-chilling cold to make sure she could be alone with me?

"I won't tell anybody," I said.

"Not even Tracey." She looked at me intently. "Especially not Tracey."

"Especially not Tracey," I said. Of course, I knew this was one thing I could never share with her.

Amanda frowned, studying my face for a moment, and then, apparently satisfied with the sincerity she found there, she pulled a wide, beaming smile. "All right," she said, grabbing my arm and pulling me toward her. I felt loose, boneless, in her grasp. "I want to show you something." As I stood close, delighting in her delicious presence, she began rifling about in one of the pockets of her coat. Then she pulled out a little box, struggled with one of her gloved hands to open it, and finally lifted the lid to show a gold locket set in the middle of a velvet cushion. "So, what do you think?" She held it a few inches away from my face.

"It's lovely," I said. It was heart-shaped, delicate, the kind of locket you'd give to someone you loved.

"Isn't it gorgeous?" she said. "Here." She thrust it into my gloved hand.

This was far more than I could even have hoped for. A gift like this said more than anyone could ever put into words. "It's . . . It's beautiful." I said, almost breathless. "Thank you." Then I threw my arms around her, pushed my face into hers, and planted a kiss on her lips.

I had written this a hundred times. In this delicious moment when I pulled Amanda to me, we wrapped our arms around each other, pressed our bodies close so that only the fabric of our clothes separated us, and our mouths melted together in a long heat-filled kiss.

But that wasn't what happened. Instead of feeling limp and eager in my arms, Amanda seemed a column of stiffness, and rather than returning my kiss gratefully, as soon as I put my lips against hers she shoved me away.

"Jesse! What the hell are you doing?"

I staggered back. She had pushed me hard. I looked at her face—her eyes were bright with outrage, her lips twisted into a tight, revolted knot. As if instinctively wiping away dirt from her lips, she wiped her hand back and forth across her mouth. I watched her and felt the earth tilt, as if all gravity were gone and I was falling sideways, my head veering toward the ground.

"What the bloody hell was that about?" she demanded. "I just wanted to show you what Stan got me."

I looked at the box, still sitting in my hand. "It's from Stan?" I asked, still unable to find my balance, my heartbeat a drum pounding inside my ears. I didn't understand. Amanda was finished with Stan. Only a couple of weeks ago she had kissed me. And now, when I tried to kiss her, she had hurled me away in horror.

"Yeah. What did you think?" Her forehead was wrinkled into a ferocious rippling question, then it suddenly smoothed. "Oh my God, you thought that I . . . you thought that you and me . . . you thought that when I kissed you . . ." Her expression changed and, instead of looking horrified she let out a loud, jagged laugh. It was a white cloud in the morning's freezing air.

A solid, sickening realization fell over me: that kiss she had placed on my lips after the disco was nothing more than a drunken gesture of gratitude. I was an idiot to imagine that it had been anything else.

"No, no, I didn't think that. . . ." I was scrambling, flailing with words. "I just thought that maybe you had got the locket for me, and that was stupid." I let out a hollow laugh. "But I didn't think. . . . Of course, I didn't think *that.*" My face was on fire, and my entire body was made of nothing more than hot liquid. Inside, I was boiling with shame.

Amanda studied my face for a moment, her brows knotted. I dropped my gaze to stare hopelessly at the ground. I knew what was coming next. I could already hear her taunts of "Lezzie, lezzie, lezzie," echoing down the high street, through all the quiet streets of the village for everyone else to hear.

"So you like it, then?" Amanda asked.

"What?"

"The locket, you like the locket?"

I looked up and met her eyes. In them, green and dazzling and as beautiful as ever, I saw that she knew my secret. She knew exactly how I felt. "I'm sorry, Amanda, I—"

She shrugged. "Forget it, Jesse."

"I didn't mean to—"

"I said forget it." Her voice was firm.

I stood there, unsure if the ground beneath me was solid. I took a breath. "So you got back together with Stan, then?" I tried to make my voice sound light, to suppress the tears I felt rising. "That's great." I forced my lips into the curve of a smile.

"Yeah." She nodded vaguely. "Yeah," she repeated, this time more brightly. "He felt really, really bad about the accident. So after he got his bike fixed he rode all the way down to Cleethorpes to see me."

"That's nice. It's a long way down to Cleethorpes," I said, my voice too loud and oddly boisterous.

"He said he was ever so sorry, and then he gave me the locket and begged me to take him back. He must have spent a lot of money on it." She took the box holding the locket from my hand. "Shame I can't wear it, really."

"Why not?"

"Well, I don't want my dad to see it. He'd go bloody nuts."

"Why?"

She sighed. "He's always on at me, anyway. But this, well, he wouldn't approve of a lad giving me something like that."

"Oh, but you should wear it. And if the chain's long enough you can just hide it under your blouse." I was stunned, even as I spoke, at what I was saying. It was as if my words had stopped being my own. But now I had to stuff all my feelings deep inside me, prove to Amanda that what she had glimpsed of me really wasn't there.

"You think so?"

"If you like, I'll help you put it on."

Amanda hesitated, tilting her head and looking at me, as if trying to discern something in my face.

"Really," I said. "It's no trouble."

"It is a bit fiddly, Jesse," she said, her tone cautious. "Maybe you should leave it."

"No, really, you should wear it." I was determined to do this. It was a test I had set myself. "I'll just take my gloves off—that'll make it easier." I removed my gloves and stuffed them into my pockets while Amanda, apparently convinced now, took the locket from the box. She handed it to me.

It was cold and surprisingly weightless in my palm. For a moment, I had the urge to close my fist around it, pull my arm back, and hurl the stupid locket into the air, across the high street, and through the bare branches of the trees into the fields beyond. I imagined myself doing this and then turning to look at Amanda, fire burning in my eyes. Then I'd tell her that I didn't care if it meant that I was a lezzie but I loved her and she was a fool for not realizing that my love meant so much more than Stan's.

I didn't throw the locket away, though. Instead, I unclasped the chain, reached up, and put it around Amanda's neck. When I'd fastened the locket, she pulled back. "Oh, I forgot to show you," she said, struggling for a moment and then popping the locket open. Inside, there was a little heart-shaped picture of Stan Heaphy. He grinned out at me from that place on Amanda's chest.

CHAPTER TWENTY

THE SATURDAY THAT UNCLE TED WAS DUE TO ARRIVE, I'D ASKED MY father to take me along to pick him up, imagining myself pacing outside a shadowy, turreted prison, waiting for the enormous gates to swing open and for Ted to walk out, blinking in the unfamiliar daytime brilliance. It turned out, though, that Ted had actually been released a couple of days before he was to come to our house and my father would pick him up at the Hull railway station after visiting Granddad Bennett for a couple of hours. Since this prospect seemed a lot less exciting, I decided to stay at home. There, however, as my mother rushed around the house putting last-minute touches to her decorating, I began to think that watching wrestling matches with Granddad and my father would have been a lot more relaxing.

In the last few weeks, she'd completed her work on the spare room and, after refurbishing her and my father's bedroom and painting it in rather alarming shades of pink and yellow, she'd required me to move out of my bedroom so that she could do it up as well. Retrieving my biscuit tin filled with my letters and my mother's pills and the whiskey bottle from my laundry basket and secreting them behind the settee, I'd spent a week and a half sleeping in the living room while she did up my room. After replacing some of the floorboards and a substantial part of the ceiling, she'd finished by covering my bedroom walls in a paisley-patterned wallpaper of purple, orange, and cream that she'd acquired in the going-out-of-business sale of a hardware shop in Hull several years earlier. While we waited for my father to return with Ted, she hung a pair of matching purple paisley curtains at my window.

"No wonder they went of out business," I said as my mother stood back to admire her handiwork and I surveyed the nightmare of swirls that had become my bedroom walls.

"Don't be so bloody ungrateful," she snapped. "There's children in Africa would kill for a bedroom as nice as this."

"And as soon as they got it they'd redecorate," I mumbled as she pushed past me into the hall.

Later that afternoon, Mabel and Frank arrived. It was the first time they'd visited since Christmas. My mother had insisted that they join us to welcome Ted home and help give him the positive new start he needed. As they followed my mother into the kitchen, they both seemed in especially cheerful moods.

"Not planning to chuck that on my trousers, are you, Evelyn?" Frank joked as my mother set the kettle on the cooker to boil.

"I told Frank we should get him a pair of asbestos underpants when he comes over here," Mabel added, nudging Frank and laughing. "That way, at least his manhood will be safe."

My mother spun around. "If you don't mind, Mabel, I'd prefer it if you didn't make distasteful jokes while you're in my house. I really don't want Jesse exposed to that kind of talk. Besides, we should set a better tone for our Ted."

"Oh, don't be ridiculous, Evelyn," Mabel scoffed. "Ted's coming home from prison, not a tour of the Commonwealth with the bloody Queen. I can't imagine he'll be shocked by anything Frank or me have got to say. . . . Or maybe by one thing," she said, exchanging a brief look with Frank. My mother caught the exchange between them and regarded them with a narrow-eyed frown. "Anyway, Jesse hears far worse than that at school every day."

"Oh, aye," Frank said, nodding. "Teenagers these days get up to larks we never even dreamed of when we were young. Don't they, Jesse, love?"

"I'm going upstairs, I've got homework to do," I said, ignoring Frank and looking instead at my mother and Mabel. "I'll come down when Uncle Ted gets here."

I did, in fact, have quite a lot of homework to do—several pages of geometry that Tracey and the Debbies were depending on me to complete so they could copy it before our maths lesson on Monday, and an essay on the War of the Roses for Miss Nutall. Neither of these activities, however, seemed particularly appealing. Instead, I decided to write a letter to Amanda.

It had been several weeks since I'd written to her. After that morning when she showed me the locket that Stan had given her, I hadn't written to her once; I hadn't even spoken to her at the bus stop very much. I couldn't bear to. I had revealed how I felt about her and she had thought me absurd, laughable, repellent. And though she remained friendly enough, just the knowledge that she had been horrified by my effort to kiss her made me shrink away. I longed for that brief period of euphoria when I'd managed to convince myself that Amanda shared my feelings. But I was alone with all my perverted yearnings for another girl. I was confused, bereft, and left without even a fantasy to cling to. This time, in my letter, I couldn't write out any more of my ridiculous stories; I simply wanted to tell her how I felt.

"Dear Amanda," I began, "I wish I could send this letter to you. Actually, I wish I could talk to you about how I feel, but if I did you would probably hate me and call me all sorts of horrible names. The thing is, I am really confused about almost everything. The only thing that I am certain of is that I love you. But I know that loving you is wrong and that if anybody found out they would say I was a lesbian. I don't even know if that is true. I just know that when you kissed me that night after the disco it was the most wonderful moment in my life and if I could stop time, the way they did in a *Star Trek* episode once, I would stop it at the exact second that we stood next to the village Christmas tree and you kissed me, and I would stay there forever. So I'm glad that you did it, and I'm glad that you danced with me at the disco, because that was really wonderful as well. But sometimes I wish that you hadn't done any of those things. Sometimes I even feel really mad at you for making me think that maybe you liked me. I suppose that doesn't matter now, because I know that you think my loving you is a horrible thing. I have never been more miserable in my life, Amanda. Even when they took my mum off to Delapole, I don't think I felt as bad as this. . . ."

The knob on my bedroom door turned, the door burst open, and I jumped in shock. It was Frank. "Oh, hello, Jesse, love," he said, pulling his thin lips into an arcing smirk.

"Don't you know to knock?" I demanded, slamming shut my notebook and scrambling to sit up. I wanted to sound confident, outraged. Instead, my voice came out thin and uncertain.

"Didn't know you were in here, did I? Your mam was telling me and Mabel about how she'd decorated the bedrooms and I thought I'd come up and take a look." He took a few steps into the room and gave the wallpaper an appraising look. "Got interesting tastes has your mam," he said, cocking an eyebrow. "Or maybe all them squiggles remind her of the state of her brain. I hope it doesn't end up driving you nuts as well."

I looked at him without comment, teeth clenched, willing him to leave and desperately aware of all those words I'd just written in my notebook—my most heartfelt confessions spelled out on the page.

"Oh, come on, now, you're not still mad with me about what happened at Christmas, are you, love?" He moved closer.

Instinctively, I ran a finger over the place where my hand had been cut. It had healed over, but there was still a perceptible ridge in my skin. "I've got homework to do," I said.

"Quite the conscientious student, aren't you?" he said, coming closer still. Now, as he stood in the light that came in through the window, I could see his expression—the wrinkled tightness around his eyes, the scornful camber of his lips.

"Not really." I willed him to stop his steady approach. But he didn't. Instead, he arrived at the bed and lowered himself to sit beside me. The mattress sank under his weight, and I felt myself tilted so that my body fell in his direction. I pulled myself away and tried to push my notebook farther from him to the corner of the bed.

"Sorry to say, I wasn't much of a student when I was a lad," he said, sighing. "And when I did read it was mostly comics. Superman was my favorite. You ever like Superman?"

I shook my head, watching him warily as I breathed in his sweat, cigarette, and aftershave smells.

"So what you writing, then?"

"Nothing," I said, pulling the notebook to me and pressing it against my chest.

"Oh," he said, his mouth turning upward in a knowing smile. "One of them teenage diaries, is it? Tell it all your private secrets, do you?"

"No," I said as I felt the blush rise in my cheeks. "It's just homework."

"Anything you want to share with your uncle Frank?"

"Actually, I'd like you to leave now," I said. "I've got to finish my homework."

Frank pulled his thin lips downward, mimicking an expression of disappointment. "Not much of a hostess, are you, love? And here's me just trying to get to know my little niece."

"I'm not your niece. And you're not my uncle."

"Will be soon," he said, grinning.

"What do you mean?" I asked softly.

"Mabel and me, we're getting married."

"Oh." I was stunned. Surely this couldn't be true. Mabel would never get married, and certainly not to Frank. He must be lying.

Frank laughed sourly. "You're supposed to say 'Congratulations!' Supposed to say 'Welcome to the family, Uncle Frank.' Actually, if you were really going to be as polite and nice to me as you should, you'd give me a kiss." He patted his hand against his whiskery cheek. "Right here."

I backed away until I felt the cold solidity of the wall against my back.

Frank threw his head back and laughed. "Oh, don't worry, love. I won't make you. But you might want to change your attitude. I mean, with me going to be your uncle—well, we'll be seeing a lot more of each other in the future. You should write that in your little diary. 'Saturday, the fifteenth of February' "—he mimicked writing in the air with his hand—" 'found out that Frank is going to marry my auntie Mabel. Oh, what happy news!' See," he said, dropping his hand to his lap and staring steadily at me. "That's the kind of welcome I'm looking for. Instead of all this ruddy rudeness and antagonism from your bloody nutcase of a mother."

"She can't help it if she doesn't like you," I said, looking at him steadily.

"Well, that's a shame. Because she's going to have to get used to me. I'm going to be part of the family now." With a grunt, he pushed himself off the bed so that he stood looking down at me. "You should probably write that down in your diary as well," he said, eyeing the notebook I was still clutching to my chest.

After Frank left, I sat on my bed for a long time holding my notebook. I sat still as his footsteps descended the stairs and as I heard his voice below, in the kitchen, a husky rumble against Mabel's and my mother's higher, lighter tones. Finally, assured that he wouldn't return, I completed my letter to Amanda. This time it didn't go on for pages and pages. This time it was short and to the point. I simply asked her why, on that cold night, she had placed her lips on mine to send my hopes soaring, then let them crash into a ditch like Stan Heaphy's motorbike, leaving me floundering, helpless, unable to brush myself off and get up.

When I was finished, I tore the letter from my notebook. Then I pulled my biscuit tin from the wardrobe, lifted the lid, and added it to my bundle. For a moment, I felt myself wanting to retrieve a box of matches from the kitchen so that I could set a little bonfire in the biscuit tin and burn all those letters. It seemed the kind of romantic gesture unrequited love demanded, and I felt a desperate desire to burn all those feelings from me, to see them ignite, flare, turn to smoke and flames. Having the letters there, hidden in my bedroom, was concrete evidence of a terrible flaw that I never wanted anyone else to find. But they were also evidence of the love I still felt. And, despite everything, I couldn't let that go. So I put the lid on the tin and put it back in its usual hiding place, but as soon as I did that I knew that I'd written the last of my letters to Amanda. I might still think of her constantly, I might still wish that she returned my feelings, but I would not write to her again.

IN ALL THE YEARS I'd known Ted, he'd never arrived at our house empty-handed. Usually, his gifts seemed extravagant—a gold watch for my father, a set of pearl earrings for my mother, a leather coat for me. Within a short while, however, we usually discovered that there was something not quite right about these items—the gold on my father's watch started peeling off to reveal a dull gray metal underneath, the pearl earrings turned mottled pink when my mother got them wet, and on the first day I'd worn my leather coat Mrs. Brockett had taken great pleasure in pointing out that it was, in fact, made of plastic. At other times, Ted brought us things that seemed more practical—a carton of six dozen lightbulbs, twenty-four tins of Mr. Sheen furniture polish, a five-gallon bucket of white paint. Soon after his departure, however, we'd invariably discover that there was something wrong with this merchandise. Only about a third of the lightbulbs had actually worked, most of the Mr. Sheen lost its aerosol propellant so quickly that we got only one or two pathetic streams of polish from each tin before they proved useless, and, upon opening the white paint we'd found it full of little gray lumps.

"Well, what do you expect when everything he gets has fallen off the back of a lorry?" Auntie Mabel said anytime my mother complained about Ted's latest offerings.

When I was younger, before I understood the meaning of this phrase, I'd imagined Ted coming upon the items he brought us in the middle of the road after they'd fallen from an overladen lorry or van. Later, even after I'd learned that Auntie Mabel was referring to the illicit ways in which Ted acquired almost everything that came into his possession, the image still stuck. Though, rather than thinking of Ted serendipitously coming upon his merchandise, I began to visualize him chasing down vehicles in the streets, or grabbing boxes and cartons out of the rear doors of lorries as they waited for the traffic lights to change. There was something about this image that seemed to sum Ted up in my mind—a dodging pilferer who was just as likely to get sideswiped by an enormous juggernaut as he was to get away with anything worthwhile.

This time when Ted arrived, he swaggered into the hallway wearing an enormous grin and what looked like a giant, sleeping animal over his shoulder.

"Uncle Ted!" I said, beaming as I opened the door to see him standing before me, wreathed in a cloud of cigarette smoke.

"Hello, Jesse, love," he said, sticking his cigarette between his lips, putting a big arm around me, and giving me a kiss on my cheek. Then he stepped back to regard me. "By heck, you've grown," he said, the cigarette, propped in the corner of his mouth, jiggling about as he spoke. "What they've been feeding you round here, rocket fuel? That'd certainly make you shoot up, eh?" He took the cigarette from his lips and let out a deep bass laugh that shuddered through my chest and echoed down the hallway. As he laughed, I studied his face. He looked a lot older than I remembered him. He was still handsome and his blue eyes had that same mischievous glow, but his greased-back hair was graying at the temples and the laugh lines around his eyes and mouth had molded themselves more firmly into his face. He was fatter, too, so that while his face looked older it also seemed softer and slightly puffy, as if it had been filled with air and then deflated slightly—like the shrunken surface of an old party balloon.

"What's that?" I asked, indicating the enormous swath of flecked brown fur slung over his shoulder.

"This? Oh, just a little something I picked up for your mam's birthday."

"But that was months ago." My mother's birthday was in November. We hadn't had much of a celebration. Though I'd made a cake and my father had bought her a bunch of flowers, my mother had refused to come downstairs. Instead, she lay under her huge mound of blankets complaining that Grandma hadn't sent her even a birthday card and that if a mother couldn't remember her own daughter's birthday, then the world was in a far worse state than she'd ever imagined and it certainly wasn't worth getting out of bed.

"I know it was months ago," Ted huffed. "But I was in the nick then, wasn't I? So I thought I'd get her something now. It's a coat. It's real fox fur, you know. Here, feel it." He pushed one of the folds of the coat toward me.

I brushed my hand over the fur. It was extraordinarily soft. "It feels nice," I said. But then I pulled my hand away. "Don't they trap and kill the foxes? Isn't it really cruel?"

The subject had come up in one of my recent English lessons, and Ms. Hastings had said that it was ridiculous that animals should suffer so that people could wear their dead skins. She'd also told us that because she was against cruelty to animals she was a vegetarian, a revelation that Tracey and the Debbies found hilarious. Later in the corridor, when they'd joked about buying Ms. Hastings a bag of rabbit food, I'd said that, really, it wasn't all that funny and that perhaps she had a point. Accompanied by a chorus of laughter from the Debbies, Tracey had responded that perhaps they should buy me a bag of rabbit food as well.

"Oh, for God's sake, Jesse," Ted said. "Don't you start. I've had your bloody dad lecturing me about fox hunting and the debauched upper classes ever since he picked me up. Though what that's got to do with fur coats I've no bloody idea. Anyway, where's your mam? I can't wait to see her face when I hand her this."

"She's in the kitchen, having a cup of tea with Auntie Mabel and Frank—that's Auntie Mabel's boyfriend."

Ted's face dropped. "Oh, no," he muttered. "Not our bloody Mabel. I was hoping to avoid her for at least a few days." He exhaled a long stream of smoke, tossed the cigarette onto the path, and marched into the house. It was wet outside, and I watched the cigarette land on the path, fizzle, and die before I turned and scrambled after him.

"Happy birthday to you, happy birthday to you, happy birthday, dear Evelyn . . ." Ted's tuneless voiced boomed down the hallway. When he reached the kitchen, he pushed open the door and concluded, "happy birthday to you." He pulled the fox-fur coat from his shoulder and, holding it out to my mother, made a bowing gesture and announced, "Your carriage awaits, madam."

"Ted!" My mother leaped from her chair and rushed across the room. "Oh, Ted," she said, taking the coat from him, holding it against her cheek and nuzzling her face into it. "It's gorgeous."

"Here, why don't you put it on?" Ted took the coat from my mother and eased it over her shoulders. My mother wriggled her arms into the sleeves and did a little twirl in the middle of the kitchen.

"Makes you look like a film star, Ev," he said.

"You think so?" my mother asked breathily as she ran her hands over the coat.

" 'Course I do."

My mother pulled a troubled frown. "Is it real?"

"Real?" Ted looked put out. "Of course it's bloody real. One hundred percent genuine bloody fox fur."

At this, Mabel, who'd been sitting silently at the kitchen table with Frank, laughed. "More like one hundred percent squirrel fur, I should think," she said, rolling her eyes.

"Oh, and I suppose you're an expert on fur coats, Mabel," Ted said.

"No, but I'm an expert on you. And either there's something wrong with that coat or there's something very dodgy about its history. Where'd you get it from, anyway? Nicked it, did you?"

"Bloody hell, Mabel. Of course I didn't nick it—"

"What, walk into the women's department in Hammonds and buy it for Evelyn, then, did you?"

"Well, no . . . I mean, who can afford to get anything from Hammonds? Mate of mine sold it to me."

"Oh, yeah, and this mate, where'd he get it from?"

"I don't know—I expect he picked it up somewhere."

"Oh," said Mabel, making her eyes wide. "Picked it up somewhere, did he? Found it on the street, did he? Just happened upon it as he was walking along Hessle Road? 'Oh, look,' he says, 'there's a fur coat—I think I'll take that home and sell it to my mate Ted.'" She laughed. "God, Ted, you think I was born yesterday?"

"No, Mabel," Ted said, pausing to light a cigarette, " 'course I don't think you were born yesterday. Let's face it, you're a bit too wrinkly for that."

"Ooh, I'll smack you, I really will," Mabel said, shaking a fist in his direction.

"You're only jealous." My mother, who had been absorbed in running her hands over the coat's smooth surface, piped up.

"What do you mean?" Mabel narrowed her eyes.

"I mean you're jealous. If Ted turned up with a fox-fur coat for you, you wouldn't say a word. But because he brought it for me—well, you can't stand it, can you?"

"Rubbish," Mabel huffed. "I'm just tired of him getting himself involved in all this malarkey. Receiving stolen property, burglary, petty theft. Christ! Surely you should know better by now."

"Oh, for God's sake, Mabel. I only brought our Ev a coat. It's not like I showed up with the takings from the local Barclays Bank, is it?"

"Same thing, you ask me," Mabel said. "I told Mike and Ev that I think they're mad taking you in like this."

"And I'm very grateful, I really am. And what better way to show my gratitude than by bringing Evelyn a nice present?"

"I'm warning you, Ted," Mabel said, wagging a finger at him. "Evelyn and Mike have enough on their plate. And they've been generous enough to give you an opportunity to finally set yourself straight. You cause any trouble while you're here and I swear, I will never, ever speak to you again." She paused as if to let this last comment sink in. "I mean it, Ted, I really do."

"Bloody hell, Mabel. I've not been here five minutes and you're giving me a lecture."

"And you've not been two days out of jail and you're bringing home stolen property."

"I don't want you to go to prison again, Uncle Ted," I said, going over to him and tugging on his arm. All this talk about Ted's illicit activity was making me nervous. I wanted him to stay, but I also wanted him to stay out of trouble, and I certainly didn't want his presence to jeopardize the sliver of stability we had in our home.

"Oh, don't you worry, love," Ted said, patting my hand. "I'm not going anywhere."

"Hah, that's a laugh, that is. You carry on like this," Mabel said, gesturing toward my mother in her fox-fur coat, "and as sure as the sky is blue and the grass is green you'll be back in the nick before Easter."

"Sky's gray today," said Ted. "Matter of fact, sky's mostly gray in England."

"Yes, well gray, blue, or pink, you'll not be seeing much of it if you don't change your ways."

"You should take the coat back, Uncle Ted," I said.

"What?" Ted looked at me incredulously.

"You should take it back. That way, you won't get into trouble and you won't go back to jail." I wanted the fur coat out of the house. With its lavish softness and rippling folds, it obviously didn't belong here. My mother didn't look like a film star when she wore it; she looked absurd. And, as Ms. Hastings had said, nobody needed to wear dead animals. "You should take it back, Uncle Ted," I repeated.

My mother, pulled from the rapture of stroking her coat, snapped, "Shut up, Jesse."

"No," Mabel said, "Jesse's right. He should take that coat back. And if he had any decency about him he wouldn't have brought it here in the first place."

"Oh, come on, now, Mabel," Frank said, reaching out to place his hand on Mabel's arm. Until now, he'd sat silent, watching the discussion attentively. "The lad's only just stepped in the door. Give him a break. There's no harm done. And Evelyn looks lovely in her new coat. Ted's right, she does look like a film star." At this, my mother beamed appreciatively at Frank, then turned to Mabel to give her a satisfied little nod. "Besides," Frank continued, "you haven't even introduced the two of us."

"I'm sorry, Frank, love. You're right." Mabel looked at Ted and pulled a taut smile. "Ted, this is my fella, Frank. Frank, this is my brother, Ted."

Frank rose and made his way across the kitchen. "Very nice to meet you, Ted," he said. I stood beside Ted as Frank extended his hand.

Ted put his cigarette in his mouth and reached out. "Thanks for calling the dogs off," he said, shaking Frank's hand enthusiastically.

"Anytime, Ted," Frank said, slapping him gently on the back. "But you know what women are like. They worry too much." He smiled at Mabel and gave her a wink. Then he lowered his voice and adopted a more confidential tone. "Don't you worry about Mabel. I'm sure you know what you're doing. That's a bloody nice coat. Must be worth a fortune. Expect you need some good contacts to be able to acquire quality merchandise like that."

As Frank spoke, my father pushed his way into the kitchen. "Bloody hell, Ted," he said breathlessly. "What the heck have you got in them cases of yours? Lead weights?"

"No, it's just my stuff," Ted began to explain. "I'd been storing it over at my mate's house and—"

"Oh, Mike," Mabel said, "don't say he's got you lugging his flipping luggage around for him? Ted, you lazy bugger, you should be doing that yourself. I hope you don't think you're going to carry on like this, do you? Because the sooner you get yourself off your lazy backside and—"

"Oh, come on, love, give the lad a break," Frank said. "He's only just got home. And Mike doesn't mind carrying Ted's luggage in, do you, Mike?"

"Well," my father said, dropping into one of the empty chairs at the kitchen table, "to be honest, it would have been nice if—"

"Let's face it, you've got to help family out when they need you," Frank interrupted. "Family is, after all, the most important thing we've got. Speaking of family," Frank said, adopting a grandiose tone, "Mabel and I have got an announcement to make, haven't we, Mabel?"

"Yes, yes we have." Mabel patted her hair and beamed around the kitchen.

I realized then that what Frank had told me upstairs earlier was true. He and Mabel were getting married.

"What sort of announcement?" my mother asked, her eyes moving suspiciously between Mabel and Frank.

"Well—" Frank began, puffing out his scrawny chest.

"They're getting married," I said flatly. I felt a moment of intense satisfaction as Frank's chest deflated and his face rumpled in annoyance. There was something immensely pleasurable about taking the wind out of his sails like that. Still, it didn't change the fact that I'd have to put up with his poisonous presence on a long-term basis. One thing I did know for certain, though: I would never call him "Uncle Frank."

"Married?" my mother said, pulling her coat protectively around her. "You're getting married?" She sounded stung.

"Yes, Evelyn, we're getting married," Mabel said, taking out a cigarette and searching around for her lighter.

"By heck," Ted said, grinning broadly. "That's a ruddy turnup for the

books. Our Mabel getting married, who'd have thought it?" He slapped
Frank across the back, the impact of his hand sounding a hollow thud
and making Frank stagger forward several steps across the kitchen.
"Congratulations, Frank! That's champion, that is. Just hope you don't
live to regret it." He bellowed out a laugh.

Mabel looked at him through narrowed eyes.

"Only joking, Mabel," Ted said, lifting his hands as if in surrender.
"Really, I think it's smashing news. About time someone had the
courage to make an honest woman of you."

"Yes, congratulations, Frank, Mabel," my father said. "That's terrific
news, isn't it, Evelyn?"

Everyone turned toward her, and for a long moment the room
seemed airless, still and filled with expectation. I watched my mother,
half hoping that she would start screaming at Frank, yell at him that she
didn't want a brother-in-law who wandered naked around her sister's
house, who brought her ridiculous gifts of sausages, who was a shame-
less degenerate who had divorced his wife and abandoned his children.
Though it was a slim hope, maybe my mother's dismissal of him might
make Mabel see some sense. On the other hand, if my mother became
as upset by Mabel's impending marriage as she had by Grandma's, then
it could send her back to languishing in bed, or worse. Barely breathing,
I waited for her reaction.

Swaddled in her massive fox-fur coat, for once my mother's physi-
cal presence seemed to match her emotional impact on the room.
"Married?" she said again.

"That's right," Mabel said, striking a light and putting the flame to
her cigarette. She took a drag, puffed out the smoke, and looked
steadily at my mother. "Married," she said firmly.

"When?" my mother asked.

"Well, we were thinking May," Mabel said hesitantly.

"I see," my mother said, still sounding dubious. Then a startling
change of expression came across her face. Her furrowed brow lifted

and her lips turned upward in a jubilant smile. "That's just fantastic!" she declared. "I'm really chuffed for you, Mabel, I am."

Mabel looked at my mother skeptically. "You are?"

"Of course I am. I'm thrilled. And a wedding—well, weddings are always wonderful. Of course," she said, striking a sudden sour note, "I wasn't even told about my own mother's wedding. Haven't even got an invitation yet."

"Well, Ev, I don't think they've set a date, I think—" Mabel started to explain.

My mother cut her off. "Not to worry about that. Mam might be marrying some too-big-for-his-boots furniture salesman in sunny Australia, but we are going to throw you the biggest, most wonderful wedding this family has ever seen. We'll show that Australian gigolo. And you know what?"

"What?" Mabel and Frank said simultaneously as they cast worried glances at each other.

"We're going to do it right here." She pointed out the kitchen window toward the garden. "We'll rent one of them big marquee tents for the reception, and we can do the ceremony on the lawn, and—"

"What lawn?" Ted asked. After she'd abandoned it in late summer, the garden had become colonized by weeds again. But now, in the middle of February, it was a barren patch of uneven shiny wet mud.

"We'd sort of been planning to get married in church, Evelyn," Mabel said.

"Oh, you can't get married in church, not with Frank being divorced—no, that wouldn't be right. Besides, just think of how lovely it would be to have your wedding here. I'll take care of everything. I'll do the food, I'll get you some lovely flowers, I'll make the clothes. And I'll do all that landscaping I'd been planning last year. It'll be the best wedding you could ever imagine. And you'll have to invite Mam, won't you, Mabel? I mean, she'll have to come home for her oldest daughter's wedding."

"Well, I'll invite her, Ev," Mabel said, "but it's a long way and I'm not sure—"

"Oh, don't be daft, of course she'll come. It's an important family event. And Jesse will be your chief bridesmaid."

"No, I won't." I had no interest in being anyone's bridesmaid, and I certainly wasn't going to participate in Frank and Mabel's wedding.

"Oh, yes you will, young lady," my mother said. "I've got this lovely pattern for a bridesmaid's dress, Mabel. I got it back when I did all that dressmaking a few years ago. Ooh, you should see it, all ruffles and pleats. Even Jesse could manage to look nice in something like that."

I imagined myself, a big, poufy bundle of satin and chiffon and pastel high heels, stumbling after Mabel, trying to hold her wedding train above the sticky mud of our back garden. After the ceremony, I'd be jostled between men in ill-fitting suits and women in outfits as ridiculous as my own while the photographs were taken. Despite the photographer's commands to say "cheese," I wouldn't smile. Instead, I'd seethe silently in my itchy underwear and tights, the solemn witness that everyone's eyes went to when they perused the wedding album years later.

"I don't believe in marriage," I said. "It makes women into men's property." I wanted to tell Mabel all the reasons that she should dislike Frank—about the things he'd said, how he'd cut my hand in the kitchen, how he was probably only marrying her for her little council house and her regular income. But I knew there would be no point. Mabel wouldn't listen to me. Nobody would listen to me. In the same way that Amanda didn't see the cruel and bullying Stan Heaphy I saw, no one in my family saw the Frank that I saw. Even Ted, who had just arrived a few minutes ago, seemed to like him. My mother had hated him, but now that he was going to marry Mabel even her opinion had changed. "Maybe you shouldn't get married, Auntie Mabel," I said.

"What, and continue living in sin? I don't think so," my mother said. "Mabel, you're doing the right thing getting wed."

"Yes, but I'm not sure about doing it in your garden, Evelyn. I mean, Ted's right—it's a bit bare out there right now."

"Oh, don't you worry. I can buy some turf and get a lawn laid in a week."

"Yes," Mabel said, "but it would be ever such a lot of trouble and expense. Don't you think, Frank?"

"Actually, I think it's a grand idea," Frank said. "And it might help save us a few bob in the end." He turned to my mother. "Mabel was wanting to rent out the Snug Room in the Snail and Whippet for the reception. I nearly had a heart attack when I heard how much they charge, and, frankly, I don't think there's room for all the guests we want to invite. The bloody church charges an arm and a leg as well. We can't afford all that. With Evelyn helping us, it'll make it a bit cheaper. And maybe Ted could help us out with one or two things, he—"

Ted beamed and opened his mouth as if to say something, but Mabel spoke sooner. "He'll do no such thing," she snapped. "If I find out he's had anything to do with supplying so much as the confetti, I'm calling the wedding off."

"All right," Frank said. "If you feel that strongly about it—"

"I do. But I suppose if Evelyn wants to help with the wedding then—"

"Great!" My mother clapped her hands together. "I'm going to start right away. While the weather's still bad, we can work on the dresses. Jesse," she said, swinging around to look at me, the coat rippling around her. "You can help me get my sewing machine out and we can measure you up for that bridesmaid's dress."

"I'm not going to be a bridesmaid," I said. "You can't make me." I felt close to tears. I held them back, but they were hot and stinging behind my eyes. My throat felt dry and my chest constricted. I had a vision of myself ripping that poofy pink dress into shreds.

"Yes, I can. And I will," she said, waving a furry arm in my direction. "You'll do as you're told. And you'll like it."

"Oh, come on, lovey," Frank said. "Don't be silly. Can't you do this one thing for your auntie Mabel and uncle Frank?"

"You're not my bloody uncle. And I'm not going to be in your stupid bloody wedding."

"Oh, Jesse," Mabel said, looking hurt. "I know you're not keen on dressing up as a bridesmaid, love, but there's no need to—"

As Mabel spoke, my mother stalked across the room. When she reached me, she pushed her face into mine so that only a couple of inches separated us. "If you weren't so big," she said, flooding my senses with her hot, slightly sour breath, "I'd put you across my knee and give you a damn good hiding. As it is, I've a good mind to get your father to tan your backside. Instead, I'm going to let you apologize to Frank and Mabel."

I moved my eyes from my mother's icy glare and swept the room to see all those other adults looking at me: Ted, a cigarette dangling from his mouth as he shifted uncomfortably from foot to foot; my father, his lips pressed together so that his mouth was nothing more than a colorless line above his dimpled chin; Auntie Mabel, her head tilted sideways, her forehead rippled with confusion; and Frank, an angled smile stretching across his satisfied mouth. They were nothing more than a solid wall of incomprehension. None of them knew me. None of them even cared to know.

"I hate you all," I said, taking them all in with a sweeping look before I turned to storm out of the room.

———

CHAPTER TWENTY-ONE

TED, LIKE MY MOTHER WHEN SHE WAS GOING THROUGH HER BAD patches, had an extraordinary capacity for sleep. During the first several weeks of his stay, he was never up when I left for school in the mornings and on several occasions he was still sleeping when I returned. I knew that he was asleep because I could hear his snores echoing through the walls of the spare bedroom, enormous reverberating snorts that sounded like the nonstop revving of a huge, ill-tuned engine. I wouldn't have minded this so much except that, while Ted was in bed, my mother insisted that my father and I should tiptoe around the house. "Be quiet! Your uncle Ted is sleeping," she'd say in hissing whispers if I dropped a shoe in the hallway or stumbled on the stairs.

My father crept around his own house like an unwelcome visitor with surprising patience. Indeed, he seemed so pleased to see my mother up and about that he didn't even mind that we were still left to make our meals now that she was spending all her time on the plans for Mabel's wedding. Every morning, by the time I made it down to the kitchen, my mother was already there, sitting at the table studying patterns for wedding dresses or sketching diagrams for landscaping the back garden. Within a week of Ted's arrival, she had also discovered the mobile library as a resource to help her with her plans.

"Such a lovely woman, that librarian is," she told me after her first visit to the mobile library. "She talks such a lot of sense. I hope you listen to her, Jesse," she said, wagging her finger at me. "You could benefit from paying attention to someone as intelligent and educated as she is." She went on to tell me how, after the two of them had discussed at length the declining cultural standards of contemporary Britain, the librarian had been only too happy to put in a request for a crateload of gardening, dressmaking, and recipe books that my mother retrieved the following week. After that, she borrowed additional volumes on a regular basis and spent hours surrounded by unsteady piles of thick hardback books, leafing through copies of *Landscape Gardening for Beginners, Turf and Lawn Care,* and *Beautiful Blushing Brides.*

When he wasn't asleep, Ted spent most of his time in the living room, watching television, smoking, and drinking cup after cup of dark, strong tea. He was almost as indiscriminate in his choice of television viewing as my mother was, and I frequently arrived home to find him staring slack-jawed at *Play School* or *Romper Room.* "Fetch us another cuppa, would you, love?" he'd say, waving his empty teacup at me, his eyes focused steadily on the screen. His trips out of the house consisted of runs to the Co-op to buy cigarettes. (I was thrilled at this additional supply of Co-op stamps.) Other than that, he rarely left the house and when he inquired about getting the dole he was delighted to find that, since we lived so far from the dole office in Hull, he wasn't required to go there after his first appointment and could continue to collect his benefits by signing the card they sent him once a week and returning it in the post.

"By, that's champion, that is," he said. "There's nothing I hate more than standing in them damn queues, having them people at the window treat you like you're a bit of rubbish, and then ending up with a couple of pounds and some change for your trouble."

"But won't they help you get a job, Uncle Ted?" I asked.

"Oh, don't you worry, love, there's plenty of time for that."

While Ted would watch almost anything on television, his favorite program by far was *Columbo.* He said that when he was in prison he and his fellow inmates never missed an episode. "He's a bloody riot, that bloke," he'd say, gesturing toward Peter Falk as he arrested yet another murderer. "To look at him, you'd think he was thick as two short planks, but he's got it all up here," he'd add, tapping an index finger to his temple and giving a knowing nod.

My father had never really liked American detective programs. "Bunch of bloody Yank rubbish," he'd mutter during the episodes of *Cannon* or *Kojak* that my mother sometimes watched. Because of this, the first Saturday night he was at our house Ted had to put up quite a battle to watch *Columbo,* but he managed to persuade my father to at least give it a chance. Much to my surprise, after seeing his first episode my father was hooked. He loved the way the disheveled and rambling detective outsmarted all those wealthy doctors, film stars, and high-flying businessmen. "Hah!" my father exclaimed when the villain was caught. "Rich bastard, serves you bloody right!"

Within a month, we'd developed a weekly household ritual to prepare for our viewing of *Columbo.* Early on Saturday evenings, Ted made an excursion to the Midham Co-op, where he'd buy bottles of beer, lemonade, crisps, and salted peanuts. While he was gone, my mother would cut up little cubes of cheese, spear them with toothpicks, and set them out on a plate. By the time the opening sequence came on to show the murder that Columbo would later solve, all four of us would be perched eagerly around the television set, chomping on salt-and-vinegar crisps. These evenings soon became some of my favorite times, and I imagined that if someone walked by our window and looked inside they'd think we looked like just another happy family gathered together on a Saturday night.

I was not very happy, however, several weeks after Ted came to stay, when Mabel and Frank dropped by a couple of hours before *Columbo* was due to start. I always liked to see Mabel, of course, but I hated the idea of Frank intruding on our cherished family ritual.

"Oh, so somebody finally decided to let us in," Frank said when I opened the door. "Thought you were going to leave us out here all bloody night." I'd been upstairs reading a pilfered book from the mobile librarian's slush pile and had expected someone else to get the door, but my father and Ted were apparently so involved in their television viewing that they hadn't wanted to leave the room. My mother was in the kitchen working on something related to the wedding plans, and these days she was so singularly focused that it wouldn't have surprised me if the knock on the door hadn't even intruded into her consciousness.

I ignored Frank, looking past him at Mabel, who was bent low, her leg lifted off the ground as she examined the tapered heel of her strappy shoe. "Hello, Auntie Mabel," I said.

"Hello, darling," she replied, looking up at me. She lost her balance and staggered forward, almost falling over before making a grab for Frank.

As she steadied herself on his arm, he tried to shake her off. "Watch the bloody jacket, won't you, Mabel? It's just back from the cleaners."

A hurt frown flickered across her face. Then, catching my eyes, she recovered herself and flashed me a tight smile.

"Are you all right, Auntie Mabel?" I asked.

She sighed as she took off both of her shoes and made her way into the house in her stocking feet. "I'm fine, but I think I've broken the bleeming heel on this shoe. It's walking up that path of yours that's done it." From the doorway she gestured to the ragged path behind her, its concrete cracked, weeds eagerly pushing upward through those cracks. "That'll never do. I don't want my wedding guests falling over and killing themselves. Not exactly an auspicious beginning for a marriage. I suppose I'll have to mention it to our Evelyn."

"Come on, Mabel," Frank said, hands shoved into his trouser pockets, a look of irritation on his face as Mabel continued to examine her broken heel. "It's just a bloody shoe."

"I know, but this pair is one of my favorites." She tossed the shoes to the floor and turned to me. "We're not disturbing you, are we, darling? We just stopped by on our way home. Frank took me for a drive up to the coast. We thought it'd be nice to get some sea air. We went to Reatton, had some fish-and-chips, and I had a few games of bingo while Frank played the one-armed bandits."

"Lost a small fortune," Frank said grimly.

"Oh, Frank, it wasn't that bad," Mabel said. "And we had a lovely walk by the cliffs afterward. Though, to tell you the truth, it was a bit of a shock to see them. I haven't been there in years, and when I was a lass there must have been—oh, I don't know—two, maybe three hundred yards more land there. There was a stable where they kept the donkeys, and there were quite a few houses overlooking the beach. It's all gone now. Fallen into the sea."

"East Yorkshire has the fastest-eroding coastline in Europe," I said. "I learned that in geography at school."

Frank rolled his eyes. "Quite a little mine of information, aren't you?"

"She's right, Frank," Mabel said. "I remember hearing something like that when I was at school. And this lad we saw there today—he lives at the caravan site—he was telling me they lost more than thirty feet just last year."

"He did?"

"Yes, poor little thing," Mabel said. "He's living in this caravan—well, more like a barrel on wheels, it is. And it's not much more than a stone's throw from the cliff edge. Said he doesn't know when his dad's going to get around to moving it."

"I know him," I said. "He's in my year at school. His name's Malcolm."

"He seemed like a nice lad. Dead friendly. But you tell him, darling, the rate those cliffs are going, he needs to get his dad to move that caravan they're living in. Either that or find a flipping decent place to live." Mabel turned to make her way to the living room.

Frank followed her, and I walked after him. After a moment, he halted and turned, blocking my way. "Bit of a girly boy, isn't he, that friend of yours?"

"He's not my friend," I said. Then, as I looked into Frank's sneering face, I added, "But Mabel's right, Malcolm's a nice person. A lot bloody nicer than you."

"OH, I'M GLAD YOU'RE HERE," my mother said as Mabel made her way into the kitchen. "I was just going to phone you. I needed to ask you about the serviettes and the tablecloths. And I want you to take a look at the garden gnomes I've decided on." My mother was sitting at the kitchen table, its surface covered with various catalogs, scraps of fabric, pieces of paper, and several half-drunk cups of tea. The room itself, which had gradually become the center of her wedding operations, was chaotic, with boxes of supplies stacked all over the floor and the counters cluttered with vases, serving plates, and half-finished sewing projects. "I think I like this one the best." She pointed to glossy pages of the gardening-supply catalog and indicated a chubby plaster gnome in a red hat and a green jacket, a fishing rod in his hands. "What do you think?"

She had already transformed the back garden, planting various shrubs and bushes, laying down turf, and installing a pond and a fountain as her centerpiece. The garden gnomes would provide the finishing touch, and she'd spent the past several days going back and forth about which ones she should order.

"Oh, bleeming heck, Ev," Mabel said, plunking herself down on one of the chairs next to my mother. "What do I care about flipping garden gnomes? They all look the same to me." I sat beside her.

"But that's just it, they don't. There's some of them that look downright bloody miserable, and you want cheerful ones for a wedding, don't you?"

"Maybe Evelyn thinks they're coming as guests," Frank said, laughing. He was lurking in the doorway, hands stuffed into his trouser pockets. "Right, Evelyn?"

I shot him an irate glare, wishing I could obliterate him with a look.

My mother ignored him. "Well, I suppose if neither of you is interested I'll just get the ones I want." She slammed the catalog closed. "But, like I said, I need to know about the serviettes and tablecloths you want. I've seen this lovely pink cotton that I think would look great."

"Oh, God, Ev," Mabel said, sinking into her chair and looking sapped. "I don't know. I suppose it sounds all right to me."

In recent weeks, I'd gathered the impression that Mabel had begun to regret her decision to let my mother run the wedding. She and Frank were always being summoned to the house by my mother, and they motored more and more frequently between Hull and Midham in the Tuggles delivery van to provide consultation on virtually every decision that needed to be made in the ever more elaborate wedding plans. While my mother could spend hours discussing the merits of carnations over roses in the bride's bouquet or the various options for marquee rentals, Mabel's patience seemed to be wearing increasingly thin.

"Oh," my mother said, apparently disappointed by Mabel's lack of enthusiasm. "If that's how you feel, I suppose I'll go ahead and order the material, then. But, before I forget, I wanted to tell you that I met with the photographer—it's the bloke that does all the fancy weddings hereabouts. He came over and I looked at his portfolio. He does a lovely job. He'll take ten years off you in his photos, Mabel."

"Terrific," Mabel said dully as she shook a cigarette out of its packet.

"And for the entertainment I was thinking of getting this smashing German oompah band. The Bavarian Swingers. Semiprofessional, they are. They played the summer season at the Bridlington Spa last year. And then for the flowers, well, I'm going to order roses and—"

"Hold on a second, Evelyn," Frank said, pulling his hands from his pockets and taking several steps into the room. "How much is this lot going to cost?"

Along with Mabel, Frank seemed to be regretting handing the wedding plans over to my mother. Not being well acquainted with my mother's fanaticism for every project she undertook, he hadn't understood that renting out the Snug Room in the Snail and Whippet would, in fact, have been a far cheaper option.

"Oh, I don't know," my mother said vaguely. "I just told them to send the bills to you."

"Jesus Christ," Frank hissed through clenched teeth. Looking askance at my mother and then at Mabel, he let out a defeated sigh. "I hope your Ted has got some beer in tonight," he said. "I could use a bloody drink."

"HE'S DEAD GOOD, that Columbo," my father pronounced as the murderer was hauled off in handcuffs and the episode ended. He was sitting in his armchair, waving a little cube of Cheddar cheese on a toothpick about as he spoke.

"A bloody genius, really," Frank declared. He sat with Mabel and my mother on the settee, and was sipping from a can of Carling Black Label lager. I'd been lying on my stomach on the newly installed fitted carpet—the final step in my father's redecoration of the living room—propped up on my elbows. Now that *Columbo* was over, I'd pulled myself up and shuffled over to the wall, where I sat with my legs out in front me.

"You're right there, Frank," Ted said, gesturing toward him with an unlit cigarette. He was slouched in the other armchair, feet planted on the floor, legs spread wide. "All them murderers he catches—well, they think they've gone and carried out the perfect crime. But, no matter what, they always end up getting caught." He struck his lighter with his thumb, put the flame to his cigarette, and took a drag.

Frank leaned toward Ted and pressed his bony face into a thoughtful frown. "So, Ted, tell me this, will you? You think there is such a thing as the perfect crime?"

Mabel groaned. "Do you have to talk to him about this? He's supposed to be sticking to the straight and narrow."

"I'm only asking," Frank protested. "After all, Ted does have more experience in the criminal world than any of us. No offense, Ted."

"None taken, Frank," Ted said.

"Anyway, if there is such a thing as the perfect crime," Mabel said, "it's not our Ted you should be asking. Clearly, with his record he hasn't discovered it yet."

Ted shifted awkwardly in his chair. "Leave off, Mabel, will you?"

"I'll leave off," she said, leaning forward to squish the butt of her cigarette into the ashtray on the coffee table with considerable force, "when you start showing some evidence that you've changed your ways. Like maybe actually getting your backside out of that chair once in a while and trying to find a job."

"Leave the lad alone, Mabel," Frank said. "I'm sure he's doing his best."

"Oh, I meant to tell you," my father said, looking over at Ted. "I heard they're taking on new workers on the night shift at that paper factory down by Hull docks. Maybe you should go down there, get yourself an application, Ted?"

"Yes, Uncle Ted," I said, giving him an encouraging smile. "Why don't you apply?"

Ted twisted his lips into a skeptical frown and slouched down farther into his chair. "Oh, I don't know about that—I'm not sure I could adapt to the night shift. I mean, I need my sleep."

"You can say that again," Mabel said, snorting.

"You get used to it," my mother offered. "Sometimes I think I should get a night job myself. Sometimes I can go without sleep for days and days."

"Yes, well, Evelyn," Mabel said, patting my mother's leg the way someone might indulgently pat an uncomprehending child. "I'm not sure that's good for anybody. Not even you. Everybody needs some sleep."

My mother shrugged, apparently unconvinced.

"Beggars can't be choosers, Ted," my father said. "And in your position you might have to take something less than ideal." There was an irritated edge to his voice. It made me wonder if he was starting to regret inviting Ted to stay almost as much as Frank and Mabel were regretting letting my mother run their wedding. After being at the office, my father came home every day to continue his repairs on the house. When he did the living room, he had to work around Ted. While my father diligently scraped old wallpaper off the walls, Ted sat on the settee watching television and offering occasional decorating tips. The only help he provided was to assist my father when he needed to move the television, taking it up to his bedroom for several days while my father painted the ceiling and installed the carpet.

"Aye, but the night shift—that's tough work, is that," Frank said. "And I don't mean to imply you're over the hill, Ted, but you're not exactly a spring chicken anymore. Working nights is all right when you're a youngster, but a man in his forties—well, it's a damn sight harder. I think Ted would be better off with something during the day."

As I listened, I couldn't help wondering why Frank was so determined to defend Ted's blatant idleness. From the moment he'd met him, he seemed eager to get in Ted's good graces, though why this was so important to him I couldn't understand. It wasn't as if Ted was a famous outlaw or a renowned bank robber. He was nothing more than a petty criminal, and he wasn't even very good at that.

"The way things are these days," Frank continued, "factories closing, the country going down the bloody drain, it's hard for anybody to get a job. Even those of us that have a job are barely scraping by. Bloody difficult to make an honest living these days, it is."

"Been difficult for Ted to make an honest living all his life," Mabel said, giving a sad, slow shake of her head.

"Well, at least he doesn't have women spending all his money left, right, and bloody center," Frank sneered, looking at my mother.

"Oh, come on, Frank, love, don't be like that," Mabel said, reaching over to rub his arm. He shrugged her away.

"Maybe you'd be better off staying single and moving back to your bedsit, Frank," I said. "Maybe you should just do your own washing and learn how to cook. Then you wouldn't have to put up with women at all."

"Quite the little joker, isn't she?" He let out a hollow laugh as he looked around the room.

"It's not a joke," I said, pushing myself to my feet.

"Jesse, it isn't like you to be so bad-tempered, darling," Mabel said, frowning over at me. "Frank was only having a laugh, love. There's no need to be so rude."

I was filled with rage, not at Frank but at Mabel. I saw how Frank treated her, and how Mabel had transformed herself into someone who would tolerate that treatment. Instead of being grateful when I spoke up to defend her from his sour comments, she defended him. For a second, I wanted to tell her to pull herself together, to stand up for herself. I swallowed my words and turned toward the door. "I'm off to bed," I said as I headed into the hall.

ABOUT HALF AN HOUR after I'd stomped upstairs, I got up to go to the bathroom. As I opened my door, I heard the low growl of male voices in the hallway below. I paused to listen and realized it was Frank and Ted, their voices animated rumblings that they seemed to be trying to keep low but which kept rising in excited little swells. Curious about what they might be discussing so heatedly, I crept along the landing until I reached the top of the stairs. I peered over the banister and saw the two of them almost immediately below me. They stood close together, puffing on cigarettes. I took a soft step back and lowered myself to the floor. Then I pressed my head against the banister, so that I was beyond their view but could look down on their heads, swathed in a misty swirl of smoke.

"See, it's ruddy foolproof, really, Ted," Frank was saying. "There's no chance that anybody would find out."

"Well . . . I don't know, Frank. If our Mabel . . . Well, she'll break my bloody neck."

"Look, you've no worries there." Frank slapped Ted on the shoulder. "She'll never know, I guarantee it. So, what do you say? Want to give it a try?"

Ted took a long drag on his cigarette. Frank moved restlessly about from foot to foot as he waited for an answer.

"Well," Ted finally said, "I don't suppose I'll get a better offer."

"You'll not regret it, Ted," Frank said, his tone obviously delighted. "Let's shake on it, shall we?" From above, I watched as they clasped each other's hands.

"Frank. Frank, what are you up to?" It was Mabel. She stepped out of the living room into the hall. I backed away, farther into the darkness.

"Nothing, love, just having a little chat with Ted here about looking for a job, that's all."

"Aye," said Ted. "He's been ever so helpful, has Frank."

"That's good," Mabel said, yawning. "Terrific. And God knows you could use some advice. Now, come on, Frank, I think it's time for us to go. Evelyn's been talking my ear off about flipping wedding china, and Mike's fallen asleep in his chair." With that, the three of them drifted back to the living room. I sat there for a while, leaning against the banister, feeling even more uneasy about Ted and Frank's blossoming friendship.

CHAPTER TWENTY-TWO

———

SPRING CAME GENTLY, A GRADUAL OPENING OF EVERYTHING THAT started with the brave white blooms of snowdrops on the verges along the roads and rose in a slow crescendo of new leaves and flowers that transformed the landscape from dismal shades of brown and gray and black to a sea of shimmering green dotted with bright flags of color. I celebrated my fourteenth birthday in the middle of a mild but rainy March, and by the time April arrived the fields were green with newly planted potatoes or emerging stalks of wheat. It seemed that the world outside our house was a place of hope, a place where, every year, the barrenness of winter was replaced by the thrill of life and emerging abundance. In the mornings, as we traveled to school, I leaned against the window and watched it flash by, wishing I could reach out and grasp all that optimism, pull it to me, and press it into my chest. But while the world around was glimmering with renewal, winter had settled inside me, a frozen fallow field.

On the seat next to me, Tracey chatted away, chirpy like the birds in the newly lush trees. And though she made me laugh sometimes, with her mocking of the teachers and her jokes about the other kids at school, much of the time I found myself tuning her out the same way I'd learned to tune out Uncle Ted's snoring, my father's rants about royalty, and my mother's monologues about bridal wear or the pros and cons of disposable tablecloths. And, like my family members, I discovered that Tracey didn't seem to mind that I wasn't really paying attention, that my absent grunts meant that I had drifted far away.

If I did pay attention to anything on those bus rides, it was to the sounds from the back, where Amanda sat, talking and laughing with her friends. I still longed to be there next to her, wanted it more than anything, but ever since that morning at the bus stop when I'd tried to kiss her I'd felt so embarrassed that I could barely even speak to her.

"You all right, Jesse?" she asked at the bus stop one April morning shortly after the Easter holidays. I'd arrived just as the bus was pulling up, and I had to run all the way along the high street to catch it. "You look worn out," she said as she waited for the boys to clamber onto the bus in front of her, bashing one another with their satchels as they fought to get on first.

I was tired. My mother, increasingly immersed in her wedding preparations, was keeping very irregular hours. Despite my best efforts, it was hard to sleep when she was thundering up and down the stairs all night. When I looked at Amanda, though, I realized that she seemed tired herself, her hair greasy and a little bedraggled; there were dark circles under her eyes.

"Jesse's fine," Tracey said, launching herself between me and Amanda. "Just sick of having to get up at the crack of dawn for school. I know I am."

In a way, I was glad of Tracey's interruption. Although Amanda had continued to be friendly enough toward me, I'd felt a new distance in her—or at least I thought I did. It was hard for me to know for certain, however, since I now found it almost impossible to talk to her. I'd felt self-conscious enough in her presence before revealing my terrible feelings for her. Now I was tongue-tied with my shame.

"I wasn't asking you, Tracey," Amanda said. "I was asking Jesse." She peered around Tracey. "You all right?" she asked again, looking into my face.

For a moment, I felt a thrill at her concern for me and wanted to shove Tracey out of the way. But then the memory of what happened when I actually tried to hold her came back to me.

"I'm fine," I said. Then, limp and unprotesting, I let Tracey take my arm and pull her with me onto the bus.

We had a grim day ahead of us—religious education and physics in the morning, an afternoon of maths followed by PE, which I found particularly excruciating these days, since our teacher had recently acquired an enthusiasm for country dancing. That afternoon, after trying to execute a swivel in the Gay Gordons and getting caught up in my partner's legs and falling flat on my face only to lift myself up to see my fellow dancers doubled up in laughter, I was relieved to make my way to our final lesson of the day.

Chemistry was taught by Mr. Matthews, who was probably the least-liked teacher at Liston Comprehensive. He had been nicknamed Adolf because he bore an unfortunate resemblance to Adolf Hitler, a resemblance that might have been significantly mitigated had he not insisted on retaining a toothbrush mustache and strutting around the chemistry lab delivering his lessons in a shrill, military bark. It was not unusual for the boys to goosestep through the door of the lab and, while his back was turned, perform *Sieg heil* salutes. But no one ever challenged him directly. Mr. Matthews kept a cane on his desk, and it took only the slightest movement of his hand toward it to command complete silence from his pupils.

That afternoon, Mr. Matthews had assigned us an experiment through which we were supposed to extract chlorophyll from a plant. We were to work in groups, and while I arranged the test tubes, Bunsen burner, and beakers, the Debbies were huddled around an article about the Bay City Rollers in the latest issue of *Jackie* and Tracey was busily decorating the cover of her chemistry exercise book with love hearts and "TG luvs GEL" (Edward, Tracey had recently discovered, was Greg's middle name) in big block letters. Mr. Matthews had disappeared into his office, which looked out on the chemistry lab.

"God, I hate chemistry," Tracey said, pushing her book away and watching me light the Bunsen burner. A fierce blue flame burst from its end. "What do we have to do this for, anyway? I mean, Adolf already told us what's supposed to happen. What's the point of us having to mess around with all this stuff?" Her eyes alighted on the small stack of filter papers I'd placed at the edge of the bench. Her face brightened. "You know, you can smoke those things."

"What?" I asked vaguely.

"The filter papers, you can smoke them."

"That's daft," I said as she picked up one of the filter papers, rolled it into a cylinder, and popped it between her lips, like a fat, empty cigarette.

"It'll be a lark." She pretended to take a drag from the empty filter paper, threw her head back, and exhaled loudly. "And, look, Adolf is tucked away in his office. He won't see a thing."

Through the open door, we could see Mr. Matthews thoughtfully leafing through a book. He seemed completely absorbed.

"Tracey," I said urgently, "if he catches you, he'll—"

It was too late. Tracey had already placed the end of the rolled-up filter paper over the Bunsen burner. At first the flame merely singed the paper's edges, but then it caught alight. Tracey pulled it away, blew out the flame, then promptly stuck it into her mouth and began puffing away.

"You'll choke yourself," I said as Tracey burst into a sputtering cough. The Debbies giggled.

"No, no, it's just like a ciggy," she said, her eyes red and watery as she waved the smoke in my direction. "You should try it." She took another puff and coughed again.

I looked at her skeptically. She didn't look as if she was having fun.

It was foolish to think that any kind of misbehavior might escape Mr. Matthews's attention, especially anything so brazen as smoking (even if it was only a filter paper) in his class. It took less than a minute for him to look up from his book, furrow his brow, and march out of his office.

"Oh, bloody hell," muttered Tracey. "I've gone and done it now." She looked around in alarm. The Debbies dived into their exercise books and feigned avid concentration. Tracey turned to me. "Here, Jesse, get rid of it, can you?"

On another day I probably would not have taken it from her, but in the wake of my humiliation in PE and my exhaustion, my reflexes weren't as sharp as they should have been. When Tracey handed the paper to me, instead of knocking it away I took it, so that, as Mr. Matthews approached, there I was in a cloud of smoke. I looked about, desperate to find somewhere that I might dispose of the burning filter paper.

"Jesse Bennett!" he barked. "What in God's name do you think you're doing?" His face was a startling shade of red. Two ropy blue veins pulsed visibly in his neck on either side of his bobbing Adam's apple.

"Nothing, sir."

"Really?" He snatched the filter paper from my hand and dunked it in a beaker of water that stood on the bench. It was extinguished with a loud hiss and a thick ribbon of dark gray smoke. "And since when, I ask, did the process of extracting chlorophyll demand that you set light to a filter paper? I'm surprised at you, Miss Bennett. I wouldn't put this kind of behavior past your friends here." Tracey was making a concentrated study of the formulas chalked on the blackboard. Everyone else in the classroom was staring at me. "Perhaps they've infected you with their idiocy? Or perhaps you think chemistry is just one big joke, Miss Bennett?"

"No, sir." My face was burning. Surely Tracey wasn't going to let me take the blame for her stupid prank.

"I'm surrounded by morons. Everywhere." Mr. Matthews swung around to indicate the group of boys sitting in the very rear of the classroom. While he was yelling at me, they had been making *Sieg heil* gestures in the air. As he turned, they dropped their arms stiffly to their sides. "Morons," Mr. Matthews repeated, eyeing them fiercely. "Any more from you lot and you can join Miss Bennett for detention tomorrow evening."

"Detention? But, sir . . ." I looked at Tracey again, but she was still frowning at the blackboard.

"Would you like to make that a week of detention, Miss Bennett?"

"No, sir."

"Good," he concluded. "So we'll see each other here tomorrow at four o'clock sharp."

"Yes, sir," I said quietly, letting my eyes drop to the bench.

"GOD, JESSE, I CAN'T believe Adolf gave you detention for that," Tracey said as we exited the chemistry lab after the lesson. "I mean, it's not like it was anything serious. . . ."

I spun around to look at her. "I told you not to do it. I told you not to light that bloody filter paper." I could feel tears, hot and stinging, behind my eyes. "And you didn't need to get me into trouble, you could have—"

Tracey gave an amiable slap to my arm. "Oh, come on, Jesse, don't go getting your knickers in a twist over nothing. It's just detention, for God's sake. It's not like he's going to chop your head off."

"But now I'll miss the school bus. I don't know how I'm going to get home."

"Oh, you can get a bus from Liston that goes to Midham. It comes by the school at half past five. Of course, it goes all over the villages round here, so you won't get home till half past six. But it's only one night."

"That's all right for you to say. But you should be the one that's in detention, not me. You got me into trouble. You deliberately—"

She sidled up to me. "Oh, come on, Jesse," she said, threading her arm through mine. "That was great what you did, taking the blame for me. I only gave you the filter paper because Adolf would kill me if he'd caught me with it. I had detention with him five times last term. I wouldn't put it past him to send a note home to my mam and dad. And then my life wouldn't be worth living. You really kept me out of the shit there, Jesse." She leaned into me and smiled.

I blinked back my tears. "You think so?" I asked, looking into her beaming face.

"Yeah," she said, giving a decisive nod. "And you know I appreciate it, Jesse, I really do." Then she tugged me forward, into the stream of students moving toward the school's main doors. "Come on, I'm supposed to meet Greg by the school gates and I don't want to be late."

BY THE TIME I arrived at detention the next day, there was already a short queue outside the door, most of them boys who were always getting into trouble, and a smattering of girls who made a habit of wearing clothes that weren't part of the regulation uniform or smoked in the bike sheds. While I wasn't shocked to see any of these usual suspects, I was a little taken aback to see Malcolm Clements standing at the very end of the line. He looked me up and down as I took my place next to him and then looked away. I was surprised at how much his contempt stung me.

"All right, you horrible little wretches," Mr. Matthews boomed, making me jump as he burst out of the chemistry lab. "Get inside. And anybody that breathes one single word without my permission during the next hour will find themselves in detention again tomorrow night. Am I making myself clear?"

A couple of minutes later we were sitting, heads bent over our exercise books, copying down the long series of indecipherable chemical formulas from the textbooks Mr. Matthews had handed out.

Time passed with excruciating slowness, expanded, it seemed, by a silence punctuated only by the scratch of pencils over paper, the turning of pages, and the hollow staccato of coughs. Eventually, five o'clock came around and we were released. Since I had half an hour before the bus arrived to take me home, I didn't gallop away like almost all my fellow students. Instead, I ambled slowly along the corridor, breathing in the pungent smells of floor polish and disinfectant as I passed mop-wielding cleaning ladies.

As I made my way to the exit, I saw Malcolm walking in front of me. His satchel was unbuckled and bounced against his hips, and as he turned the corner of the corridor its flap flew wide and something fell from it and fluttered to the floor. When I reached the corner, I bent down to pick it up. It was several pieces of paper folded together, covered in tight paragraphs of tiny, scrawled writing. Without thinking, I picked up my pace.

"Malcolm," I called.

He spun around. "What do you want?"

I waved the papers at him. "You dropped this."

"Oh." He took it from me. "Thanks."

Without knowing why, I realized that I wanted to keep him there. "It's probably not important," I said, "but I thought . . . I thought . . . Well, you never know what someone has written on those little bits of paper. I write things all the time and I, well . . . I just thought you might need it, that's all."

Malcolm looked at me steadily, as if he were trying to solve a puzzle in my face. Then he let his lips ease into a slight smile. "Actually, those are my notes for the history essay I have to write tonight. I spent ages writing these. I'd be sort of lost without them. So, really, thanks a lot." He put them back into his satchel.

"I'm glad you didn't lose them," I said as he buckled up the flap. Then, not knowing what else to say, I turned to make my way to the school's main doors. I was surprised, though, when Malcolm matched my pace to walk beside me. I was also surprised and rather pleased when he seemed to want to make conversation.

"So why did you get put into detention?" he asked.

"Nothing."

"Yeah, that's what they all say."

"No, really, I didn't do anything," I said with conviction. Then, more softly, I asked, "What did you do?"

"I got caught running in the corridor, but it wasn't really my fault. I know better than to run in the corridors when Adolf is on patrol." He looked at me and grinned. "See, I had to stay behind after registration, and when I got out I ran because I didn't want to be late for French. Miss Greenly hates it when you're late. Of course, there was no point trying to explain that to Adolf. You know, I actually think he'd make a good dictator, that man."

"He is a bit of a wanker," I ventured.

"You can say that again." Malcolm laughed. "So, anyway, why did you end up in detention?"

I hesitated.

"Come on," he said, nudging me gently with a skinny elbow. "You can tell me."

For a moment, I wondered if I should just tell Malcolm that I'd set fire to the filter paper and tried to smoke it, if it would be disloyal to Tracey if I told him the truth. But while I'd taken the blame with Mr. Matthews, I wasn't prepared to let Malcolm think I'd done such a stupid thing. So I told him what happened. Malcolm said nothing as I spoke.

"Do you want a lift home?" he said as we pushed out into the chill and he pointed to a car standing by the entrance, the headlights on and the engine running. "That's my dad. He can drop you off in Midham if you want. It's on our way."

I looked around the school grounds. There were still a few kids from detention crossing the car park. And by the gates I could see a little crowd. I wondered if Tracey was among them, still chatting with Greg, waiting for him to give her a lift home on his motorbike. I wondered, too, what she would think if she saw me pass the school gates with Malcolm in his father's car.

"No, no, it's all right," I said. "Really, I don't mind getting the bus."

"But that's daft. It'd be much quicker for you if—" Malcolm paused, following my gaze.

"Thanks for the offer, but I don't want to be any trouble." I smiled at him. He didn't smile back. For a moment, he looked hurt. Then his expression shifted to that same look of disdain I'd seen when I joined him earlier outside the lab.

"I get it," he said. "You don't want your precious friends to see you with me. Is that it?"

I said nothing.

"Your lovely best friend, the one who deliberately dropped you in it with Adolf—you don't want her to see you with Malcolm Poofter Clements?" He imitated Tracey's sour and mocking tone. "What would she say if she saw you with a pathetic little nancy boy like me?" He tossed his head and waved his hand loosely through the air, the way Tracey did when she made fun of him.

"No, it's just that . . ." I wanted to explain to him. It wasn't really like that. It was just that I couldn't bear to go back to what had gone before. I couldn't be like him, teased and ridiculed, and withstand it.

"You know something? You're the one that's pathetic. Look at you." He jabbed a finger in my direction. "So busy worrying about what other people think. Did it ever occur to you to start thinking for yourself?" For a second, his expression was a burning accusation, and then he turned and stalked toward his father's car.

CHAPTER TWENTY-THREE

—

Not long after Mabel and Frank joined us to watch *Columbo*, Frank started to make far more frequent visits to our house. Most of the time, he came without Mabel. Chugging up the driveway in the Tuggles delivery van, he often arrived just after I got home from school. The only positive thing about these visits was that he didn't stay long. Instead, he and Ted would leave together, returning late when he dropped Ted at the end of our driveway and sped off down the road. Sometimes, when I heard the distinctive churn of Frank's van as it approached in the evening, I'd peer out my bedroom window to watch Ted make his way up our path—now a smooth gray band of new concrete after my mother had replaced the old one. In the dark, I could see his silhouette and the glowing orange dot of his cigarette end sweeping back and forth from his mouth.

"Frank's being ever so good to Ted," Mabel said to my mother one Sunday afternoon a couple of weeks after Frank's more frequent visits had commenced.

Mabel was standing on a chair in the kitchen while my mother, a handful of pins clenched between her lips, adjusted the hem of her wedding dress. The dress was hot-pink satin with a bell-shaped skirt, huge puffy sleeves, and a deeply plunging neckline—a feature that my mother and Mabel had argued about for weeks, with Mabel (unusually, as far as decisions for the wedding were concerned) finally winning out. Up on the chair like that, I thought Mabel looked more like an enormous cake decoration than a bride.

"I'm sure Ted doesn't appreciate it, but Frank's doing him a whopping big favor," Mabel said.

"What do you mean, Auntie Mabel?" I asked. I was sitting at the table, leafing through the Littlewoods catalog. I'd been instructed by my mother to look at two pairs of shoes she'd circled, the ones she thought would go best with my bridesmaid's dress. Both pairs were pink—one satin and pointy-toed, the other shiny plastic with a three-inch heel. I'd already decided that I'd rather walk barefoot on burning coals than wear either. "How's Frank helping Uncle Ted?"

"He's trying to help Ted get a job."

"He is?" Somehow, I doubted this. After having had the opportunity to observe Ted for a couple of months now, I'd concluded that he would prefer to attend his own execution than engage in anything resembling legitimate work. And, after overhearing his surreptitious conversation in the hallway with Frank, I'd developed various theories about what sort of shady activity the two of them might be up to, finally concluding that Frank, worried about all the expense of the wedding, had engaged Ted in getting some of the supplies on the cheap. I wanted to confide my suspicions to Mabel, knowing that she'd be livid with Frank if this was, in fact, true. Maybe she'd even break off her relationship with him. But I wasn't sure how my mother would take any blowup so close to the wedding, so I'd decided to keep my suspicions to myself. Still, I couldn't help trying to sow a few seeds of doubt about Frank in Mabel's mind. "How's he helping Uncle Ted find a job?" I asked.

"Every day, after Frank's finished at the Tuggles factory, he comes over here, picks Ted up, and takes him out to look for work. Bloody angel for doing it, you ask me."

"But that doesn't make any sense," I said. "Shouldn't Uncle Ted be looking for a job during the day?"

"Frank says he's trying to help Ted get a job working nights, says they need to go then so they can talk to the shift supervisors."

"But I thought Ted said he didn't want to work nights," I said. "And Frank agreed. He said it would be too hard on a man Ted's age."

"Oh, I don't know, darling," Mabel said, wrinkling up her nose. "Anyway, whatever sort of work he's helping Ted to look for, I've told Frank that he's wasting his time. The day I see our Ted in a normal job will be the day that pigs get wings. And, once the wedding's over, I've told Frank—" Mabel paused, looking excited, as if another thought had dawned on her. "Speaking of the wedding, Ev, I meant to tell you. I got a reply yesterday to the invitation I sent to Mam. And guess what—she says she's going to come. She's coming to the wedding, Ev."

My mother stood up, spitting the pins from her mouth so that they spattered, like silver threads of spittle, down her dress to land on the linoleum with bright little *pings*. "Really? Mam's coming here, all the way from Australia? She's coming?" Her features simmered with excitement.

"Yep, she's coming all right. Unfortunately, she says she was late making a booking and the only flight she could get is one that gets her into London the night before. So she won't be able to get here until the actual day of the wedding. Still, she'll be here."

"That's great, that's brilliant," my mother said, bouncing up and down on her heels, her face filled with the kind of delight she usually reserved for eating Mr. Kipling cakes. Within a couple of seconds, though, her expression changed. "She's not bringing that bloody Australian gigolo with her, is she?"

Mabel looked sheepish. "Well, I think so. I mean, he is her fiancé. And I did include him in the invitation." She winced in apparent anticipation of my mother's reaction.

"You invited him?"

"I had to invite him, Evelyn," Mabel said, lifting and then dropping her shoulders in such a dramatic shrug that the billowy satin dress rustled as if it, like Mabel, were letting out an exasperated sigh. "You never know, maybe you'll like him once you meet him."

"Right," my mother said, crouching toward the floor as she began to search for the pins she'd spat out. "I'd say that's about as likely as Frank getting our Ted a job."

AS APRIL TURNED to May and the wedding came closer, the pace of activity in our house rose to a previously unknown level of frenzy, which, given my mother's history of frenetic focus, was really quite breathtaking. During the final fortnight before the ceremony, I got the impression that she never really slept. She was working on the wedding when I went to bed and she was working on it every morning when I got up, and it became increasingly common for her to wake me with some noise or disturbance during the night.

Even my father, who was usually pleased when my mother was engaged in some new all-consuming project, was concerned at the ceaseless pace with which she continued to work. "Don't you think you should take a day off, Evelyn?" he asked her one Sunday afternoon as she sat at her sewing machine in the kitchen, her foot pushed down on the pedal as if she were a racing-car driver in the final stretch. I was standing at the counter, making myself some toast and jam for an afternoon snack. I cringed as my father shouted from the doorway over at my mother. But he had to yell; otherwise she would never have heard him above the roar of the sewing machine's motor.

"Take a day off?" my mother yelled back, pausing to straighten out the rose-patterned material she'd been pushing under the flash of the sewing-machine needle. "I haven't got time to take a day off. I've got to get these tablecloths finished. And then I've got the place mats and serviettes to make. Then there's the decorations to buy, and the booze to order. I haven't even got around to finishing the menu. And, of course, I'm going to have to fit in some time to make the wedding cake."

"But do you have to do it all, Evelyn?" my father said, recoiling as my mother pressed her foot down and the sewing machine roared again. "I mean, can't we just order the food and the cake? Can't we get some help from somebody else?" He was shouting at the top of his voice, trying to make himself heard above the sewing machine's harrowing bawl.

"Somebody else?" My mother lifted her foot from the pedal again and the machine stopped. "Somebody else?" Her voice was high, far more ear-piercing than the sewing machine. "What do you mean, get somebody else?"

As she yelled, I noticed how disheveled she appeared. Her clothes were unwashed, food-splattered and rumpled, her hair stood out in matted greasy lumps. But it was her expression that disturbed me most. Her face was pale and drawn and, except for the dark shadows beneath her eyes, almost without color, while her eyes seemed immensely big and bright. They were filled with such a ferocious energy that, as I regarded her, she made me think of a trapped animal, desperate and possessed by fear.

"I was only trying to help, Ev," my father said, putting his hands out in front of him as if he were trying to stave my mother off.

"Help? Help?" she shrieked. "Do I look like I need bloody help? Are you saying I can't manage this on my own?"

"No, but . . ." My father had started to back away toward the door. I was planning on following him just as soon as I'd finished spreading the jam on my toast.

"Well, then, leave me to get on with this!" she screamed, slamming a fist down on the kitchen table then springing to her feet. "Unless you want me to end up in bloody Delapole again."

At this, my father flinched and staggered backward, dazed, like a man who had just taken a blow to the chest.

I looked at him, at the overwhelming weariness in his face. Then I looked at my mother, at the way her eyes blazed like tiny infernos, as if there was a fire raging in her head.

"Get out!" my mother yelled. "Both of you!"

"Come on, love," my father said to me softly. "Let's go see if there's anything on the telly and get out of your mother's way."

I WAS WORRIED about my mother, but I was also worried about myself. At least when I'd been writing my letters to Amanda they'd offered me a place I could go to when everything else seemed so awful.

I hadn't even been able to sneak anything interesting from the mobile library to distract me while my mother had been visiting it regularly herself. She and the librarian spent ages at the little checkout desk chatting about weddings, gardening tips, and the terrible state of the world, and since the slush pile was right there, behind the librarian, it was far more difficult to grab something from that stack without being seen. In the final weeks leading up to the wedding, however, my mother stopped visiting the little van, declaring that she now knew everything she needed to know about planning a wedding and, once Mabel and Frank's ceremony was over, she planned to write a book about it herself.

Once I was able to steal more interesting titles from the slush pile again, my life became a little more bearable. A week before the wedding, I saw a book there that I absolutely had to have. I had been pretending to browse and had pulled down a couple of random books before approaching the checkout desk to get a closer look at the slush pile when I saw there, at the very top of the forbidden volumes, a book with the title *Modern Homosexuality,* in bold red letters along its spine. I felt a bolt of burning interest surge through me, and as the librarian lifted her date stamp to check out the titles I had taken from the children's shelves I knew that I had to get my hands on that book.

"Erm, excuse me," I said, coughing.

"Yes?"

"I was wondering if you have any books by Beatrix Potter. I couldn't see anything on the shelf."

"Couldn't see anything on the shelf?" The librarian looked at me, aghast. "Of course, we have books by Beatrix Potter."

"Well, I couldn't see anything and I thought—"

"Here, let me show you," she said, dropping her date stamp and marching over to the children's shelves.

While she began pulling out various volumes of Beatrix Potter stories, I reached behind the counter and grabbed the book that I wanted. By the time the librarian returned with copies of *The Tale of Peter Rabbit*, *The Tale of Squirrel Nutkin*, and *The Tale of Jemima Puddle-Duck*, I had *Modern Homosexuality* securely stuffed under my anorak. As soon as I got to the house, I ran upstairs into my bedroom, sat down on my bed, opened the book, buried my face in its pages, and started to read.

I'd never even seen a book before with the word "homosexuality" in its title and, now that I had, I was expecting it to offer definitive answers to all my tormenting questions, all those questions I had about what my feelings for Amanda actually meant. What I was really hoping for was something along the lines of the quizzes in *Woman's Weekly*. "Is your husband lying to you? Are you a good communicator? What's your personality type? Answer the questions below, rate your answers, and find out!" I wanted to write down my answers to the pertinent questions, run down a list at the bottom of the page, and discover what I really was. All A's: Yes, you're definitely a homosexual and there's nothing you can do about it. B's: Probably, but there's still time to change. C's: Probably not, it's just a phase you're going through and you'll get over it soon. D's: Definitely not, stop worrying and get on with your life!

Unfortunately, it didn't seem to be that simple. First, the book was written in dense, unfamiliar jargon. Second, for the first two chapters it talked almost exclusively about rats, which I didn't find at all relevant to my quandary. And third, when it did finally get to talking about humans, it was all about men, something that left me wondering if women could actually be homosexual at all or if it was something that mani-fested only in the male of the species. Despite those housewives in the problem pages, perhaps I was a terrible oddity after all.

It was probably because I was so absorbed in the book that I didn't hear a vehicle pull up outside the house. It was also why I didn't hear the front door open, the footsteps on the stairs and along the hallway, and probably why I didn't hear someone turn the knob on the door of my room.

"*Modern Homosexuality,* eh? I tell you, times have certainly changed since I was a lad."

I looked up to see Frank standing in the open doorway. "It's for homework," I blurted, dropping the book into my lap.

"That right?" he asked, a grin blooming across his bony face.

"Yes." My voice sounded far away. My heart was hammering in my chest.

"So you're not one of them queers, then?"

I shook my head. This time, I found I couldn't even speak.

"Good job, that. Because, you know, there really is nothing more terrible for a parent to find out than their kid's a pervert. If I ever found out either of my little ones was queer—well, I think I'd rather kill 'em. I know it sounds harsh, but really, it's a parent's worst night-mare, that is. And your mam, her being so fragile, I can't imagine she'd take news like that very well at all."

I tried to meet his eyes, but I couldn't. Instead, I looked down at the dense text in the pages of the book.

"So," Frank said, "you seen your uncle Ted? I came up here looking for him. He's supposed to be out job hunting with me."

"He's sleeping," I said.

Frank laughed. "Should do well on the night shift, Ted, don't you think? I mean, he certainly has no trouble sleeping during the day."

"You're not helping him get a job, are you?" I had closed the book and pushed it away from me, to the far side of my bed. Somehow, dis-tancing myself from it like that gave me courage and allowed the anger

I felt at Frank to flare alive. "You're doing something else. Something you shouldn't. Something Mabel wouldn't like."

Frank's features became stiff. He took a couple more steps into my room. "It's none of your bloody business what Ted and me are doing, you hear me? None of your business at all. And if you say one word to upset Mabel, one bloody word, I'll make you sorry." He let his eyes flicker down to my feet and then he slid them slowly over my body until they finally rested on my face. "More sorry than you have ever been. Understand me?"

"Yes," I replied quietly.

"Good. Glad to hear it. Now, why don't you get back to your reading? You looked real wrapped up in it before I disturbed you." He nodded at the book. "A shame you've gone and lost your place."

As soon as I heard Frank and Ted leave the house and drive toward the road, I dived into my wardrobe and retrieved the biscuit tin I'd hidden there. Again, I considered burning the letters, but again I just couldn't bring myself to destroy them. I also knew that I couldn't keep them there at the bottom of my wardrobe any longer. Frank was an ever more frequent visitor now. If he wandered into my bedroom when I wasn't there, I wouldn't put it past him to rifle through my things. I didn't want him to find the whiskey or the pills that I'd put in my laundry basket, of course, but if he did I could live with the consequences of that. What I wouldn't be able to live through, however, was his reading my letters. I had to prevent that happening at all costs. So I went downstairs and retrieved a large brown paper bag from the kitchen and placed all of my letters inside. Then I stuffed the bag into my school satchel, determined that, from now on, I would keep it with me at all times.

CHAPTER TWENTY-FOUR

I RETURNED *MODERN HOMOSEXUALITY* TO THE LIBRARIAN'S SLUSH PILE the following week, which was the week of Mabel and Frank's wedding. The ceremony, to be held that Saturday afternoon, was supposed to have been led by the vicar of Midham, but two weeks earlier some-one had broken into the Midham church, made off with the silver collection plate and the candlesticks, and vandalized the altar by spray-painting STATUS QUO FOREVER! on the church's massive oak table. The vicar, no more knowledgeable about popular heavy-metal bands now than he had been after the Black Sabbath fan defaced his church, apparently thought this was some sort of political statement and stormed into the monthly meeting of the local Young Conservatives Club to make several ugly accusations about its stunned members. Shortly after this, we were told that the vicar had been placed on indef-inite leave by the bishop and sent off to recuperate in a rest home in Whitby. For a few days, this seemed to leave the entire wedding in jeopardy, sending my mother into a terrifying conniption and the house into complete anarchy, until Reverend Mullins stepped in and agreed to take the vicar of Midham's place.

On the Tuesday evening before the wedding, my mother made me do a final fitting of my bridesmaid's dress. I stood in the kitchen, surrounded by piles of boxes, stacks of folding chairs, and teetering mountains of plates, cups, glasses, and dishes on almost every surface.

"For God's sake, Jesse, breathe in, can't you?" she said as she tugged at the zip in the back of the dress and I felt it press against my sides.

"I *am* breathing in," I protested.

"Well, breathe in more." She tugged again, but the zip got stuck at my waist.

"I can't."

"You've gone and bloody grown again, haven't you?" she said, looking over my shoulder to peer at me in the full-length mirror she'd placed in the corner by the door.

"I don't know," I said glumly, staring at my grotesque reflection. The dress, hideous under even the best of circumstances, looked absolutely awful on me. Next to the wan pink satin, my face looked sallow, and my hair seemed completely without shine. My mother was right— I must have grown, since she'd made the dress for me almost three months ago; my body seemed about to burst the seams. I reminded myself of one of the raw pink Tuggles sausages that Frank continued to bring over on a regular basis, all unruly mottled flesh pressing against its tight skin.

"Well, I haven't got time to take the dress out," my mother declared. "And, to be honest with you, I don't know that there's enough give for that in the seams. But I think if we can get rid of that flab on your stomach, that should do the trick." She slapped a hand against my abdomen and I looked down at my belly, the sheeny fabric wrinkled and misshapen over its bulge.

"I'll have to phone our Mabel and tell her to go and buy you a girdle," my mother said.

I turned on her, pulling myself out of her grip. "I am not wearing a girdle!" I felt close to tears. Having to wear this dress was humiliating enough. I was not going to wear one of those ridiculous items of underwear—that was more than I could bear.

"Yes, you are, young lady!" she screamed. "You'll do as I bloody well say! I've worked my sodding socks off for this wedding. And, come hell or high water, it's going to be our Mabel's perfect day. If you or anybody else ruins it, there'll be hell to pay. I've put my lifeblood into it, do you hear?" She held her arms out toward me, her palms turned upward, as she looked down at her wrists. The scars were healed over and far fainter now but still vivid against her pale and veiny skin.

AT SCHOOL THE FOLLOWING afternoon, Tracey was in a horrible mood after hearing that Greg Loomis had been observed sharing a cigarette with a fourth-year girl, Margery Pearson, in the bike sheds during break. Margery was known throughout the school for her willingness to flash her extraordinarily large breasts in return for a couple of bites of a Mars Bar or a few drags on a cigarette, so Tracey considered herself justifiably irked. She was frustrated, too, because Margery was one of the most ruthless girl fighters in the school, leaving anyone foolish enough to challenge her with black eyes, missing teeth, and noticeable bald spots where she'd yanked out whole handfuls of hair. So while Tracey wasn't about to get into a confrontation with Margery, she stomped around the school corridors, barked angrily at the Debbies and me in response to any question, and seemed quite determined to take out her anger on someone before the day was out. It was Malcolm Clements who ended up getting the brunt of it.

We were in our English lesson and Dizzy, Malcolm, and a few other students had been engaged in an animated discussion about the most recent book Ms. Hastings had assigned us: *To Kill a Mockingbird*. I'd enjoyed the book and I was interested in the discussion, listening attentively as Malcolm talked about how he thought Atticus Finch was a hero for going against all the other small-minded people in his town to defend the black man who had been accused of rape. Sitting next to me, Tracey yelled across the room to interrupt him. "Oh, for God's sake, shut your gob, you stupid bloody nancy boy! Nobody cares what you think, you little poof!"

"Shut up yourself," Malcolm said, waving his hand at her.

Tracey laughed and gave a limp-wristed flap of her hand in imitation of him. "Hah! Look at the state of you, you nasty little queer."

Her laugh fell from her face, however, as Ms. Hastings, in a few sweeping strides, marched across the classroom to stand next to her desk. "What did you just say, Tracey?" she asked in the quiet voice she reserved for the moments when she was most angry.

"Nothing, Ms. Hastings." Tracey dropped her eyes to make a study of her desk.

"Really?" Ms. Hastings folded her arms and looked at Tracey steadily. "Because that's not what I heard."

"I didn't say anything, Ms. Hastings," Tracey said, still not looking away from her desk.

"I see. So I must be delusional, then, is that it?"

"What?" Tracey looked up, a perplexed frown on her face. A ripple of stifled giggles rolled across the room.

"Are you suggesting I'm hearing voices in my head, Tracey?" The giggles grew louder, but stopped abruptly when Ms. Hastings swept the room with her eyes.

"No, Ms. Hastings."

"Good. Because I know what I heard, which was you insulting a fellow pupil in the most offensive manner."

"I only called him a poof and—" This time the giggles erupted into a ragged wave of laughter.

"I know exactly what you called him, Tracey," Ms. Hastings said. "I think we've established that there's nothing wrong with my hearing. And if anyone else thinks there's anything funny about using those words they can join you every afternoon next week in detention." She lifted a single eyebrow and looked around the room. All the laughter ceased.

"Detention? Every day?" Tracey looked at Ms. Hastings with an expression of horror. "But Ms. Hastings, I—"

"Detention, a week of it," Ms. Hastings said firmly. "And I do not want to hear those words cross your lips again."

"No, Ms. Hastings," Tracey muttered. Her features compressed into a picture of simmering rage, she dropped her eyes to her desk again.

Ms. Hastings returned to the front of the classroom, placed her hands on her hips, and sighed heavily. "I am very disappointed to see any of you using these sorts of words as insults," she said gravely. "Making fun of someone because they're different, or because you think they're different, is hurtful and cruel and very, very wrong. I would have hoped that from our reading you'd already learned this, but I see that some people are slower than others." One of the boys raised his hand. "Yes, Andrew?"

"But being a homo, that's not the same as being black like the man in the book. Being a homo is . . . well, it's perverted." He turned his lips downward in an expression of disgust.

"The term, Andrew, is homosexual. And it's a natural part of the human condition."

I leaned forward in my seat. While Tracey grumbled beside me, I wanted to make sure I could hear every word Ms. Hastings said. "Homosexuality," she continued, "has certainly been around for a long time, and in some societies—like ancient Greece, for example—it was considered quite normal. All those famous Greek philosophers and thinkers, a lot of them were homosexuals. Plato, Socrates, Aristotle—"

"Who the hell were they?" a boy shouted from the back.

"They were some of the most influential men of Western culture. And it wasn't just men who were homosexual." At this, I felt a bolt of excited interest rush through me. "One of the most talented women poets in ancient Greece was also gay. Sappho. She lived on the island of Lesbos." At this, a few sniggers rippled around the classroom. Beside me, Tracey snorted. But I wasn't paying any attention to Tracey at all. She could have disappeared into thin air as far as I was concerned.

"There have also been many, many writers and famous people since then who've been gay," Ms. Hastings continued. "Oscar Wilde, Gertrude Stein, James Baldwin, Alexander the Great, to name just a few. In fact, homosexuals have often been some of the most influential and talented people in society."

"But why are they like that?" another boy yelled.

With a musical jingle from her colorful bangles, Ms. Hastings folded her arms in front of her and pressed her face into a thoughtful frown. "Well, no one really knows what makes some people homosexual. There are many different theories but no definite answer. Homosexuality could be the result of social forces or it could be the result of biology. All we do know is that it occurs in humans, in every society, and during every time in history. Estimates are that about one in ten people are homosexual." She looked around the room. "Yes, that means among the thirty of you here it is likely that three of you are gay."

At this, everyone began looking around, and a few of the boys began pointing fingers at one another, whispering, "It's you, it's you," under their breath. I looked about, afraid to discover any of those fingers pointing in my direction; I was immensely relieved to see that they were not.

Ms. Hastings sat on her desk. "Okay, okay, enough of that. Clearly, you are not getting what I am trying to say, which is, Tracey," she said, raising her eyebrows and looking pointedly over at Tracey, "that there is absolutely nothing wrong with being gay. It is a normal part of human nature, and it certainly should not be used as an insult against anyone." Ms. Hastings paused, looking more solemn now. "I for one do not want to hear it being used in such a fashion in my classroom again. And, if I do, I will give the guilty party a weeklong detention, just like Tracey here. Any questions?" No one spoke. "All right," she said. "Let's get back to our discussion of *To Kill a Mockingbird.* Malcolm, could you continue the point you were making before you were so rudely interrupted?"

Malcolm nodded. "What I was saying was that people like Atticus Finch, people who stand up for other people's rights, no matter what they look like or where they come from or how much everybody else hates them—well, those people are heroes." He looked around the classroom, daring anyone to contradict him.

"Excellent point, Malcolm," Ms. Hastings beamed. "Anyone else have any thoughts on that?"

I might have ventured to say something myself, but I was far too distracted as I tried to recall every word that Ms. Hastings had just said and to fathom the implications of those words. If being gay wasn't perverted, as Frank and everyone at school seemed to think—if it was, as Ms. Hastings asserted, "natural" and "normal"—I wondered what that meant for me. And if my feelings about Amanda did mean that I was gay, then, according to Ms. Hastings I wasn't alone.

I was still preoccupied with these thoughts when the lesson ended and we straggled out of the classroom and into the corridor. Consequently, I wasn't paying much attention to Tracey at all. It was impossible, of course, not to notice that she was very unhappy about the prospect of detention for all of next week, since she'd mumbled complaints about it throughout the remainder of the lesson. But I hadn't realized how angry she was until I looked up to see her, a few feet away from me in the corridor, jostling against Malcolm.

"You fucking little poofter," she said, sticking her finger into his face. "Getting me into trouble like that. Well, I'm not going to put up with it. A whole fucking week of detention. That's your fucking fault, that is."

"It's your own fault," Malcolm said, swiping her hand away. "You should keep your big mouth shut for a change."

"Oh, is that right?" Tracey said. "Well, we'll see about that, won't we?"

"Get lost," Malcolm said, trying to push past her. "You don't scare me, Tracey Grasby."

Tracey shoved herself into him. "Well, you'd better be scared. You bloody well better be!" And with that she spun on her heels and stalked off down the corridor, her whole body rigid with rage.

THE NEXT MORNING when I entered the chaos of the kitchen to make some breakfast, I looked out the window to see my mother in the back garden. Although there were a couple of workmen coming to the house later, she'd already begun putting up the massive marquee tent alone, swinging an enormous sledgehammer to sink the metal tent stakes into the ground. Each blow she landed made the glass in the kitchen window shiver in its frame. She looked a strange sight through the quivering glass, partly because she had an odd technique for using the hammer that involved making little jumps every time she delivered a blow, and partly because her face, neck, and arms (exposed because she'd stripped down to her white cotton vest for the task) were a very unsettling color.

When I'd returned home the previous afternoon, I'd found her in the bathroom, a bottle of Tanfastic in her hand. "This'll make your grandma think twice," she'd said as she smoothed the gelatinous beige cream over her face and arms. "I'll tell her we've had such good weather this spring that I've been sitting out in the garden getting a tan." She let out a high yodeling laugh, as if she were telling herself an enormously funny joke. "If she sees me like this, who knows, maybe she'll change her mind about staying in Australia."

The bottle had said, "Get all the tan without all the trouble. Achieve a natural-looking glow without sitting in the sun for hours. You'll be the envy of all your friends!" However, "natural-looking" was one thing my mother was not, and I doubted that friends, relatives, or enemies would envy the way she appeared. Almost as soon as she applied the Tanfastic, it turned her skin a rather disturbingly bright and very streaky orange. Fortunately, my mother didn't realize how very bizarre she looked. In fact, she seemed quite satisfied with the results, declaring, as she admired her reflection in the bathroom mirror, "I can't wait to see the look on your grandma's face when she gets here and sees this." Neither could I.

As I stood by the window sipping a cup of tea and eating a few stale chocolate digestives and watching my mother work, I took in the transformation of the garden. It really was quite spectacular. What had been a virtual jungle of thistles, bramble bushes, and overgrown shrubs less than a year ago had become a wide green lawn with a complicated pond and fountain at its center. The surrounding trees—except for the dead and dying elms—were clothed in leaves, lush with burgeoning life. One side of the garden was bordered completely by a hawthorn hedge, and though my mother hadn't planted it, she had cleared the garden so that it was now possible to see the blossom there that had begun blooming in late April. Creamy white against the dark hawthorn leaves, it filled the air with a sweet, heady aroma that made me want to close my eyes and breathe deeply whenever I caught its scent. The lawn itself was bisected by a stone path and surrounded on all sides by neat little borders filled with flowers that included, much to my delight, bright-faced little pansies, as well as white and pink alyssums, yellow primroses, and golden marigolds. She'd even planted rosebushes, which had started to develop slim little buds that I knew would open into fat, fragrant blooms as soon as summer came. The pond, finished only a couple of weeks before, was now filled, and the fountain at its center—an enormous fake-marble affair sporting chubby-cheeked little cherubs with fig leafs on their groins—merrily spilled water over its three wedding cake–like layers. A week earlier, my father had purchased a dozen huge goldfish at a pet shop in Hull, bringing them home in several buckets he'd put in the boot of his car. Although the water had slopped about as my father drove the curvy road home and half of it had ended up in the boot rather than in the buckets, the fish had miraculously survived. Now, in the pond, they wove serenely between clumps of slimy green weed, their big convex eyes staring sideways, bodies flashing as they moved.

As I finished my tea, I thought of going into the garden to look at the fishpond before I went to school. But with my mother out there wielding her sledgehammer it was hard to imagine that even the fish felt protected as she slammed those stakes into the shuddering ground. So, instead, I put on my coat, lifted the strap of my satchel over my shoulder, and headed out the door.

When I arrived at the bus stop, Tracey was already there and, much to my relief, in a considerably better mood than she'd been in the previous day. Apparently, she and Greg had patched things up the night before.

"I gave him a right good telling off for smoking with that slag Margery Pearson." She was splayed across the bench, her elbow resting on its wooden arm, her head propped on her palm. I sat down beside her and dropped my satchel, which was overstuffed and very heavy, since I'd begun lugging all my letters around. "He promised me he'd never do it again. Said he doesn't like her anyway. He was just cadging a cig off her, that's all. Anyway, I made him drive me home and we rode right by Margery Pearson's bus on the way back. With a bit of luck, she'll have seen him with me and she'll know to keep her greasy hands off him from now on."

Just then Dizzy arrived, shuffling up to the bus stop without even looking at us.

"Hiya, Dizzy," Tracey said brightly.

Dizzy, who was used to being either completely ignored by Tracey or the target of her insults, blinked at Tracey. Her brown eyes, magnified through the thick lenses of her glasses, made me think of the saucer-shaped stares of goldfish as they eased themselves beneath the water of our pond.

"You all right?" Tracey asked, tossing her ponytail over her shoulder.

Dizzy nodded cautiously. "Yeah."

"Hey, why don't you come and sit down here, on the bench." Tracey pulled herself out of her slouch so there was more space between the two of us. "There's plenty of room for you here," she said, patting the wooden slats next to her and flashing Dizzy another smile.

Dizzy looked at me, as if seeking some hint as to why Tracey was being so uncharacteristically pleasant. I gave a little shrug. I had no idea what had got into her. I could only think that perhaps making up with Greg had made her so happy that she was prepared to be warm and friendly toward even those she normally despised. "I'm fine here," Dizzy concluded, taking a step back and stuffing her hands into the pockets of her scruffy anorak.

"Suit yourself," Tracey said. "I just wanted to ask you something, that's all. You're still friends with Malcolm Clements, aren't you?" Tracey's tone was cheery, not a hint of a threat in it.

"Yeah." Dizzy gave me another suspicious glance. Then, finding no clue there, she looked back at Tracey. "What about it?"

"Nothing, really. It's just that I want you to give him a message. Can you do that?"

"I suppose so," Dizzy said.

Naturally, I expected Tracey to issue another threat to Malcolm, or ask Dizzy to convey another slew of insults. So I was taken aback when I heard her speak to Dizzy in her sweetest tone. "Can you tell him that I want to apologize to him? That I'm sorry about what I said."

"You are?" I burst out, unable to contain my surprise. This was certainly a first for Tracey. Particularly after the display she'd put on yesterday in the corridor after Ms. Hastings's lesson, it came as quite a shock.

"Yeah, I've been thinking about what Ms. Hastings said yesterday and I realized that what I said to Malcolm wasn't very nice." Tracey regarded Dizzy with a look of unwrinkled sincerity. "I mean, calling him a poof and all that. It's . . . well . . . I realize that Ms. Hastings is right—I shouldn't use words like that."

The idea that Tracey had given Ms. Hastings's remarks such consideration warmed me. It wasn't that I expected to confide in her about my confused feelings for Amanda, but the idea that she was even open to thinking about these things gave me a little thrill of hope.

"Will you tell him?" She looked at Dizzy expectantly.

Dizzy shrugged. "I'll tell him. I don't know what he'll say, but I'll tell him."

Tracey beamed. "Thanks. Because I probably won't see him in school. I haven't got any lessons with him today." She put her hand in one of her coat pockets and pulled out a packet of chewing gum. "Want a piece of chewy?" she said, offering the packet to Dizzy.

Dizzy shook her head, and Tracey took out a piece and started un-wrapping it. Before she was done, though, she looked up at Dizzy, as if a thought had suddenly come to her. "Hey, maybe you could tell Malcolm I'd really like to make up for things by apologizing to his face? It'd be nice if we could clear the air. I'll be by the gates, right after school. Can you tell him that?" Her voice was high, filled with eagerness. It seemed, amazingly, as if she really wanted to put things right.

"I don't know if he'll want to talk to you," Dizzy responded. She was blinking fast, and I noticed how pale and sparse her eyelashes were. Under her glasses they looked frondlike and alive.

"Yeah, I understand. But, really, I do want him to know how bad I feel."

Dizzy's blinking eased. "I'll definitely tell him," she said.

A smile eased across Tracey's face. "Thanks a lot. And, er . . . now that I'm saying this, I want to say I'm sorry for all the horrible things I said about you as well." I was struck by the profound contrition in her voice and expression. I felt such warmth toward her. She might be hard-edged a lot of the time, but underneath she could be soft and car-ing, the kind of person you wanted as a best friend.

"Thanks, Tracey," Dizzy said. The suspicious look fell completely from her face. A smile itched at the edges of her mouth.

"Yeah, well, don't you forget to tell Malcolm that I want to say the same thing to him as well. I want him to know I mean it." She finished pulling the wrapping off the chewing gum and popped it into her mouth. "Sure you don't want a piece?" she said to Dizzy, offering her the packet again.

"Okay," Dizzy said, moving closer to Tracey and taking a piece of gum.

"What are you up to, Tracey? Picking on Dizzy again?" It was

Amanda. Normally, I watched out for her approach, but I'd been so taken aback by Tracey's dramatic change of heart that I hadn't noticed her walking up the street. She was almost at the bus stop now. I was surprised to see her carrying a black suitcase. It had silver buckles on the sides and looked heavy. Before she reached us, she put the suitcase on the ground, took a deep breath, then switched hands to lug it the last few steps.

"I'm not picking on anybody," Tracey said gruffly.

"That'll be the day," Amanda said. When she reached us, she dropped the suitcase onto the ground next to my satchel; it hit the pavement with an enormous thud. Then, panting, she fell onto the bench, in the space between Tracey and me. "Hiya, Jesse," she said.

"Hiya." There on the bench her body was pushed against mine. I shuffled uncomfortably. "Where are you going?"

"Oh, that?" Amanda said, looking down at the suitcase as if she'd only just noticed it there. "I'm going away for the weekend, to Leeds. It's a trip with school, with my drama class. We're going to see a couple of plays."

I frowned at the suitcase. It was huge—a small adolescent could have folded herself into it and there would still be room for several items of clothing.

"Oh, I know," she said, giving the suitcase a little kick. "I've never been very good at packing. I end up taking everything except the kitchen sink. That's right, isn't it, Tracey?" She turned to her sister, giving her a gentle dig with her elbow.

"How the bloody hell would I know?" Tracey said, slapping Amanda away. "And why would I care? You can go away forever for all I mind."

"Yeah, well, I'm not, am I? I'm going for a weekend, on a school trip."

"Which plays are you going to see?" I asked.

"You know what, Jesse," Amanda said, her eyes still on Tracey, "I don't really remember." Then she turned to me, smiling. "Something by Shakespeare, I think. I'll tell you when I get back, all right?"

"All right," I said, hoping and fearing that we could sit like this, pressed together, when she returned and told me about her trip.

When the bus arrived, I leaped up and grabbed Amanda's suitcase. "I'll carry it on for you," I said.

"No, Jesse, really—"

"It's all right." As I lifted the suitcase, Amanda bent down to pick up my satchel. "No," I said, dropping the suitcase and snatching the satchel from her grasp. For a second, I clung to it, and then, realizing how odd this behavior probably seemed, I eased my grip and tried to evoke a more casual attitude as I slung the strap across my shoulder.

Amanda laughed. "What's wrong, Jesse? Carrying top-secret documents for the government or something?"

"No," I said, my face burning as the weight of all my letters to Amanda hung there at my side. "I just . . . I just didn't want you to strain yourself. It's very heavy."

"Come on, Jesse," Tracey said, pushing past me to join the rest of the little crowd as they climbed onto the bus. "Keep messing about like that and you're going to make us late."

"Maybe it's best if we take our own bags, eh?" Amanda leaned across me to grasp the suitcase's handle. She hoisted it up and made her way over to the bus. I followed behind, feeling like an idiot. As Amanda reached the door of the bus, she set the suitcase on the ground and turned to me. "Thanks, Jesse," she said.

"For what?" I asked. After all, I hadn't even helped her with her suitcase.

"For wanting to carry my case for me. And for just . . . well, for being so nice, so sweet." She smiled.

I shrugged, but inside I was singing. Amanda still liked me. Despite knowing that I had tried to kiss her, despite everything she might suspect about my feelings for her, she still liked me.

Her expression became more serious. "Listen, Jesse, you take care, now, won't you? Don't let our Tracey pick on you. And don't . . . well, you take care, all right?"

"I will," I said, confused by the intensity in her face. The last time she looked at me like this was that night after the disco, when she had kissed me. For a moment, I felt awash in all the feelings I'd had then, wanting to reach out and run my hand over the impossible softness of her cheek, the sleekness of her hair. Instead, I watched as she turned to lift her suitcase again and struggled up the stairs. "Have a nice trip, Amanda!" I called after her as she struggled to the back of the bus.

AS SOON AS THE bus pulled away from the bus stop, I looked at Tracey, excited. "You know, I think that's really great what you said to Dizzy, Trace," I said. "And I know Malcolm will be—"

"Oh, for God's sake, don't be so bloody stupid, Jesse," Tracey interrupted, shoving me against the window with both hands. She lowered her voice to a whisper. "I'm not going to say sorry to that stupid little tosspot. And that fat four-eyed lump Dizzy can go to hell as far as I'm concerned."

"So why did you apologize to her? Why did you—"

Tracey gave me an exasperated look. "God, Jesse, for somebody that's supposed to be clever, you're right bloody thick sometimes."

"But I thought—"

"Yeah, I know what you thought." She grinned, keeping her voice to an animated whisper. "And I suppose it was all right that you did, because that means I did a good job of convincing Dizzy as well. But I didn't mean a bloody word of it."

"You didn't?" I tried not to reveal my pitching disappointment.

"Of course I didn't. God, Jesse, don't you know me by now?"

"So why did you say it?"

She looked at me, her face aglow. "Because I want to get him outside the school gates tonight. Because Stan and Greg are going to be there as well. And when that little poofter arrives they're going to beat the living daylights out of him. It's perfect, see. With goody-two-shoes Amanda gone on her stupid school trip, there'll be nobody who'll try to stop them. Stan and Greg are going to teach that little queer a lesson that he will never forget." She looked utterly gleeful. "Great, isn't it?" she said, jostling me with her arm. When I didn't respond, she jabbed me with her elbow. "Hey," she said, "don't you say a word to anybody about this, Jesse. I'm not telling anyone, not even the Debbies. They'll never keep their mouths shut, and then that poof will find out. But you're my best friend. I know you can keep a secret."

I SAW MALCOLM once that morning, across the playground as Tracey and I made our way to the gym for P.E. Later, at lunchtime in the dining hall, I didn't see him or Dizzy at their usual table by the door. During the afternoon break, I thought I caught sight of him moving among the crowds in the cloakroom in front of me and I had a momentary urge to push my way through all those uniformed bodies so that I could warn him not to go to the gates after school. But I didn't. Instead, while Tracey became ever more excited as the end of the day approached, I felt my stomach fill with a sour and rising dread.

There had been only one occasion on which I had felt quite as torn as I did now, and that was in the cloakroom at the Christmas disco, when I watched Stan threaten to burn Kevin and beat up Malcolm, and gave Dizzy the opportunity to seek help by spraying the whiskey around the room. But even that surreptitious act had cost me dearly and, until Greg Loomis asked her to dance, I'd spent the rest of the evening convinced that Tracey would never be my friend again. I knew that if I did anything to help Malcolm escape her wrath today and Tracey found out she would never forgive me. But as the day went on I felt more and more uneasy, so that by the time our final lesson came along I realized, with sudden perfect clarity, that I did not want to see Malcolm hurt.

With only fifteen minutes left until the bell sounded the conclusion of our final lesson of the day, Tracey was finding it hard to concentrate on her work. "I can't wait to see that little poofter's face when he gets it," she said as she doodled in the textbook *The Wonders of Tudor England,* drawing an enormous fist that looked as if it were about to punch a ruffle-collared Sir Francis Drake right in the face.

"Tracey," I said cautiously.

"What?"

"Maybe you shouldn't get Malcolm like this. I mean, Stan and Greg—well, they're a lot bigger than him. They could really hurt him."

She dropped her pen and looked at me, flabbergasted. "That's the bloody point, Jesse."

"But why? He hasn't done anything to anyone. He hasn't really done anything to you. He's just being himself, he just—"

"Jesse, he's a poof."

"But Ms. Hastings said—"

Tracey batted my arm. "God, don't tell me you actually listen to what that stupid hippie cow has to say? I told my dad what she said about that stuff and he was dead mad. Said she shouldn't be filling our heads with all that rubbish. Said she needs a bloody good hiding." She laughed. "God, I'd like to see that, I would."

I looked at Tracey, at her grinning hunger, and I felt defeated. Short of betraying her and telling Malcolm not to show up at the school gates, there was nothing I could do. And that, I knew, was a step I was not prepared to take.

"Maybe he won't be there," I said. "Maybe he'll realize that you're just pretending to be sorry."

"Yeah, maybe," Tracey said. "But, whatever he thinks, I bet he ends up showing up. I know that little nancy boy. He might be weedy, might be a big bloody queer, but he likes a challenge and, even if he's wetting his knickers, he doesn't like to look as if he's scared."

THOUGH IT HAD BEEN warm and sunny that morning, by the time we left the school building the air had turned cold. I shivered as I trudged after Tracey and the Debbies toward the school gates, pulling my coat tight around me and trying not to think about what lay ahead. It had crossed my mind to make some excuse so that I could leave them and walk instead to the car park, where I could wait for the bus. There, I could pretend I didn't know what was about to happen, that this was just another ordinary day. No matter how tempting that prospect was, however, I felt oddly compelled to go with Tracey. Besides, I knew she expected me to accompany her, that this was another required duty of her best friend.

As we walked, swept along in the river of students exiting the school, I thought about Malcolm and what he said to me after we left detention together, how he'd been so angry at me for worrying about what other people thought. I'd considered what he said many times since then, imagining how light I'd feel if I said what was on my mind. I'd tell Tracey to stop being so petty and mean-spirited; I'd tell the Debbies that they needed to start doing their own homework and I never wanted to hear another word about the Bay City Rollers again. I'd tell Stan Heaphy that he was a coward and a bully, and I'd tell Greg Loomis that he was vain and shallow and that he looked a complete moron in his ridiculous clothes. I'd tell Mabel I thought she was a fool for marrying Frank, and I'd take great pleasure in telling Frank how much I hated him. I'd tell Uncle Ted to get up early, go out, and not come back until he had a job. I'd tell my father to stop pretending that my mother wasn't bonkers, and I'd tell my mother that she was ruining my life. Of course, I'd tell Amanda that I loved her. I'd say all of this and more, loud and without inhibition, relishing the way my voice carried through the air. Except all of this was nothing more than an impossible fantasy. The punishment Malcolm was about to get for speaking out, for simply being himself, was evidence of that.

When we reached the gates, I felt a surge of hope when I saw that Stan and Greg weren't there and their motorbikes were nowhere to be seen, but when Tracey's expression brightened and she gave a little fluttery wave I turned to see Stan and Greg standing about thirty yards away, their bodies tucked behind a stand of trees. She rapidly explained her plan to the Debbies. "Stan and Greg are hiding," she told them, "until nancy boy shows up. Wouldn't want to frighten him off, now, would we?" The Debbies nodded, exchanging eager looks.

As I watched Tracey strut about, the picture of impatience, I stood rooted to the spot while my heart resounded through my body, as loud as my mother's sledgehammer when she'd driven those metal stakes into the ground. I kept hoping that Malcolm would see through Tracey's ruse, make his way instead to the car park, get on his bus, and go home. But this was not to be. And when I saw Malcolm leave the main entrance of the school and begin walking toward us, his long-limbed gait unmistakable even from that distance, it was as if one of those cold metal stakes had been driven into my gut.

Tracey, on the other hand, let out a joyful little gasp, and as Malcolm came closer she smiled and waved at him, as if she were greeting a long-awaited friend. Then she turned to the Debbies and me. "Move back from the gates a bit," she said, gesturing us to follow her as she stepped a few yards from the entrance. "I don't want anyone in the school to see us. Besides, I want to get closer to Stan and Greg." The two of them had ducked all the way behind the trees now.

"Hiya," Tracey said when Malcolm was within a few feet of us. "I'd almost given up on you. Thought you weren't going to show up." She swung her ponytail and smiled. I gnawed on my lip as I watched.

"I heard that you wanted to talk to me," he said.

"Yeah," Tracey said. "There's something I want to tell you." She stepped toward him. I clenched my hands into fists so tight I could feel my fingernails pressing like tiny blades into my palms. "I just wanted to say—" And then Tracey reached out and grabbed hold of both of Malcolm's arms.

"What the hell are you doing?" he said, jerking his arms about and trying to shake her off.

Tracey held on tight, clutching at the thick woolen fabric of his blazer. "I've got him, I've got him!" she yelled over her shoulder.

At this, Malcolm ceased his struggle for a moment. "What the hell—?" And then his voice faltered as he saw Greg and Stan charge out from behind the stand of trees.

"You're going to get your head kicked in." Stan sang the words as he galloped over the grassy verge and onto the path. As he ran his blond hair flared behind him, his lips twisted into a lopsided snarl, and his eyes, narrowed and focused completely on Malcolm, glinted like coins catching the sun. He moved faster than Greg, who was wearing plat-form shoes and stumbled clumsily over the uneven grass before reach-ing the pavement to clunk along the asphalt after Stan.

Malcolm struggled to free himself from Tracey's hold, fighting more fiercely now, his arms flailing while he kicked and shoved and tried to pry her fingers from his sleeves. Even next to Tracey he looked slight, but in contrast to the looming forms of Greg and Stan he seemed scrawny, hopelessly light, as if with a single blow they might send him flying into the air and he would land lifeless on the pavement.

This was not, however, what made me do it. It was the look Mal-colm gave me as he wrestled with Tracey. At first I saw his fear, a sheer animal panic. It blazed, a conflagration in his cheeks, flames in his eyes. But beneath that fear I saw the fire of his accusation. When, that look demanded of me, will you stand up for what you know is right? So it was then, with Stan fast approaching me on the footpath, that I lifted my satchel from my shoulder, grabbed the strap, swung it back, and hurled it with as much strength as I could muster, right into Stan's face.

First there was the sound, an enormous hollow thud as the satchel struck him, and then there was Stan's roar—a simultaneous cry of pain and consternation. I saw his head snap upward, his back arch, and then he took two, three, four staggering steps back. My satchel continued upward, spinning on itself, sweeping loose, so that for a moment it looked as if it might take flight and never return to earth. Then, caught by the tug of gravity, it ceased spinning and fell, like a rock, to the ground.

It was just at this moment that Greg caught up with Stan. He'd seen me slam Stan with the satchel, and he was enraged, yelling at the top of his lungs. "What the fuck do you think you're doing, you stupid cow?"

I stood there gaping at Stan as he floundered, appearing for a moment to find his balance before teetering forward, and then, like one of those unfortunate murder victims shot during the opening sequence of *Columbo,* he crumpled to the ground. I looked up, horrified, expecting now to feel the full force of Greg's fury. But Greg, like me, hadn't expected my blow to have such an impact, and he hadn't anticipated Stan's sudden fall. So, as he continued to run forward, pulling back his arm, readying to land his fist on me, he careened into the buckling Stan and fell with him, headlong onto the ground.

I simply stood, blinking, staring at the bundle of tangled arms and legs at my feet. Then I looked around, feeling as disoriented as if I'd been woken from a deep sleep. Everyone's eyes were on me—Tracey, the Debbies, Malcolm. They were all motionless as they gawked, mouths flaccid and wide open, eyebrows arched high, foreheads creased with shock. And then Greg let out a little moan and began trying to haul himself up. I felt a surge of fear and energy, and I began to run.

"Run!" I yelled at Malcolm as I approached him. I saw him turn and try to move away, but he was pulled to a halt as Tracey grabbed him again.

"Come on!" she cried at Greg, who was pulling himself to his feet. "I've still got him, Greg. Come and get him. Smash this little poofter's face." Then she let go of one of Malcolm's arms only to grab hold of a hank of his hair. "I've got him!" she yelled, her voice shrill and victorious. "Come on, Greg, he's not going to get away!" Malcolm flailed and pummeled at Tracey, then yelped in pain as she twisted his hair around her clenched hand and yanked his head back, hard. At the same time, I saw Greg finally lift himself off the ground, and I saw the Debbies move closer to Tracey, apparently readying to help her hold Malcolm down. So I did the only thing I could think of. As I came level with Tracey, I halted, swung my leg back, and issued the hardest kick I could muster to her shin. As she screamed, I prepared to kick her again, but she relinquished her grip on Malcolm to double over and grab her leg.

"Run!" I yelled at Malcolm again as Greg ran toward us. We both turned on our heels and ran back along the path and through the school gates. We kept running at full tilt into the car park, sweeping over the dark asphalt and easing to a stop when we reached the single bus still standing there, its passengers already loaded, all of them staring out the windows at us.

"That's my bus," Malcolm said, panting. "Quick, get on. It's leaving." He tugged at my arm.

I hesitated and looked back. Greg and Tracey hadn't pursued us. They were standing just inside the school gates, their faces furious. "You fucking bitch, Jesse!" Tracey yelled.

"Come on," Malcolm said, pulling at my arm again. "Otherwise you'll be left here with them."

I followed him onto the bus, flopping down into the nearest seat as the doors swished shut and the engine rumbled to a start.

"Are you all right?" Malcolm asked me. There were no other empty seats close to mine, and he stood over me in the aisle.

I nodded. "Are you?" I asked.

"Yeah, my head's a bit sore." He patted the place on his head where Tracey had pulled so viciously on his hair. "I think I—"

"Hey, can you sit yourself down?" It was the bus driver. He frowned over his shoulder at Malcolm, his brows knotted into a single heavy line. "As you know full well, lad, I can't move this bus an inch until you put your bum on one of them seats."

"Sorry," Malcolm said. But before moving away he looked down at me again. "Thanks, Jesse," he said. "That was really—" He paused in apparent embarrassment. "Well, I just want you to know that I thought you were really brave."

As he smiled at me I felt pride, a burst of glorious yellow light, flood through me.

"You want chucking off this bus, lad?" the bus driver bellowed.

"Sorry," Malcolm said again, and shuffled along the aisle to find an empty seat.

I didn't look out the window at Tracey and Greg as we drove through the school gates. Instead, I closed my eyes and let my head loll against the seat back. As the bus pulled away, my heartbeat slowed and my breaths began to lengthen, while a feeling of utter satisfaction thrilled through my veins. I had stopped something terrible from happening. For once, the fear of consequences hadn't left me silent and afraid. I had, as Malcolm said, finally been brave. I knew I ought to be worried about Tracey's anger, the threat of reprisals from Stan Heaphy and Greg Loomis. I knew that I'd stepped over a line that would separate me from them, and that now that I'd done it there would be no going back. But instead of worrying I felt deliciously carefree. I felt weightless, unhampered, as if, like my satchel after I'd thrown it into Stan's face, I could defy gravity, dance upward, spinning, through the air.

And then I remembered. The thought plummeting into me with all the force of something heavy falling and then crashing to the ground. I had left my satchel behind.

CHAPTER TWENTY-FIVE

—

I GOT OFF THE BUS IN REATTON HIGH STREET. "JESSE, WHY DON'T YOU come to the caravan?" Malcolm said, pushing his way through the other kids on the pavement to reach me. "When my dad gets back, he can give you a lift home."

I shook my head. I felt dull, dazed; there was a hollow dread pushing from my stomach into my chest. "I'm going home," I said, turning and striding toward where the road veered off to Midham.

Malcolm jogged after me. "He won't be long, Jesse. You'll probably get home sooner if you wait for him. And I don't know about you, but I'm a bit—well, I'm still a bit shaken up."

His face was flushed, mottled red, his clothes rumpled where Tracey had grabbed and pulled at them, his hair messy and snarled. His eyes were wild and watery. But it wasn't fear that held him now; he was flying high on the thrill of victory. I felt a surge of anger at him for still being able to occupy that place.

I said nothing. I kept on walking. The wind, brisk and cold, pushed my hair back from my face and sent grit into my eyes.

"Slow down, Jesse," Malcolm said as he strained to keep up with my rapid march. "You don't need to leave. It'd be nice if you stayed. We could look at some of my library books. I've this really good one right now about London. . . ." He touched my arm.

"Get off me!" I yelled, swinging my arm away as I spun around to face him. "Just because I helped you it doesn't mean I want to be your friend, you stupid little poof!" I stood there watching as his expression changed from concerned to confused, then to bemused and stung. I stared at him, daring him to say something. When he stayed silent, I turned on my heels and marched off down the road.

I DIDN'T SLEEP MUCH that night. This was partly because of my mother, who had decided that the outfit she'd made for herself for Mabel's wedding—a beige-colored smock that looked more like a sack than a dress—didn't do enough to show off her newly acquired fake tan. So she'd pulled out a bolt of bright yellow Crimplene from her stash of dressmaking supplies and at ten o'clock that evening had begun pinning out the tissue-paper pattern pieces for a sleeveless frock and a matching bolero jacket. At midnight, Ted arrived home after another excursion with Frank. I heard him slam the front door behind him, trudge up the stairs, then sing tunelessly in the bathroom until he flushed the toilet and marched off to bed. By one in the morning, my mother had started assembling her new outfit, the sewing machine roaring below. Had the house been completely silent, however, I probably would have found it impossible to drop off.

My mind roared almost as wildly as my mother's sewing machine. First, of course, there were the thoughts of my abandoned satchel. When I wasn't silently berating myself for putting all my letters to Amanda in it, I was raging at myself for leaving it behind. Then I would wonder where it was, and who might have it. For seconds, my mind would soar on the hope that a stranger had found it, that he or she would leave it securely buckled, and simply hand it in to the school secretary the next day. Then my thoughts would take a flailing dive, as I was sure that Stan Heaphy had found it and that he'd spent the entire evening amusing himself by reading every one of my letters. And then—and this was the most terrible thought of all—I'd imagine him showing the letters to Amanda, and how, then, she would really hate me. She might be able to brush away what it meant when I'd tried to kiss her, but she couldn't ignore all those terrible confessions on the page.

I knew the satchel had been retrieved by someone, because as soon as I returned home from Reatton I'd made my father drive up to Liston Comprehensive to see if we could find it. Though he'd complained all the way there that he was missing a "damn good documentary about Tricky Dick and that bloody Watergate what-have-you," he actually helped me search for the satchel along the grass verge outside the school. It was nowhere to be seen.

As I lay in bed, when my thoughts weren't taken up with the whereabouts of my satchel, I was thinking how foolish I'd been to write those letters in the first place, and how, more than ever, I wished I'd simply been able to erase my feelings about Amanda from my mind. And, when I wasn't thinking that, I was mulling over what an idiot I'd been to clobber Stan and kick Tracey for the sake of one of the most loathed pariahs in the school.

Now that bright euphoria I'd felt as the bus pulled away from the gates simply felt like another symptom of my idiocy. I hadn't been brave; I'd only been stupid. I tossed and turned for hours, until my mother finally finished her sewing and light began seeping, wan and gray, through my curtains. I considered getting up, but, finally exhausted, I must have fallen asleep, because the next thing I knew I opened my eyes to see that the clock on my bedside table said a quarter past eight. In my tumult the previous night, I'd forgotten to set the alarm; I'd slept in and I'd missed my bus.

"Dad, Dad," I said, scurrying into the kitchen, still in my pajamas. "Can you give me a lift to school?"

Amid the chaos of the wedding preparations and the leftovers from my mother's late-night sewing, he had cleared a little scrap of space for himself at the kitchen table. He was reading the previous day's Hull *Daily Mail,* a teacup and a plate of toast set before him. "Oh, for God's sake, Jesse," he groaned from behind the paper. "I'm not looking for that bloody satchel again. If we didn't find it last night, we won't find it this morning. Besides, I've got to get to work." He crunched the newspaper down in front of him. "Somebody's got to make a living round here, you know." He looked at the ceiling, in the direction of Uncle Ted's snores.

"But, Dad, I need a lift, I—"

"And I can't be late, because your mother wants me home early tonight," he continued, ignoring my pleading look. "Says she needs me to help her arrange the furniture in the tent. Honestly, I don't know how many bloody people we've got coming to this thing. Must be a hundred and fifty at least. I think Mabel's invited her entire bloody bingo club. And Frank seems to have more of a tribe than a family."

I tried again to interrupt him. "Dad, I—"

But he kept on going. Apparently, he felt the need to get it off his chest. "Honestly, it looks more like a bloody circus than a wedding out there." He nodded toward the window and the huge billowing marquee that covered almost half the lawn. "Mind you, it wouldn't surprise me if your mother rented out a couple of performing elephants, a gang of clowns, and a troupe of trapeze artists. Heck, maybe we'll even have a ten-bloody-cannon salute when the bride and groom make their vows. To be honest, I'm just glad it's Frank and not me that's having to pay for all of it. I know she's always a bit over the top when she does things, but this"—he took a slow, sweeping look around the room—"it takes the bloody biscuit, does this. Honestly, I don't know why I bothered doing up this kitchen—you can't see any of it for all the bloody crap she's put everywhere." He sighed. "But at least the hall and the living room still look nice, eh? Your mam might have got done all the bedrooms, but I did a nice job of the downstairs." He smiled, but it quickly faded and he let out a long-suffering sigh, his shoulders sinking so that he seemed to melt into his chair. "I know your mam has poured her heart and soul into this wedding. And, frankly, I'm a bit nervous about the whole bloody thing. For both our sakes, Jesse," he said, looking at me, anguish gripping his features, "I just hope everything goes all right. Otherwise . . ." His eyes drifted to the window, through which we could see my mother, her face a brighter and streakier orange after apparently applying another treatment of Tanfastic, staggering under a stack of metal folding chairs as she carried them across the lawn. "Well, let's just say I'll be glad when tomorrow is over and things can get back to normal again."

"Dad," I said, ignoring the temptation to grab my father by the shoulders, shake him, and demand when, exactly, he thought things had ever been normal in our house. "I really need a lift to school. I've missed my bus. Please, will you take me?"

He shook out his paper, swept the pages together, then folded it in half and slapped it down on the table. "I suppose so. But you'd better get back upstairs and get yourself dressed. I haven't got all day, you know."

I DID NOT WANT to go to school. It was, in fact, the last place I wanted to be that morning. Were it not for my desperation to retrieve my satchel and my letters, I would happily have hidden under my blankets. Like my mother in one of her bad patches, I could easily have spent my day in bed. But I was driven now by a desperate urgency, and as I dressed, then launched myself downstairs to follow my father out the door, I felt that I was on a mission to save myself.

Though the fact that I was late for school made me more anxious, I was relieved that I didn't have to face Tracey at the bus stop and could sweep instead along the winding road to Liston Comprehensive in the safety of my father's car. It was a cool morning, and, though it was sunny, a brisk breeze had painted high clouds in delicate brushstrokes against an otherwise startling blue sky. I leaned my head against the car window and looked at the vivid landscape while I let the tart tones of

the BBC radio announcers wash over me, along with my father's occasional snorts and mumbled responses. There were reports of war and
protests, bombs and riots, strikes and strife. Listening, I was struck by
the realization that these were not just stories of distant places; they
were the actual facts of people's lives. For a moment, my anguish for
myself melded with all the anguish found elsewhere, so that it seemed
that I held that roiling world inside me, all those struggles to survive. It
made me think of my mother—of her flailing desperation, the way she
so often seemed on the verge of going under, and then how she'd somehow tap that fiery well of energy she held within her to soar upward,
like a bird discovering its wings. In those glorious times, when she was
pouring herself into some project or hobby, she did not care what anyone else might think of her; the only world she lived in was her own. As
the car sped along the road and my dread churned at the prospect of my
feelings for Amanda being discovered, for the first time that I could remember I found myself envying my mother. Consumed with the
preparations for the wedding, she might be delirious, ridiculous, and
completely distracted, but she was absolutely herself.

"See you tonight, then, Jesse," my father said as he pulled up outside
the school.

The exterior was quiet, and, apart from a couple of other stragglers
plodding toward the main entrance, there was no one else around. As
soon as I walked inside, however, I entered another world.

By the notice board outside the cloakrooms there was a huge
milling crowd. At least four deep, they pressed against one another in a
scramble to see some new notice that was apparently pinned up there.
Despite my urgency to find my satchel, everyone seemed so excited
that I felt myself drawn to find out what all the fuss was about.

As I approached, I saw a girl from my class standing on the edge of
the crowd. When I caught her eyes, they widened and she sputtered a
giggle into her hand. Within moments I heard the whispers, spreading
around me as if those voices were a ripple and I was a stone dropped
into a pond. Then, as I stepped closer, the crowd quieted and began to

part. I walked through the silence, past the grinning faces, all those shoes shuffling to make way.

I knew what was coming, the same way I had known that something dreadful had happened to my mother when we lived in Hull and I found that gathering of neighbors outside our house. In that awful hush, pregnant with held breaths and stifled laughs, it was a certainty that gripped me, a fist clenched around my heart. I was moving again, steadily, toward disaster, unable to turn around or stop.

"Lezzie!" Tracey said the word before I had made my way past the assembled group. "Lezzie!" she yelled again, standing triumphant in front of the notice board as I looked at the several sheets of paper pinned up there. "Lezzie!" she screamed as I looked at the familiar writing on those pages. I took in only the words "Dear Amanda," then I spun around and hurled my way back through the jostling, jeering crowd.

CHAPTER TWENTY-SIX

—

I DIDN'T CRY WHILE I TRUDGED THE SIX MILES FROM LISTON TO MID-ham. I didn't shed a single tear. There was no reason to cry, because I was a shell holding only humiliation. I had nothing now. No friends and no protection. The worst thing I could imagine had happened, and all I could do was put one foot in front of the other and make my way home.

By the time I arrived at the top of our driveway, the weather had become bleaker. A cold wind had risen to make the branches of the trees by our house sweep and thrash. As I traipsed up the driveway, a scrap of pink fabric danced through the air toward me.

"Grab it, Jesse!" my mother yelled, careening down the path. "Grab it—that's one of the wedding serviettes!"

I halted to watch it flutter like a pink butterfly, sail upward, dip so that it almost brushed my head, then soar up and away again.

"I told you to grab it!" she screamed, crashing into me so that I staggered back. "What the hell is wrong with you?" Her astoundingly orange face leaned into mine. I caught the scent of her breath, warm and yeasty, before she pulled away. Then she continued onward, chasing the serviette as it swooped low, then was pulled high into the air yet again.

For some reason, she was wearing her new yellow wedding outfit, apparently not quite finished, as the hem was frayed and slightly jagged, and one of the sleeves of her bolero jacket hung loose. Since I had seen her earlier that morning, she had dyed her hair, transforming herself into a tufty-headed platinum blonde. She was bare-legged in her slippers and, because she hadn't put any Tanfastic on her legs they were a ghostly white in contrast to her arms and face.

As I watched her, I felt strangely mesmerized, taking in the stark contrast of all that color—the vivid pink, the blazing yellow, the streaky orange flesh—against the inky sky. I was filled with complete indifference, as if I were watching something on the television, as if this were not my life. I simply no longer had it in me to care about anything—not my mother or this stupid wedding, not even Amanda, and certainly not myself.

My mother ran down the driveway, the serviette just out of her grasp until, as if the wind had finally became bored with teasing her, it tugged the little flag of fabric far upward and swept it away into the black branches of one of the dead elm trees that stood on the other side of the road. There it caught, a beautiful pink pennant, flapping far beyond my mother's reach.

I SPENT THAT afternoon in bed. All about me I could hear the clatter of my mother's frantic preparations, and the wind as it shuddered against my window. Sometime in the early afternoon, I heard the familiar growl of the Tuggles delivery van as it entered the driveway and then Mabel's and Frank's voices in the hall. Later still, I heard Ted thump about in the bathroom and stomp down the stairs. Then the boom and bellow of male voices until I heard the front door bang, Frank's and Ted's laughter as they made their way down the path, the cough of the van's engine as it started and then chugged off. A little later, I heard my father's car arrive and then more voices—my mother's shrill, Mabel's loud and steady, my father's a burdened distant drone.

Throughout this, I lay, eyes closed, unmoving. It was nice to be there, I found, weighted down by blankets, swaddled in my body's warmth. With no one to taunt me, no faces grinning with hungry accusation, I felt safe, half buried, hidden from the dangers of the world. It was comforting, too, to hear the voices, the sounds of life going on without me, knowing that, while I lay there, the world continued on. I wondered now if this was how my mother had felt during all her hibernations in the daytime dusk of her curtained bedroom. If, held in place by the bedclothes, she'd felt protected, soothed by the slow rhythm of her own breathing and the dark walls that kept the passing time at bay. As I listened to her rampaging about the house below me, I realized that her frenzied projects were just another means of giving herself shelter, another barrier to stave off what she feared. I also understood what drove her to it—it was the harshness and unpredictability of everything. While landscaping a garden or planning a wedding were infinitely manageable, life itself was a chaos we could not control.

I had thought it required only willpower. But, in the same way that I knew my father could not will my mother to normality, I knew now that I could not will the same for myself. I had wanted, more than anything, to fit in with Tracey and the Debbies, to shed and leave behind my difference in the same way that a hermit crab might crawl into another shell. But my difference was a thing I held inside me, and I could not simply discard it. I was flawed and terrible and, again, everyone knew it. This time, though, I could not blame my mother. The only person I could blame was me.

"JESSE!" IT WAS EARLY evening and my bedroom door flew open. "Jesse! For God's sake, what the hell are you doing in bed?" I peered over the top of my blankets to see my mother standing, hands on hips, in the doorway. She was wearing a pair of her paint-spattered overalls, with a headscarf over her hair.

"Leave me alone, I don't feel very well," I said, heaving the bedclothes over my head and flopping onto my side.

"Rubbish!" I heard her walk across the room. "Don't think I'm falling for that, young lady. What, you think you can get out of being a bridesmaid by pretending to be poorly? I wasn't born yesterday, you know."

"I don't feel very well," I repeated, my words dull and hot and muffled against the blankets.

"Don't be so bloody daft. Me and Mabel and your father are working ourselves to the bone for this wedding. It's bad enough that Ted and Frank have cleared off, never mind you lolling around in bed. We could use your help, young lady. Now come on, get yourself up."

"I don't want to."

"Hah! We'll see about that," she said, yanking the bedclothes off me.

"Leave me alone," I said, cradling my head and drawing my knees to my chest.

"Oh, I don't think so," she said, grabbing my arm.

"Leave me alone." My voice was distant, defeated, as I tried to pull away from her grasp.

My mother tightened her grip so that her nails pressed into my flesh. "Look!" she yelled. "If you don't get yourself out of bed bloody sharpish, I'll get your father up here to tan your backside."

"I don't care," I said, still trying to twist away. But my mother had grown stronger from all her home repairs and gardening; it was impossible for me to shake free.

"Oh, you will bloody care," she said, tugging me upward. "Or I'll slap you myself." She shook my arm so that I flopped about like something without substance.

"All right, all right," I said. She loosened her grip, and I was finally able to pull away.

She folded her arms across her chest. "Come on, then."

"I'm not going to get dressed in front of you," I declared. "I'm not a child anymore, you know."

"Well, you're not too old to get a damn good hiding. So don't you forget that!" She stalked to the door, but turned around before she left.

"Ten minutes and I want you downstairs," she said, stabbing a finger in my direction. "Otherwise, I'll be back."

I HAD HEARD THE wind while I was in my bedroom, and I knew it was loud, but when I entered the kitchen I realized that it was far stronger than I'd thought. Through the window, I could see the big marquee tent moving like something breathing, its sides billowing out, drawing inward, then bulging out again. The ropes that attached it to the stakes were pulled taut, as if in a tug-of-war with the wind. The plants my mother had put out in the garden lurched, like frenzied dancers, the colorful heads of all the pansies dipping toward the ground and then, hurled upward by a sudden gust, flapping down again. The bare branches of the elms slashed the air like whips.

"There's going to be a storm," I said, plunking myself down at the kitchen table across from my mother. She was sitting, pen in hand, frowning over the seating plan for the wedding reception. She'd drawn it out on the back of a length of wallpaper. There were teacups on either side holding the paper down.

"No, there isn't." She looked up at me, irate.

"Yes, there is." I leaned across the table and scowled at her. I hated her for bullying me out of bed and forcing me into the blaze of daylight. If she was going to pull me from my little envelope of safety, I wanted to tear her out of the one she'd constructed for herself.

"I don't know, Ev," Mabel said. She stood over a couple of pans on the cooker, one of them sizzling and spitting. The smell of frying sausages filled the room. "Maybe Jesse's right." She waved a spatula toward the window. "Them's real dark clouds out there. I wouldn't be surprised if we're in for some rain. I watched the weather forecast on the telly a couple of days ago, and it said it was going to be quite nice, but . . . Well, maybe we should listen to the forecast now."

"There's no use in listening to them," my mother snapped. "What do they know? They're always getting it wrong. Trust me, Mabel," she said, vehemently scribbling across her seating map, "it's only a bit of un-settled weather. By tomorrow the sun will come out and everything will be fine."

I laughed, but my mother ignored me and continued her writing. I felt an itching urge to snatch the pen from her grasp.

"I just wish Frank and Ted were back," Mabel said. "Frank said they were only going to run a couple of errands. I hope nothing's happened. There's too many bleeming accidents on all these little country roads." She pressed her lips into a firm, thin line and turned back to the cooker, where she began to prod agitatedly at the contents of the pans.

Just then I caught some movement in the window and I looked over to see my father staggering across the garden, a wavering stack of plates in his arms. The strands of hair he usually combed over his bald patch were being blown into his eyes, and the oversized parka he wore flapped about him like something feral. The way he leaned and battled the gusts seemed almost comical; it made me think of a chalky-faced mime artist pretending to walk into the wind.

"It is really windy out there," I said, enunciating each of my words.

"It's just a strong breeze, that's all," my mother countered, crossing out a name and writing in another one in its place. As soon as she'd spo-ken, we heard the sound of something loud and metallic clatter away from the house.

"Ooh, heck," Mabel said, jumping at the noise and dropping her spatula on the floor.

"It's not a bloody breeze," I said, enraged now at my mother's capac-ity for self-delusion. "It's blowing a bloody gale."

"You watch your language, young lady!" my mother yelled, rising out of her chair and lifting her hand high in the air, as if she were about to strike me.

"Go on," I said, meeting her eyes and rising with her. "Go on, just hit me." I pushed my face across the table and lifted my cheek toward her palm. More than anything, I wanted her to do it. I wanted her to hit me hard, again and again and again. I wanted to feel her stinging blows fall upon me, knowing the pain would erase the numbing distance I felt from my body, knowing it was exactly what I deserved.

"Now, now, you two," Mabel said, sweeping across the kitchen to stand between us. "Come on, I don't want you to have a fight." She'd retrieved her spatula from the floor and now thrust it between us. She placed a hand on my mother's shoulder. My mother continued to glare at me, but she let Mabel push her down into her chair. "I'm feeling nervous enough," Mabel continued. "All this nasty weather and Frank not back. The last thing I need is you two going at each other. Tomorrow is supposed to be my big day, you know."

"Oh, don't you worry, Mabel," my mother said, standing up suddenly and sending her chair crashing to the floor. "This," she declared, swinging her arm in a wide arc around the kitchen, "is going to be the wedding to beat them all." Then, leaving the chair there on the floor, she stomped across the room. "I'm off to see how Mike's getting on putting out the place settings. He doesn't know his bloody arse from his elbow, never mind where to put the salad forks." When she reached the door, she swung around to look at me. "For God's sake, Jesse, make yourself useful. Finish off the cooking for your poor auntie Mabel and make us all a pot of tea." Then she flounced into the hallway and slammed the door behind her. Mabel flinched and dropped the spatula again.

The judder of the slamming door had sent a bolt of energy through me. Like the slap that I had longed for my mother to deliver, it jarred me into feeling. Tears rose, like boiling liquid, into my eyes and spilled down my face.

"Are you all right, Jesse?" Mabel asked. She sat down in the chair next to me.

I said nothing. My cheeks were wet, scalded with sudden emotion.

"Oh, I'm sorry, love," she said, putting her arm around my shoulder and pulling me to her. "I know your mother can try the patience of a saint sometimes. She's just about driving me mad." She placed her hand on my face and brushed away one of my tears. "I don't know what on earth I was thinking when I said she could do this bleeming wedding. I suppose I was just trying to humor her, keep her happy. But now . . ." She looked out the window again.

Mabel's hand on my cheek was warm, her fingers soft. The heat of her skin made me want to press myself closer to her, into the welcoming give of her body, the familiar comfort of her smells. I remembered all the times I had found solace there, and I yearned for that solace again. But it was too late for that now. There was no sanctuary for me with Mabel now that she was about to marry Frank.

"Those sausages are going to burn," I said, shaking Mabel's arm from my shoulder and rising from my chair. I gulped back my tears and ran my sleeve across my eyes. Then I turned off the gas under the sausages, picked up the kettle, and walked over to the tap. After I had filled it and put it on the cooker, I turned on the radio just as the shipping forecast was being read.

"There are warnings of severe gales in all areas except Irish Sea and Shannon," the announcer said.

Mabel looked nervous as she picked up her cigarettes from the table.

"Viking, North Utsire, South Utsire," the announcer continued, "Northeast severe gale nine to storm ten. Very rough. Rain. Poor."

The shipping forecast had always been almost indecipherable to me, but I knew what severe gale warnings were. I wondered how far we were from all those oddly named places.

"Forties, Cromarty, Forth, Tyne, Dogger, Northeast storm ten to violent storm eleven. Very rough. Rain. Poor. Fisher, German Bight, Humber, Northeast ten to violent storm eleven . . ."

Without thinking, I turned off the radio.

"Humber," Mabel repeated. "Ooh, heck. We're right near the

bleeming Humber. Violent storm eleven," she said, staring out the window at the flapping, billowing tent. "I don't think that sounds very promising."

THE RAIN BEGAN a little after eight o'clock. When the first drops streaked the windows, my mother announced that it was just a shower, the sort we often got at this time of year. Even when it started to pour, the rain driven by the raging wind to batter the windows and drum audibly against the walls, she continued to prance about the house, issuing orders to my father, making encouraging comments to Mabel, and occasionally glowering at me. In fact, the harder the rain fell, the higher her energy seemed to rise, so that she ran from room to room, her voice shrill, her eyes huge and wild. While the storm outside was a shrieking, howling monster, we had a hurricane indoors.

"I should have seen this coming," Mabel said. She was sitting at the kitchen table, smoking. It had been raining for well over an hour. "Should have known it would end in disaster. I mean, let's face it, anything that our Evelyn's involved in usually does. I know she can't control the weather, but a wedding, in a tent, in her bleeming back garden—I must have been bloody mad." She crushed the butt of her cigarette in the overflowing ashtray and took another one out of the packet. "And I'm ever so worried about Frank and Ted. They were supposed to be back hours ago."

As Mabel spoke, a huge crack sounded from just beyond the window. We both looked out, but it was almost dark now and all we could see was our own frowning reflections in the glass. We heard something outside thrashing about.

"It's the tent," I said. "One of the stakes must have come out."

We ran into the hallway and found my father sitting, head in hands, on the stairs. "Come on, Mike," Mabel said, pulling him up by the arm. "No time for moping, we've got to get outside."

"What's wrong?" It was my mother. She'd changed into her wedding outfit again. This time, though, it was finished and she'd completed the ensemble with a pair of yellow tights and yellow high-heeled shoes. Her brittle bleached hair sat on her head, like little clumps of white moss. "What's going on?" she demanded.

"It's that tent, that's what, Evelyn," Mabel said as she pulled her coat down from the hanger in the hall. "The bleeming thing is blowing away." I grabbed my anorak and shoved my arms into the sleeves. Beside me, my father grappled with his parka.

"Everything is going to be fine," my mother said, as if we were being ridiculous, as if we were the panicking passengers and she was the captain who was steering us competently through a couple of choppy waves.

It was her dismissive tone that infuriated me, sparking an anger that turned, in a single second, into a firestorm. And with it came a realization: Of everyone I had struck out at in the past couple of days—Stan, Greg, Tracey, Malcolm—there was no one that I wanted to hurt more than my mother.

"Nothing is going to be fine!" I yelled. "Nothing! The weather, the tent, the whole bloody wedding—it's all a disaster. All of it!"

"Now, now, Jesse," my father said, putting a hand on my shoulder. "No need for that. No need to upset your mum."

I batted him away. "No need to upset her?" My voice held a howl far stronger than the wind's. "No need to upset her?" I repeated. "What about me?" I yelled. "Why doesn't anyone care about upsetting me?" For a moment I stared at my father, my eyes an outraged accusation. He returned my look, blinking, as if a blinding light had been directed into his eyes. I dared him to speak, but he said nothing, and then I spun around to face my mother. "You!" I shouted, fueled by the delicious energy that coursed through me. "You are the biggest disaster of all."

I took a couple of steps toward her, standing so close now that I could see the pale area of her pores where the Tanfastic hadn't penetrated, a stripe of dark hair next to her ear where she'd failed to get the bleach all the way to the roots. I stood so close that our bodies were touching. Her breasts, unyielding in the pointy bra she wore under her yellow dress, pressed against my barely curved chest.

"You want to know a secret, Mum?" I asked, lowering my voice so it was just above a whisper, so that, against the backdrop of yowling wind, she'd be the only one to hear. My mother frowned, her eyes vague and distant, as she moved her head up and down in a jerky little nod. I leaned closer to her and spoke into her ear. "When they took you out of the house on that stretcher," I said, "I wished that you'd really killed yourself." I pushed out the words with a soft viciousness, enjoying the way they rolled, like the lines of a song, so easily off my tongue. "I still wish it now," I said.

It was true, it was there inside me. It was complete and utter certainty. I wished they'd taken her off in that ambulance and never brought her back. Or, more accurately, I wished that Mrs. Brockett had never found her, that she'd been left to bleed slowly into the bath, and that I'd discovered her there when I came home from school, drained of life, made soft and wrinkled by the bloody water.

I pulled away slightly to look into her face, exhilarated. And then I let the words out slowly. "It would make me really happy if you were dead."

For a moment, my mother's expression flared with indignation. She took a couple of steps back, balled her hands into fists, and lifted them to her chest, like a boxer preparing to deliver a blow. But, in the next moment, she dropped them again, so that her arms flopped loose at her sides and her face fell slack. Then she staggered backward a few steps on her teetering heels before turning away from me to walk slowly down the hall.

WE DID OUR BEST to rescue the tent. Mabel, my father, and I battling the gale to reach the back garden, then struggling across the waterlogged lawn as the rain hit our faces like needles and the gale howled like something alive. But the huge marquee, broken free from several of its stakes now, reared and bucked like a liberated wild animal; it was like trying to pin a roaring elephant down. We could hardly hear one another; our voices were blown from us and drowned.

"It's no good!" Mabel yelled, a few inches away from me, as the rope she'd been able to grab jerked away from her hand.

"I know!" I yelled back. Then both of us fought our way over to my father, who was clinging to the front flap of the tent and looked as if he might be tugged away and into the air at any moment.

"Come on, Mike!" Mabel shouted, pulling at him so that he loosened his grip and the fabric flew upward. "The bloody wedding's off!"

We'd been working in the pale yellow light that shone from the windows of the house. As I turned and began making my way back to the house, I saw my mother watching us from the kitchen window. The next moment, all the lights went out and I was plunged into darkness.

I stood there, wavering in the wind, as I tried to get used to the dark. But the seconds went by, and in the stinging rain I could make out nothing but shadow outlines. The entire world seemed to have turned into looming silhouettes. From somewhere, rippling on the wind, I heard Mabel's and my father's voices. They were both calling out my name. I realized that I didn't want to go to them, that I wanted to stay there, shivering and sodden, alone. I imagined the water seeping ever deeper into me, so that it would wash me clean, all the way down to my bones.

"Jesse!" It was my father. He had stumbled into me.

"Is that Jesse?" Mabel yelled. She was holding on to my father.

They both grabbed me and tried to pull me onward. I resisted.

"For God's sake, Jesse!" Mabel cried. "We need to get inside!"

I let her tug me forward, joining her and my father to struggle toward the house.

It took us a long time to find our way to the door. But finally we got there, and as soon as my father turned the door handle the wind caught the door and flung it wide, into the hall. The three of us stumbled inside, breathing hard, and then turned round to grapple with the door, shoving against it until we were finally able to close it with an enormous, resounding slam. We fell against it, panting and dripping, our backs resting on the wood. It was then that I saw a pale flickering light coming from the kitchen, and a moment later that I heard the heavy thuds, the sound of metal striking something hollow and dull. The noise reverberated through the house half a dozen times, followed by the sound of wood splitting, a bright and aching yawn.

"What the bloody hell . . . ?" my father said, a dark shadow beside me. He pushed himself off and began walking down the hall. Mabel stayed behind, still panting, apparently winded, while I followed, pressing my palm against the cold, flat surface of the wall as I tried to guide myself through the darkness. As the banging continued, I felt it shudder through the wall and into my hand. It was as if the entire house were being beaten in a series of violent, body-crushing blows.

When my father reached the living-room doorway, I heard him knock into something, let out a little bark of pain, then stumble onward again. When I reached the obstacle he had encountered, I realized it was the living-room door, hanging half off its hinges, leaning into the hall. I let out a sharp gasp and continued on after my father. He halted a few seconds later outside the kitchen, and I joined him there to peer into the room.

It was the candle I noticed first, upright in a saucer in the middle of the table. Its flame flickering slightly, it gave out a pale illumination that made the room all soft-edged shadows and blocks of darkness against the shuddering light. Everything else was indistinct except my mother, her jaw clenched and her eyes gleaming buttons of conviction as she swung her sledgehammer up, grunted, and then smashed it against the kitchen wall.

"Jesus Christ almighty!" my father whispered, his words coming out like the slow hiss of a leaking tire. Then the hammer hit the wall with an enormous thump, and there was the sound of plaster tumbling in fragments; it made me think of teeth falling from a cartoon character's mouth.

As we stood in the kitchen doorway I turned to look at my father, but all I could make out were the hollows of his eyes. Then he took a breath and stepped past me, into the kitchen. "Evelyn," he said as she swung the hammer over her shoulder. "Evelyn," he repeated, this time louder as he tripped on something. In the tangle of his feet I thought I made out the outline of a broken chair. "Stop!" he shouted as my mother, a flat silhouette, began to lift the hammer above her. "Don't you think you've done enough damage?" His voice was loud, but pleading, like a child's.

She turned to him. I saw her arms twitch slightly, as if she were about to swing the hammer at him. Then she let it go so that it dropped behind her and fell to the floor.

CHAPTER TWENTY-SEVEN

—

I SPENT THAT NIGHT WITH MABEL AND MY FATHER AMONG THE BAT-
tered remains of the living room. None of us wanted to spend the night
alone. I sat on our now legless armchair, my legs stretched out on the
floor in front of me, while my father slept on the tilting settee and
Mabel paced back and forth across the littered floor. When she wasn't
smoking, she gripped the diamond engagement ring on her finger,
twisting it nervously round and round.

"Oh, God, Jesse, I can't believe this is happening. It's like one of
them bleeming disaster films, is this. But I tell you, I can take canceling
the wedding. I can even take our Evelyn acting like a one-woman de-
molition crew. But I'm worried to death about Frank and Ted being out
in this." She swept an arm toward the window and the cacophony of
the still raging storm. "They could be off in a ditch somewhere. They
could be injured. Oh, God, they could be . . ." She sobbed, then added
softly, "I just wish we could phone the police."

We had discovered that the telephone was dead when my father
tried to ring my mother's doctor, though what advice the doctor might
have offered in the wake of her fit of destruction I did not know. When
he hadn't been able to reach the doctor, my father had searched out a
bottle of her pills, given her a couple with a glass of water, and made her

swallow them down. Then he and Mabel had taken her upstairs to her bedroom, where she'd rapidly fallen asleep. After walking through the house with a torch to survey the full extent of the damage my mother had carried out, my father had collapsed in a defeated bundle onto the settee. When he finally fell asleep, he slept fitfully, letting out little murmurs and grumbles as his limbs jerked and his features twitched.

"I'm sure Frank and Uncle Ted are fine, Auntie Mabel," I said, trying to sound reassuring. "Maybe they stopped off somewhere to get out of the weather."

"I hope you're right, Jesse," Mabel said. "I really do. But I've got this awful feeling. I just know something terrible has happened." She pressed a fist into her stomach. "I can feel it, right here, in my guts."

I WAS JERKED OUT of sleep by the sound of loud banging, and for a moment I thought my mother must have found her sledgehammer again. But then, as I opened my eyes, I realized that it wasn't the noise of a hammer that had woken me; there was someone banging on the front door. I pushed myself out of the broken armchair.

It was no longer dark. Light seeped through the curtains, so that the room was cast in a silvery pall. My father still lay sleeping on the settee, his mouth open, his breath coming out in snuffled gasps. Mabel was flopped into the other armchair, her head thrown back, her arms draped limp over the chair's sides. As the pounding on the door continued, she groaned, her eyelids flickered, and then she suddenly opened her eyes wide. The next moment, she was on her feet.

"It must be Frank and Ted," she said. "Oh, thank God! They must have forgotten to take a key." She marched across the room, pausing for a moment to check her reflection in the mirror above the mantel, now hanging at an angle, a massive crack across its middle. She cupped her cheeks in her hands, groaned again, then patted her hair. "Crikey," she said. "I look like I've been through a bleeming war." Then she added, mumbling, "Feel like I've been through one as well."

I followed her out into the hallway, hanging back as she raced to the door.

"Where the heck have you—" she began as she opened the door. Apparently shocked at what she saw there, she took a step back. The door swung wide, and I saw two policemen standing on our front step. One was tall, with a jutting chin and an enormous swell of a belly that pressed against the shiny buttons of his midnight-blue uniform. The other was thin and much younger, his conical helmet too big, so that it hid a good part of his smooth-skinned face and made me think of a bucket turned upside down onto his head.

"Are you . . . Mrs. Bennett?" the tall policeman asked, pausing as he consulted the notebook he held. He had a deep, authoritative voice, the sort that seemed appropriate for a representative of the local constabulary.

"No . . . she's . . . she's in bed. I'm Mabel Pearson," Mabel said, her voice shaky as she pressed her hand against the wall.

The tall policeman looked grave. The younger one shuffled about, his expression invisible as he made a study of his feet. "Well, Mrs. Pearson—"

"It's Miss . . . Miss Pearson," Mabel said.

I moved along the hallway to stand next to her.

"Well, I'm afraid, Miss Pearson, that we've got a bit of bad news."

"Oh, God," Mabel gasped. "I knew it. I just knew it. What is it? What happened? Has there been an accident? Are they both . . . are they dead?"

The two policemen exchanged looks.

"Erm . . . If you're referring to"—the tall man looked at his notebook again—"Mr. Edward Pearson and Mr. Frank Shipton, no, Miss Pearson, they're not dead. They're fine. But I'm sorry to say that they've been arrested."

"Arrested?" Mabel's voice rose close to a shriek. "For what?"

He looked down at his notebook. "Stealing. And I'm afraid there may be a charge of conspiracy to defraud."

"Oh, God," she said, grappling with her cigarette packet. "I'll kill our bloody Ted, I will. Dragging poor Frank into trouble." She pulled out a cigarette, waving it about, unlit, as she spoke. "So, what's he been stealing? What's he been defrauding?"

"It's both of them that's being charged, Miss Pearson," the policeman said solemnly. "They've been stealing Tuggles sausages."

AS SOON AS THE police were gone, I left Mabel smoking and pacing the hallway, ran upstairs to my bedroom, gathered up a few things, and put them into a duffel bag that I slung across my shoulder. Then I galloped down the stairs again, launched myself past Mabel, and out the front door.

It was a different world now. The storm had transformed everything. The hedgerows were battered and the fields beaten. The wheat, silvered with rain, lay flat like the fur of a damp animal. The road was pocked with wide, shimmering puddles and strewn with debris—ragged leaves, broken branches. Huge shape-shifting clouds, dense and gray at their bottoms, rolled across the sky. Next to where our driveway opened out into the road, a tree had fallen, blocking one lane of the narrow little thoroughfare. It was one of the dead elms, stark and bare, a felled corpse sent sprawling. As I made my way around it, I noticed, in the fine fingers of its upper branches, a pink serviette splayed on the ground, tattered, streaked with dirt, and darkly wet.

I walked purposefully, breathing in the cool, stark air. The wind, far less powerful than during the night, but still strong, was coming off the coast. As I moved against it, I felt myself pushing into a force that was so much larger than me, urging it to welcome me into its arms. And while my body moved forward, I let my thoughts skim over the bedraggled landscape. After such destruction, it seemed a miracle that the world remained intact, resilient. I only wished that I could say the same of myself. Instead, I felt undone.

I had tried so hard. Tried to make a new life for myself, tried to fit in. Tried to take care of my mother, to rein in her maniacal energy, to keep her afloat. I had tried, too, to love someone. And, finally, when pushed to it, I had even tried to stop brutality and bullying, to stand up, to speak out. I'd failed in all of it. Instead of making myself loved and popular and normal, I'd become the worst thing there was. At school, I was a "lezzie," a "homo," a "pervert," but at home I was something even more dreadful. I had said the cruelest thing I could think of to my mother. I had told her that I wished that she were dead. And I'd told her knowing full well the state she'd worked herself into over Mabel's wedding. I might as well have lifted that sledgehammer and smashed the walls and doors and furniture myself.

IT WAS STILL EARLY when I reached Reatton-on-Sea. The little high street was empty, the shops still closed, the only movement the squeaky flapping of a dislodged metal sign above the amusement arcade. I saw no one on the road that led to the cliff edge. The only sounds were the wind and the roar of the waves. The sea was a strip of slate gray, widening as I came closer, and flecked with white ruffles, like shreds of lace. I didn't see the dramatic change in the shape of the cliffs until I was almost at the end of the road. It was only then that I noticed that the jutting little peninsula at the edge of the caravan park was no longer there. Where that tongue of cliff had stuck out, there was nothing more than air. Malcolm's battered caravan was gone.

My duffel bag bounced hard against my back and its stringy strap bit into my shoulder as I ran past the entrance of Holiday Haven. I sped across the sodden grass, splashing through puddles, sliding over greasy mud, until I stopped as close as I dared get to the cliff edge, to the place where that peninsula had been. Then I craned my head to peer over the rim, to see where the sea had ripped the land away. The clay, dark and moist, seemed poured downward, like suddenly frozen liquid. At the bottom, it was held in the tumultuous caress of the waves.

The sight finally made me certain, tipped me, too, over the edge. As

I gazed down at the place where Malcolm and his family must have plunged to in the middle of the night, I knew what I had to do. I had come looking for him, I now realized, hoping that there might be at least one person who could understand me, who could keep me attached to this place. But he was gone now. Sucked down, sucked under by the insatiable waves.

As the high tide swirled below and gnawed eagerly at the base of the cliff, I thought about Mr. Cuthbertson's stories in my geography lessons, of whole towns and villages pulled under, of ports and people washed away. There were ancient graveyards in the silt and mud off the East Yorkshire coast. A sea full of bodies. I was sad that Malcolm had to drown there, but it seemed a fitting place to end.

I stepped back from the cliff and pulled the duffel bag from my shoulder. Then I tugged back the string fastening its mouth and tipped its contents onto the wet ground—a pillowcase holding a hundred little pills and a whiskey bottle containing a couple of inches of bright, coppery liquid.

It didn't take long to push it all into me. A handful of pills, a stinging mouthful of the whiskey, another handful of the pills. I did it so fast that by the time I was done I didn't feel the effects of any of it, just the raw and glorious burn of the whiskey all the way from my lips down my throat and into my stomach.

I began walking. Back along the cliff, gazing at the turbulent water, until I reached the path that led to the beach. As I made my way down, my limbs began to feel stretched out, loose. The noise of the waves became deafening, a percussion orchestra in my ears. And then a bright stretch of sky opened up on the horizon. It glistened across the silvered water, dazzling. I kept blinking. My eyes, now heavy and aching, couldn't bear all that light. But I kept plodding downward until I reached the bottom, and a little patch of sand not quite covered by the tide. For a moment—or perhaps for a long, long time—I stood there, watching the waves sweep onto the sand, over and across one another, like crescendos of music, or rising and falling floods of hope. Then, as I felt dizziness start to overtake me, I kicked off my shoes, and in my stocking feet I stumbled over the wet sand and into the water, its cold fingers welcoming me, pulling me into a startling embrace.

I waded deeper, into history, into memories, toward swallowed land and drowned villages, inundated lives. I waded into stories about myself. The chubby-cheeked three-year-old my mother had talked about, thrilled to run away from her into the churning waters of the North Sea. It occurred to me then that I'd always been determined to run toward a dazzling, distant horizon. As the water clasped me to it, I decided that this was the one thing I loved about myself.

A wave came in, fast and tumbling, and I was underwater, limbs flailing, clothes flapping, sagging, dragging me downward. I gasped for air and took in choked-down mouthfuls of salt water. I felt my lungs burn, I felt my stomach lurch, I felt a shuddering convulsion. Then, buoyed up and pushed above the surface, I took in a breath.

Then I opened my eyes and saw Malcolm's ghost swim over to greet me. He wrapped his arms around me and pulled me to him. And, even though I fought him, I was happy to see him. It was nice, I realized, to finally find a friend.

———

CHAPTER TWENTY-EIGHT

"AM I IN DELAPOLE?"

An old lady was hovering over me. Veiny-faced and smiling. She took my hand. The room behind her was creamy, gloss-painted. At my feet I could see the grim metal frame of a hospital bed.

"You're safe now, lovey." She had a voice that was scratchy and vaguely familiar. She smelled of eau de cologne and washing detergent. She had wrinkly tan skin and white, almost invisible eyebrows, and the palest blue eyes I'd ever seen.

"I didn't drown?"

She shook her head and squeezed my fingers. "No, love. You're still with us." I saw a tear roll down her cheek, and I thought of the taste of salt water. I felt my stomach rise then lurch back, like a wave.

"Who are you?" I asked. She looked too old to be a nurse, and besides, she was wearing a flowery dress and big button earrings that covered her earlobes. There was a brooch pinned to her chest, a cluster of bright-colored feathers and little pearls.

While another tear rolled down her face, she let out a soft laugh. "Me? I'm your grandma, darling. I've come back from Australia. Looks like you could have used me a lot earlier. Still, better late than never, eh?"

She sniffed and I examined her face more closely, thinking back to all those photographs she'd sent us from Australia. But she didn't look familiar, and I could discern no family resemblance in her face. Except for her deep tan, she looked just like any other old lady, with permed white hair and a lined and saggy neck.

"You came for Mabel's wedding," I said. "It was supposed to hap-pen. . . ." I realized that I had no idea what day it was, whether I'd lain in this bed for a few hours or been here unconscious for days. I tried to push myself up off my hard little.pillow to get a better view of the room. But my limbs felt pathetically weak, without substance, and every inch of my body ached. I could lift myself high enough only to see a long row of beds and the window, tall and many-paned, next to the bed opposite mine.

"No need to worry yourself, love," Grandma said. She smoothed back the hair at the side of my face. "You just lie down and rest."

I fell back onto my pillow and looked at the distant white ceiling.

I WOKE AGAIN TO the sound of rain, an insistent metallic patter, the beginning of a storm on a caravan's roof. I opened my eyes and was sur-prised to see openness instead of a cramped interior. When I turned my head, I saw an old lady knitting something in pastel pink, the *click-click-click* of the needles just like falling rain. For a moment, I wondered if she was making wedding serviettes. Then I remembered that the wedding was off.

"Are you my grandma?" I asked, faintly recalling a previous conver-sation.

"That's right, darling," she said, looking over at me and dropping the knitting into her lap.

"Oh," I said, glad that I could at least remember this while every-thing else seemed a shifting blur. "How did I get here?"

"In an ambulance, love. From Reatton, from the beach."

"But who? How?" I was confused. I knew that I had stepped into waves, that I had been pulled under, toward all those buildings and bodies consumed by the sea. "I thought I . . . I saw a ghost. I saw Malcolm. He was taking me with him . . . he—"

"Malcolm? Is that the stringy lad that lives at the caravan park?"

I nodded as I remembered the cliff devoured by the sea and the blank place where his caravan had stood.

"Well, I don't know about any ghost, darling," Grandma said. "But Malcolm was the one who pulled you out. He said you put up such a struggle that he thought he might not be able to bring you in. He was worried that you both might drown. But you let him help you, eventually. I suppose with all them pills and what-not you'd taken, you didn't have that much fight left."

"He saved me?"

"That's right, love. He saved you."

"So he's alive?"

"Well, he was last time I saw him." She squinted at a tiny-faced gold watch on her wrist. "About an hour ago, at about half past five. Poor little thing, he was ever so worried about you. He wanted to come to see you. But the nurses wouldn't let him. It's only family members allowed right now. But, as much as his dad wanted him to go home, he wouldn't leave until he knew for certain that you were going to be fine."

"Oh," I said, remembering how I'd thrashed and kicked and gulped in all that seawater, how I'd known, as I felt Malcolm's ghost dragging me under with him, that I really didn't want to die.

I FOUND I RATHER liked being in the hospital. The nurses were very nice to me, smiling and speaking softly; they pressed warm fingers to my wrist to take my pulse and tucked my covers tight so I felt swaddled, like a baby, in my bed. And though she was only vaguely familiar, it was reassuring to have Grandma Pearson sitting at my bedside, a solid presence that I kept coming back to as I drifted in and out of sleep. I was also pleased when I found out that I wasn't in Delapole but in Bleakwick General Hospital. Most of all, I liked that, exiled there, I was capable of lying back and keeping my mind completely blank.

"Oh, Jesse, I finally managed to get here when you're awake. It's such a relief to see you, love."

It was morning. Or at least I thought it was. The light from the window was bluish; I could hear the distant clatter of teacups, the busy slap of shoes on hard, tiled floors. Mabel came into view at the foot of my bed. Her sheeny hair and vivid makeup were dazzling against the colorlessness of the room. She hurried to the side of my bed, looming over me to wrap her arms around my shoulders.

"Oh, for goodness' sake, Mabel, you'll stifle the lass," Grandma said, her voice muffled by Mabel's springy flesh. I hadn't realized she was still there, at my bedside. I wondered if she'd been there all night.

Mabel eased her grip and let me drop onto the pillow. "I'm sorry, love. It's just that you gave me the biggest scare of my entire life. I can't tell you how pleased I am to see you. Awake. Alive." She punctuated these words by slapping at the bare V of her chest above her plunging neckline a couple of times. "You don't look well, but at least you're with us. Thank God." She began rummaging about in her huge, shiny handbag.

"You can't smoke here, Mabel," Grandma said.

Mabel rolled her eyes, dropped her bag to the floor with a thud, and sank into the chair next to Grandma's. "Probably just as well," she said. "I've smoked four bleeming packets in the last twenty-four hours. Maybe it's time I gave up smoking. What do you think, Jesse? Might as well give up my two bad habits at the same time—cigarettes and men."

"But you're getting married—"

"Married? Oh, no, I don't think so, love. The wedding's off. Permanently. I'm not marrying a liar and a thief. The coppers are still investigating, but turns out Frank wasn't helping our Ted get a job at all. He was driving over to your house with that bleeming van filled up to the brim with Tuggles sausages. Apparently, they were delivering to butchers and grocers from Reatton-on-Sea all the way up to Flamborough.

No wonder they were driving about until all hours." She shook her head slowly and pursed her lips into a glossy knot.

"One thing I'll say about Teddy is that he's always been enterprising," Grandma said, her scratchy voice coming out in a soft, roiling laugh.

"Enterprising and about as thick as two short planks," Mabel huffed. "Not the best combination. But turns out that Frank was the bleeming criminal genius behind this one. He'd got one of the Tuggles managers to help him by cooking the books. You know, so they wouldn't be able to keep track of all them missing sausages. He recruited Ted for his criminal contacts. That way, he was able to find all the shops and suppliers that'd take the sausages cheap, no questions asked. Unfortunately for them, Ted thought he'd got himself a good contact at the Midham Co-op. Some woman he'd become friendly with while he was staying at your house. Knowing our Ted, I'm sure he thought he had her charmed. But when he offered her some stolen sausages she went straight to the cops and turned him in."

I wondered if the woman who turned Ted in had been Mrs. Franklin, the woman who'd banned me. If it was, I was sure my entire family would never be allowed to shop at the Midham Co-op again.

"Such a shame Teddy's got to go back to prison," Grandma said. "I was hoping I'd get to see him without having to pay a visit to Bradford jail."

"Yes, well," Mabel said, "despite Ted's record, Frank's likely to get the longer sentence. The coppers know that Frank's the one that organized everything. So Ted will probably get just a few months. But if Frank's found guilty he'll be in for three or four years." She sighed and closed her eyes for a moment. Then she looked over at me. "I should have listened to you all along, Jesse. I've had it with men. People can think what they like, but I've decided to call myself a Ms."

MY FATHER ARRIVED just after Mabel left. When I saw him, I felt a little jolt of excitement, and then, remembering what I had done and everything that had happened, I felt the urge to press my face into my pillow, as if by doing so I could hide away.

"Jesse! Oh, Jesse. It's so good to see you awake." He leaned over and kissed me, soft as a whisper, on my cheek. Then, just as he seemed about to pull back, he plunged himself against me. I was muffled in my father's sweaty smell and the wooly scratch of his pullover. As he held me, I felt jerky sobs move through his chest.

"I'm sorry, Dad," I said when he finally pulled back.

"Sorry?" He was red-eyed, ragged, and rumpled. His pullover was stretched out and lopsided. The long strands of his hair hung loose, while his bald patch shone like a pale polished apple under the glaring hospital lights.

"I didn't mean to—" I felt my own tears rise. I was no longer a blank mind registering nothing. Regret and sadness and aching guilt flooded through me.

"I know, love," my father said. "I know. But, Jesse, love, I thought we'd lost you. Please," he said, his eyes big watery saucers, "don't ever do anything like that again."

"I won't," I promised.

"Good. Because if you did I know I'd never forgive myself. I'd know it was because I let you down. And you have to realize, Jesse, that though I might not show it sometimes, I . . . well, I love you, Jesse, I really do."

For the first time since I'd found myself in that hospital bed, I filled my lungs with a long, deep breath. Though the air was thick and stale and tasted of bleached sheets and disinfectant, I was glad to pull it into me all the same.

My father took the seat next to Grandma, who was knitting again.

"Where's Mum?" I asked. It was the question that had been on my mind ever since I'd first woken.

My father eyed Grandma. She returned his look, raising her almost invisible eyebrows, then gave a subtle nod.

"Well . . ." My father brushed his palms over his thighs, hard, as if he were trying to smooth the map of creases out of his trousers or to wipe something sticky from his hands. "That's why I couldn't stay here with you, love. That's why your Grandma's been here. I've . . . Well, your mum had to go back to Delapole, Jesse."

"She didn't . . . ? She didn't try to . . . ?" I couldn't bring myself to say the words. I knew if she had tried to kill herself again, then I had propelled her to it. I was the one who had wished her dead.

My father shook his head. "No, love. She didn't do anything like that. It's just . . . Well, Jesse, love, your mum has an illness. There's something wrong inside her head. She has to get treated by the doctors. The way they might treat someone who's got a bad heart or a broken leg. So she's going to stay there, in the hospital, for quite a while."

"Will she be cured when she comes home, then?" I asked. I felt myself clinging to a thread of hope. A lifeline thrown to someone drowning.

Grandma dropped her knitting into her lap and rested her hand on my wrist. "Your mum has the kind of illness that they can't really cure, darling. Not now, not yet. But they think they can help her, give her medicines that will make her a lot better, able to cope more easily with life." She leaned closer to me, holding me steady in her pale blue eyes. "She wasn't always like this, you know, darling. When she was much younger, she was just a normal lass. She might have been a little more moody than Ted or Mabel, but most of the time she was like anyone else. So you have to understand, love, that the person she is right now, it's not really Evelyn. It's like a storm that happens inside her head. It's like the weather. There's nothing that you can do or say to stop it. And there's no point in trying. You're just a lass—a bairn, really. You've got your whole life ahead of you. You've got other things you need to think about."

I lay silent, letting these words sink into me. After a few moments, I tilted my head toward my father. "Is Malcolm all right?" I asked.

"He's fine," my father said.

Then I asked him how it had happened, how it was that while Malcolm's caravan had been pulled down the cliff side, Malcolm was still alive. My father explained that, unlike my family, Malcolm's had been regularly checking the weather forecast. When Malcolm's father heard there was such a big storm coming in, he'd moved their caravan far back from the cliff, among the other caravans there. Though the storm had kept them awake all night, they'd been safe.

When Malcolm went outside that morning, he'd seen me walking along the cliff, unsteady on my feet. He'd called to me and, when I didn't seem to hear, had followed me. He was there, on the cliff, looking down on me as I stood on the beach. When he saw me stagger into the water, he ran down the path and went after me, into the waves.

"You were very lucky, Jesse," my father concluded. "All the seawater that you drank made you vomit up a lot of those pills. It took quite a while for them to get an ambulance all the way out to Reatton. Even if you hadn't drowned, you could easily have ended up dead. Of course, it's Malcolm you've got to thank for everything. You wouldn't think it to look at him, but he's a brave little bugger, that lad."

TWO DAYS LATER, my father brought Malcolm to see me. I was feeling much better by then, and when they arrived I was sitting, propped against fluffed-up pillows, absently leafing through the *Woman's Weekly* Mabel had left behind. My first instinct was to dive beneath my covers or to tell Grandma, still knitting at my bedside, that I didn't want any visitors. Instead, I sat frozen in embarrassment as he loped across the shiny tiled floor.

"Here's the little hero," my father announced as he reached my bedside. His chest was thrown out and he was smiling so broadly that his dimples looked like two little handles in his cheeks. Next to him, Malcolm was silent.

"Hiya," I said, pressing myself against the pillows, shuffling down in my bed.

"Hiya," Malcolm said. "How are you feeling?"

"I'm all right." I shrugged and let my eyes fall to the *Woman's Weekly* in my lap.

"Is that all you've got to say to this young man, Jesse?" my father said. "I know you're still a bit out of sorts, love, but, come on, now. I mean, he did save your life."

"Thank you," I mumbled, unable to lift my gaze. I was, in fact, unbearably grateful, but I was also swathed in shame—not only at all the ways in which I'd stood by and let Malcolm be mistreated, even calling him a poof myself, but also at the fact that he'd found me drunk, drugged, and delusional and had to pull me out of the sea. While he'd been strong and able to withstand everything, I had been pathetically weak.

"Oh, come on, Jesse," my father said. "You can do better than that. This lad here"—he patted Malcolm's shoulder—"well, he could have drowned trying to help you. But he didn't think about himself for a second. You need to tell him—"

"It's all right, Mr. Bennett," Malcolm interrupted. "When I helped Jesse, I was really only returning a favor."

I looked up.

"What do you mean?" my father asked.

"There was a group of bullies at school," Malcolm said. "They were going to beat me up. It was Jesse that stood up to them. She helped me escape. She fought them off."

"She did?"

Malcolm nodded and looked at me, smiling. "Yeah, see, when I went in that water after her, really, I was only repaying a friend."

—

CHAPTER TWENTY-NINE

AFTER A STAY OF SEVERAL DAYS IN THE HOSPITAL, I'D RETURNED home to a place that was completely different. Though there were still holes in the walls from my mother's fit with the sledgehammer and some of the furniture had been clumsily nailed back together, all other evidence of her tempestuous presence was gone. In the mornings I slept late, until after my father had left for work. When I came downstairs, Grandma was cooking breakfast while her fiancé, Bill—an almost bald and jowly seventy-year-old who looked about as un-gigolo-like as I could imagine—filled out the crossword in the previous evening's Hull *Daily Mail.* Our days were spent in a quiet routine punctuated by washing dishes, cleaning, and cooking. In the afternoons, we'd drink tea and listen to the play on Radio 4. If there was a cricket match, Bill would turn on the television to watch it, Grandma would pull out her knitting, and I'd get out a book. In the evenings, when my father came home, he and Bill would repair the various holes and cracks in the walls. Upstairs, I'd lie on my bed reading until I fell asleep. A couple of times a week, Malcolm and Dizzy would come over and we'd sit together in the kitchen, or, if the weather was nice, we'd go into the garden and talk until the long June evenings descended into dark. There were no highs, no lows, no screaming fits or pits of hopeless desperation. But during all this time the dread of returning to Liston Comprehensive hung there, a lurking menace in my mind. I could imagine it all so clearly—the trail of titters I'd leave behind me as I walked through the playground, the snarled comments in the corridors, the gangs of vicious, angry girls. I could clearly hear the choruses of "lezzie" and "loony" as I pushed my way through jostling crowds in the cloakrooms. Even the teachers would look at me with sneering pity— the pathetic case who'd written secret love letters to an older girl student, and who'd tried to kill herself when she was found out.

Finally, after I'd been at home for three weeks, my father told me that I had to return to school. "But I can't," I protested, unable to imagine leaving the refuge of our house. "I can't go back."

"You've got to, Jesse," he said. "You've got no choice. The doctor only wrote you a sick note for three weeks, love. If you don't go back, they'll be sending the truant officer out."

I WALKED ALONG the road into the village as if I were walking to my own funeral. For the first time since I'd woken at the hospital, I wondered if it might have been better if I had drowned. When I rounded the corner onto the high street, there was already a group gathered at the bus stop. I saw Tracey staring eagerly at me. The boys hovered around her, all elbows and knees, shoving and sputtering as they watched my approach.

"Hello, lezzie girl," Tracey called when I was still several feet away. "Didn't think we'd see you again. Heard you'd tried to walk on water. What, think you're some kind of bloody saint? Too bad you didn't realize that lezzies sink!"

The boys around her laughed, and one of them started chanting, "Saint Lezzie, Saint Lezzie."

I'd been hoping that Dizzy would be at the bus stop, but more than anything I was also hoping to see Amanda. I'd been hoping to see her almost as soon as I woke at the hospital, hoping she'd show up among my little string of visitors. When Mabel swept into the ward, I'd peer around her, wanting to see Amanda in her wake. And when my father arrived I looked past him, wishing more than anything that she had tagged along. Even when Malcolm came to see me a second time, whisked into the ward by one of the silky-voiced nurses, I thought how perfect it would have been if Amanda accompanied him and I could lie there, basking in the attention of my newfound friend and the girl I still loved. After I'd been discharged, though I was soothed by the un-eventful routine of my days, I kept looking out the window, yearning with an impossible ferocity for Amanda to appear at the end of our driveway and wave cheerily to me as she made her way to the house.

If she had come to see me, I'd know that she forgave me for writing all those things about her in my letters, that she cared that I had tried to drown myself, that, even if she didn't return my feelings, she was glad that I was still alive. But, as the days and then weeks went by and I did not see her, I began to realize that perhaps she really did hate me for what I'd done. It was this I feared more than anything. When they came to visit, I wanted to ask Malcolm and Dizzy if they'd seen her, if she'd asked after me, but I couldn't bring myself even to say her name. Now, as I approached our old meeting place, I felt hopeful once again. Even if she'd decided she hated me, I knew she would never be as cruel as Tracey.

"Looking for your little lezzie girlfriend, are you?" Tracey asked, ap-parently catching me glance toward the end of the street.

I'd been avoiding her eyes, but now I looked straight at her. She was simmering, energized. Her pupils shone like gleaming coals.

" 'Dear Amanda,' " she began, making her voice all soft and squeaky as she imitated writing in the air. " 'I love you *soooo* much. You are *soooo* wonderful. And *sooo* beautiful. Let me ride up on my big white horse and rescue your big fat beautiful arse. . . .' " She turned to the boys and cackled. Then she put her hands on her hips and whipped back to face me. "Too bad you're not going to see her again, isn't it?"

I frowned. What was she talking about?

"Yeah, bet you didn't know that, did you?" She flicked back her ponytail with a toss of her head. "Hah! So much for all your lovey-dovey-lezzie letters. She's cleared off with Stan."

"What do you mean?"

"She's left home. Buggered off. Gone."

Surely Tracey was lying. It would be just like her to want to see me suffer at the thought of Amanda running off with Stan Heaphy. "I don't believe you," I said.

Tracey shrugged. "Believe what you want. See if I care. I'm sorry she broke your little lezzie heart, but what I'm saying's true. She went on a school trip but she sneaked off, met up with Stan. Cleared off with him, she did. Left a note for the teacher, and another for my mum."

I thought back to that enormous buckled suitcase Amanda had hauled to the bus stop, how she'd seemed so intense when she said goodbye to me before getting on the bus.

"I'm bloody glad she's gone. She's sixteen—she doesn't need any-body's permission. And, you ask me, she'd better not come back. If she does, my dad will give her a bloody good belting again. She never got on with him anyway, was always aggravating him. She thought she was badly done to, but you ask me, she deserved every bloody smack she got."

As I looked at Tracey, her face jubilant and flaming, I remembered the first time I'd met her, standing in front of that neat little house among all those other neat little houses, the rows of identical windows, the brightly painted doors. I thought of Tracey's mother in her apron, the smell of fresh-baked cakes, the glamorous photographs on the wall. And I thought of Amanda telling me there were a lot of things more important than appearances.

"Where did they go?" I asked.

"Timbuktu, for all I care."

I imagined Amanda clinging to Stan on his motorbike, her enor-mous suitcase strapped on the back as they raced along an unwavering straight thread of narrow road. I imagined her helmetless, her bright blond hair streaming behind her, her chin leaning on Stan's shoulder as she stared, unblinking, into the future, into what lay ahead. And I imagined myself standing at the roadside, watching as they became ever distant, until they disappeared into the landscape, until they were just a tiny speck against the asphalt's gray.

"What, you going to cry now your lezzie friend has left you?" Tracey sneered. "Or maybe you should jump off a cliff, try to drown yourself again?"

Beside her, the boys continued giggling and shoving, but now I saw that they were only noise. And Tracey, though she could puff herself up until she was enormous and frightening, really, she was like a balloon expanding. I realized then that we were all like that, our skin only a thin membrane of protection for all the secrets we held inside.

I took a couple of steps toward her, so that I was only inches from her face. "Shut your face, Tracey," I said. "I'm sick and tired of listening to the bloody rubbish that comes out of your big mouth." Then I pushed past her and the little bevy of boys, to take a seat on the bench while I waited for the bus to arrive.

I SAT NEXT TO Dizzy on the bus and in most of my lessons. During break time and at school dinner, we met up with Malcolm, and the three of us sat together. It wasn't easy to continue our conversations amid the laughter and whispers and occasional paper pellets, the insults tossed down corridors and echoing against the classroom walls. But somehow we managed it. And though the day passed with glacial slowness, the last lesson of the day came around.

"Are you all right, Jesse?" Malcolm asked me as we made our way to English, the only lesson that the two of us shared.

"I don't know," I said as I heard a group of third-year girls giggling behind us and a chant of "lesby-friend, lesby-friend" coming from a couple of boys peering out of an open classroom door.

It wasn't just the taunting. It was the stunning knowledge that

Amanda was gone, and that while I'd been writing letters filled with ridiculous fantasies of rescuing her she really had needed to escape. Now she had left with a stupid, horrible bully. I just hoped that Stan treated her better than her father had. My only consolation was that at least she'd left before she could learn about my letters, that I wouldn't have to see her turn around and hate me like almost everyone else. I could still hold on to her warmth, the kindness of her smile.

"I don't know if I'm all right," I said to Malcolm. "But I think I feel strong."

"You should," he said.

"I should?"

"Yeah. I mean, the sea ate a whole bloody cliff, but you, it spat you back up."

"JESSE, CAN I SEE you for a minute?" Ms. Hastings said.

It was the end of her lesson, and though I was itching to leave now that the school bell had sounded I'd rather enjoyed sitting in the back of the classroom between Malcolm and Dizzy, while the class talked about *Lord of the Flies*. I'd even raised my hand and made my own comment during the discussion, and, despite scornful looks from Tracey and the Debbies, I liked what I said. Now, though, with Ms. Hastings looking at me solemnly and asking me to stay behind, it was obvious that I must have done something wrong.

"I'm not quite sure how to say this, Jesse," she said as soon as she'd closed the classroom door after the last student. I dropped my eyes to the scuffed-up floor. "It's just that I'm very surprised at you. Shocked, really." She was standing a few feet away from me. I could see her big leather boots and the jagged hem of her pale cotton skirt. "You see, I took down those letters you wrote that someone put on the school notice board."

My stomach plummeted. I was suddenly hot. I focused on Ms. Hastings's boots.

"I know they were private, Jesse. And I'm sorry that they were stolen from you, but I have to confess that I ended up reading those letters myself."

I wanted to dissolve into the floor.

"Like I said, I was very shocked. Jesse," she continued, taking a step closer so that her boots and skirt filled my vision. "What you wrote, it was remarkable. Beautifully written. I've never seen you produce anything like that in my lessons. If I didn't know your handwriting, I might not have believed those letters were written by the same girl."

I let my gaze flicker upward, so that my eyes rested on the bright stripes that zigzagged across Ms. Hastings's blouse.

"Young woman, you really are quite a talented writer." She paused, and when I lifted my eyes to her face she was looking at me intently. "Do you realize that?"

I knew that she expected an answer, but I was flabbergasted. Those letters were nothing more than my absurd imaginings. They were ridiculous. Everyone at Liston Comprehensive thought so.

"I'm perfectly serious about this, Jesse Bennett. I'm not sure why you've been handing in such mediocre work in my lessons when you're clearly capable of so much more. But I won't stand for it any longer. Really, young woman, if you can produce such wonderful stories outside my lessons I don't see why you can't start doing the same here. Am I making myself clear?" She folded her arms across her chest.

"Yes, Ms. Hastings." I studied her face. She was completely serious. She really thought my writing was good.

"Good. I'm glad we understand each other." Then she turned away from me and walked over to her desk, where she picked up a sheaf of creased paper. "I believe these are yours," she said, returning the little stack to me.

It wasn't all of my letters to Amanda, but from its weight I guessed it was a good portion of them. "Thank you," I said, taking them from her tentatively.

"That's all, Jesse. Now go on—I know your friends are waiting for you." She tipped her head toward the little window in the door. Malcolm's and Dizzy's heads were bobbing about as they peered through the glass.

"Yes, Ms. Hastings," I said, my body surprisingly light as I turned toward my desk, gathered my things, and hastened across the classroom. As I put my hand on the door handle, she called to me.

"Jesse."

I turned around.

"There's nothing wrong with what you said in those letters. Nothing you should feel ashamed of. No matter what anyone else says, Jesse, I want you to know that."

For a moment, I looked at her. Hands planted firmly on her hips, legs astride, in the swell of her flared skirt and sturdy boots, she looked so solid, so full of certainty, a dark X in the middle of the quiet room.

"Yes, Ms. Hastings," I said, before darting out the door.

CHAPTER THIRTY

—

"WELCOME HOME, EVELYN," GRANDMA SAID, RAISING HER TEACUP.

We were sitting around a big wooden table in the garden. It was August, a beautiful sunny afternoon—"perfect," Grandma had declared, for the party she'd insisted on organizing for my mother's return. When my father had objected, suggesting that my mother might find the idea of coming home to a house full of people a little overwhelming, Grandma had dismissed him. "She'll be happy to have her family around her. And, besides, I want to let everybody know my news."

"What news?" I'd asked.

"You'll have to wait until the party, Jesse," Grandma had answered, giving me a wink and tapping her nose.

Although this coming-home party was not quite the enormous affair my mother had planned for Mabel's wedding, the garden was a lovely setting. The lawn had long recovered from its battering during the storm, and, aside from a sizable gap in the hawthorn hedge where a portion of it had been blown down, the place was lush, filled with lavish growth. The borders spilled over with flowers and the rosebushes were a concert of color—all dark green leaves against oranges, reds, pinks, and yellows. The humid summer air was alive with their scent. As Grandma proposed her teacup toast, behind her the fountain gurgled and the fish slid below the surface of the water, their scales catching the light like shimmering sequins on a ball gown. The few remaining garden gnomes—those that hadn't been smashed in the storm—grinned over at us. As I took this all in, I realized what a truly incredible transformation my mother had wrought. We'd arrived in Midham a little more than a year ago to a jungle of thistles and brambles. Out of that she had created a haven far more soothing than any neat patch of lawn surrounded by a few pansies.

"Welcome home, Evelyn," my father echoed, jerkily lifting his cup, so that some of his tea sloshed out onto the front of his shirt. While the brown stain seeped into the crisp white cotton, he smiled at my mother and then drank the entire cupful down.

"Welcome home," said Bill. While my mother sat on one side of Grandma, he sat on the other. As he spoke, my mother's beaming smile fell into a narrow-eyed frown. Ever since she'd arrived home a couple of hours earlier, she'd been staring daggers at the poor man. If looks could kill, he'd already have been transformed into nothing more than a pile of bones, a few strands of hair, and an oversized pair of glasses on the ground.

Across from me, Granddad Bennett mumbled something under his breath. He'd been complaining for the past half hour, ever since Mabel dragged him away from the living room, where he'd been sitting with her new fella, Charlie, watching the Saturday afternoon sports with the curtains closed. Mabel shoved her elbow into Granddad's arm. "Welcome home, Evelyn," he said, grimacing in my mother's direction. Then he popped another mini-sausage roll into his mouth and started to chew loud and open-mouthed.

"She looks grand," Charlie declared, nodding up the table at my mother. "Mind you, Mabel, you look a bloody knockout yourself." He reached his arm around Mabel and pressed a set of stubby fingers into her side.

"Give over, Charlie," she said, laughing and knocking his hand away. "Don't go creasing up my dress."

"That's not what you said in the car on the way over." He waggled a set of thick black eyebrows.

I turned to Malcolm and Dizzy and rolled my eyes as Charlie leaned into Mabel and she sputtered out a laugh.

"Where's your mum been, Jesse?" Malcolm asked, speaking softly so the adults around us wouldn't hear. Next to him, Dizzy looked at me. Beneath her glasses, her eyes looked enormous, expectant.

It was Grandma who'd suggested that I invite Malcolm and Dizzy, and for a long time I'd resisted. But just a couple of days ago I'd relented. Somehow, despite all my turbulent fear of what they would make of my family and of this gathering, I'd decided I wanted to have them there.

"I knew she was gone," Malcolm continued, "but I was never sure where."

My mother was sitting next to Grandma, and now, no longer scowling at Grandma's fiancé, she had a smile, slim and bright as the crescent of a brand-new moon, etched across her face. It had been four months since I'd last seen her, and when I heard my father's car pulling into the driveway after picking her up, I was afraid I'd forgotten what she looked like. But the second she stepped out of the car, I realized that she was as familiar to me as the sound of my own voice, or the smell of my own skin. She looked different, though, as she made her way along the path to the front door—her face plumped up, her cheeks pinked with color, her movements measured rather than jagged and wild or painfully lethargic. Now her smile so wide that it made little fans of the creases around her eyes, I wondered if it was really possible that this most recent stay in Delapole might actually have done her good.

"She's been in the hospital," I said, keeping my voice low. And then, surprising myself, I added, "In Delapole."

I saw a look flicker between the two of them, a little flame of knowledge that leaped within their eyes. I gripped the edges of my chair.

"Is she better?" Malcolm asked.

"I don't know."

"She looks well, Jesse," he said. "I bet she's probably all right."

"Yeah, she looks great," Dizzy agreed.

They were both smiling at me, hopeful, buoyant. I felt them holding me up the way I'd always thought that friends might.

For a while, everyone focused on eating. There was the clatter of knives and forks on china, the chomping of jaws, the gulping down of tea. Then, after working his way through an enormous slab of pork pie, Granddad turned to Malcolm. "Play football, do you, lad?" he asked, leaning across the table and jabbing a fork in Malcolm's direction.

"Only at school, but I'm not really interested in sports."

"Not interested in sports?" Granddad said, as if Malcolm had just confessed to a murder. "Lad of your age? Not interested in sports?" Granddad looked around the table, apparently seeking affirmation of his outrage from the other guests. Next to Granddad, my father sighed and lifted his eyes skyward.

"Malcolm's a very good swimmer," I chirped.

Granddad huffed. "Swimming? That doesn't count. I'm talking about real sports. The sort that develops the body and the character, that makes a boy into a man. See, my lad Brian, he was a terrific footie player. Mike here"—he stabbed his fork in my father's direction—"he was like you, no interest, no skill in sports. Tell you the truth, don't think he's much of a swimmer, either, are you, Mike?"

My father didn't bother to answer Granddad. Instead, he looked down at the table and his shoulders slumped forward, into his chest.

"But Brian, well, he was an athlete, he was. Best footie player you're ever likely to see. Could do magic with that ball, he could. Aye," Granddad said, nodding to himself. "You've never seen a footballer like our Brian."

My father looked up and caught my eye. Then he turned to Malcolm, and looked back at me. As he did so, I noticed a muscle in his cheek twitch, a flicker of something in his eyes. Then, as if he'd come to a decision, he put his hands on the table and pushed himself up in his chair. "Dad," he said, sitting straight, looking at Granddad across the table.

"If you got a chance to see Brian play," Granddad continued, jabbing his fork in the air, apparently not hearing, "well, you'd understand what I was saying. See, he ran around that field like—"

"Dad," my father bellowed. He lifted his hands and then slapped them down hard on the table, making the cups rattle in their saucers, the glasses jolt, and the cutlery bounce. Everyone was stunned into silence.

"What?" Granddad asked, his tone irritated.

"Brian's been dead almost twenty years," my father said.

"So?"

"So I'm just plain tired of hearing about how bloody wonderful he was. And I swear, if you extol the virtues of my dead brother once more in my presence, today or any other day, I will never, ever speak to you again. So either drop the subject now or I'll drag you from that chair, drive you home, and you can spend the rest of your days staring at pictures of Saint bloody Brian."

Granddad, at a loss for words for the first time I'd ever witnessed, let his mouth flap wide to gape at my father. After a couple of seconds, the hand holding his fork dropped loosely to the table. "Well, if that's the way you feel . . ." he finally muttered. Then he shrugged and glanced around the table, his eyes finally settling on Dizzy. "So, lass," he said, picking up his fork again and gesturing toward her, "what rubbish are they teaching you at school these days?"

While Dizzy tried to convince Granddad of the importance of learning a foreign language (Granddad's theory on the matter being that, since English was clearly the best language on the planet, there was no reason for us to learn anything else), I looked over at my father. He was smiling to himself as he stuck his fork into a slice of tomato, and he continued smiling as he shoved it into his mouth. Next to him, my mother studied him, perplexed. Then, as her eyes moved over to Granddad, she pulled a small but nevertheless jubilant grin.

IT WASN'T AN elaborate meal, but Grandma had made sure it included all my mother's favorites—the pork pies, the mini-sausage rolls, the coleslaw she had made with raisins and Heinz Salad Cream, the little hot-dog sausages, the pickled onions, the cubes of Cheddar cheese. But when she brought out an enormous plate filled with a selection of Mr. Kipling cakes—chocolate éclairs, vanilla slices, bakewell slices, custard tarts—she had clearly outdone herself. For the first time since she'd sat down at the table, I heard my mother speak.

"Oh, look at that!" she said. "I haven't had a Mr. Kipling's in weeks." Then she reached over and took two vanilla slices and a chocolate éclair and put them on her plate. Within a couple of minutes, she had eaten them and, after wiping her mouth with one of the pink serviettes Grandma had set out on the table, she reached over to take a custard tart and another vanilla slice.

"So, listen everybody," Grandma said, rising from her seat after the Mr. Kipling cakes had been polished off and more tea had been poured. "Bill and me, we've got an announcement to make." Beside her, Bill rose to his feet and Grandma took hold of his arm. "As you all know, we're planning to get married. . . . Well, we've decided to have our wedding here in England, in that nice little church in Reatton-on-Sea. That lovely Reverend Mullins has agreed to do the ceremony. In a few months, when our Ted's not . . . indisposed."

I looked at my mother. She was glowering at Bill. My father was watching her warily, his mouth pressed in an anxious lipless line.

Across the table, Granddad mumbled, "I'd have thought this family would've had enough of weddings. Tempting fate, you ask me, planning another one so soon."

After silencing him with a look, Mabel turned to my mother. "Ooh, won't that be lovely, Ev?" Her booming tone and beaming smile making me think of the presenters on *Play School,* trying to pump enthusiasm into an audience of five-year-olds beyond the television screen. "We'll all get to be at our mother's wedding. You ask me, that'll be just great."

My mother said nothing while she studied Bill stonily. Beside Grandma, Bill looked extremely wary. I got the distinct impression that if Grandma hadn't been holding on to him the poor man might have tried to make a run for it.

"Yes, but that's not the only thing we wanted to tell you," Grandma said, giving Bill a reassuring pat on the arm. "See, the two of us have talked about it a lot, and we agreed that we're not going back to Australia. We're going to settle down here, in England. Get us a house somewhere between Midham and Hull. Bill suggested it, and I agree. Right now, my family needs me here."

My mother was on her feet, throwing her arms around Grandma's shoulders. "Oh, Mam, that's smashing, that's brilliant," she said, pressing her face into Grandma's neck. Then, after a few seconds, she pulled back and looked at Bill. "Welcome to the family," she said, and leaned over to place a loud smacking kiss on the astounded man's cheek.

AFTER EVERYBODY HAD LEFT, I joined Grandma in the bustle of clearing away dishes, washing up, drying, putting things away. It was nine o'clock by the time we were done. I was tired, but it wasn't dark yet and I felt drawn to go outside. As I made my way down the hallway, behind the living-room door I heard the drone of the newsreader on the television, and then a voice shouting, "Bunch of bloody codswallop!" in an Australian accent. "You tell him, Bill!" my father yelled.

I went out the door and into the garden. It wasn't until I had wandered halfway across the lawn that I realized my mother was there as well. She was sitting in one of the chairs at the table. I walked over and took the seat beside her.

"It was a nice party, wasn't it, Mum?" I said, looking at the flower beds and the faces of the pansies. In the grainy light, it was easy to imagine them as animals, a long row of fierce little sentries standing guard.

"It was lovely," my mother said. "I'm a bit full now. I think I ate too much, to be honest. But I did have a terrific time. It's nice to be home. Nice to be back." There was a new steadiness in her voice. It melded, like the day's fading colors, into the falling dusk.

"I missed everybody so much," she said. "When you're away like that, it's hard to remember that you have a home."

As she spoke, I felt a hard stab of guilt for not visiting her. Grandma and my father had both asked me many times to go with them, but I'd always refused. Though it had been impossible to soothe myself by imagining her on a world cruise or some other exciting adventure, I hadn't been able to face her in the hospital.

"I'm glad you're back, Mum." I said it although I wasn't quite sure I meant it.

"Yes," my mother said. "So am I." Then she turned in her chair so that she was looking right at me, her eyes glassy bright in the blurred contours of her face. "You know what helped me more than anything when I was in there? More than the doctors and the pills and all that silly arts and crafts they make you do?"

I shook my head.

"It was those letters you sent me, love. They were just wonderful. They kept my spirits up something marvelous. I looked forward to getting them ever so much."

"You did?"

"Oh, yes. I was reading them again just now, until it got too dark." She lifted a little stack of papers she'd been holding in her lap. "And in the hospital, when I got them—well, reading about all those countries and places you wrote about . . . You made everything seem so real."

"I looked it all up, in the main library at Bleakwick. I thought you might find it interesting. I thought it might help cheer you up."

"Oh, it did, love. Made me feel like there was something to look forward to, once I got better, once I got out." Then she reached over and placed her hand, loose and cool, over mine.

"I liked writing to you," I said.

My mother nodded. "Yes, love, I could tell."

Then we sat there, not speaking. And, for the first time in my mother's presence, I took in the delicious stillness of a warm summer evening—the slowly shifting shadows, the steady rhythm of my own breath. I let myself simply be there, wrapped in nothing but the evening's drawn-out perfection, and the reassurance that beyond the leafy barrier of our garden the world was waiting, beautiful and immense.

ACKNOWLEDGMENTS

—

My thanks go first to Cindy Spiegel and Mike Mezzo at Spiegel & Grau for their invaluable insights and skillful editing, and to my agent, Eric Simonoff. I am deeply grateful to Poets & Writers and the California Writers Exchange Program and, in particular, Cheryl Klein and Jamie Fitzgerald. For their excellent feedback and sage advice, I'd like to thank Teresa Burns Gunther, Margo Perin, and Rebecca Chekouras. And for their enthusiastic support of my writing, I'm very grateful to Jennifer Fechner, Rosemary Christoph, Terry Glavin, and Bev Parrish. I am also enormously grateful to my wonderful friends and all the ways in which their presence has helped me do what I love. Above all, I am deeply thankful to my partner, Suse Herting—a solid, steadfast presence and a beautiful soul.

I'd also like to thank my father, who gifted me with his love of books; I wish you could read this one, Dad.

ABOUT THE AUTHOR

Born and raised in East Yorkshire, England, ELAINE BEALE is the winner of the 2007 Poets & Writers California Writers Exchange contest, a competition she won for a partial draft of this novel. Her fiction and nonfiction have appeared in several anthologies. She lives in Oakland, California.

This book was set in Requiem, a typeface designed by the Hoefler Type Foundry. It is a modern typeface inspired by inscriptional capitals in Ludovico Vicentino degli Arrighi's 1523 writing manual, *Il modo de temperare le penne.* An original lowercase, a set of figures, and an italic in the "chancery" style that Arrighi helped popularize were created to make this adaptation of a classical design into a complete font family.